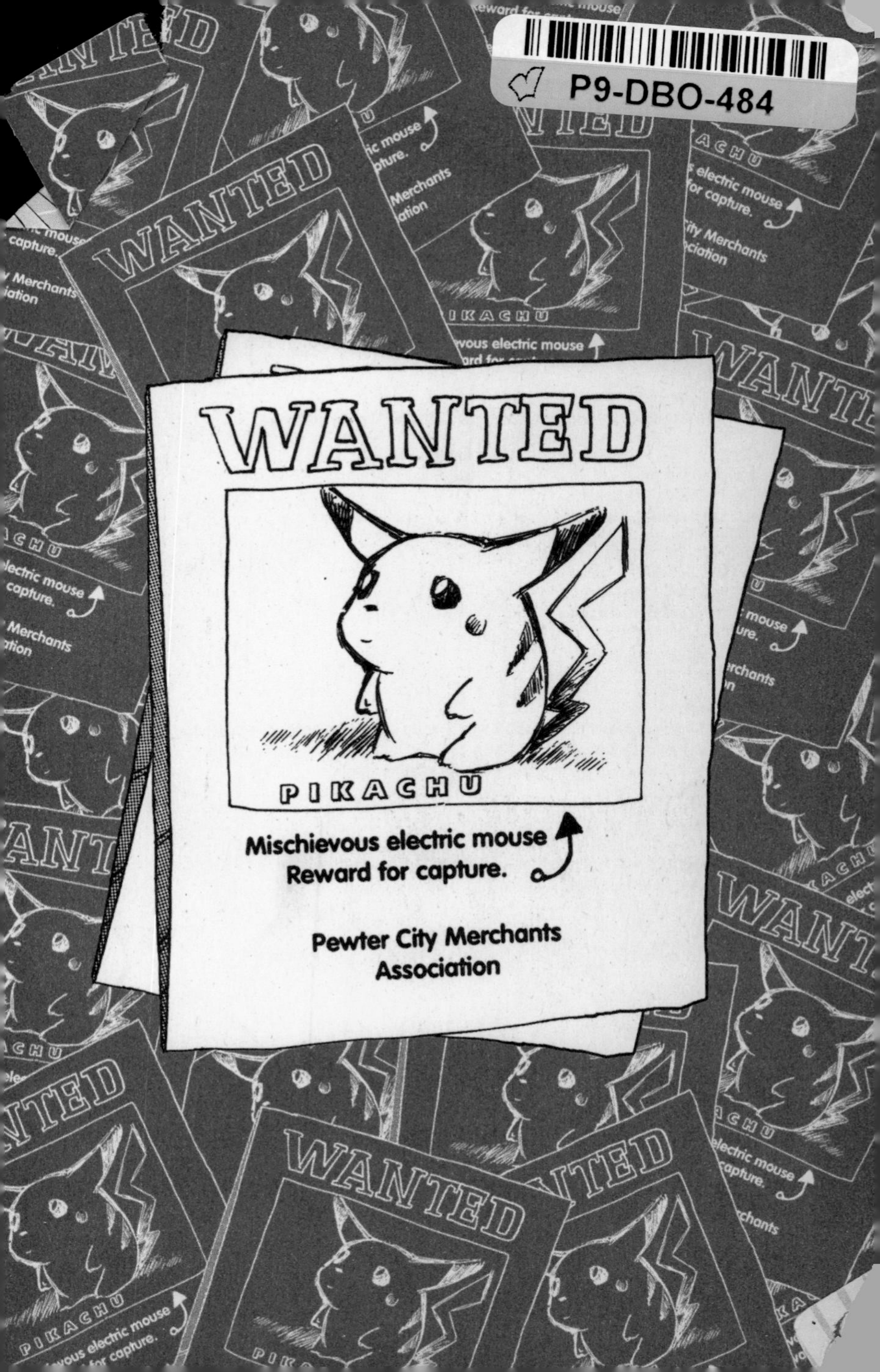
WANTED
PIKACHU
Mischievous electric mouse
Reward for capture.
Pewter City Merchants
Association
P9-DBO-484

THE BEST OF POKÉMON ADVENTURES

RED
VIZ Kids Edition

Story by **Hidenori Kusaka**
Art by **Mato**

From VIZ Graphic Novels *Pokémon Adventures* Vol.1-Vol.3 published by VIZ Media.

[1st Edition]
Translation/Kaori Inoue
Touch-Up & Lettering/Dan Nakrosis
Graphic Design/Carolina Ugalde
Editor/William Flanagan

[VIZ Kids Edition]
Cover & Graphic Design/Izumi Hirayama

Editor in Chief, Books/Alvin Lu
Editor in Chief, Magazines/Marc Weidenbaum
VP of Publishing Licensing/Rika Inouye
VP of Sales/Gonzalo Ferreyra
Sr. VP of Marketing/Liza Coppola
Publisher/Hyoe Narita

Printed in the U.S.A.

Published by VIZ Media, LLC
P.O. Box 77064
San Francisco, CA 94107

VIZ Kids Edition
10 9 8
First printing, October 2006
Eighth printing, April 2008

For advertising rates or media kit, e-mail advertising@viz.com

store.viz.com

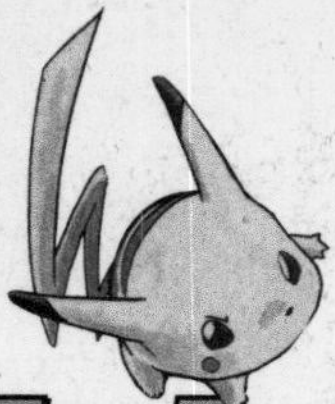
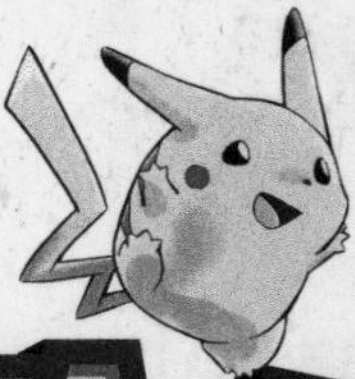

The Best of Pokémon Adventures®

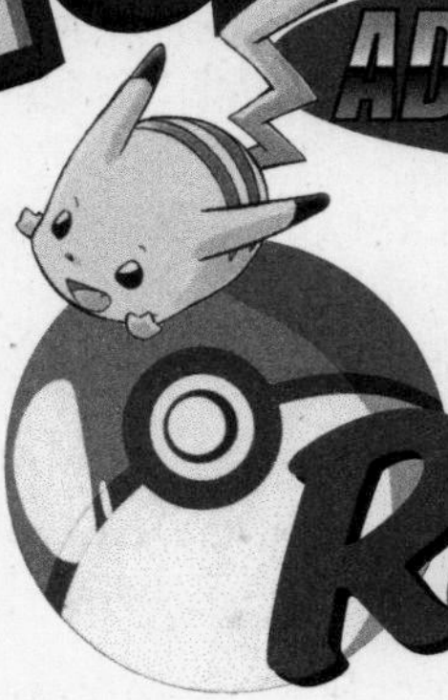

Red

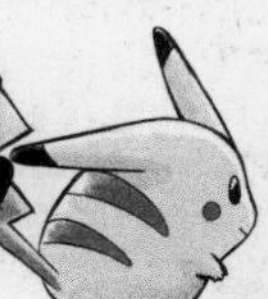

VIZ Kids Edition

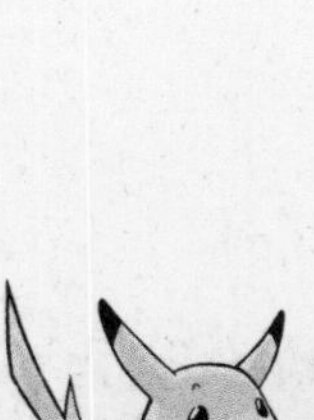

Story by Hidenori Kusaka
Art by Mato

CONTENTS

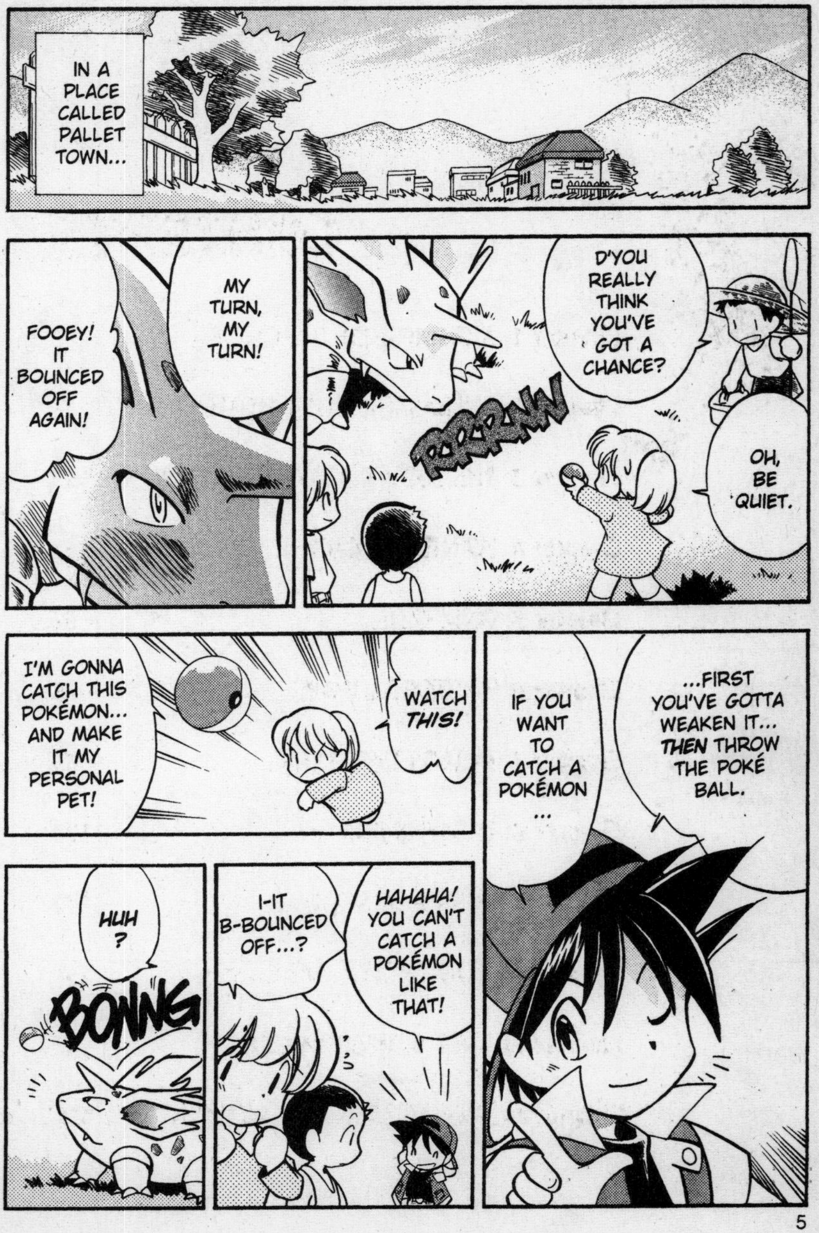
IN A PLACE CALLED PALLET TOWN...
FOOEY! IT BOUNCED OFF AGAIN!
MY TURN, MY TURN!
D'YOU REALLY THINK YOU'VE GOT A CHANCE?
OH, BE QUIET.
I'M GONNA CATCH THIS POKÉMON... AND MAKE IT MY PERSONAL PET!
WATCH *THIS!*
HUH?
BONNG
I-IT B-BOUNCED OFF...?
HAHAHA! YOU CAN'T CATCH A POKÉMON LIKE THAT!
IF YOU WANT TO CATCH A POKÉMON...
...FIRST YOU'VE GOTTA WEAKEN IT... *THEN* THROW THE POKÉ BALL.

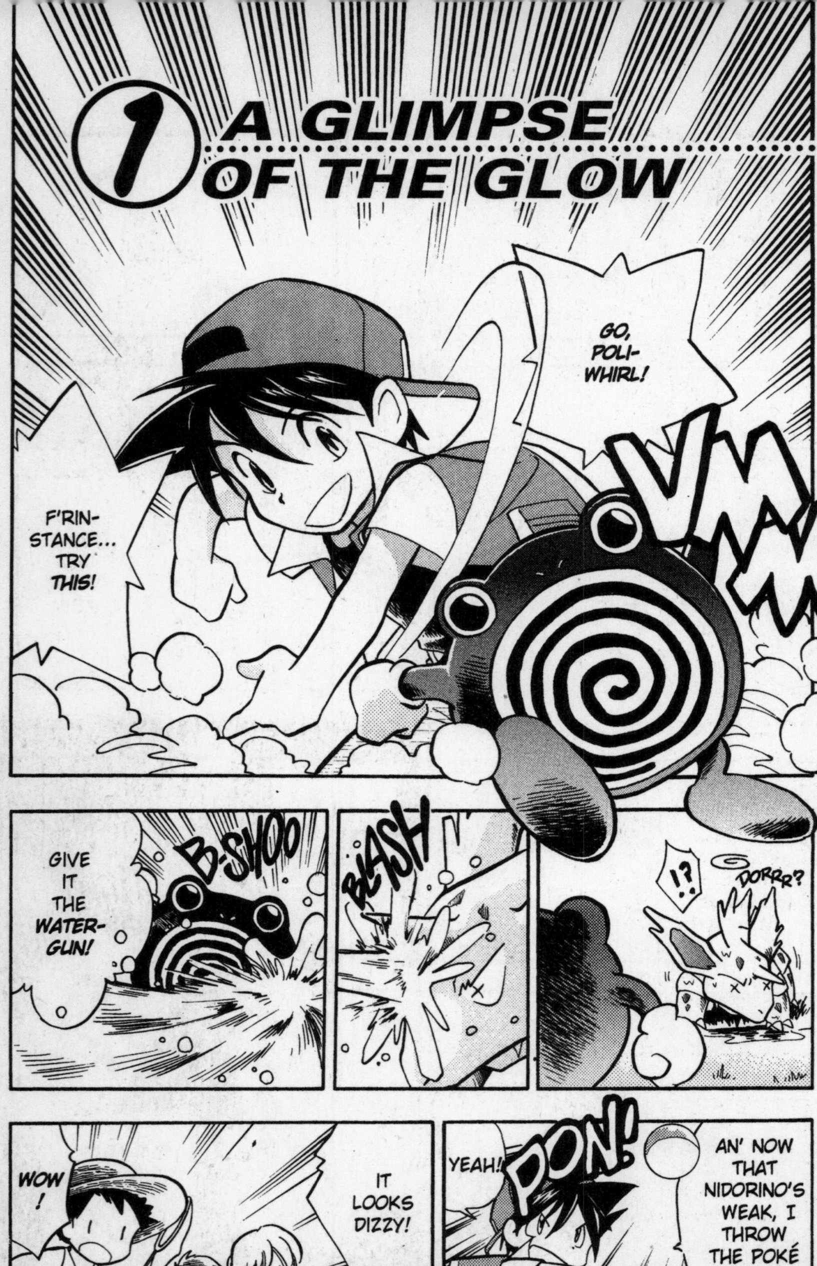
1 A GLIMPSE OF THE GLOW
F'RIN-STANCE... TRY THIS!
GO, POLI-WHIRL!
VMM
GIVE IT THE WATER-GUN!
B-SHOO
BLASH
!?
DORRR?
WOW!
IT LOOKS DIZZY!
YEAH!
PON!
AN' NOW THAT NIDORINO'S WEAK, I THROW THE POKÉ BALL.

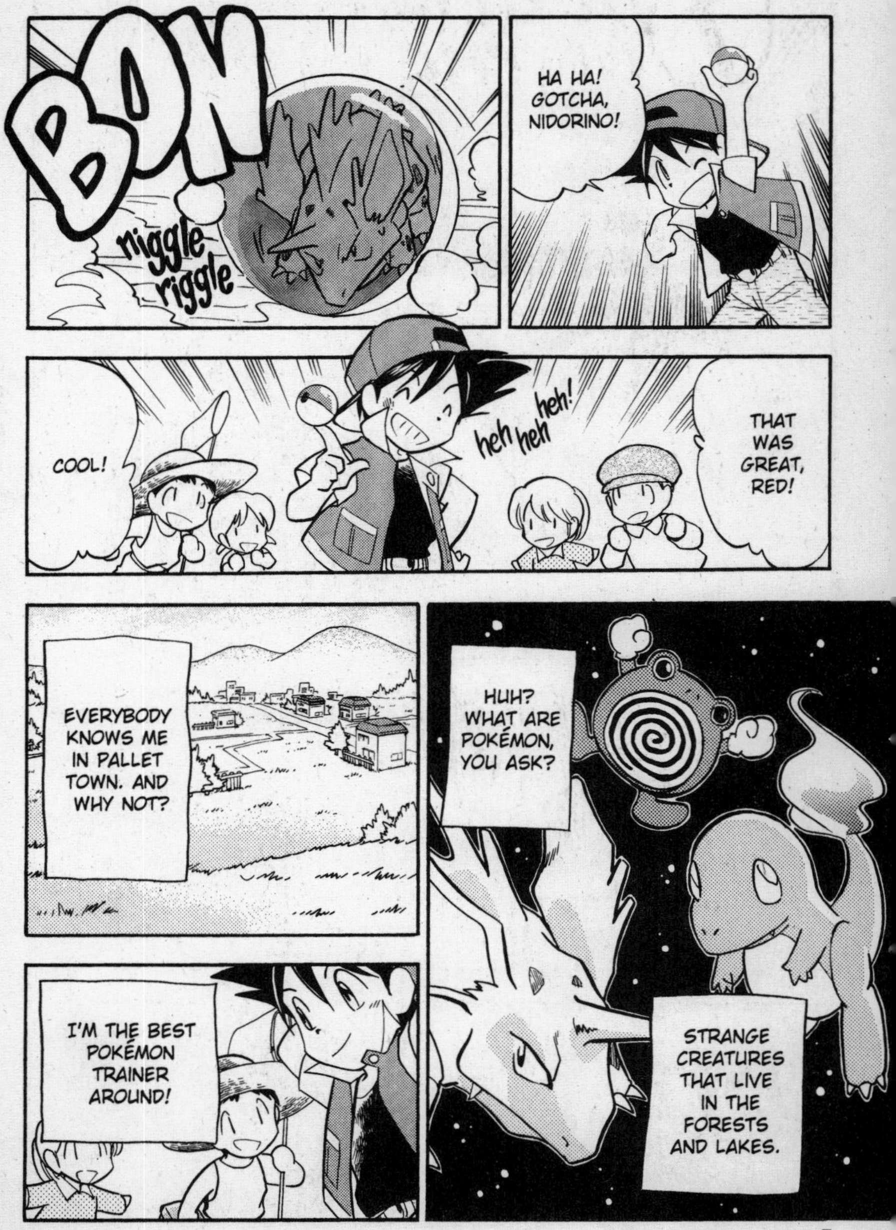
BON
riggle riggle
HA HA! GOTCHA, NIDORINO!
COOL!
heh heh heh!
THAT WAS GREAT, RED!
EVERYBODY KNOWS ME IN PALLET TOWN. AND WHY NOT?
I'M THE BEST POKÉMON TRAINER AROUND!
HUH? WHAT ARE POKÉMON, YOU ASK?
STRANGE CREATURES THAT LIVE IN THE FORESTS AND LAKES.

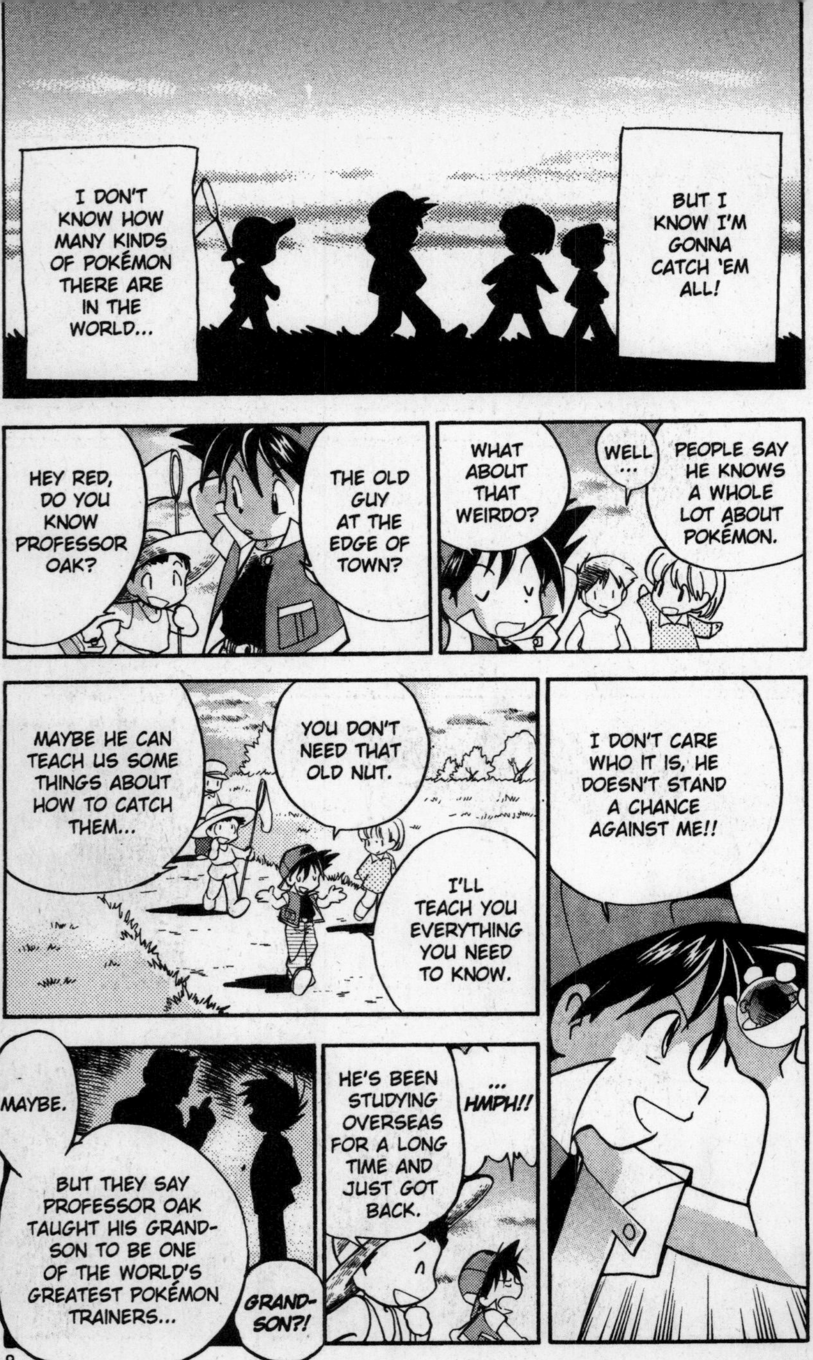
I DON'T KNOW HOW MANY KINDS OF POKÉMON THERE ARE IN THE WORLD...
BUT I KNOW I'M GONNA CATCH 'EM ALL!
HEY RED, DO YOU KNOW PROFESSOR OAK?
THE OLD GUY AT THE EDGE OF TOWN?
WHAT ABOUT THAT WEIRDO?
WELL...
PEOPLE SAY HE KNOWS A WHOLE LOT ABOUT POKÉMON.
MAYBE HE CAN TEACH US SOME THINGS ABOUT HOW TO CATCH THEM...
YOU DON'T NEED THAT OLD NUT.
I'LL TEACH YOU EVERYTHING YOU NEED TO KNOW.
I DON'T CARE WHO IT IS, HE DOESN'T STAND A CHANCE AGAINST ME!!
MAYBE.
BUT THEY SAY PROFESSOR OAK TAUGHT HIS GRAND-SON TO BE ONE OF THE WORLD'S GREATEST POKÉMON TRAINERS...
GRAND-SON?!
HE'S BEEN STUDYING OVERSEAS FOR A LONG TIME AND JUST GOT BACK.
... HMPH!!

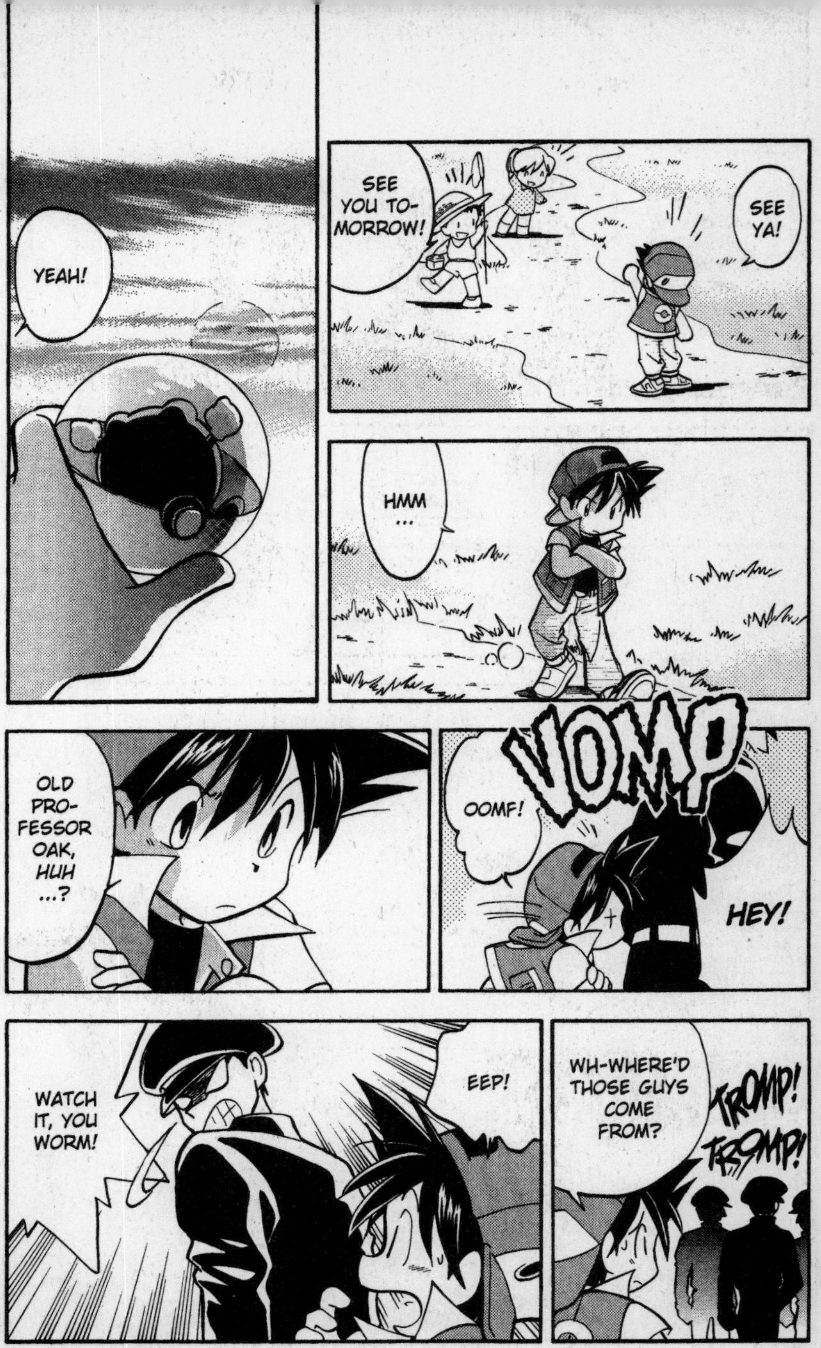
YEAH!
SEE YOU TO-MORROW!
SEE YA!
HMM...
OLD PRO-FESSOR OAK, HUH...?
VOMP
OOMF!
HEY!
WATCH IT, YOU WORM!
EEP!
WH-WHERE'D THOSE GUYS COME FROM?
TROMP!
TROMP!

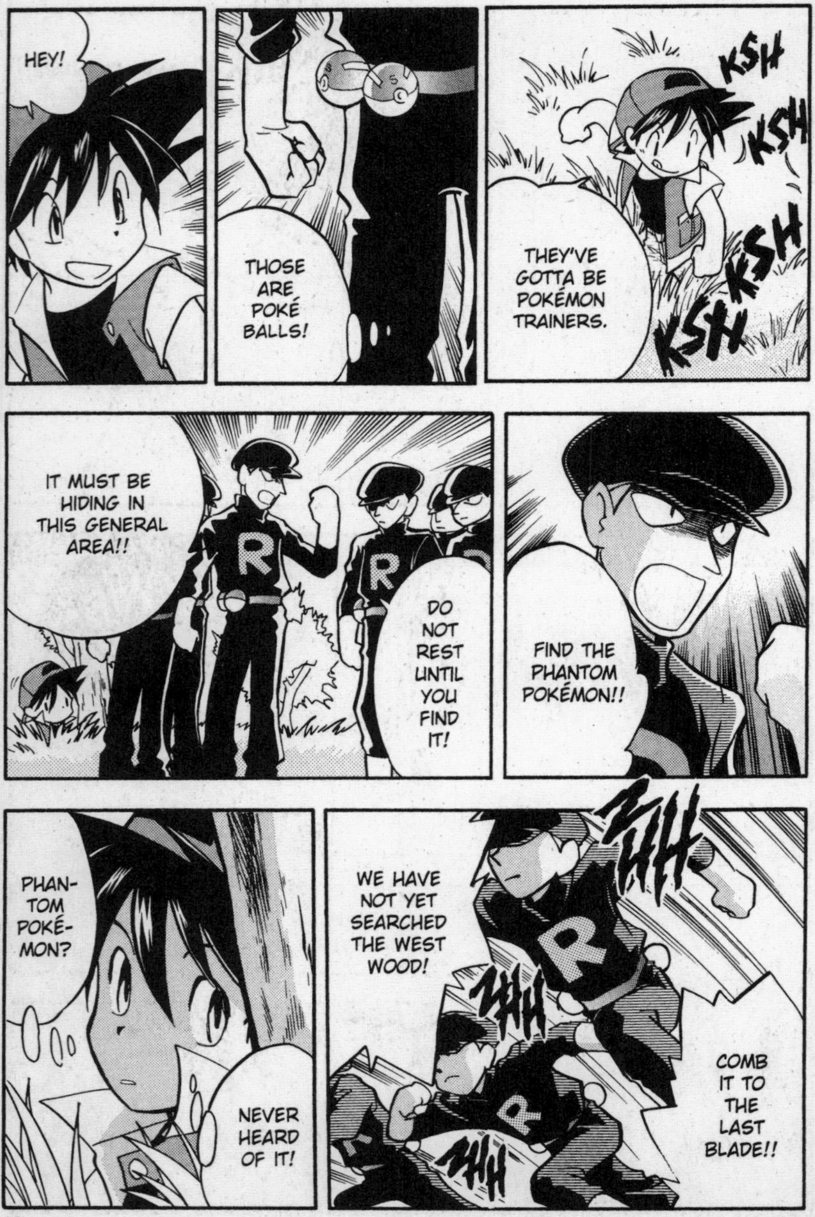
HEY!
THOSE ARE POKÉ BALLS!
KSH KSH KSH KSH KSH
THEY'VE GOTTA BE POKÉMON TRAINERS.
IT MUST BE HIDING IN THIS GENERAL AREA!!
DO NOT REST UNTIL YOU FIND IT!
FIND THE PHANTOM POKÉMON!!
PHANTOM POKÉMON?
NEVER HEARD OF IT!
WE HAVE NOT YET SEARCHED THE WEST WOOD!
COMB IT TO THE LAST BLADE!!

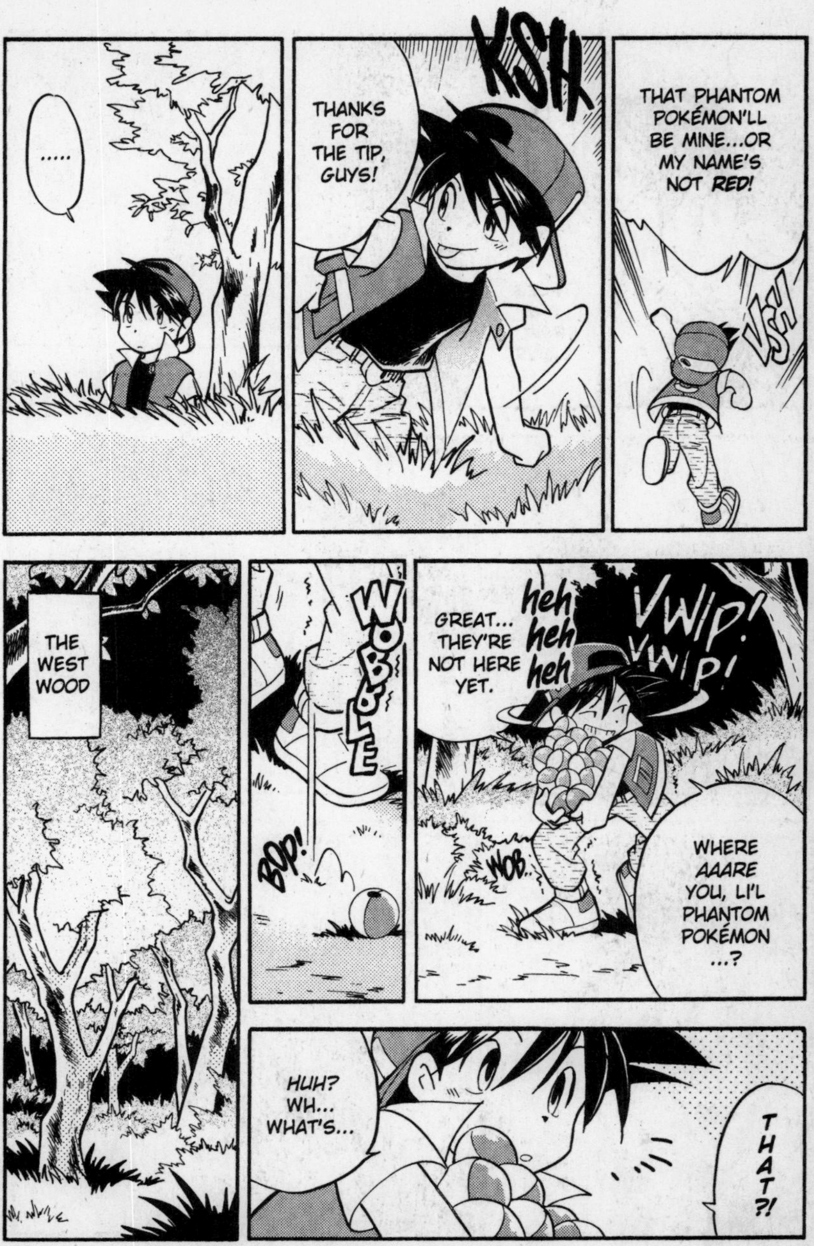
.....
THANKS FOR THE TIP, GUYS!
KSH
THAT PHANTOM POKÉMON'LL BE MINE...OR MY NAME'S NOT RED!
VSH
THE WEST WOOD
WOBBLE
BOP!
GREAT... THEY'RE NOT HERE YET.
heh heh heh
VWIP! VWIP!
WOB..
WHERE AAARE YOU, LI'L PHANTOM POKÉMON ...?
HUH? WH... WHAT'S...
THAT?!

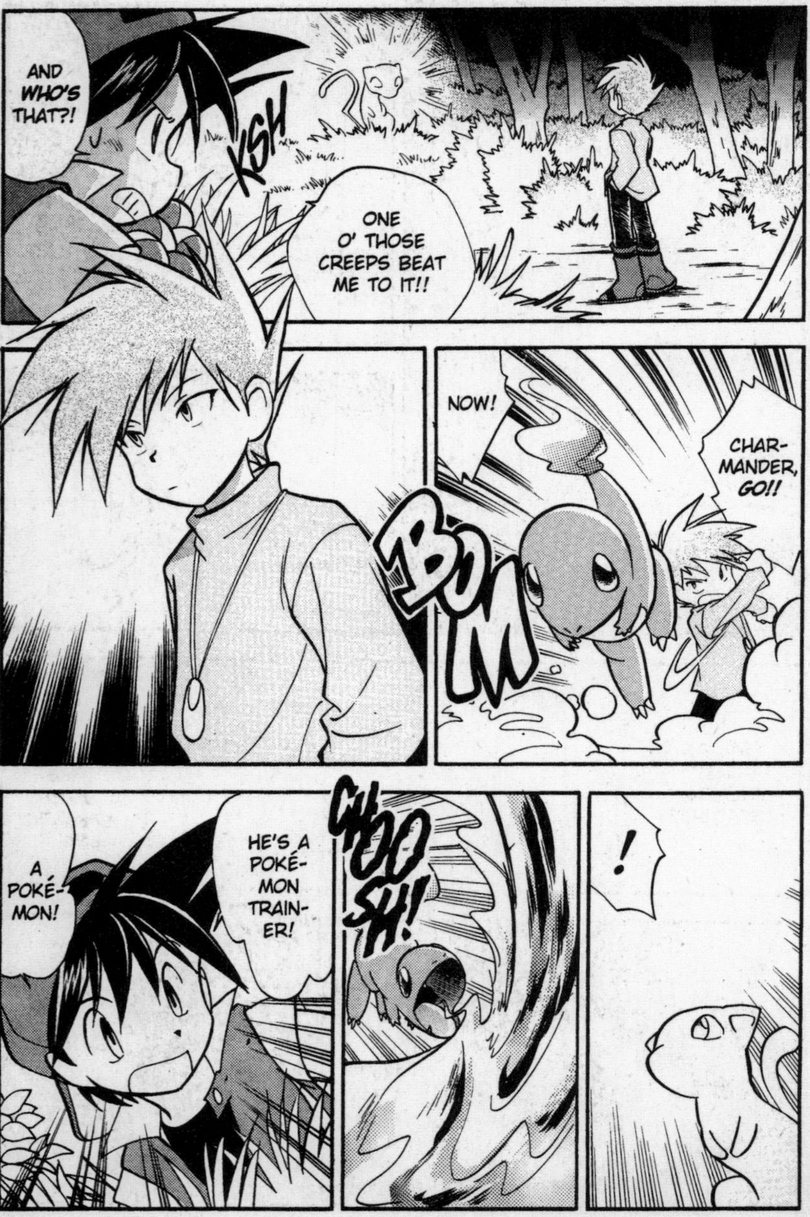
ONE O' THOSE CREEPS BEAT ME TO IT!!
KSH
AND WHO'S THAT?!
CHAR-MANDER, GO!!
NOW!
BOOM
HE'S A POKÉ-MON TRAIN-ER!
A POKÉ-MON!
!
CHOOSH!

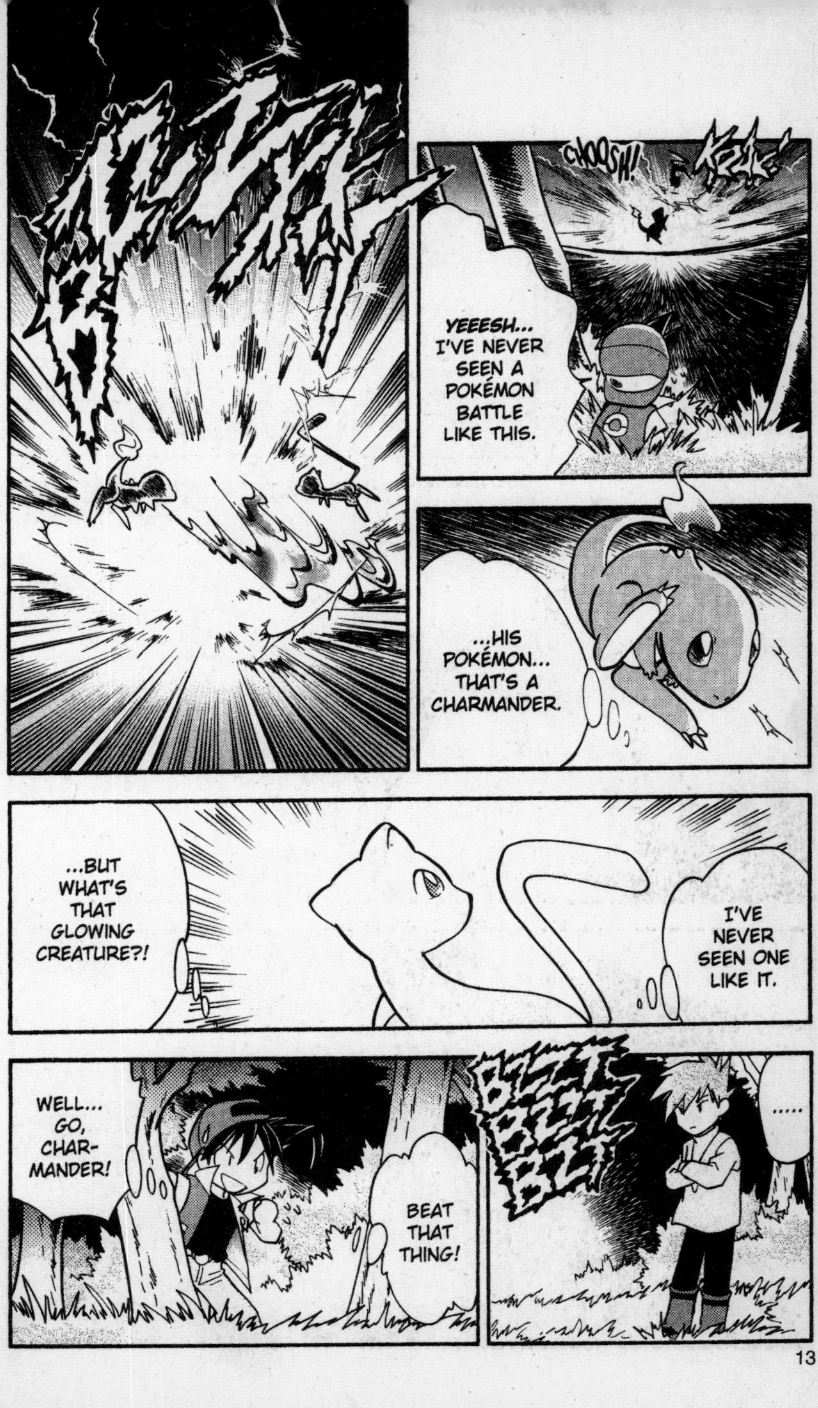
CHOOSH!
KRAK!
YEEESH... I'VE NEVER SEEN A POKÉMON BATTLE LIKE THIS.
...HIS POKÉMON... THAT'S A CHARMANDER.
...BUT WHAT'S THAT GLOWING CREATURE?!
I'VE NEVER SEEN ONE LIKE IT.
WELL... GO, CHAR-MANDER!
BEAT THAT THING!
.....

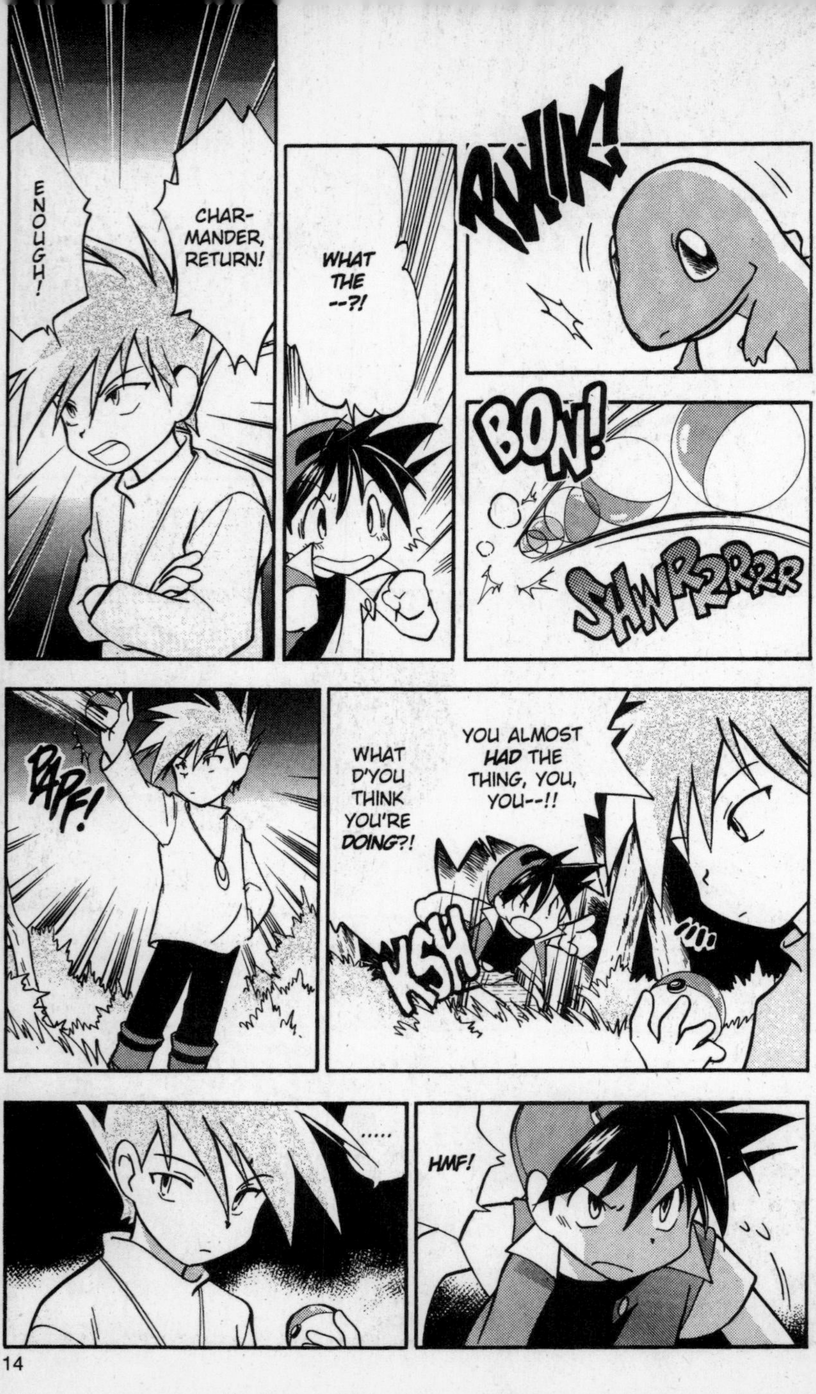
ENOUGH!
CHAR-MANDER, RETURN!
WHAT THE --?!
RWIK!
BON!
SHWRRRRR
BAPF!
WHAT D'YOU THINK YOU'RE *DOING*?!
YOU ALMOST *HAD* THE THING, YOU, YOU--!!
KSH
.....
HMF!

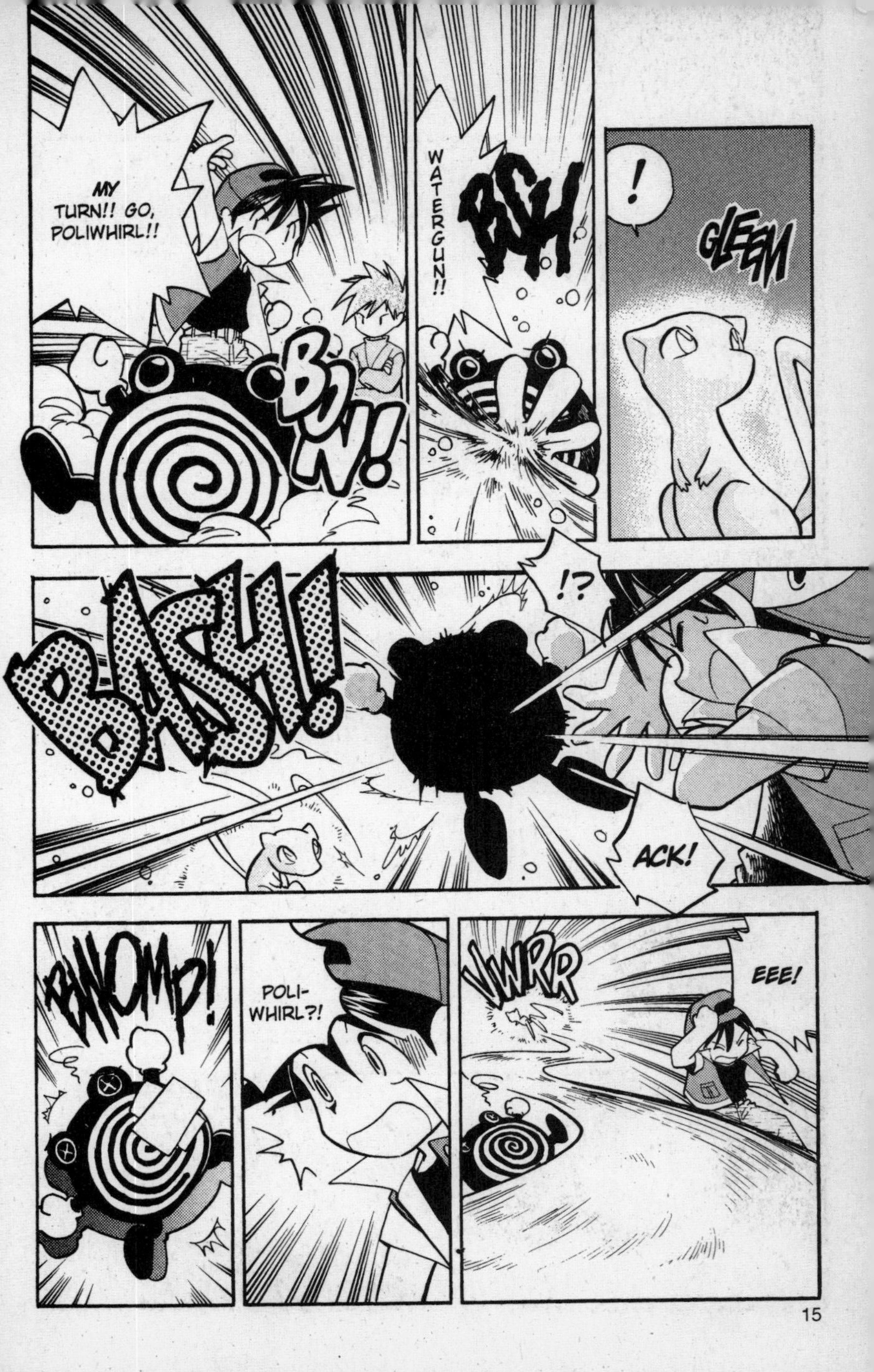
MY TURN!! GO, POLIWHIRL!!
BOON!
WATERGUN!!
BSH
!
GLEEM
BASH!
!?
ACK!
BWOMP!
POLI-WHIRL?!
VWRR
EEE!

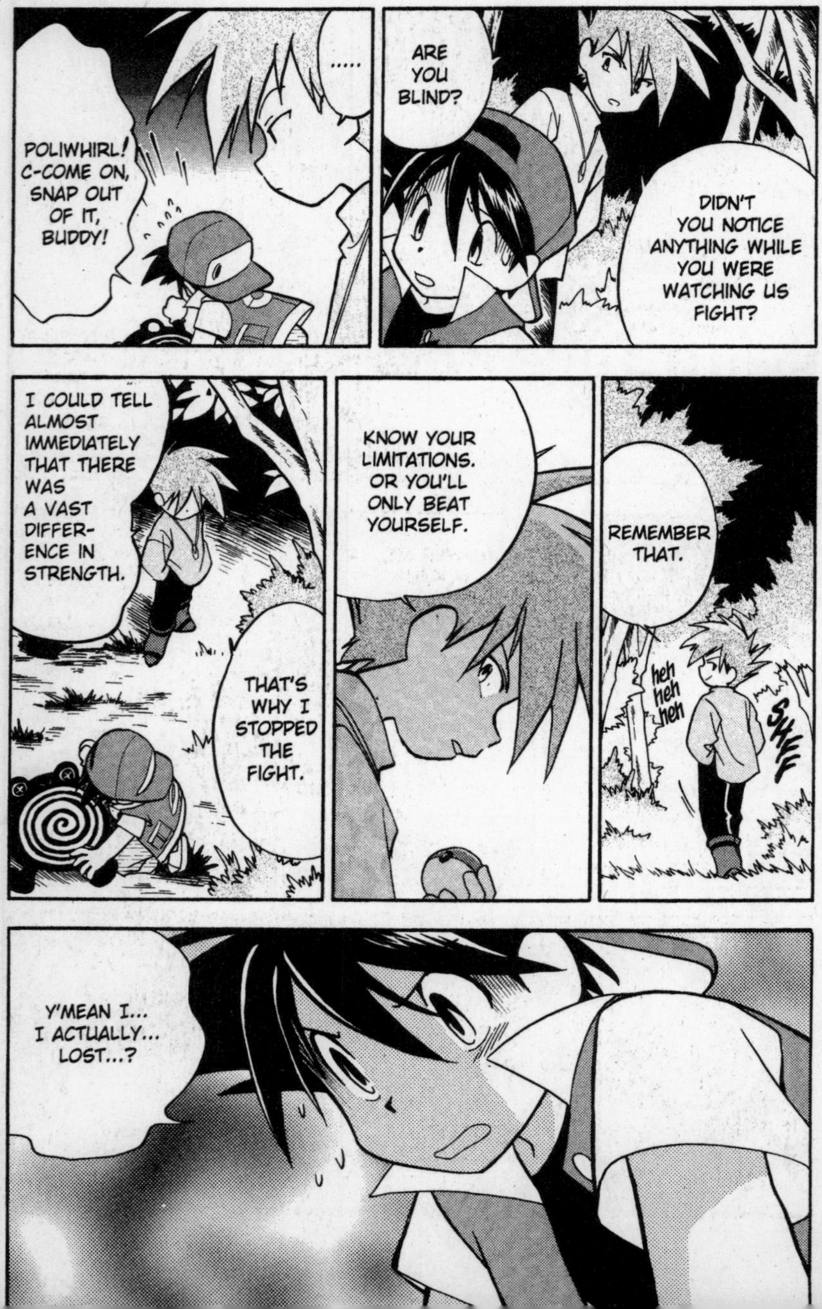
POLIWHIRL! C-COME ON, SNAP OUT OF IT, BUDDY!
.....
ARE YOU BLIND?
DIDN'T YOU NOTICE ANYTHING WHILE YOU WERE WATCHING US FIGHT?
I COULD TELL ALMOST IMMEDIATELY THAT THERE WAS A VAST DIFFERENCE IN STRENGTH.
THAT'S WHY I STOPPED THE FIGHT.
KNOW YOUR LIMITATIONS. OR YOU'LL ONLY BEAT YOURSELF.
REMEMBER THAT.
heh heh heh
Y'MEAN I... I ACTUALLY... LOST...?

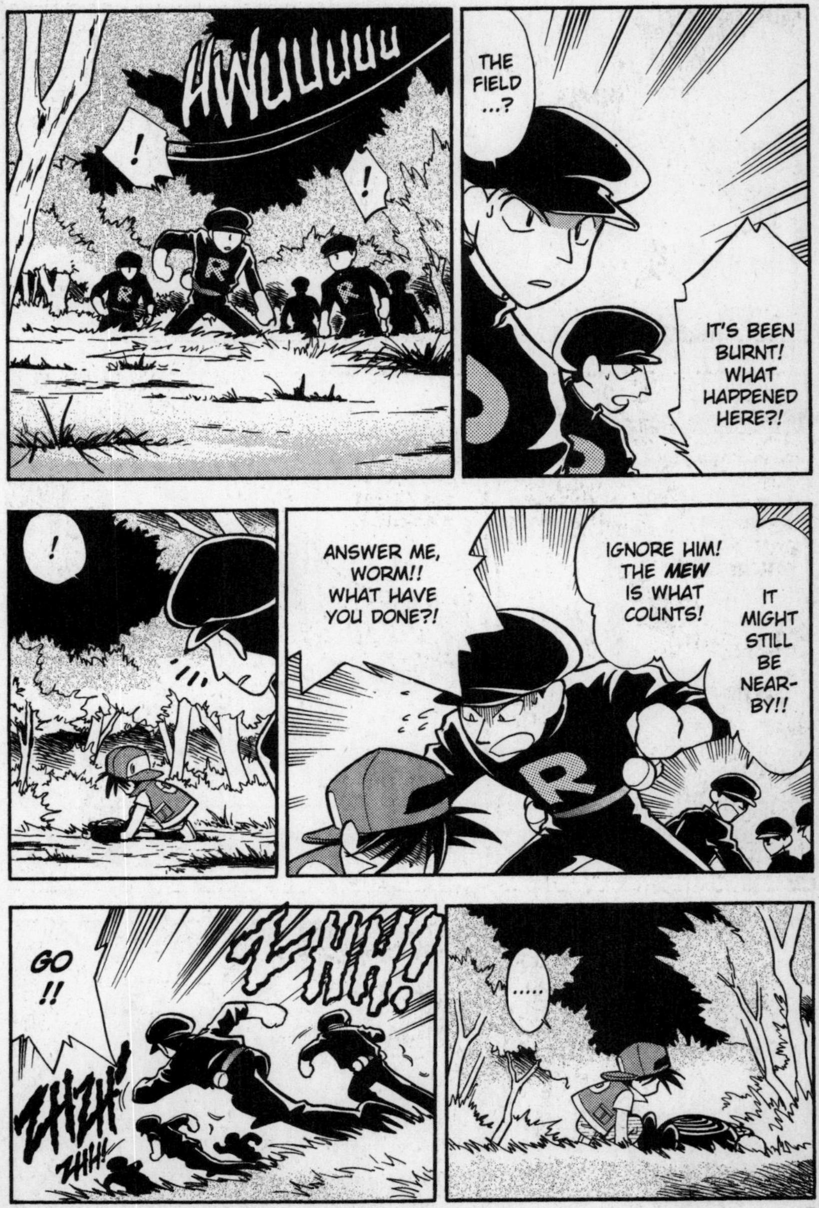
HWUUUUU
!
!
THE FIELD ...?
IT'S BEEN BURNT! WHAT HAPPENED HERE?!
!
ANSWER ME, WORM!! WHAT HAVE YOU DONE?!
IGNORE HIM! THE MEW IS WHAT COUNTS!
IT MIGHT STILL BE NEAR-BY!!
GO !!
ZHHH!
ZHZHH
ZHH!
......

SO THIS IS OL' PROF OAK'S LAB...

OAK POKÉMON RESEARCH LAB

THEY SAY HE'S A MEAN OLD GUY...

...SO I ALWAYS KEPT AWAY...

BUT I GUESS THE ONLY PLACE I'LL LEARN TO BE A GREAT POKÉMON TRAINER...

IS HERE.

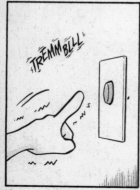

TREMMBLL

Bing Bong!

GULMP

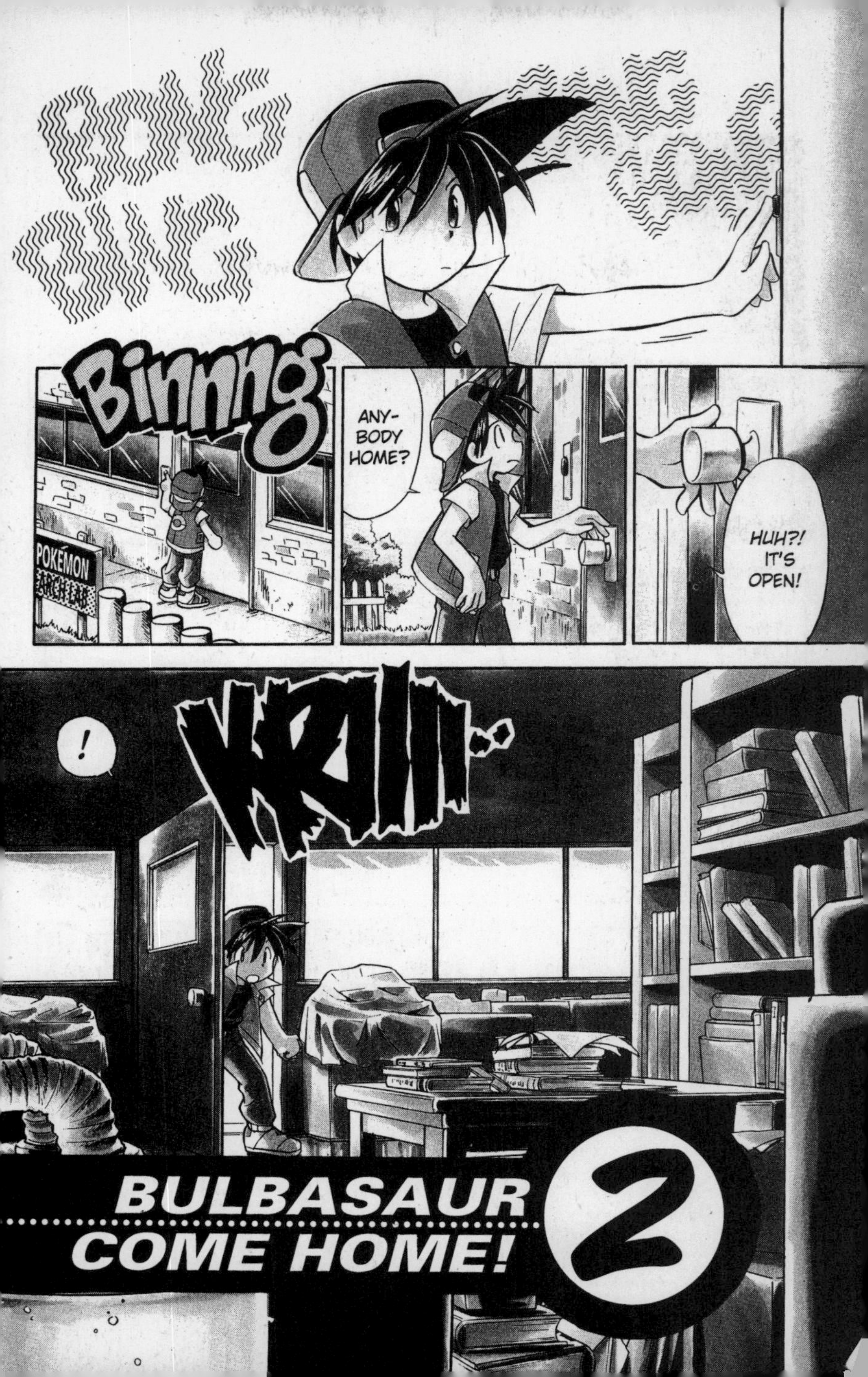
Binnng
POKÉMON
ANY-BODY HOME?
HUH?! IT'S OPEN!
!
2
BULBASAUR COME HOME!

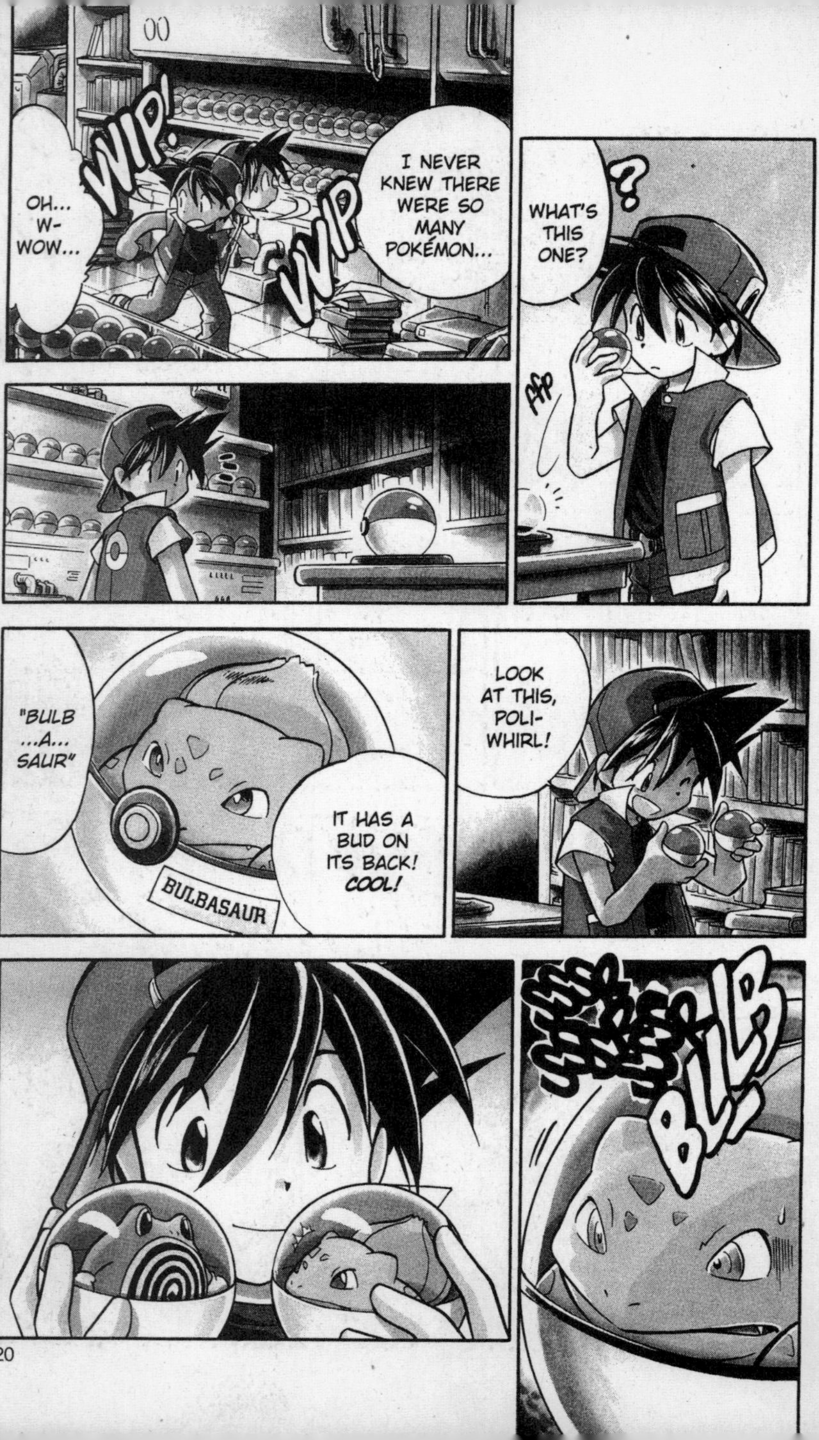
OH... W-WOW...
I NEVER KNEW THERE WERE SO MANY POKÉMON...
?
WHAT'S THIS ONE?
"BULB ...A... SAUR"
BULBASAUR
IT HAS A BUD ON ITS BACK! *COOL!*
LOOK AT THIS, POLI-WHIRL!

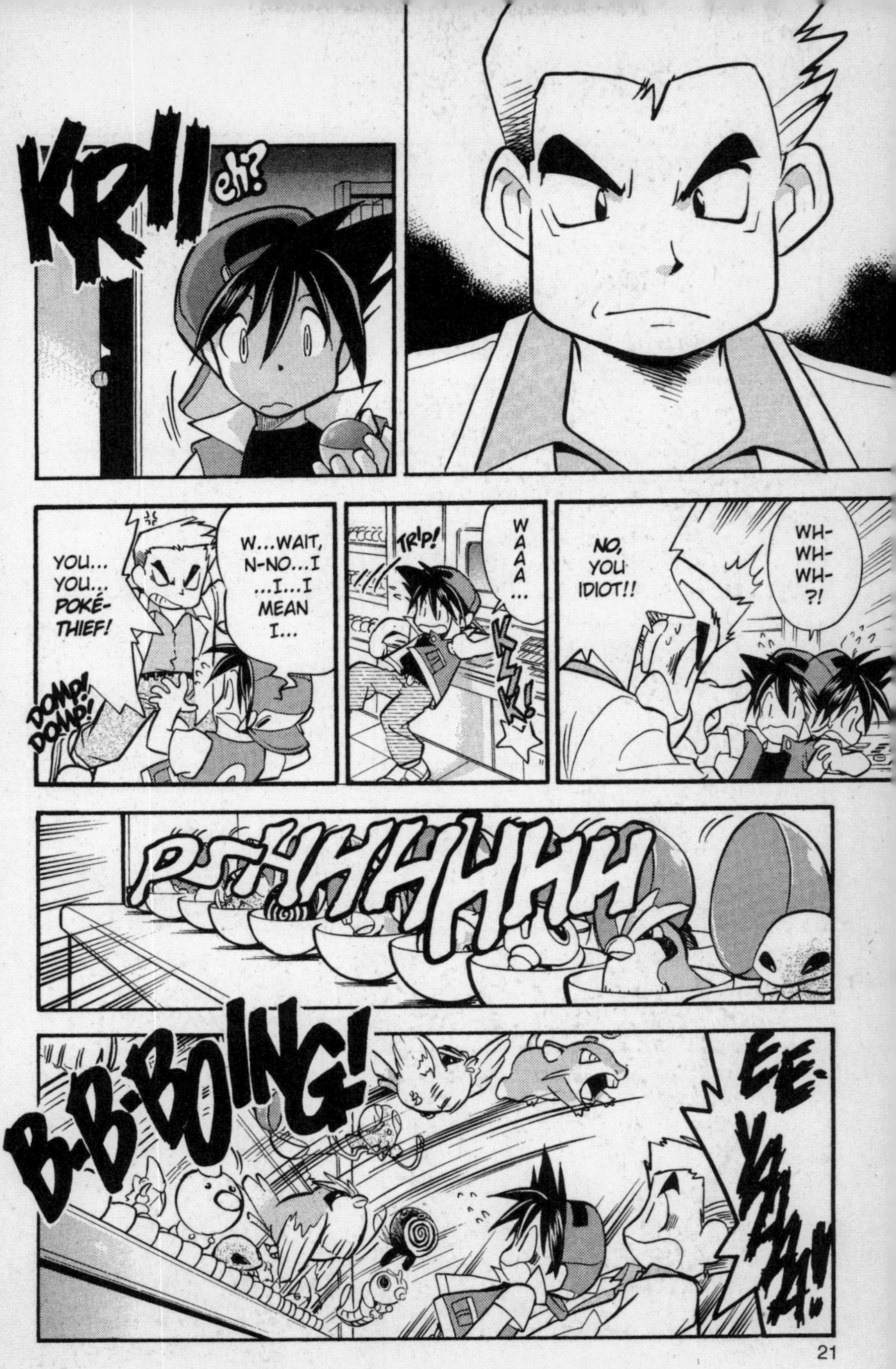
KRAK
eh?
YOU... YOU... POKÉ-THIEF!
W...WAIT, N-NO...I ...I...I MEAN I...
DOMP! DOMP!
TRIP!
WAAAA...
NO, YOU IDIOT!!
WH-WH-WH-?!
PSHHHHHHH
B-B-BOING!
EE-YAAAA!!

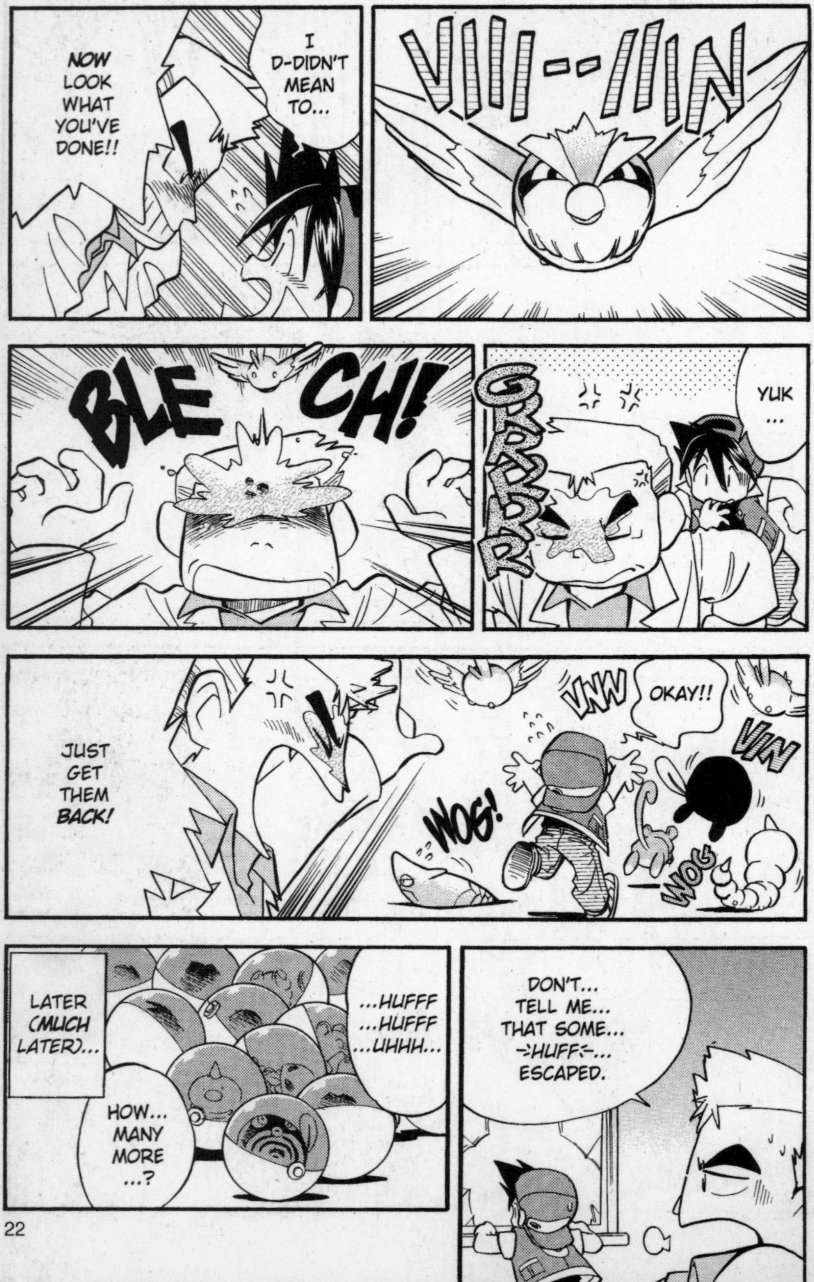

NOW LOOK WHAT YOU'VE DONE!!
I D-DIDN'T MEAN TO...
VIII--IIIN
BLE CH!
GRRRRR
YUK ...
JUST GET THEM BACK!
VNN
OKAY!!
VIN
WOG!
WOG
LATER (MUCH LATER)...
...HUFFF ...HUFFF ...UHHH...
HOW... MANY MORE ...?
DON'T... TELL ME... THAT SOME... ~HUFF~... ESCAPED.

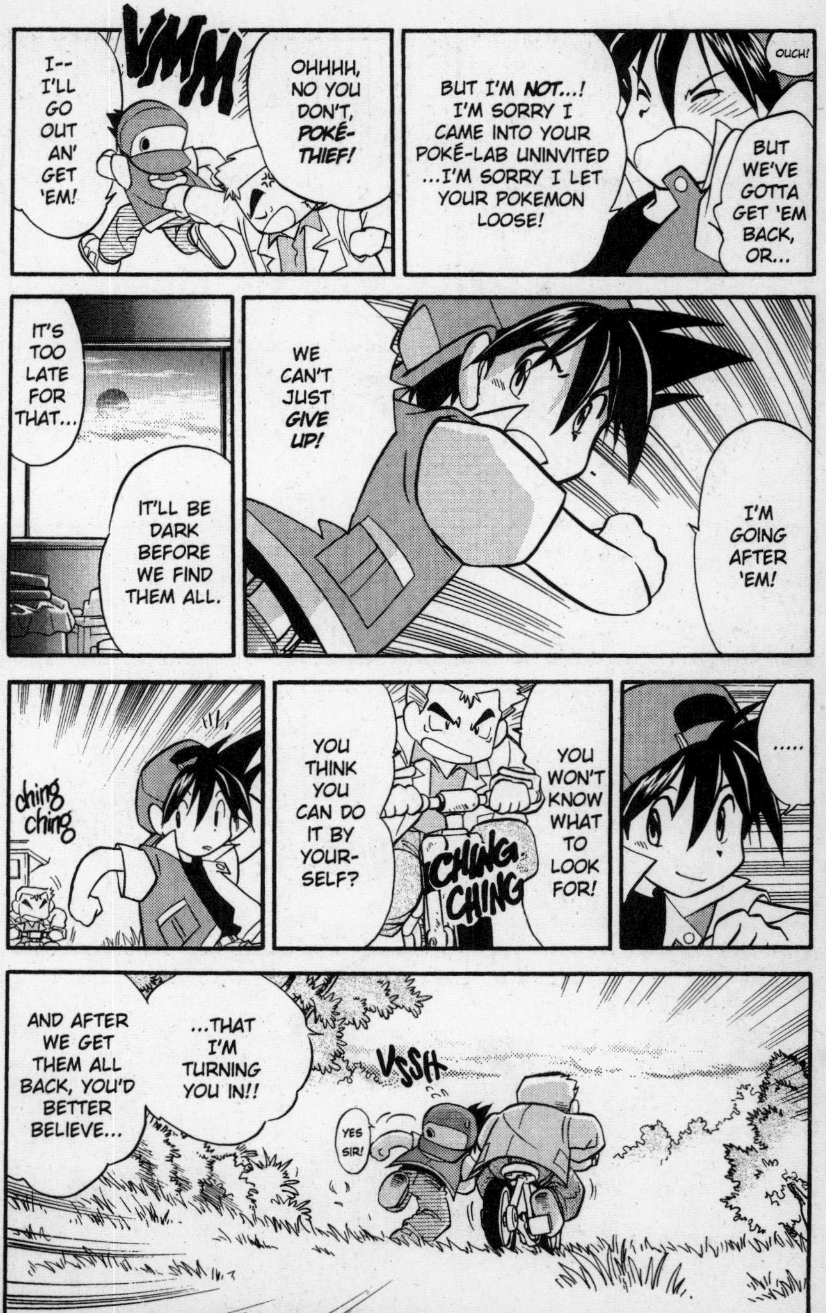
VMM
I-- I'LL GO OUT AN' GET 'EM!
OHHHH, NO YOU DON'T, POKÉ-THIEF!
BUT I'M NOT...! I'M SORRY I CAME INTO YOUR POKÉ-LAB UNINVITED ...I'M SORRY I LET YOUR POKEMON LOOSE!
OUCH!
BUT WE'VE GOTTA GET 'EM BACK, OR...
IT'S TOO LATE FOR THAT...
IT'LL BE DARK BEFORE WE FIND THEM ALL.
WE CAN'T JUST GIVE UP!
I'M GOING AFTER 'EM!
ching ching
YOU THINK YOU CAN DO IT BY YOUR-SELF?
CHING CHING
YOU WON'T KNOW WHAT TO LOOK FOR!
.....
AND AFTER WE GET THEM ALL BACK, YOU'D BETTER BELIEVE...
...THAT I'M TURNING YOU IN!!
VSSH
YES SIR!

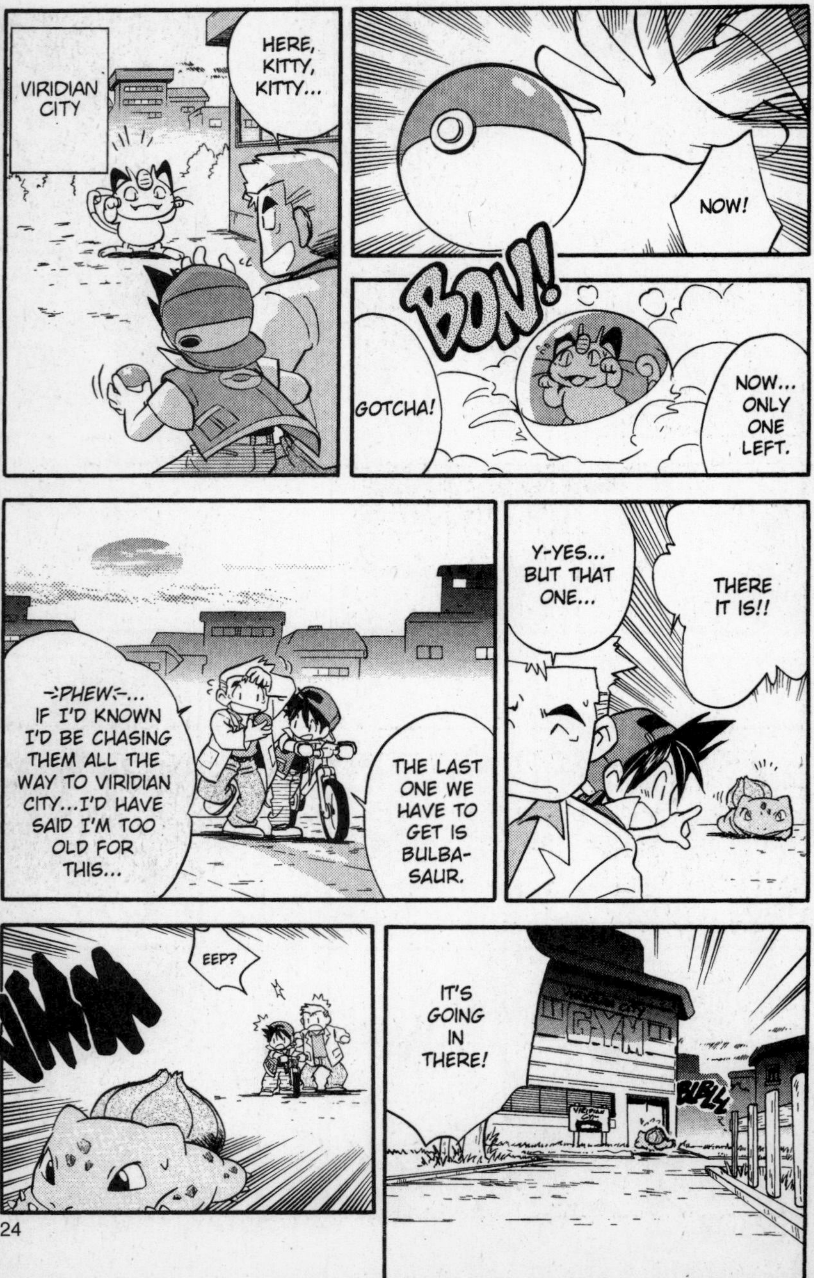

VIRIDIAN CITY
HERE, KITTY, KITTY...
NOW!
BON!
GOTCHA!
NOW... ONLY ONE LEFT.
-PHEW-... IF I'D KNOWN I'D BE CHASING THEM ALL THE WAY TO VIRIDIAN CITY...I'D HAVE SAID I'M TOO OLD FOR THIS...
THE LAST ONE WE HAVE TO GET IS BULBA-SAUR.
Y-YES... BUT THAT ONE...
THERE IT IS!!
EEP?
IT'S GOING IN THERE!
GYM

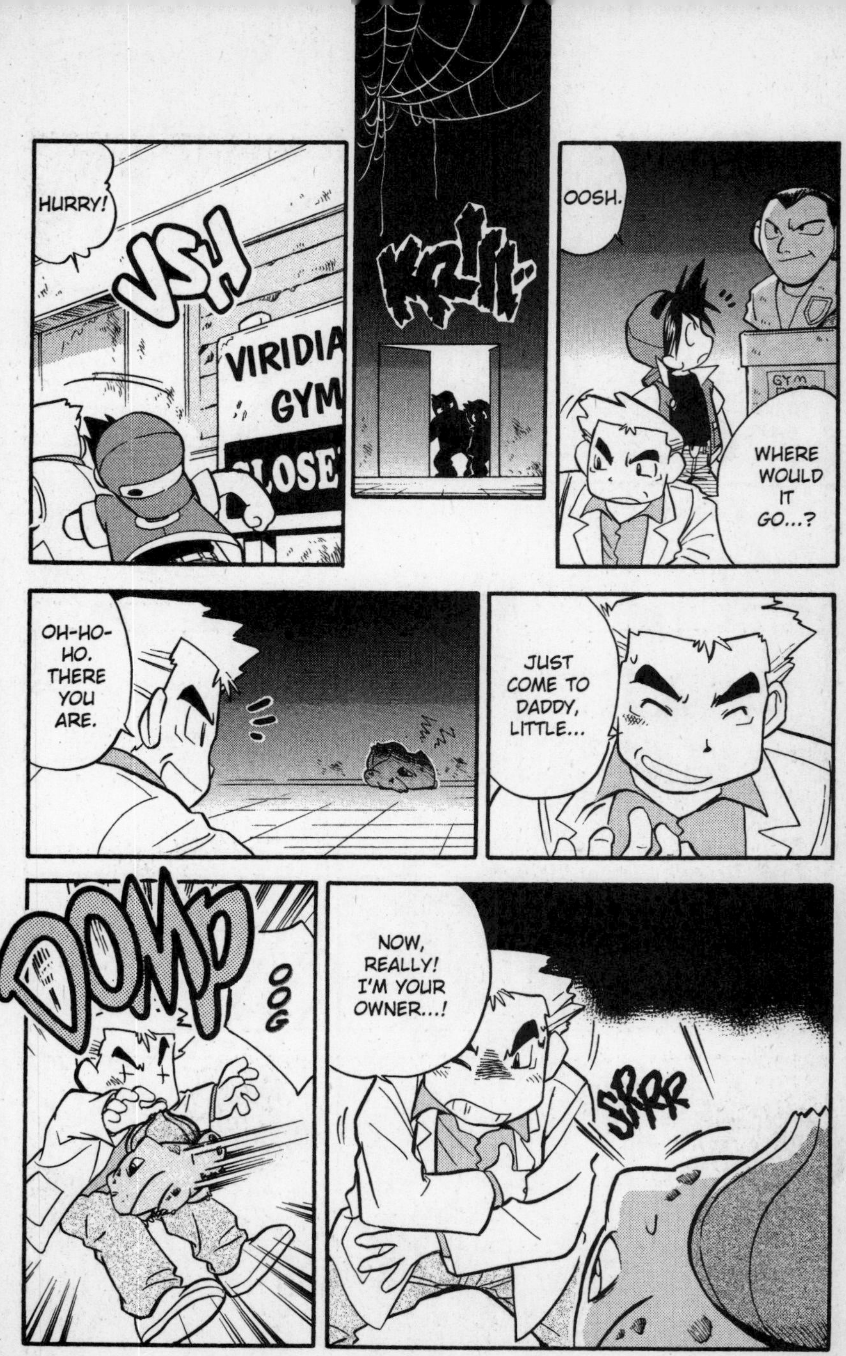
HURRY!
VSH
VIRIDIA
GYM
LOSE
OOSH.
WHERE WOULD IT GO...?
OH-HO-HO. THERE YOU ARE.
JUST COME TO DADDY, LITTLE...
DOMP
OOG
NOW, REALLY! I'M YOUR OWNER...!
SRRR

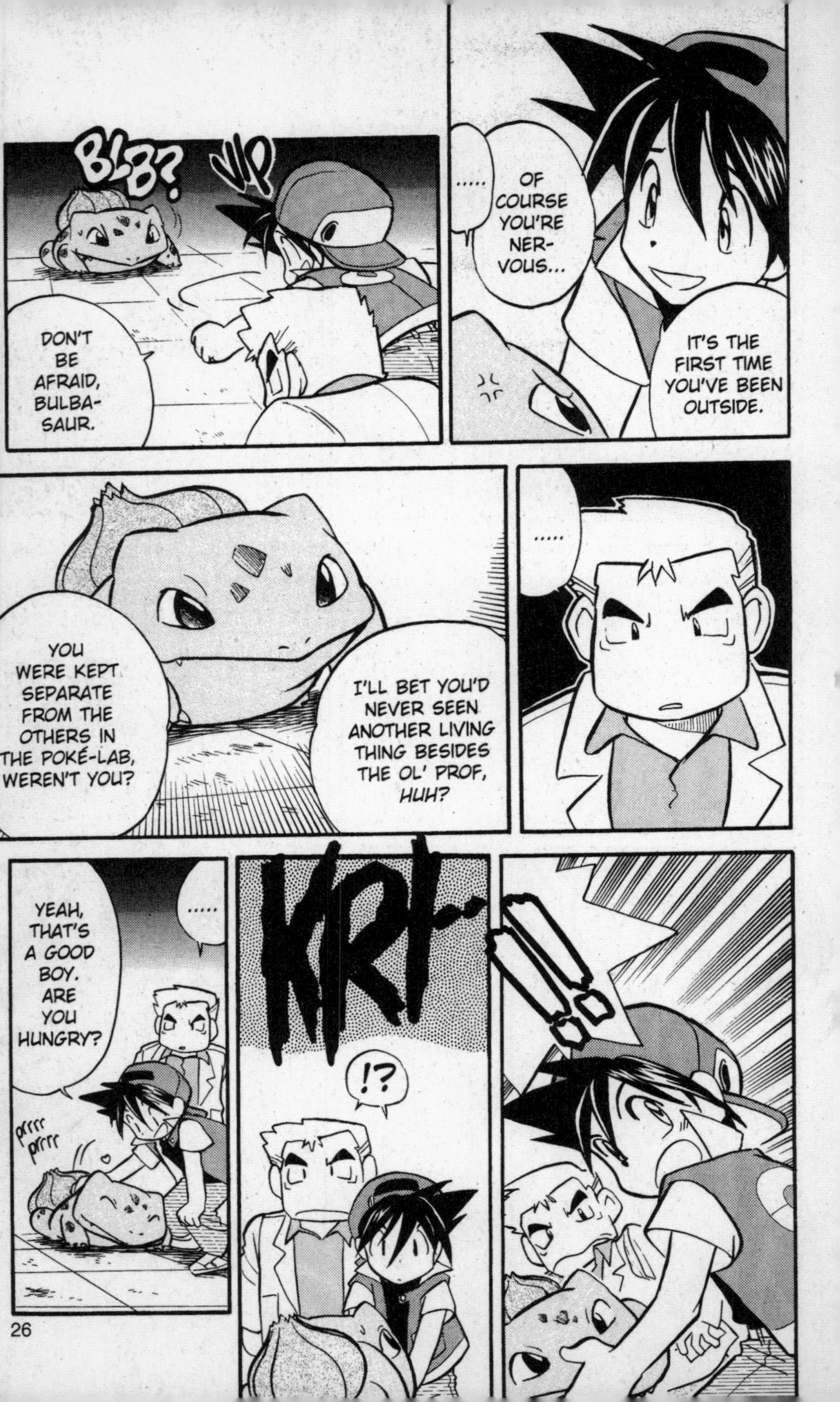
BLB?
JIP
DON'T BE AFRAID, BULBASAUR.
.....
OF COURSE YOU'RE NERVOUS...
IT'S THE FIRST TIME YOU'VE BEEN OUTSIDE.
YOU WERE KEPT SEPARATE FROM THE OTHERS IN THE POKÉ-LAB, WEREN'T YOU?
I'LL BET YOU'D NEVER SEEN ANOTHER LIVING THING BESIDES THE OL' PROF, HUH?
.....
YEAH, THAT'S A GOOD BOY. ARE YOU HUNGRY?
.....
prrrr prrrr
KRI
!?
!!

GASP!

I-IT'S ...

A WILD MACHOKE !!

MMMMMAAAAA

YAA !!

VOOOO

SSSRRRR

BU

CHKK

PROF!! D'YOU SEE THAT?!

WHAT'S THE BULBASAUR'S BEST ATTACK?!

N'YONGG

EEP

OH, GREAT... WHAT NEXT?

WAIT... IF IT'S GOT A BULB...

HMMM

CHOK!

MYAAA BAM!

WUP!

MMMM...

TH-THERE'S NO WAY...

ARRG!!

GLINT!

!! GLINT

WAIT...

WH-WHAT IF...? I GUESS ...I GOTTA...

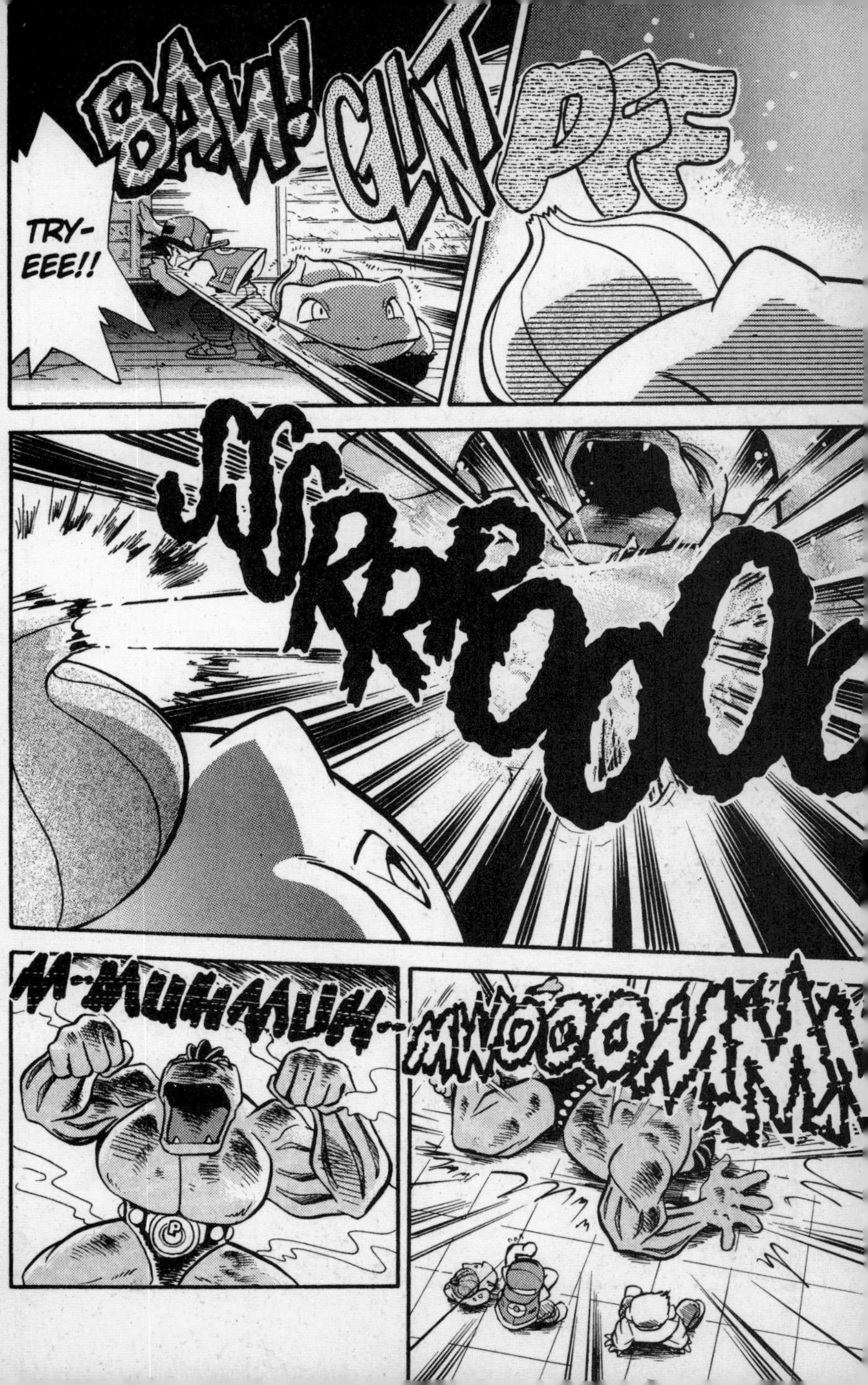
BAM!
CLINT
POFF
TRY-
EEE!!
WURRROOO
M-MUHMUH-
MWOOOWWW

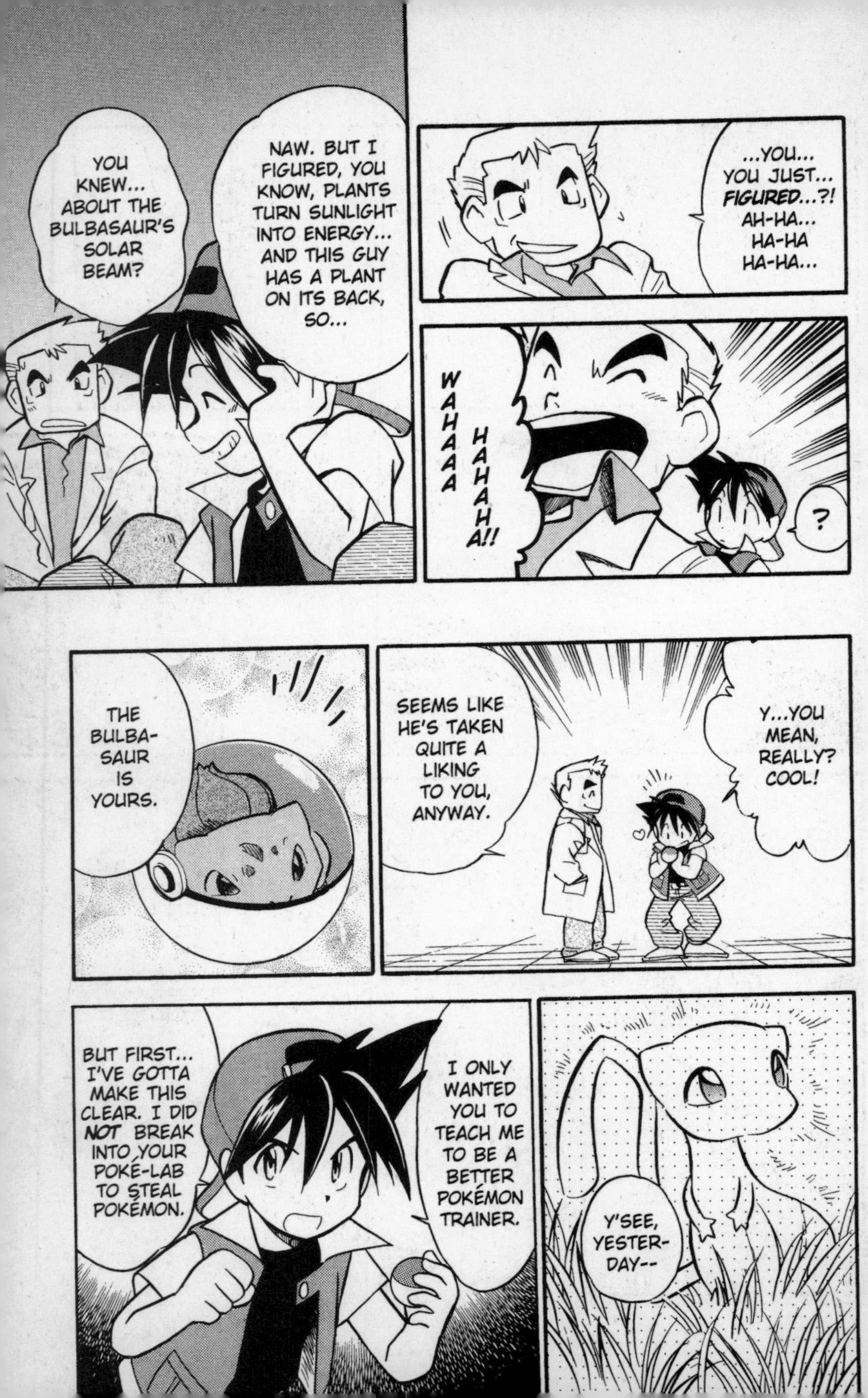
YOU KNEW... ABOUT THE BULBASAUR'S SOLAR BEAM?
NAW. BUT I FIGURED, YOU KNOW, PLANTS TURN SUNLIGHT INTO ENERGY... AND THIS GUY HAS A PLANT ON ITS BACK, SO...
...YOU... YOU JUST... FIGURED...?! AH-HA... HA-HA HA-HA...
WAHAHAA HAHAHAHA!!
?
THE BULBASAUR IS YOURS.
SEEMS LIKE HE'S TAKEN QUITE A LIKING TO YOU, ANYWAY.
Y...YOU MEAN, REALLY? COOL!
BUT FIRST... I'VE GOTTA MAKE THIS CLEAR. I DID NOT BREAK INTO YOUR POKÉ-LAB TO STEAL POKÉMON.
I ONLY WANTED YOU TO TEACH ME TO BE A BETTER POKÉMON TRAINER.
Y'SEE, YESTERDAY--

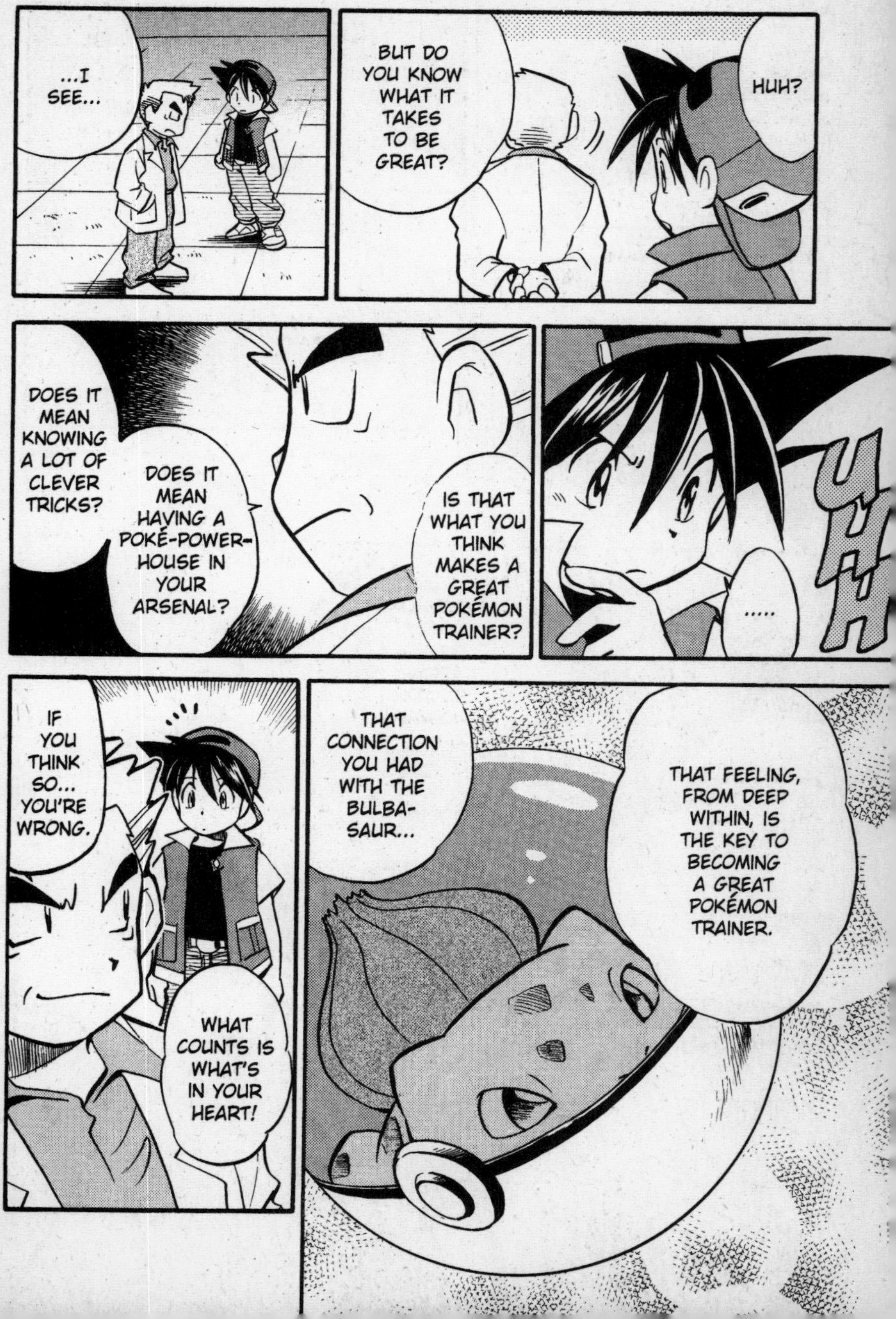

...I SEE...
BUT DO YOU KNOW WHAT IT TAKES TO BE GREAT?
HUH?
DOES IT MEAN KNOWING A LOT OF CLEVER TRICKS?
DOES IT MEAN HAVING A POKÉ-POWER-HOUSE IN YOUR ARSENAL?
IS THAT WHAT YOU THINK MAKES A GREAT POKÉMON TRAINER?
UHH
.....
IF YOU THINK SO... YOU'RE WRONG.
WHAT COUNTS IS WHAT'S IN YOUR HEART!
THAT CONNECTION YOU HAD WITH THE BULBA-SAUR...
THAT FEELING, FROM DEEP WITHIN, IS THE KEY TO BECOMING A GREAT POKÉMON TRAINER.

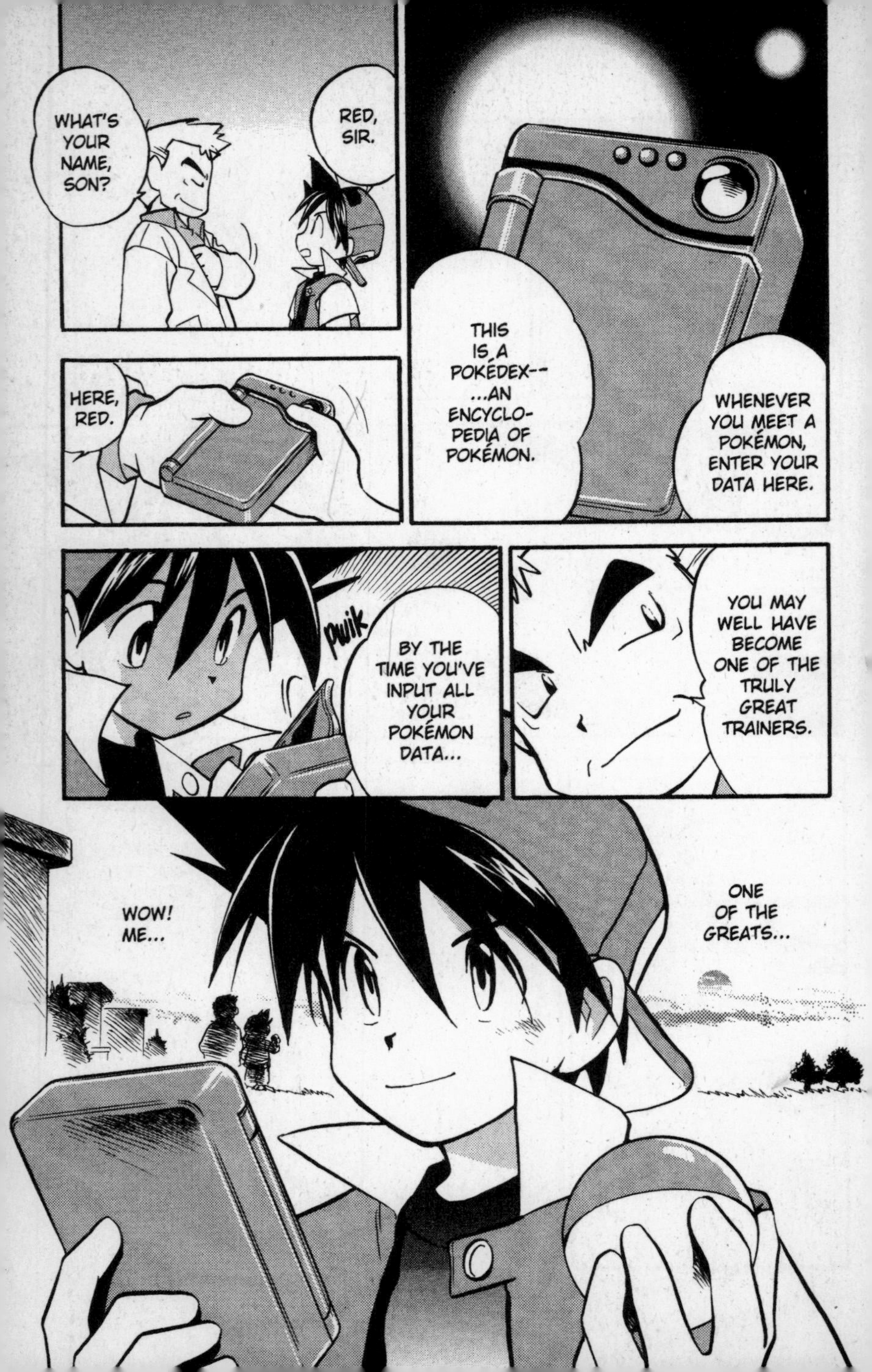
WHAT'S YOUR NAME, SON?
RED, SIR.
HERE, RED.
THIS IS A POKÉDEX-- ...AN ENCYCLO-PEDIA OF POKÉMON.
WHENEVER YOU MEET A POKÉMON, ENTER YOUR DATA HERE.
pwik
BY THE TIME YOU'VE INPUT ALL YOUR POKÉMON DATA...
YOU MAY WELL HAVE BECOME ONE OF THE TRULY GREAT TRAINERS.
WOW! ME...
ONE OF THE GREATS...

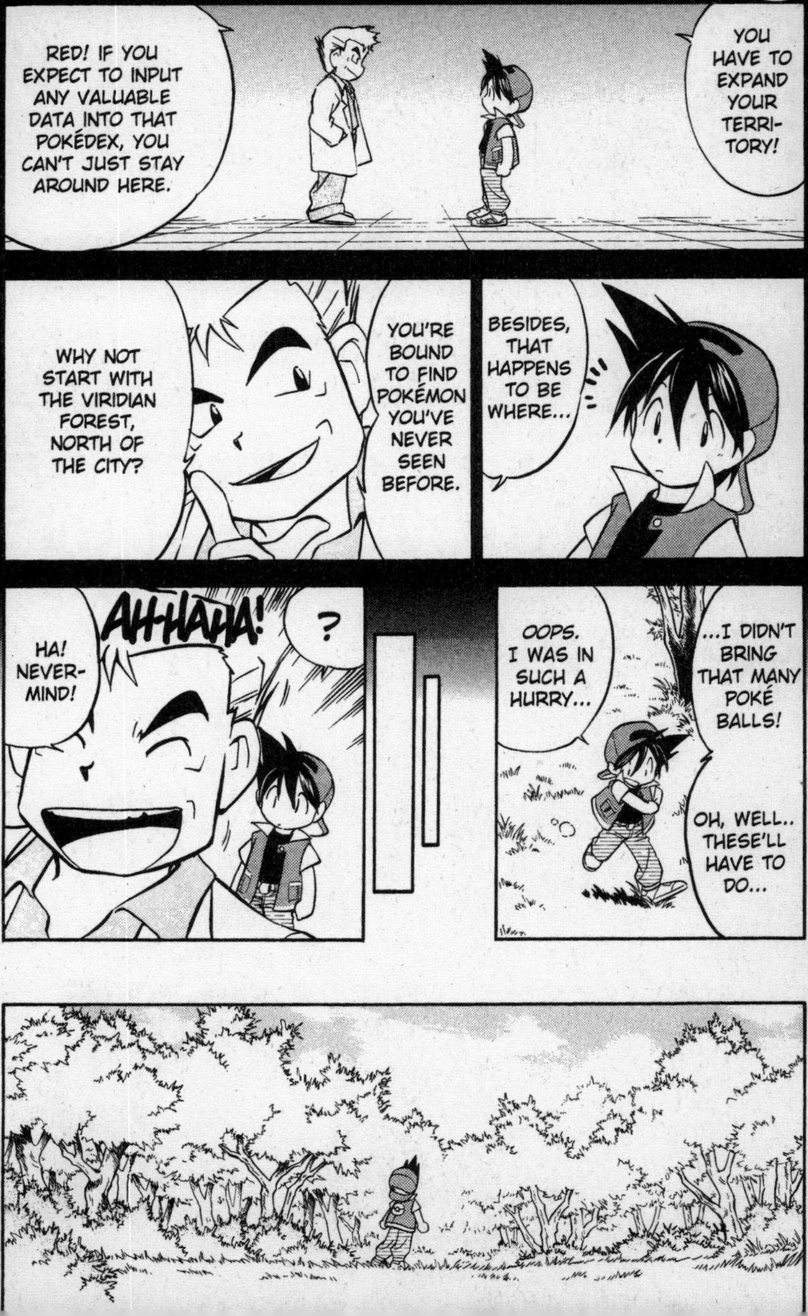

RED! IF YOU EXPECT TO INPUT ANY VALUABLE DATA INTO THAT POKÉDEX, YOU CAN'T JUST STAY AROUND HERE.
YOU HAVE TO EXPAND YOUR TERRITORY!
WHY NOT START WITH THE VIRIDIAN FOREST, NORTH OF THE CITY?
YOU'RE BOUND TO FIND POKÉMON YOU'VE NEVER SEEN BEFORE.
BESIDES, THAT HAPPENS TO BE WHERE...
AH-HAHA!
HA! NEVER-MIND!
?
OOPS. I WAS IN SUCH A HURRY...
...I DIDN'T BRING THAT MANY POKÉ BALLS!
OH, WELL.. THESE'LL HAVE TO DO...

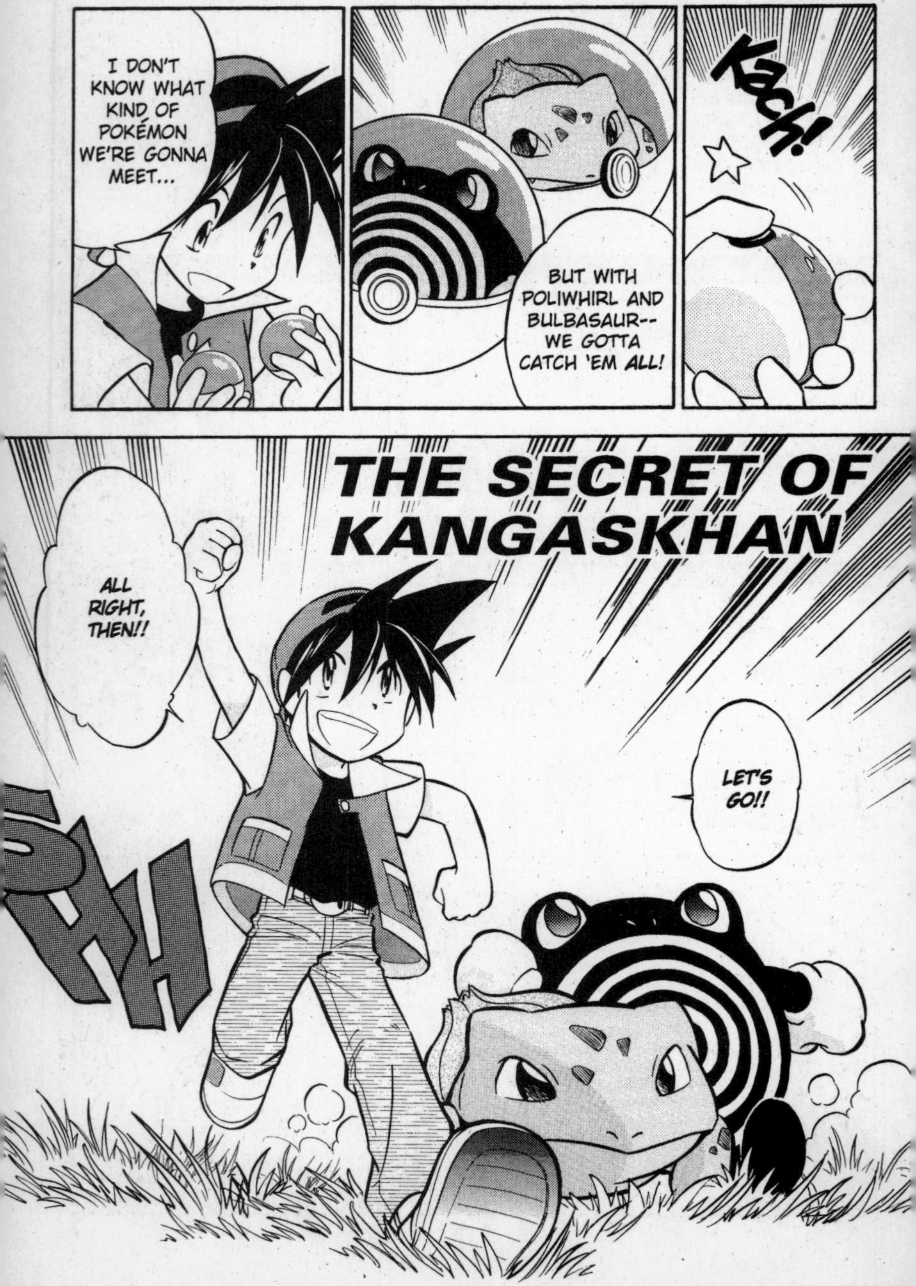
I DON'T KNOW WHAT KIND OF POKÉMON WE'RE GONNA MEET...
BUT WITH POLIWHIRL AND BULBASAUR-- WE GOTTA CATCH 'EM ALL!
KACH!
THE SECRET OF KANGASKHAN
ALL RIGHT, THEN!!
LET'S GO!!

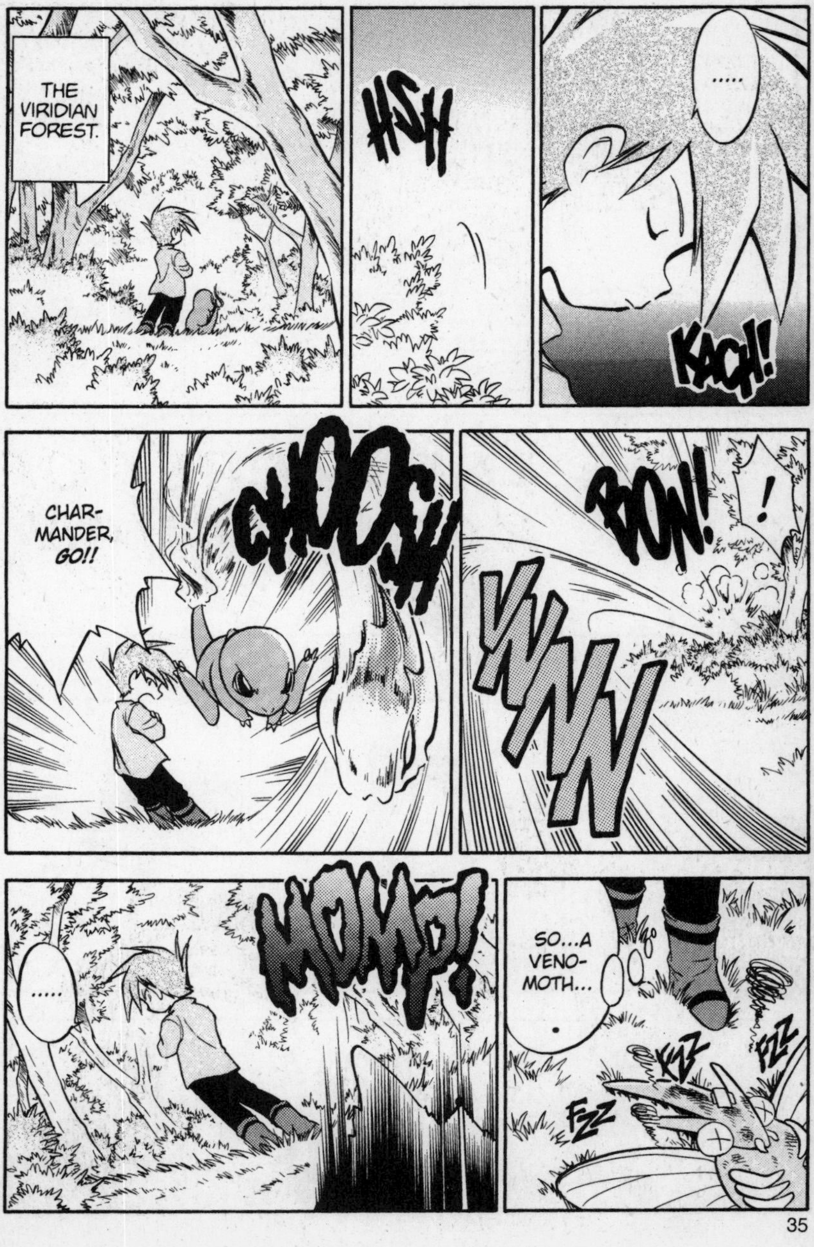
THE VIRIDIAN FOREST.
HSH
.....
KACH!
CHAR-MANDER, GO!!
CHOOSH
BON!
!
VNNN
.....
WOMP!
SO...A VENO-MOTH...
KZZ
FZZ
FZZ

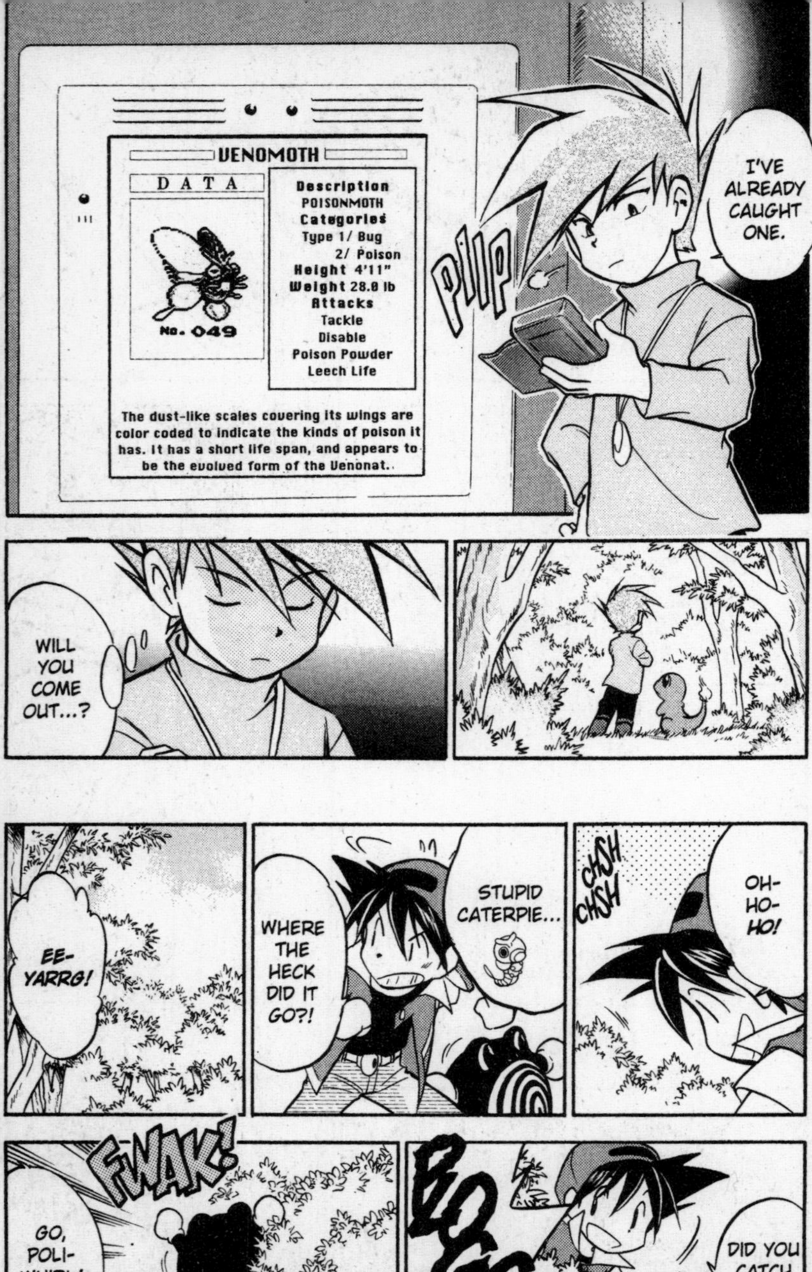
VENOMOTH
DATA
Description
POISONMOTH
Categories
Type 1/ Bug
2/ Poison
Height 4'11"
Weight 28.0 lb
Attacks
Tackle
Disable
Poison Powder
Leech Life
No. 049
The dust-like scales covering its wings are color coded to indicate the kinds of poison it has. It has a short life span, and appears to be the evolved form of the Venonat.
PLIP
I'VE ALREADY CAUGHT ONE.
WILL YOU COME OUT...?
EE-YARRG!
STUPID CATERPIE...
WHERE THE HECK DID IT GO?!
CHSH CHSH
OH-HO-HO!
FWAK!
GO, POLI-WHIRL!
BOGG
DID YOU CATCH IT?! DID YOU--

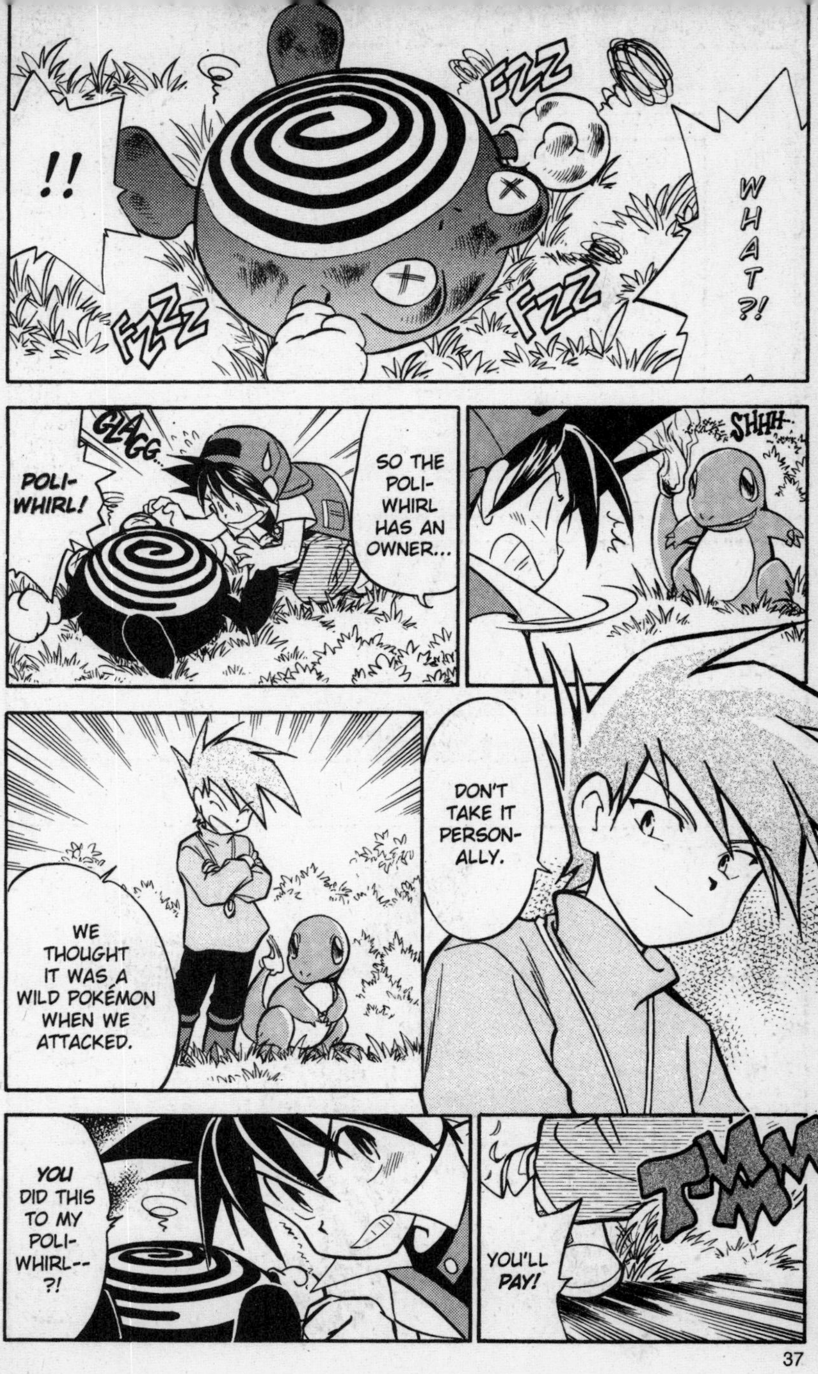
!!
FZZZ
FZZ
FZZ
WHAT?!
GLAGG...
POLI-WHIRL!
SO THE POLI-WHIRL HAS AN OWNER...
SHHH
WE THOUGHT IT WAS A WILD POKÉMON WHEN WE ATTACKED.
DON'T TAKE IT PERSONALLY.
YOU DID THIS TO MY POLI-WHIRL-- ?!
TMMM
YOU'LL PAY!

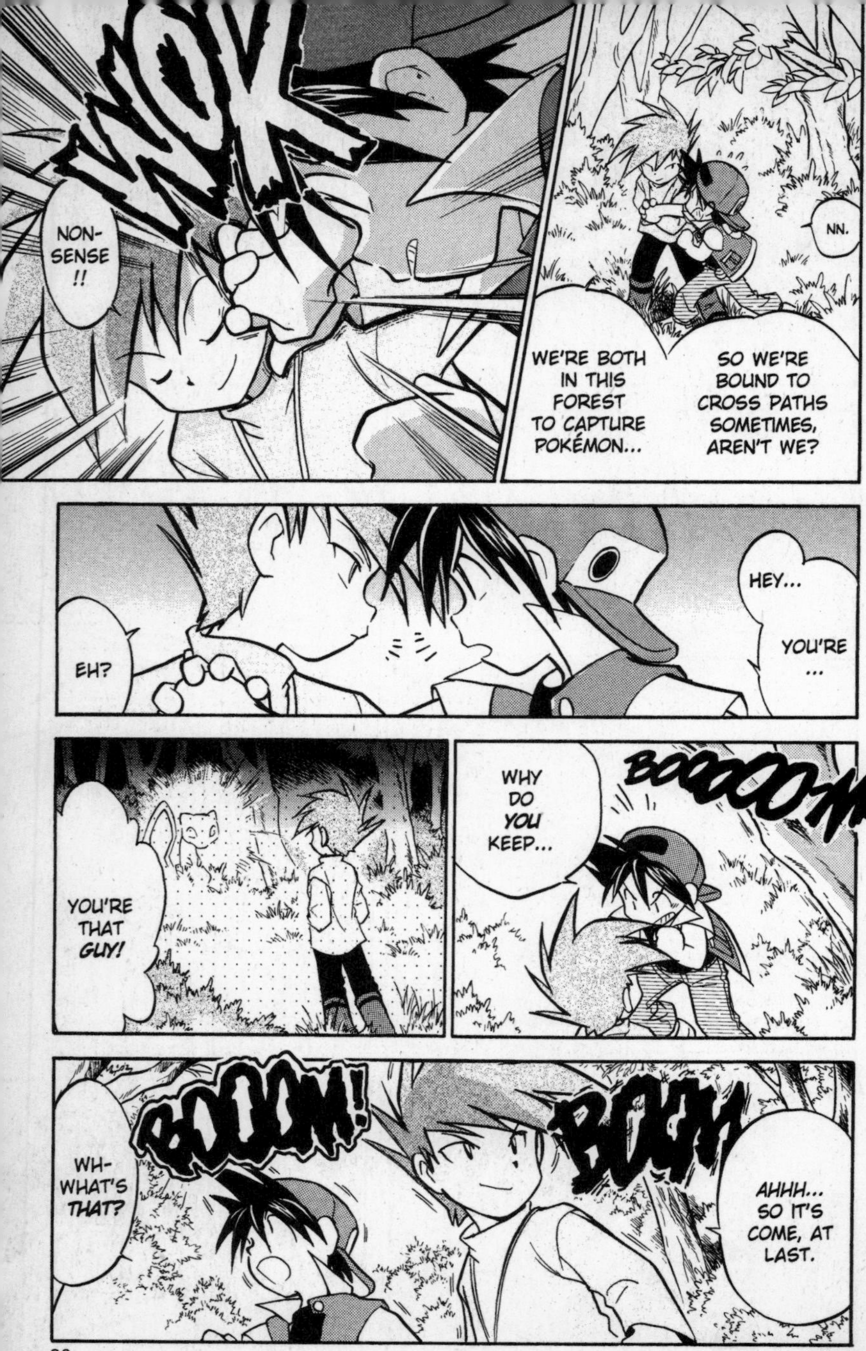
NON-SENSE!!
NN.
WE'RE BOTH IN THIS FOREST TO CAPTURE POKÉMON...
SO WE'RE BOUND TO CROSS PATHS SOMETIMES, AREN'T WE?
EH?
HEY...
YOU'RE ...
YOU'RE THAT GUY!
WHY DO YOU KEEP...
BOOM!
WH-WHAT'S THAT?
BOOM
AHHH... SO IT'S COME, AT LAST.

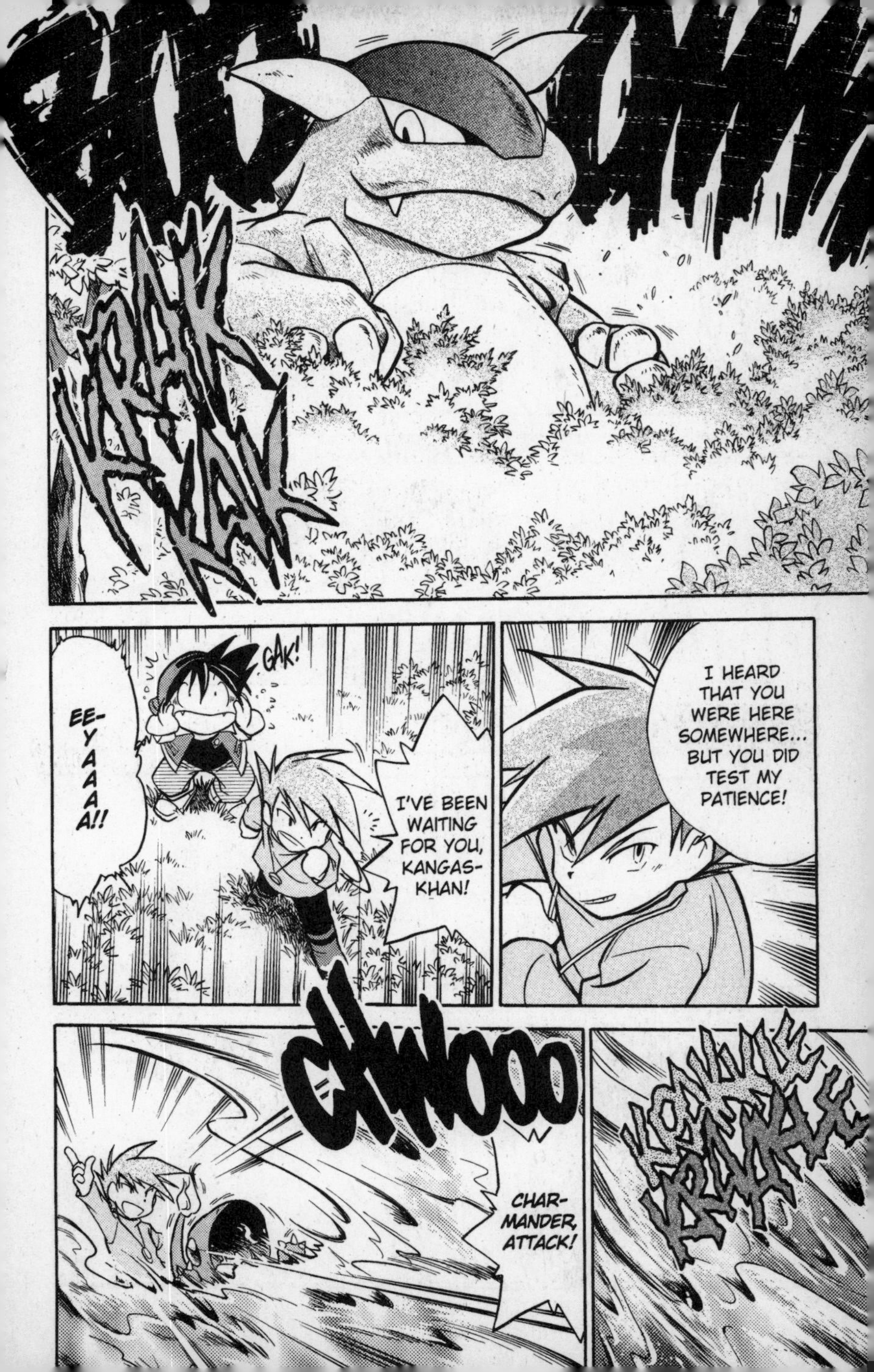
GAK!
EE-YAAAAA!!
I'VE BEEN WAITING FOR YOU, KANGAS-KHAN!
I HEARD THAT YOU WERE HERE SOMEWHERE... BUT YOU DID TEST MY PATIENCE!
CHAR-MANDER, ATTACK!

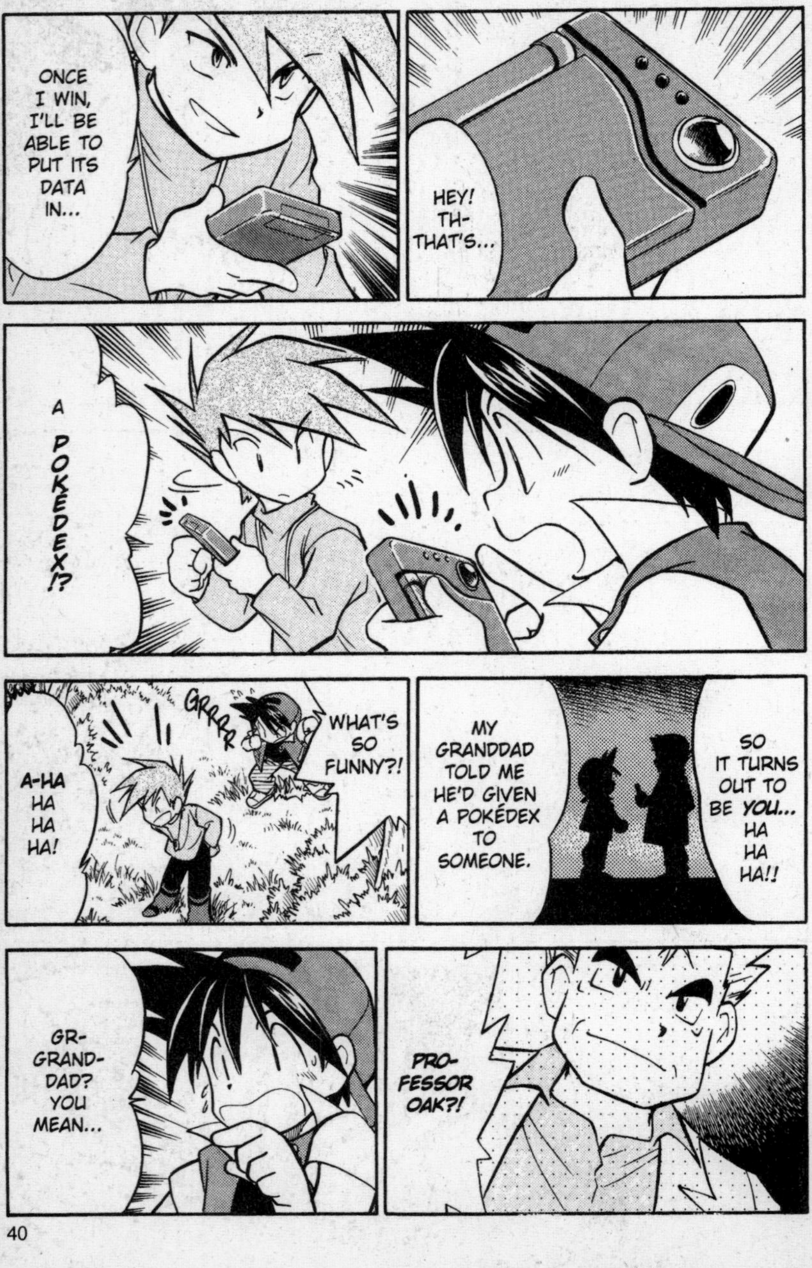
ONCE I WIN, I'LL BE ABLE TO PUT ITS DATA IN...
HEY! TH-THAT'S...
A POKÉDEX!?
A-HA HA HA HA!
GRRRR
WHAT'S SO FUNNY?!
MY GRANDDAD TOLD ME HE'D GIVEN A POKÉDEX TO SOMEONE.
SO IT TURNS OUT TO BE *YOU*... HA HA HA!!
GR-GRAND-DAD? YOU MEAN...
PRO-FESSOR OAK?!

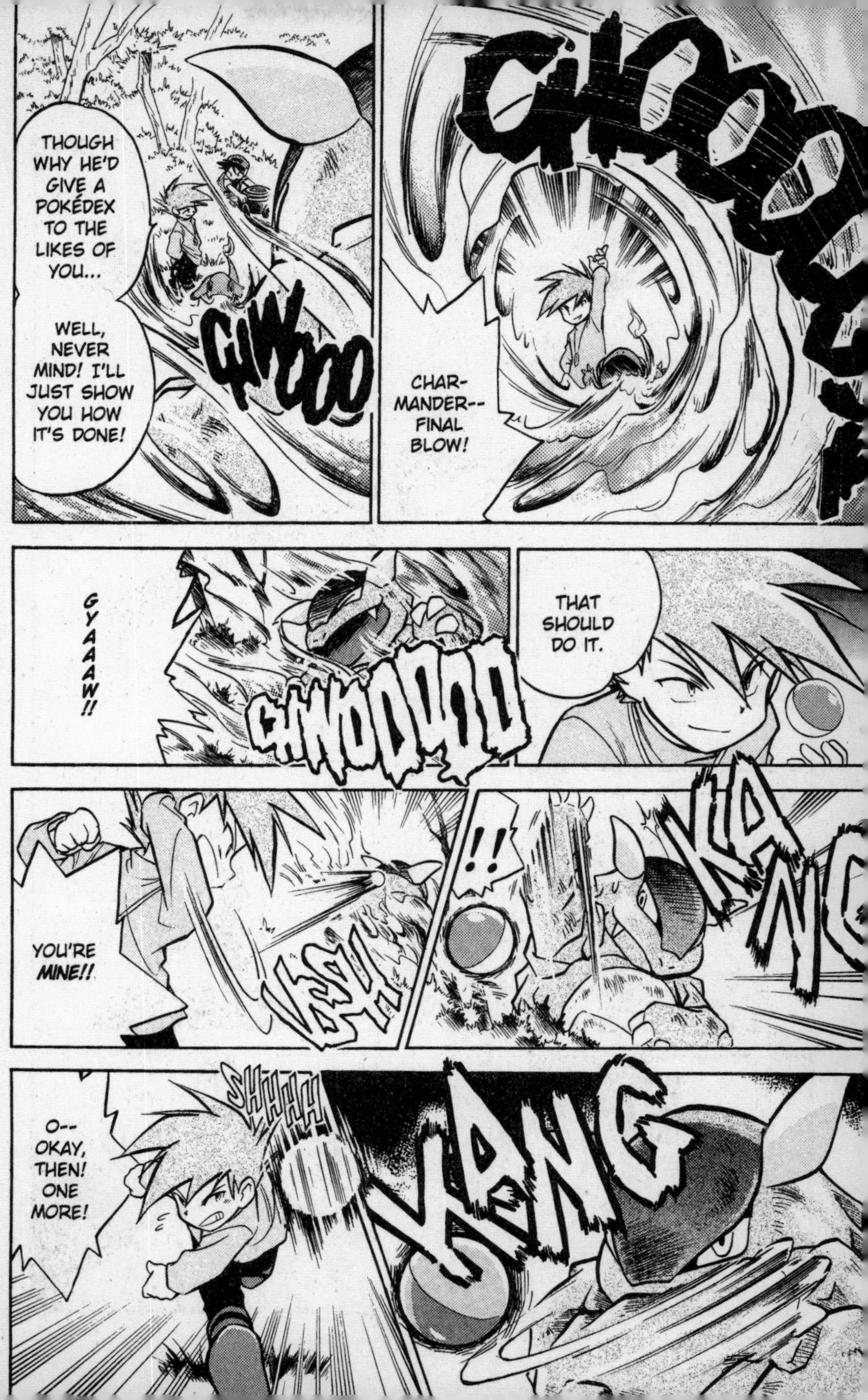
THOUGH WHY HE'D GIVE A POKÉDEX TO THE LIKES OF YOU...
WELL, NEVER MIND! I'LL JUST SHOW YOU HOW IT'S DONE!
GWOOO
CHAR-MANDER--FINAL BLOW!
GYAAAAW!!
GWOOOOO
THAT SHOULD DO IT.
YOU'RE MINE!!
!!
KANG
O--OKAY, THEN! ONE MORE!
SHHHH
YANG

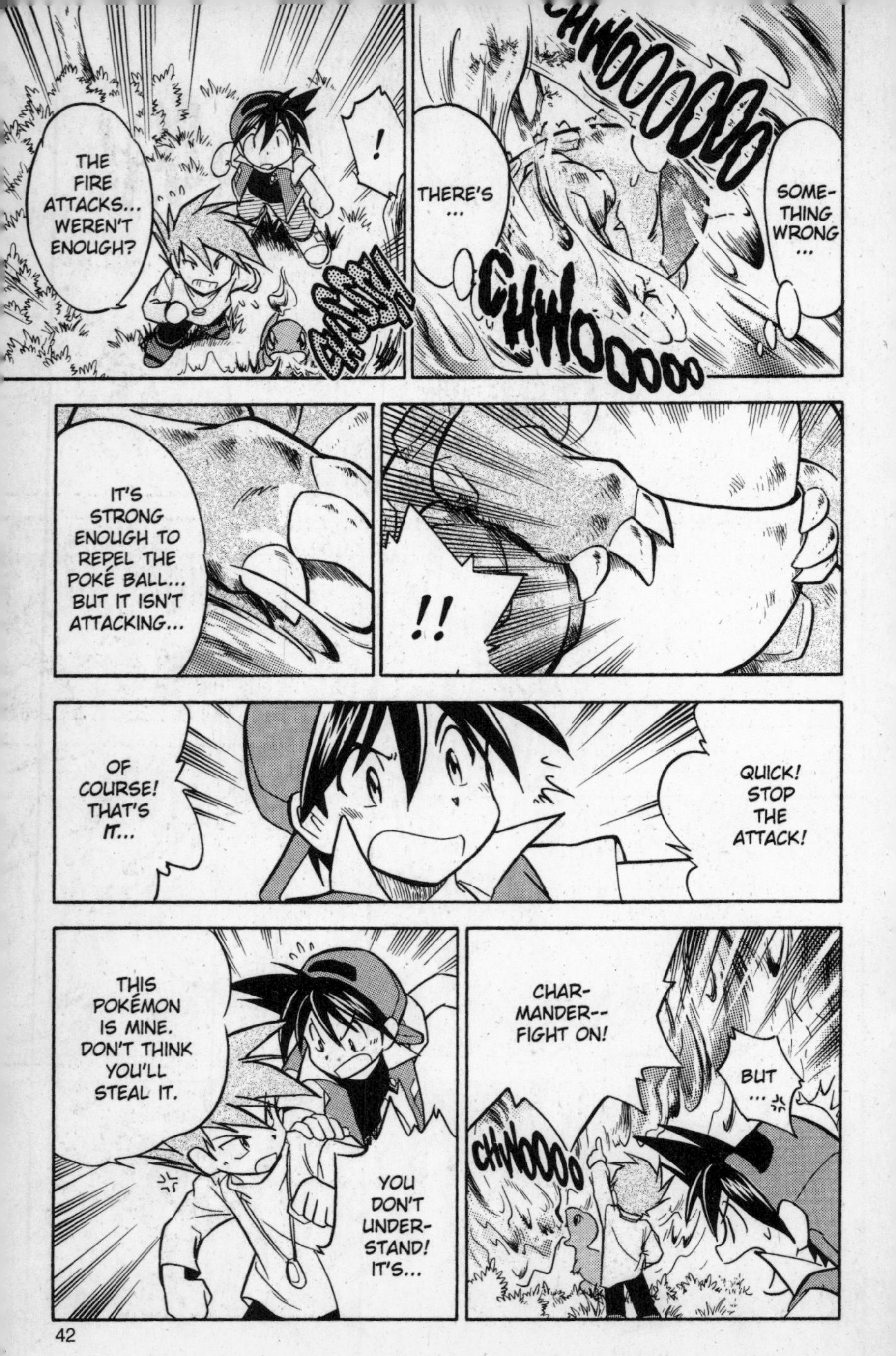
THE FIRE ATTACKS... WEREN'T ENOUGH?
!
CHWOOOOOOO
SOME-THING WRONG ...
THERE'S ...
CHWOOOOOO
IT'S STRONG ENOUGH TO REPEL THE POKÉ BALL... BUT IT ISN'T ATTACKING...
!!
QUICK! STOP THE ATTACK!
OF COURSE! THAT'S IT...
CHAR-MANDER-- FIGHT ON!
BUT ...
CHWOOOOO
THIS POKÉMON IS MINE. DON'T THINK YOU'LL STEAL IT.
YOU DON'T UNDER-STAND! IT'S...

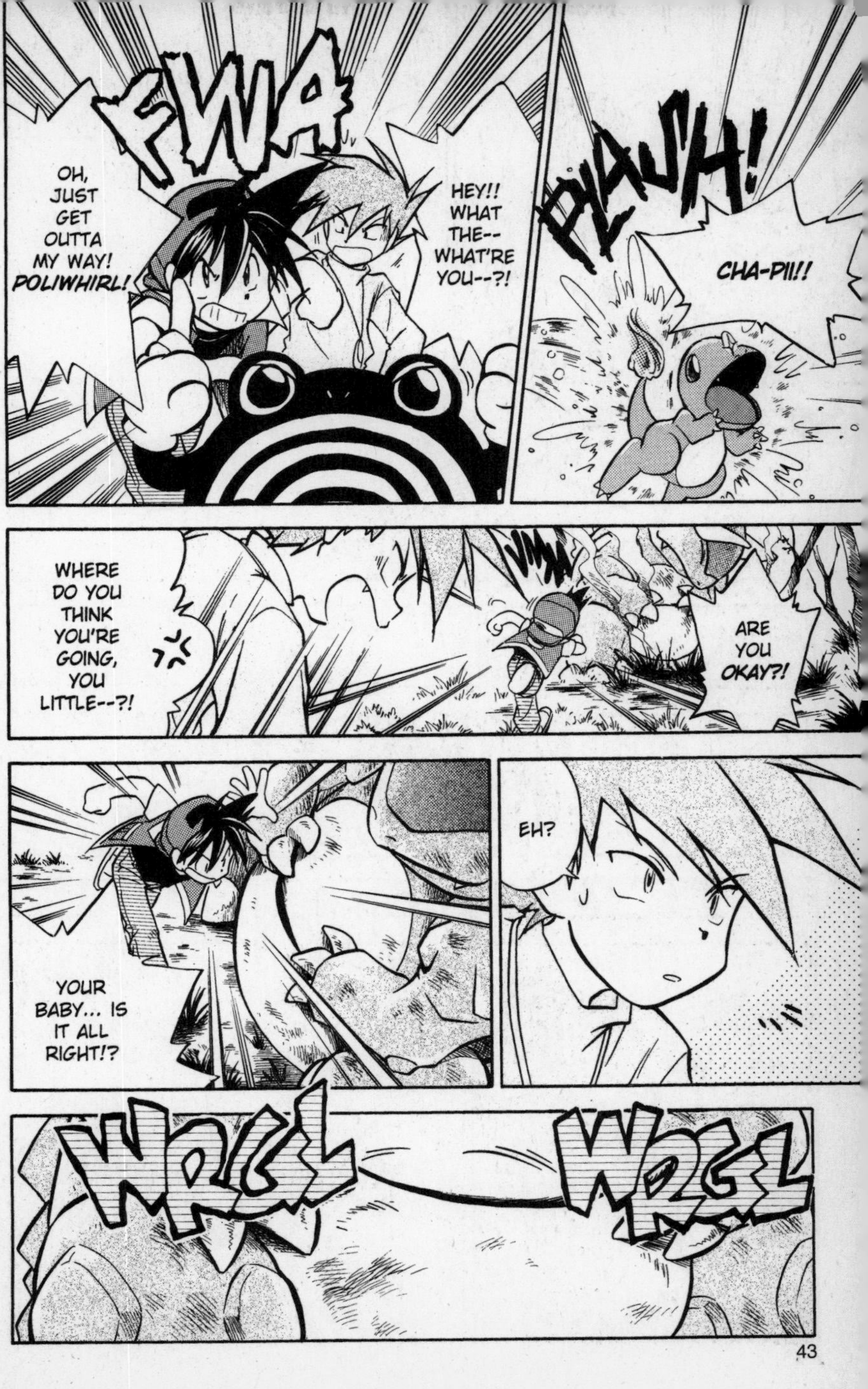
FWA
OH, JUST GET OUTTA MY WAY! POLIWHIRL!
HEY!! WHAT THE-- WHAT'RE YOU--?!
PLASH!
CHA-PII!!
WHERE DO YOU THINK YOU'RE GOING, YOU LITTLE--?!
ARE YOU OKAY?!
YOUR BABY... IS IT ALL RIGHT!?
EH?
WRGL
WRGL

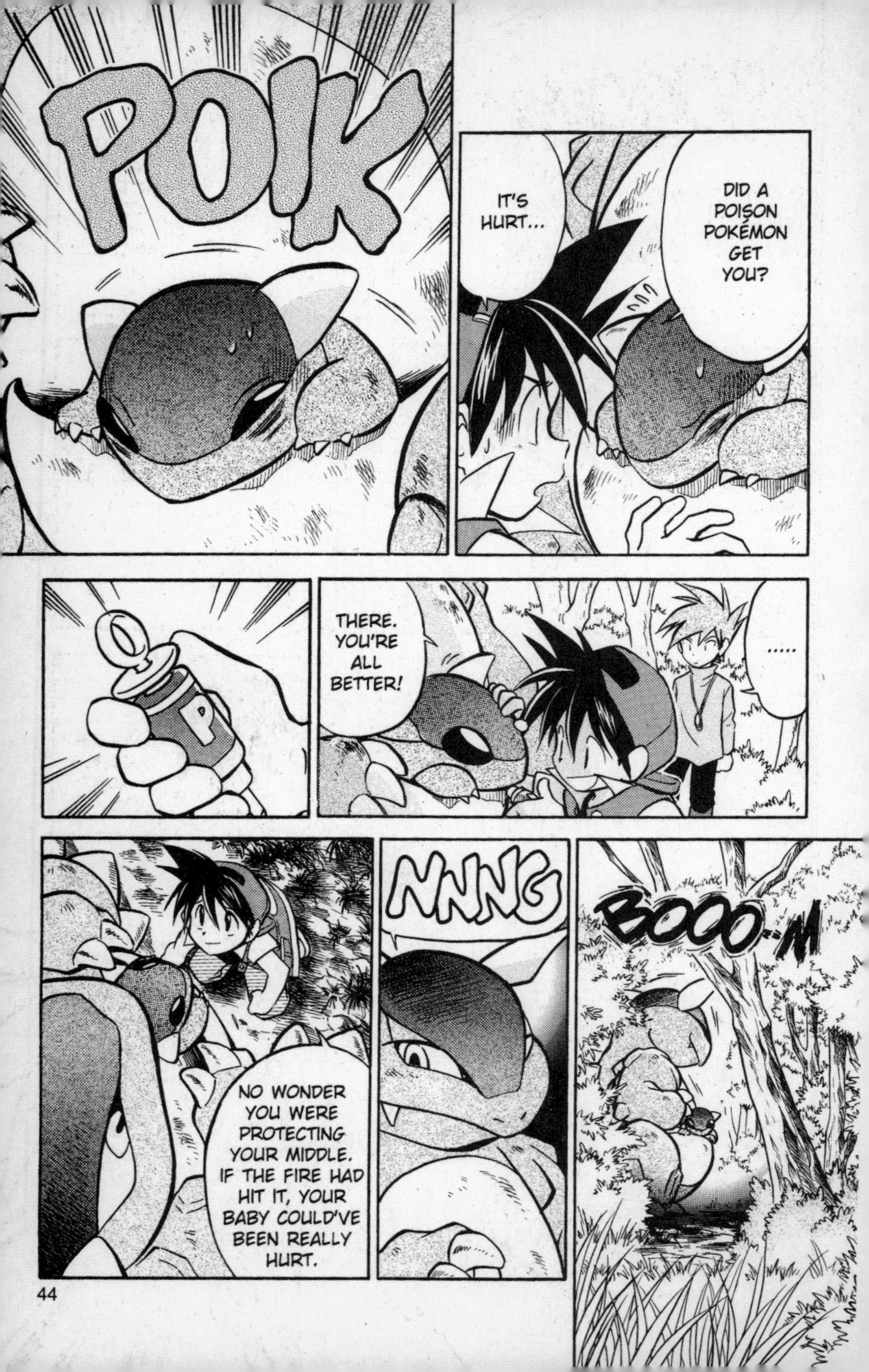
POK
IT'S HURT...
DID A POISON POKÉMON GET YOU?
THERE. YOU'RE ALL BETTER!
.....
NO WONDER YOU WERE PROTECTING YOUR MIDDLE. IF THE FIRE HAD HIT IT, YOUR BABY COULD'VE BEEN REALLY HURT.
NNNG
BOOOM

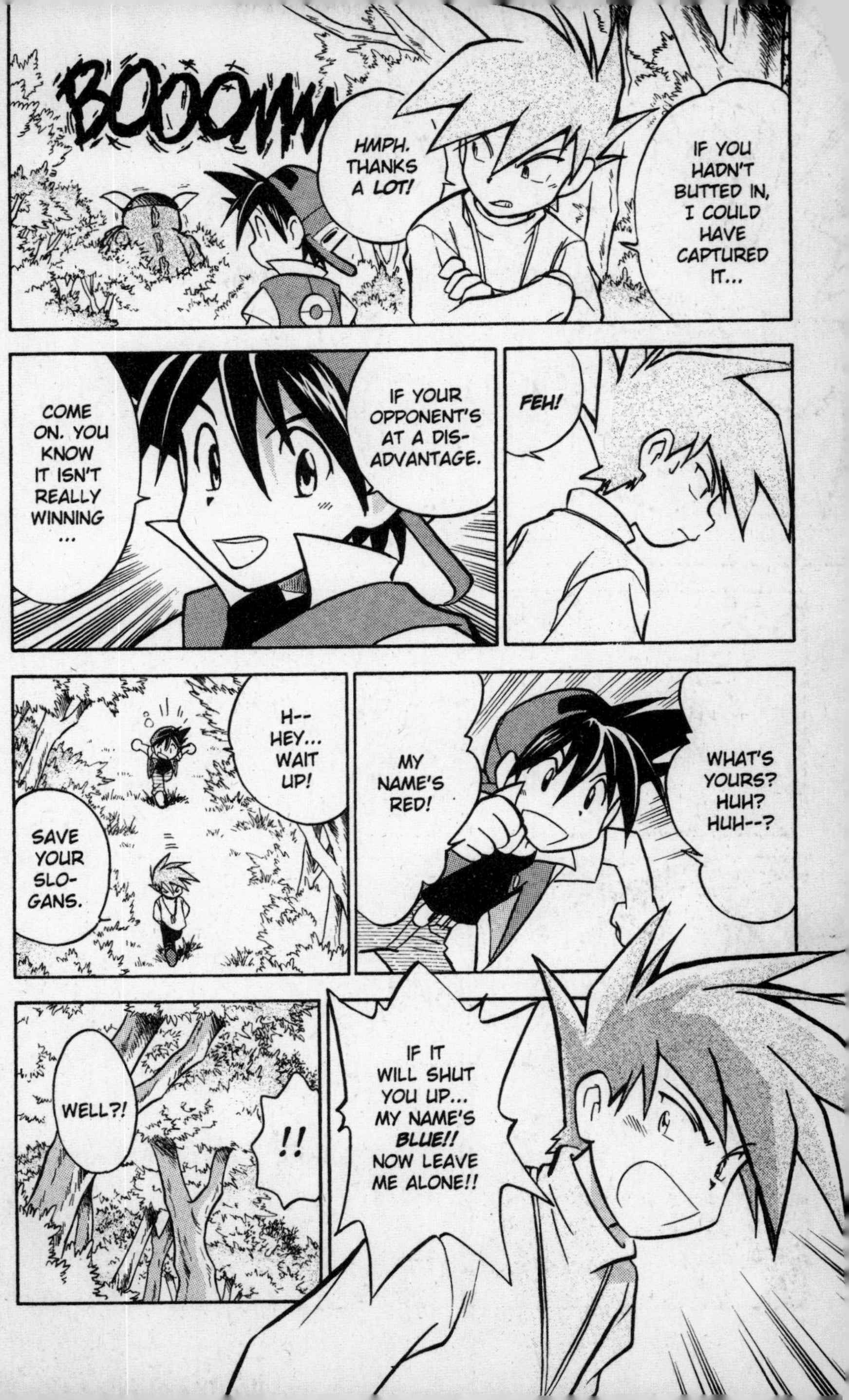
BOOOOM
HMPH. THANKS A LOT!
IF YOU HADN'T BUTTED IN, I COULD HAVE CAPTURED IT...
COME ON. YOU KNOW IT ISN'T REALLY WINNING...
IF YOUR OPPONENT'S AT A DIS-ADVANTAGE.
FEH!
H--HEY... WAIT UP!
SAVE YOUR SLO-GANS.
MY NAME'S RED!
WHAT'S YOURS? HUH? HUH--?
WELL?!
!!
IF IT WILL SHUT YOU UP... MY NAME'S BLUE!! NOW LEAVE ME ALONE!!

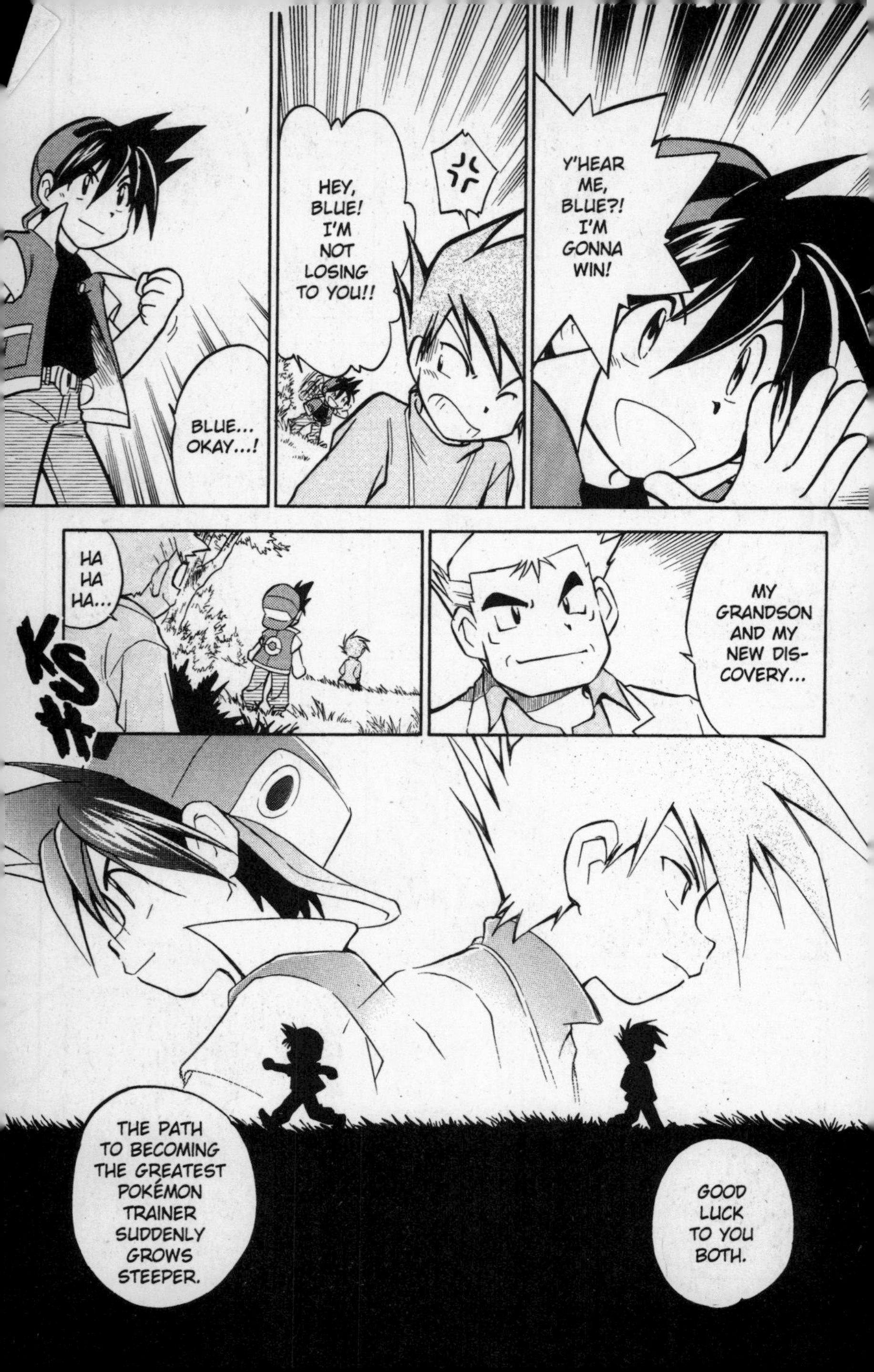

Y'HEAR ME, BLUE?! I'M GONNA WIN!
HEY, BLUE! I'M NOT LOSING TO YOU!!
BLUE... OKAY...!
MY GRANDSON AND MY NEW DIS-COVERY...
HA HA HA...
KSH
GOOD LUCK TO YOU BOTH.
THE PATH TO BECOMING THE GREATEST POKÉMON TRAINER SUDDENLY GROWS STEEPER.

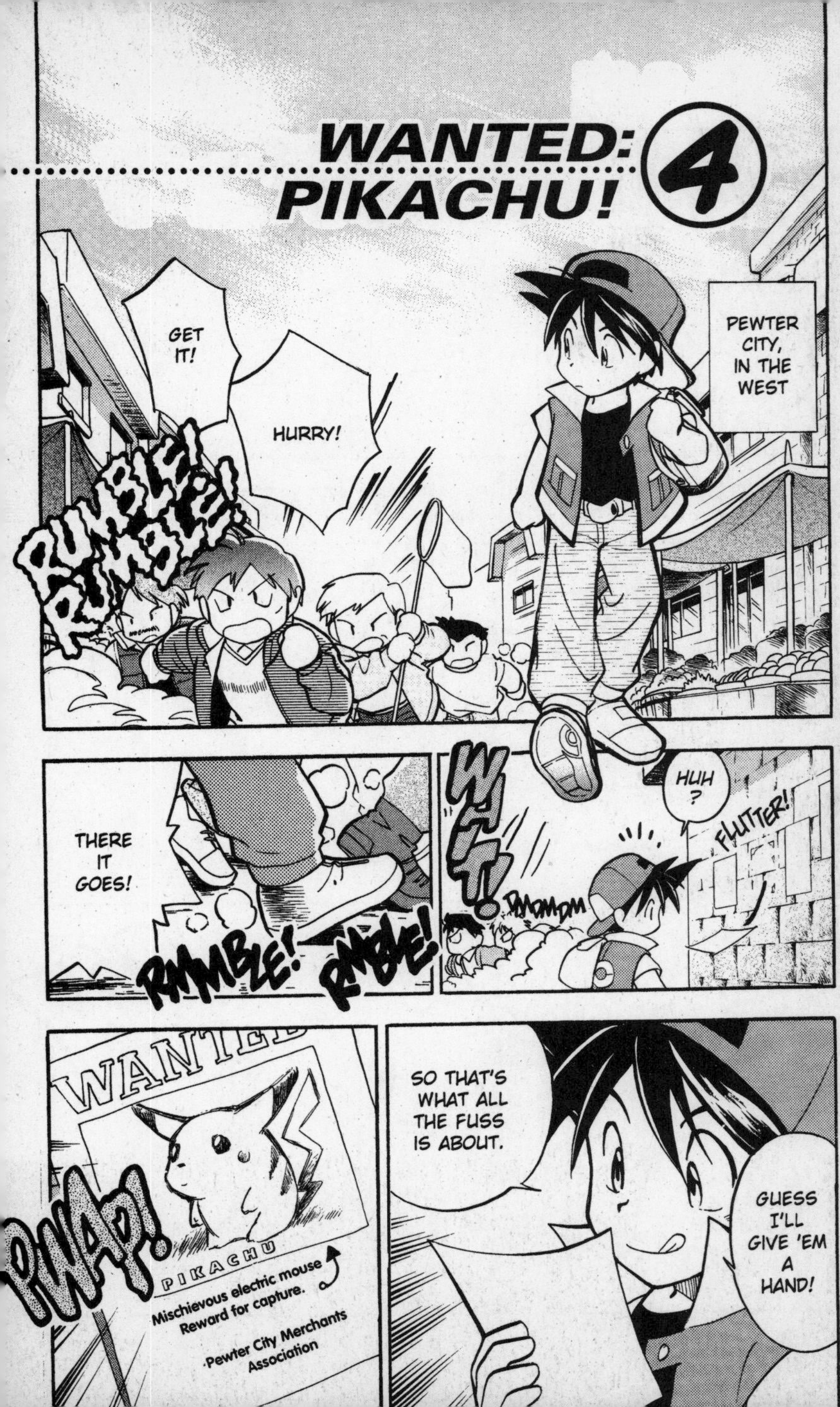
WANTED: PIKACHU!
4
PEWTER CITY, IN THE WEST
GET IT!
HURRY!
RUMBLE! RUMBLE!
THERE IT GOES!
RAMBLE!
RAMBLE!
WHAT!
HUH?
FLUTTER!
WANTED
PIKACHU
Mischievous electric mouse
Reward for capture.
-Pewter City Merchants Association
PWAP!
SO THAT'S WHAT ALL THE FUSS IS ABOUT.
GUESS I'LL GIVE 'EM A HAND!

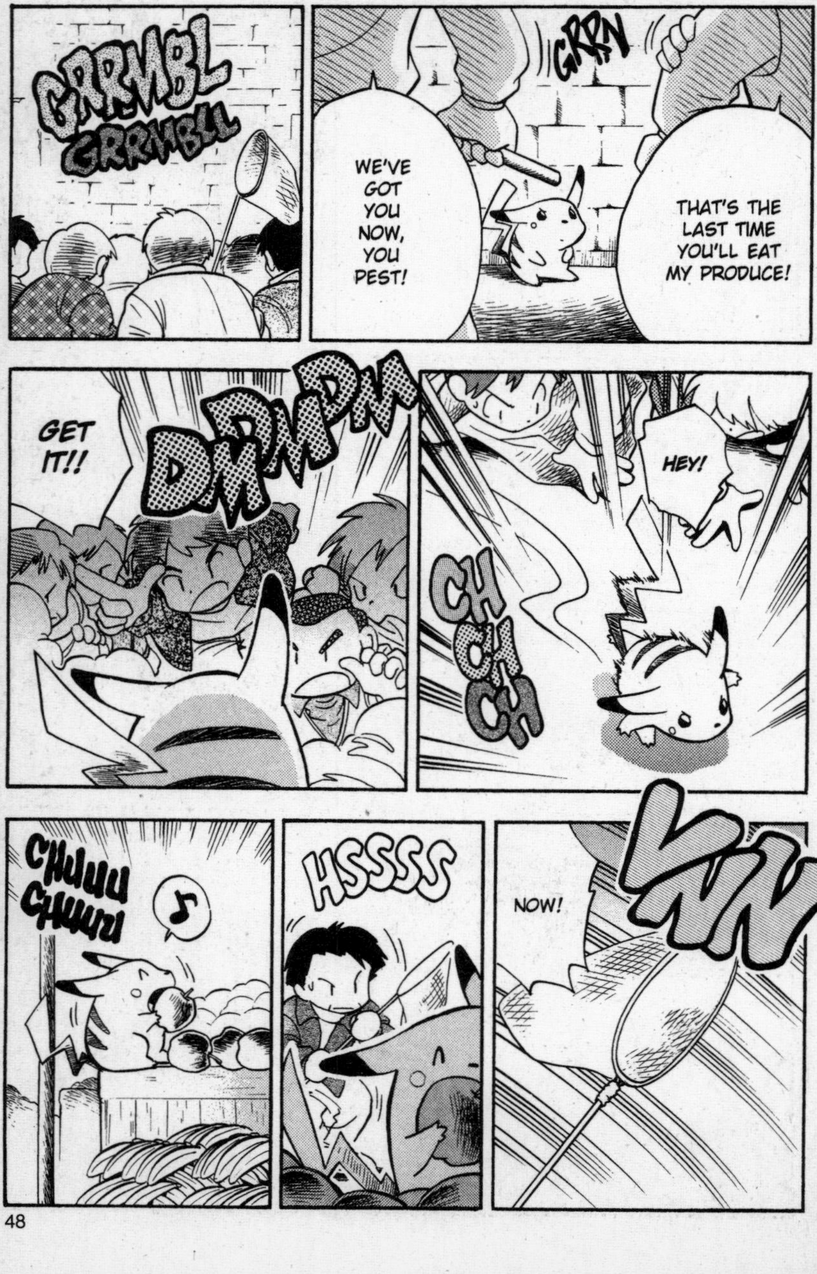
GRRMBL
GRRMBLL
GRRN
WE'VE GOT YOU NOW, YOU PEST!
THAT'S THE LAST TIME YOU'LL EAT MY PRODUCE!
GET IT!!
HEY!
CH CH CH CH
♪
HSSSS
NOW!

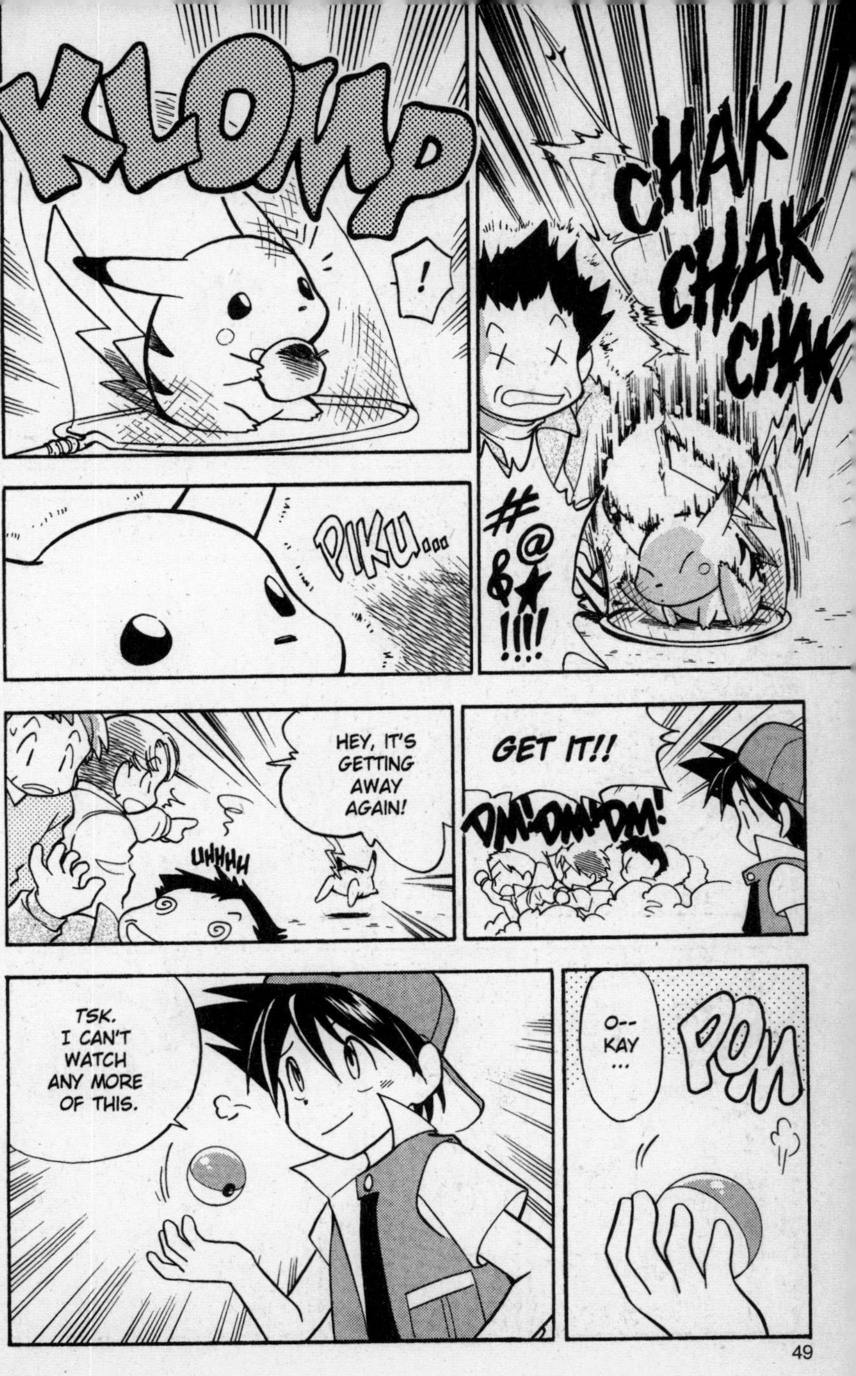
KLOMP
!
PIKU...
CHAK CHAK CHAK
#@&★!!!!
HEY, IT'S GETTING AWAY AGAIN!
UHHHH
GET IT!!
DM DM DM!
TSK. I CAN'T WATCH ANY MORE OF THIS.
O-- KAY ...
POM

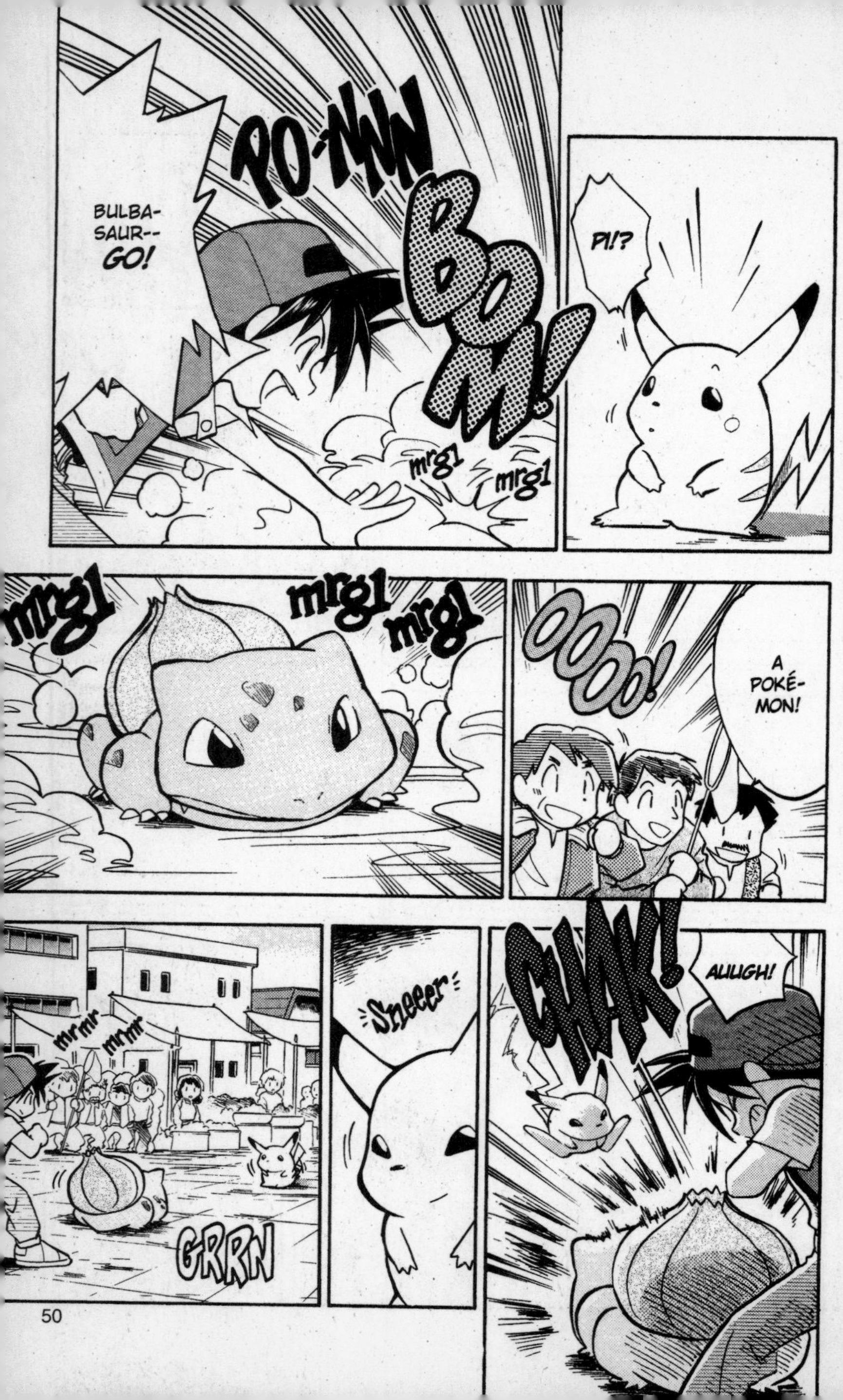
PI!?
BULBA-
SAUR--
GO!
PO-NNN
BOOM!
mrgl
mrgl
A
POKÉ-
MON!
OOOO!
mrgl
mrgl
mrgl
AUUGH!
CHAK!
Sneeer
mrmr
mrmr
GRRN

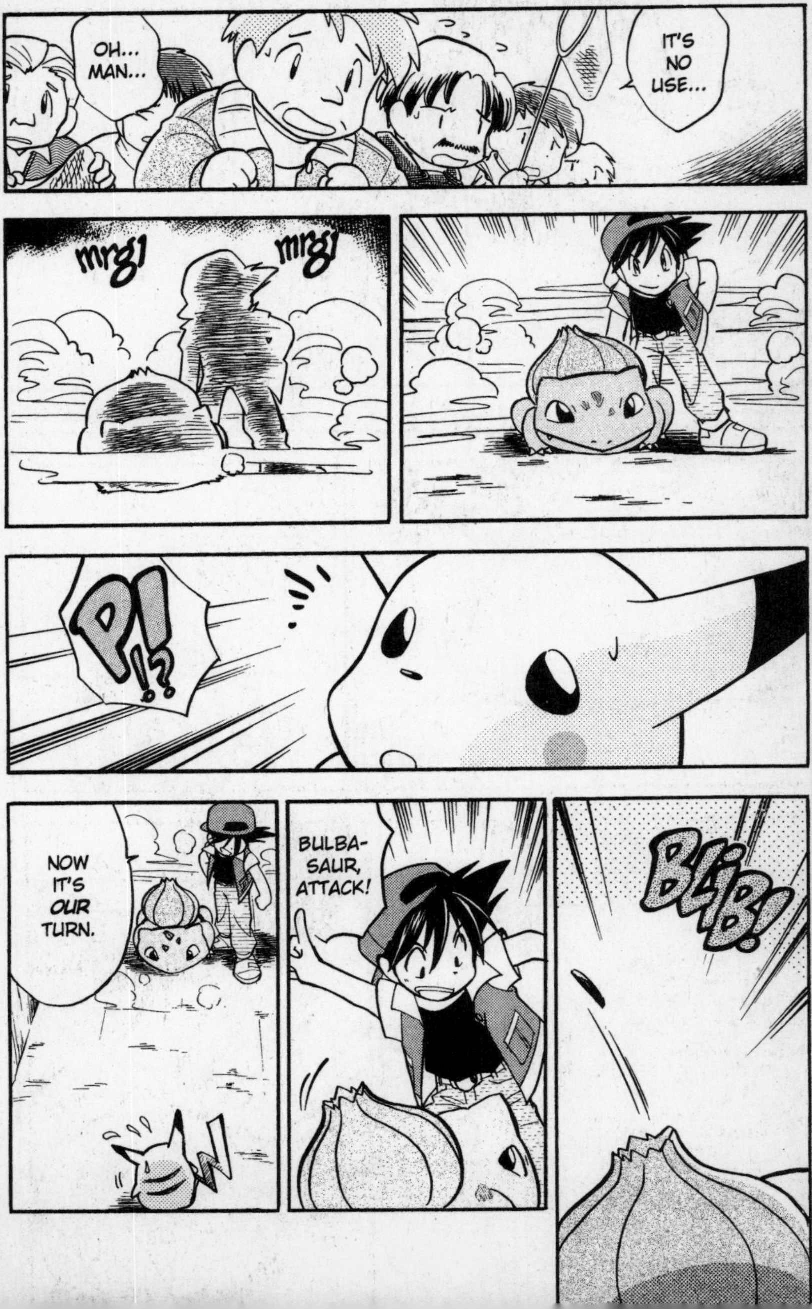
OH... MAN...
IT'S NO USE...
mrg1
mrg1
P!
!?
NOW IT'S OUR TURN.
BULBA-SAUR, ATTACK!
BLIB!

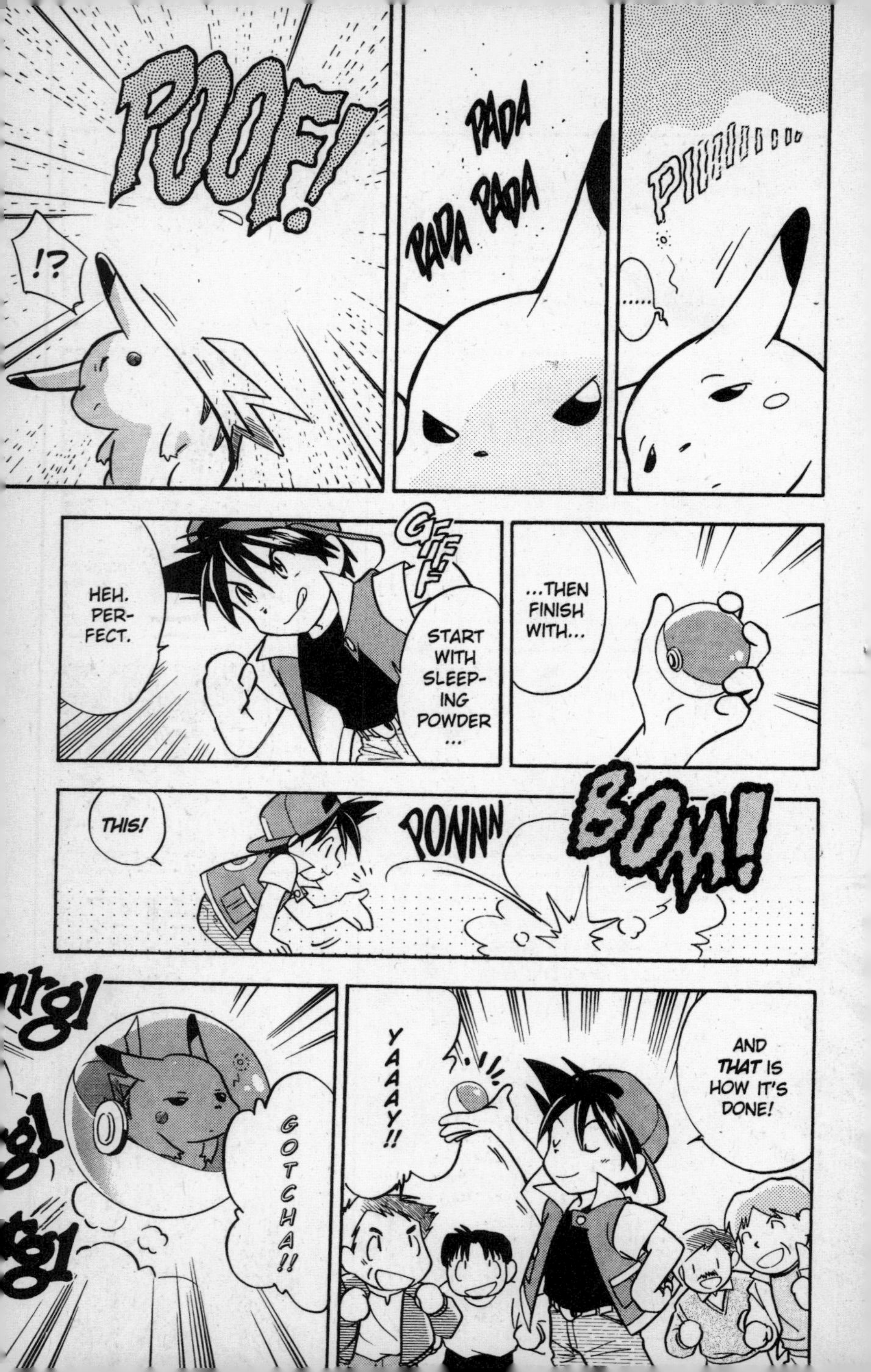
POOF!
!?
PADA PADA PADA
PIIIIIII...
HEH. PER- FECT.
GFFF
START WITH SLEEP- ING POWDER ...
...THEN FINISH WITH...
THIS!
PONNN
BOW!
nrg!
rg!
rg!
GOTCHA!!
YAAAAY!!
AND THAT IS HOW IT'S DONE!

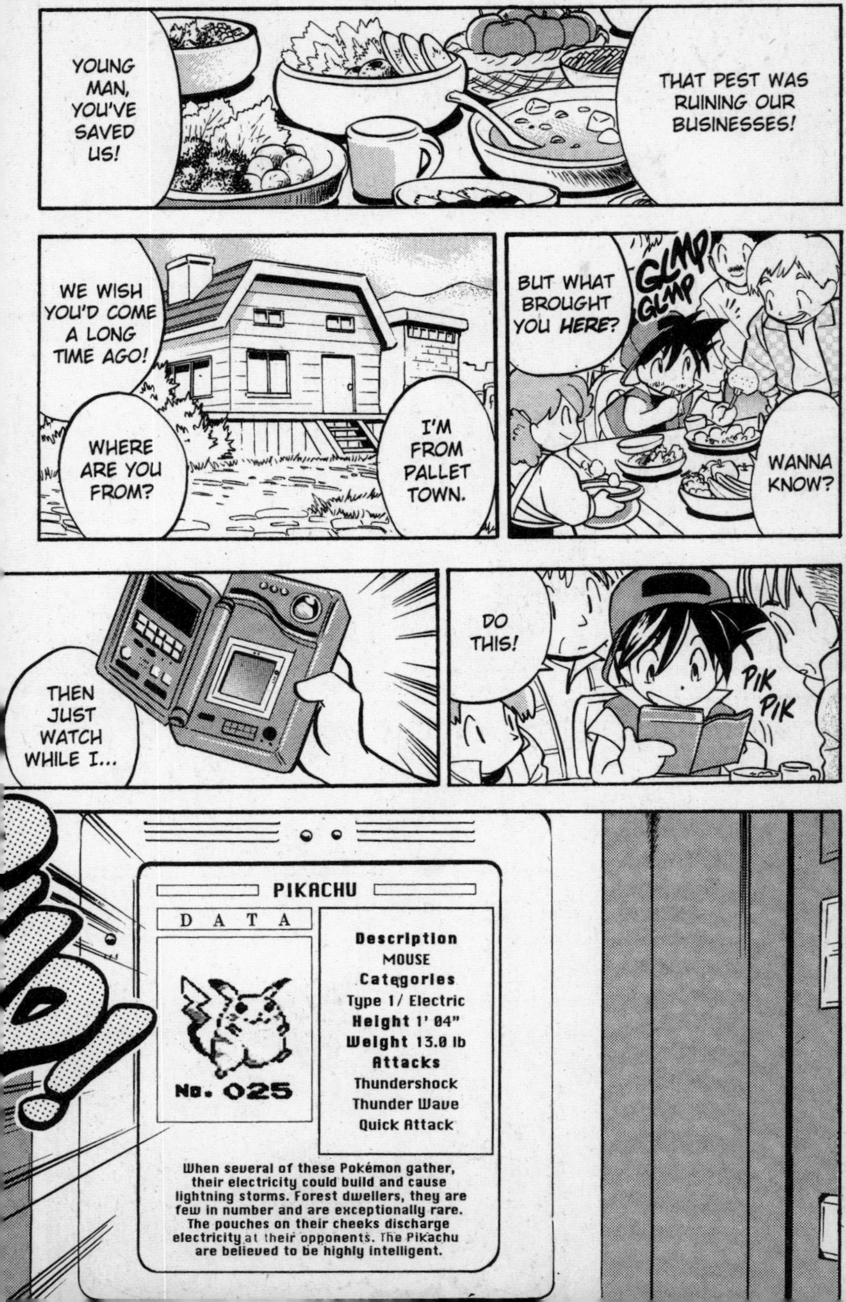
YOUNG MAN, YOU'VE SAVED US!
THAT PEST WAS RUINING OUR BUSINESSES!
WE WISH YOU'D COME A LONG TIME AGO!
WHERE ARE YOU FROM?
I'M FROM PALLET TOWN.
BUT WHAT BROUGHT YOU HERE?
GLMP GLMP
WANNA KNOW?
THEN JUST WATCH WHILE I...
DO THIS!
PIK PIK
PIKACHU
DATA
No. 025
Description
MOUSE
Categories
Type 1/ Electric
Height 1' 04"
Weight 13.0 lb
Attacks
Thundershock
Thunder Wave
Quick Attack
When several of these Pokémon gather, their electricity could build and cause lightning storms. Forest dwellers, they are few in number and are exceptionally rare. The pouches on their cheeks discharge electricity at their opponents. The Pikachu are believed to be highly intelligent.

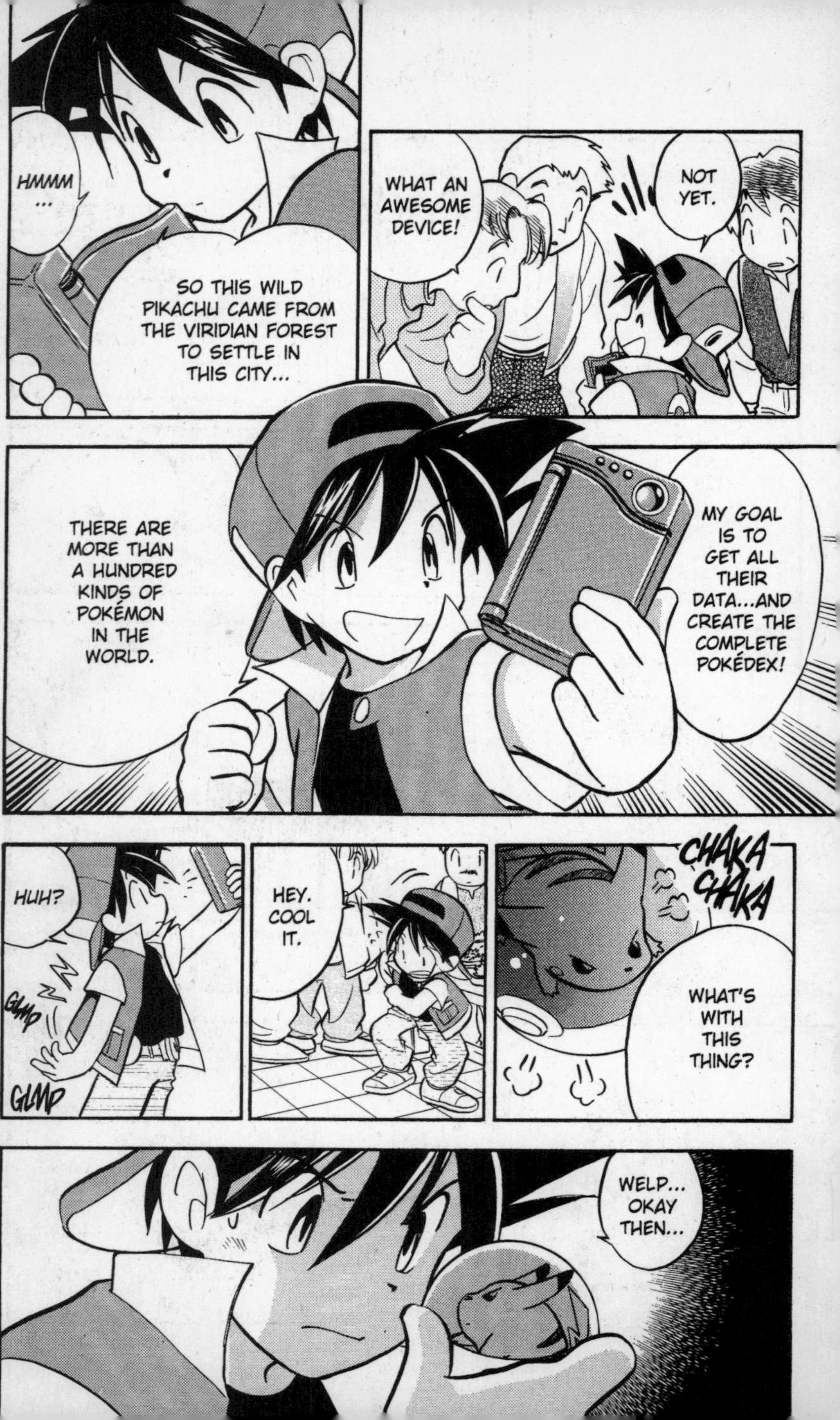
HMMM ...
SO THIS WILD PIKACHU CAME FROM THE VIRIDIAN FOREST TO SETTLE IN THIS CITY...
NOT YET.
WHAT AN AWESOME DEVICE!
MY GOAL IS TO GET ALL THEIR DATA...AND CREATE THE COMPLETE POKÉDEX!
THERE ARE MORE THAN A HUNDRED KINDS OF POKÉMON IN THE WORLD.
CHAKA CHAKA
WHAT'S WITH THIS THING?
HEY. COOL IT.
HUH?
GLMP
GLMP
WELP... OKAY THEN...

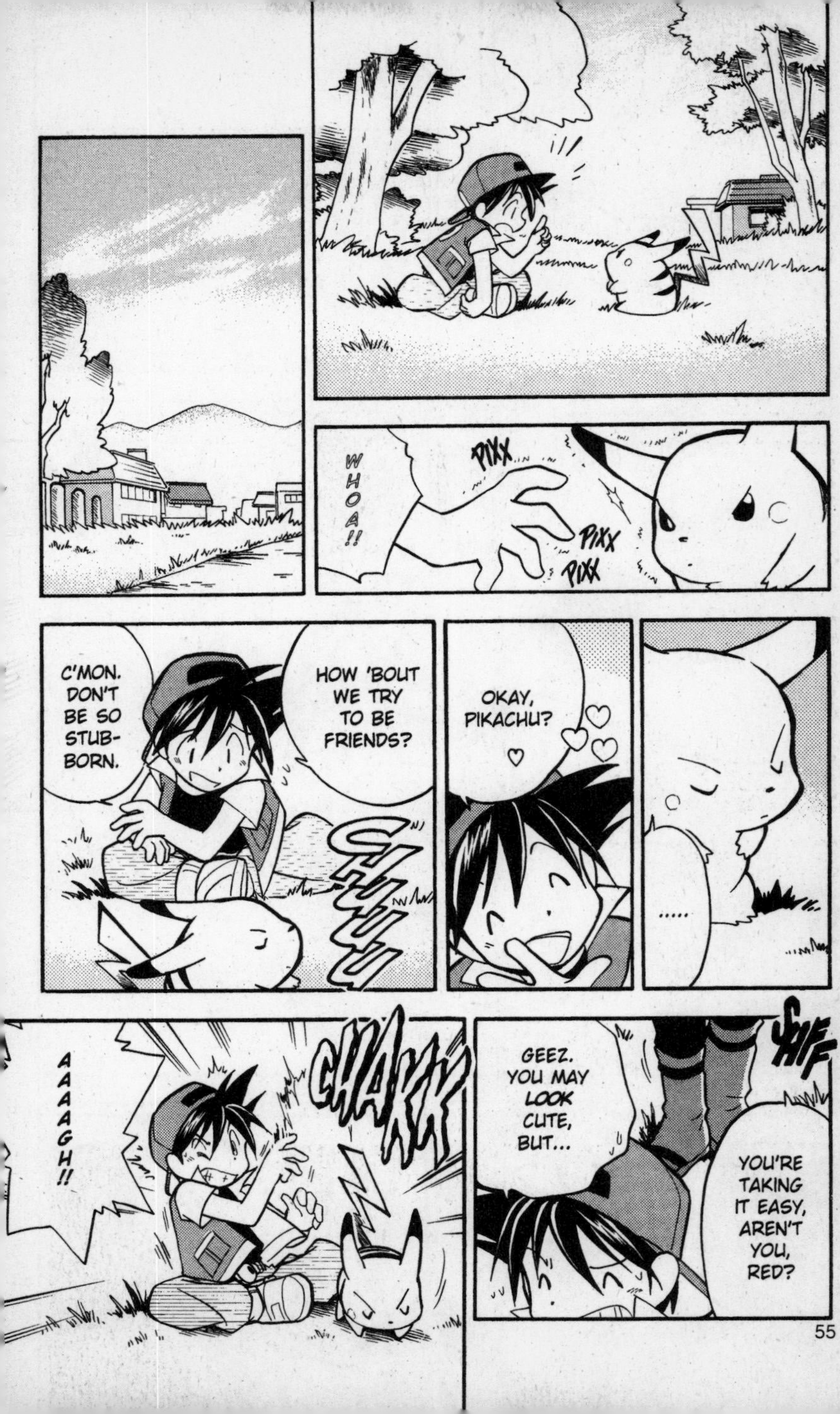
WHOA!!
PIXX
PIXX
PIXX
C'MON. DON'T BE SO STUBBORN.
HOW 'BOUT WE TRY TO BE FRIENDS?
CHUUU
OKAY, PIKACHU?
.....
AAAAAGH!!
CHAKK
GEEZ. YOU MAY LOOK CUTE, BUT...
SHFF
YOU'RE TAKING IT EASY, AREN'T YOU, RED?

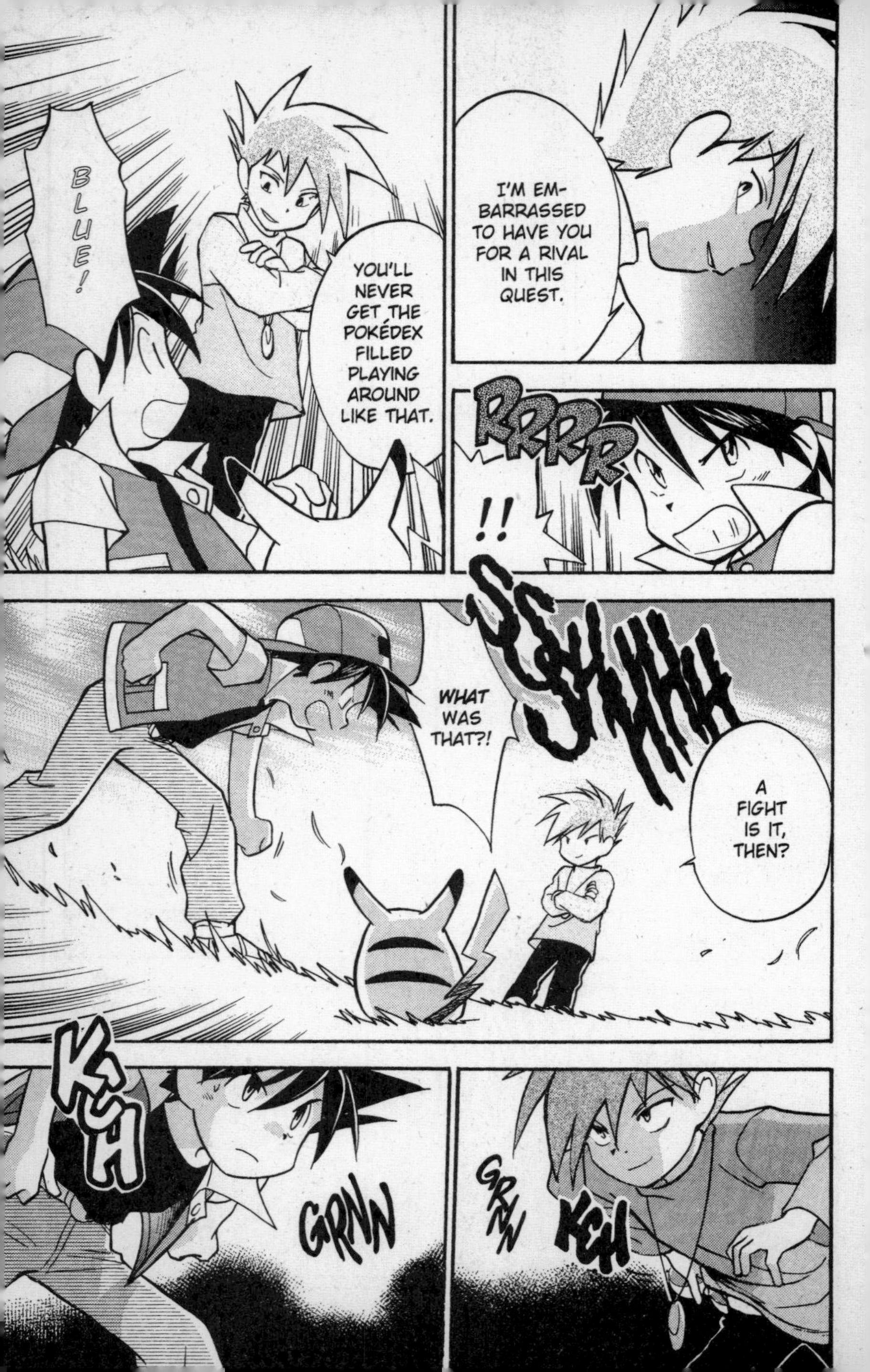
BLUE!
YOU'LL NEVER GET THE POKÉDEX FILLED PLAYING AROUND LIKE THAT.
I'M EM-BARRASSED TO HAVE YOU FOR A RIVAL IN THIS QUEST.
RRRR
!!
SSHHH
WHAT WAS THAT?!
A FIGHT IS IT, THEN?
KUH
GRNN
GRNN
KEH

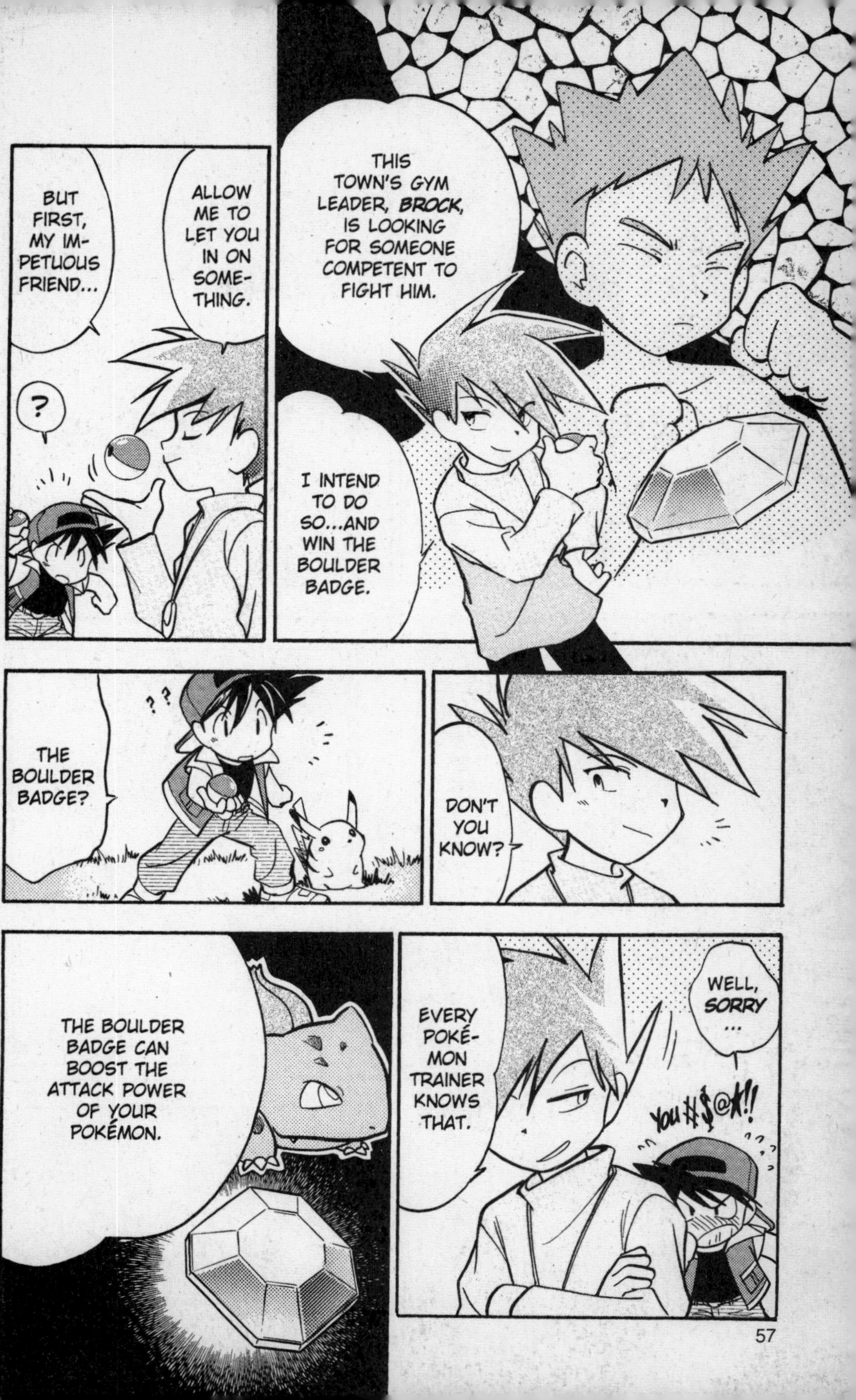
ALLOW ME TO LET YOU IN ON SOME-THING.
BUT FIRST, MY IM-PETUOUS FRIEND...
?
THIS TOWN'S GYM LEADER, BROCK, IS LOOKING FOR SOMEONE COMPETENT TO FIGHT HIM.
I INTEND TO DO SO...AND WIN THE BOULDER BADGE.
THE BOULDER BADGE?
DON'T YOU KNOW?
THE BOULDER BADGE CAN BOOST THE ATTACK POWER OF YOUR POKÉMON.
EVERY POKÉ-MON TRAINER KNOWS THAT.
WELL, SORRY...
YOU #$@*!!

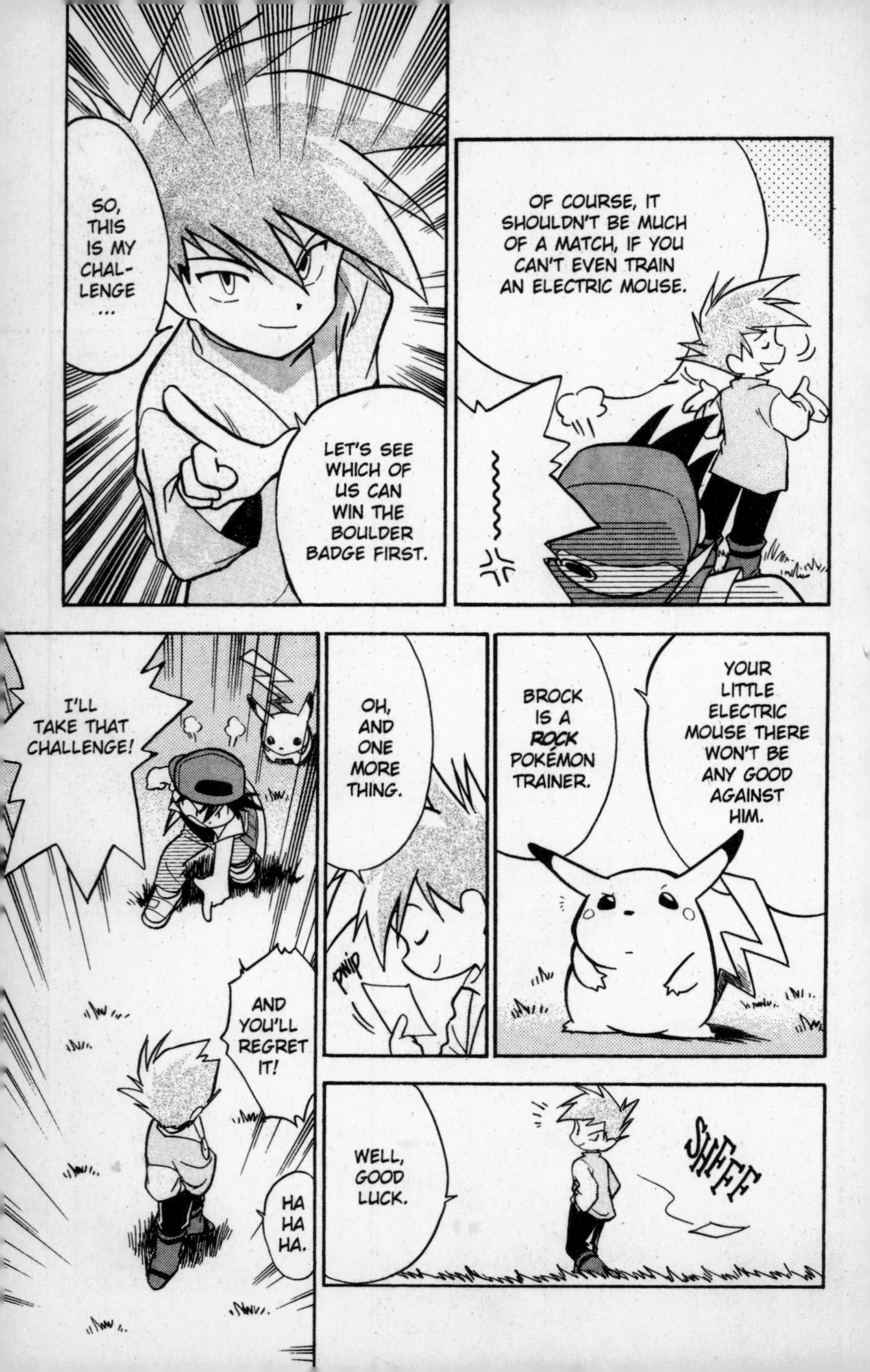

SO, THIS IS MY CHAL-LENGE...
LET'S SEE WHICH OF US CAN WIN THE BOULDER BADGE FIRST.
OF COURSE, IT SHOULDN'T BE MUCH OF A MATCH, IF YOU CAN'T EVEN TRAIN AN ELECTRIC MOUSE.
I'LL TAKE THAT CHALLENGE!
AND YOU'LL REGRET IT!
HA HA HA.
OH, AND ONE MORE THING.
FWIP
BROCK IS A ROCK POKÉMON TRAINER.
YOUR LITTLE ELECTRIC MOUSE THERE WON'T BE ANY GOOD AGAINST HIM.
WELL, GOOD LUCK.
SHFFF

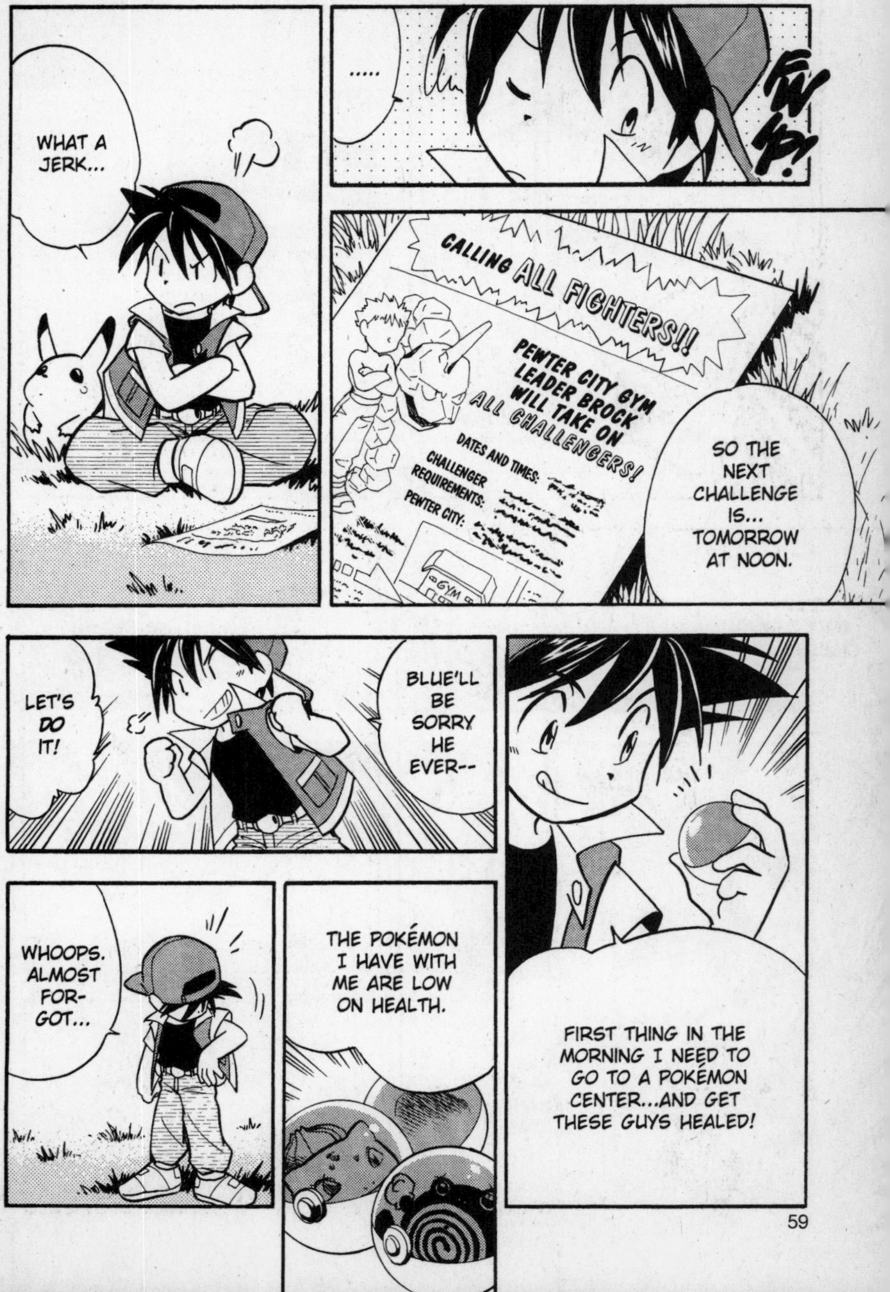

.....
FWIP!
WHAT A JERK...
CALLING ALL FIGHTERS!!
PEWTER CITY GYM LEADER BROCK WILL TAKE ON ALL CHALLENGERS!
DATES AND TIMES:
CHALLENGER REQUIREMENTS:
PEWTER CITY:
GYM
SO THE NEXT CHALLENGE IS... TOMORROW AT NOON.
BLUE'LL BE SORRY HE EVER--
LET'S DO IT!
FIRST THING IN THE MORNING I NEED TO GO TO A POKÉMON CENTER...AND GET THESE GUYS HEALED!
THE POKÉMON I HAVE WITH ME ARE LOW ON HEALTH.
WHOOPS. ALMOST FOR-GOT...

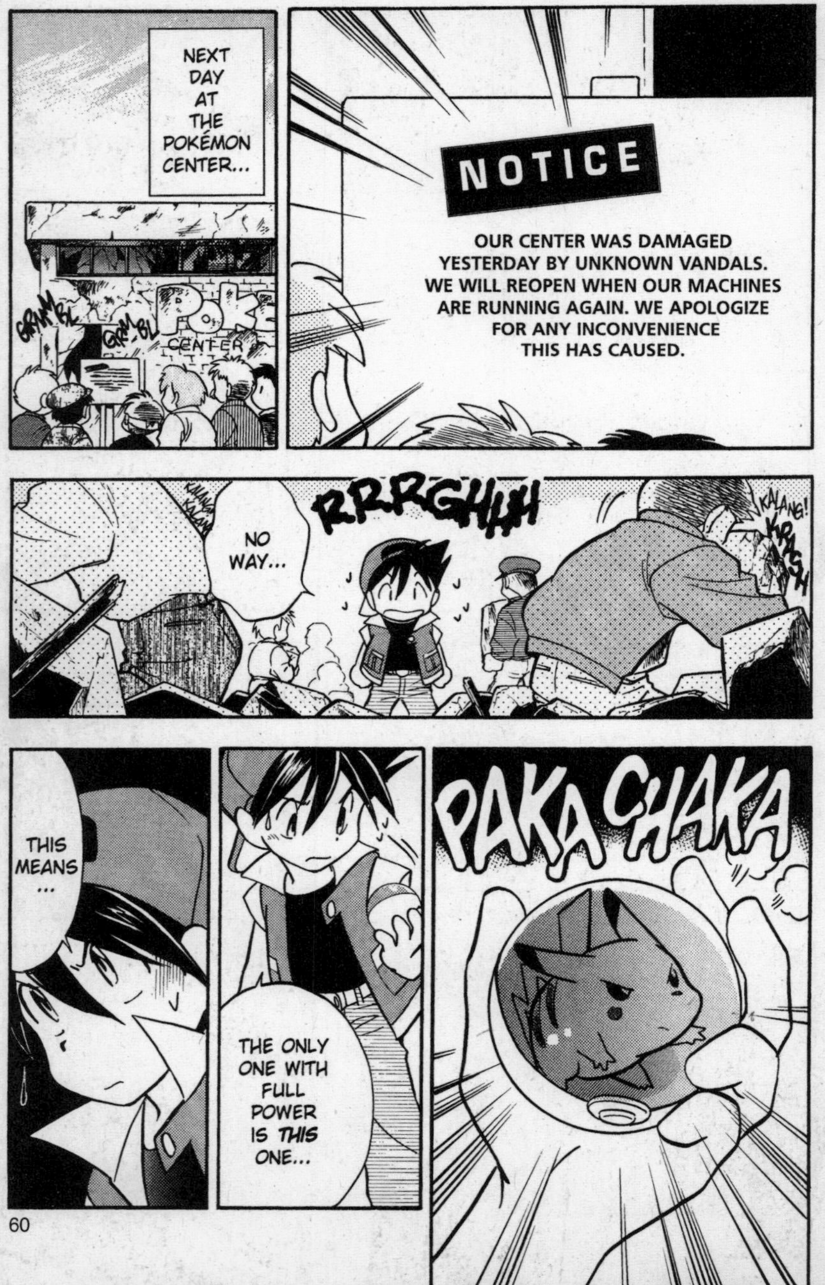
NEXT DAY AT THE POKÉMON CENTER...
CENTER
NOTICE
OUR CENTER WAS DAMAGED YESTERDAY BY UNKNOWN VANDALS. WE WILL REOPEN WHEN OUR MACHINES ARE RUNNING AGAIN. WE APOLOGIZE FOR ANY INCONVENIENCE THIS HAS CAUSED.
NO WAY...
RRRGHHH
KALANG!
KRASH
THIS MEANS ...
THE ONLY ONE WITH FULL POWER IS THIS ONE...
PAKA CHAKA

CHAPTER 5

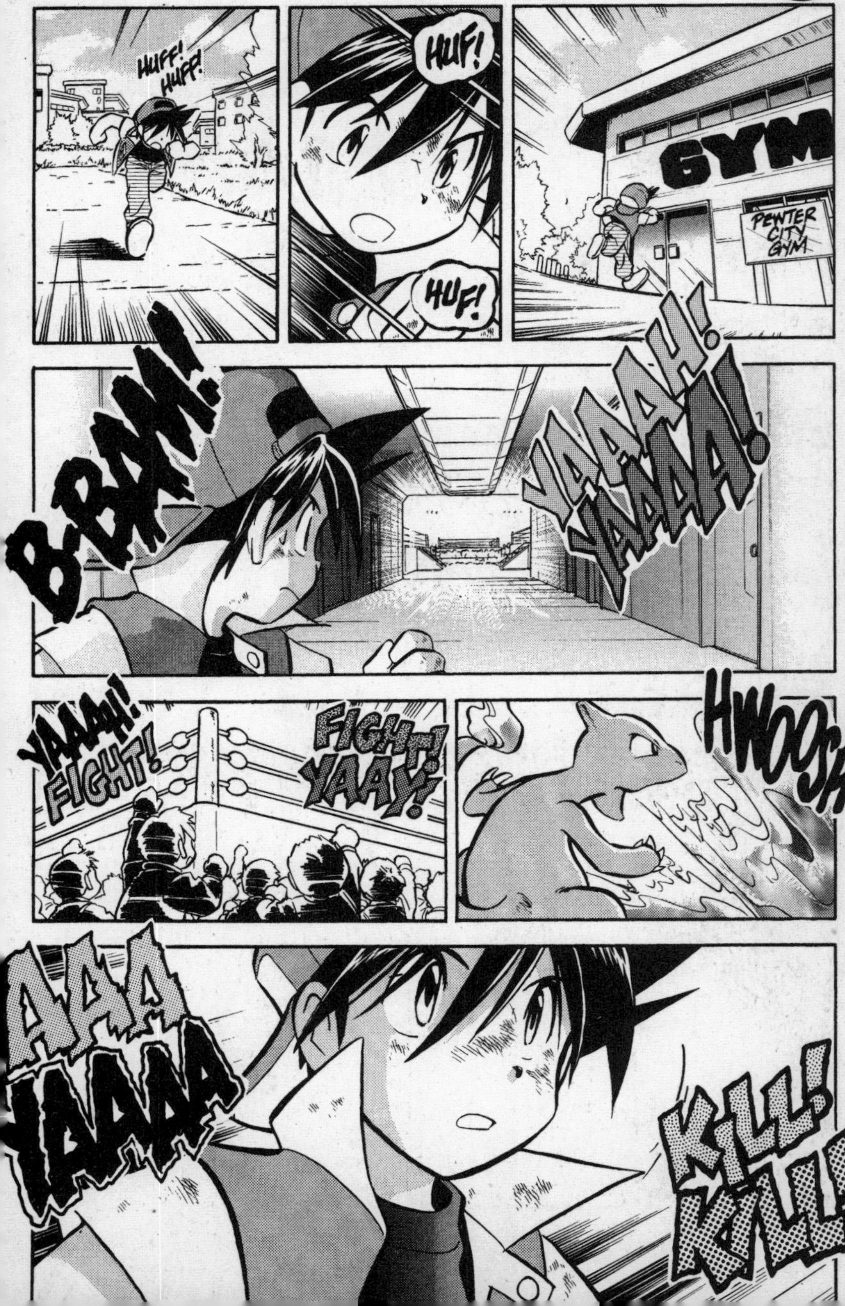
HUFF! HUFF!
HUF!
HUF!
GYM
PEWTER CITY GYM
YAAAH! YAAAA!
B-BAM!
YAAAH! FIGHT!
FIGHT! YAAY!
HWOOSH
AAA AAAA
KILL! KILL!

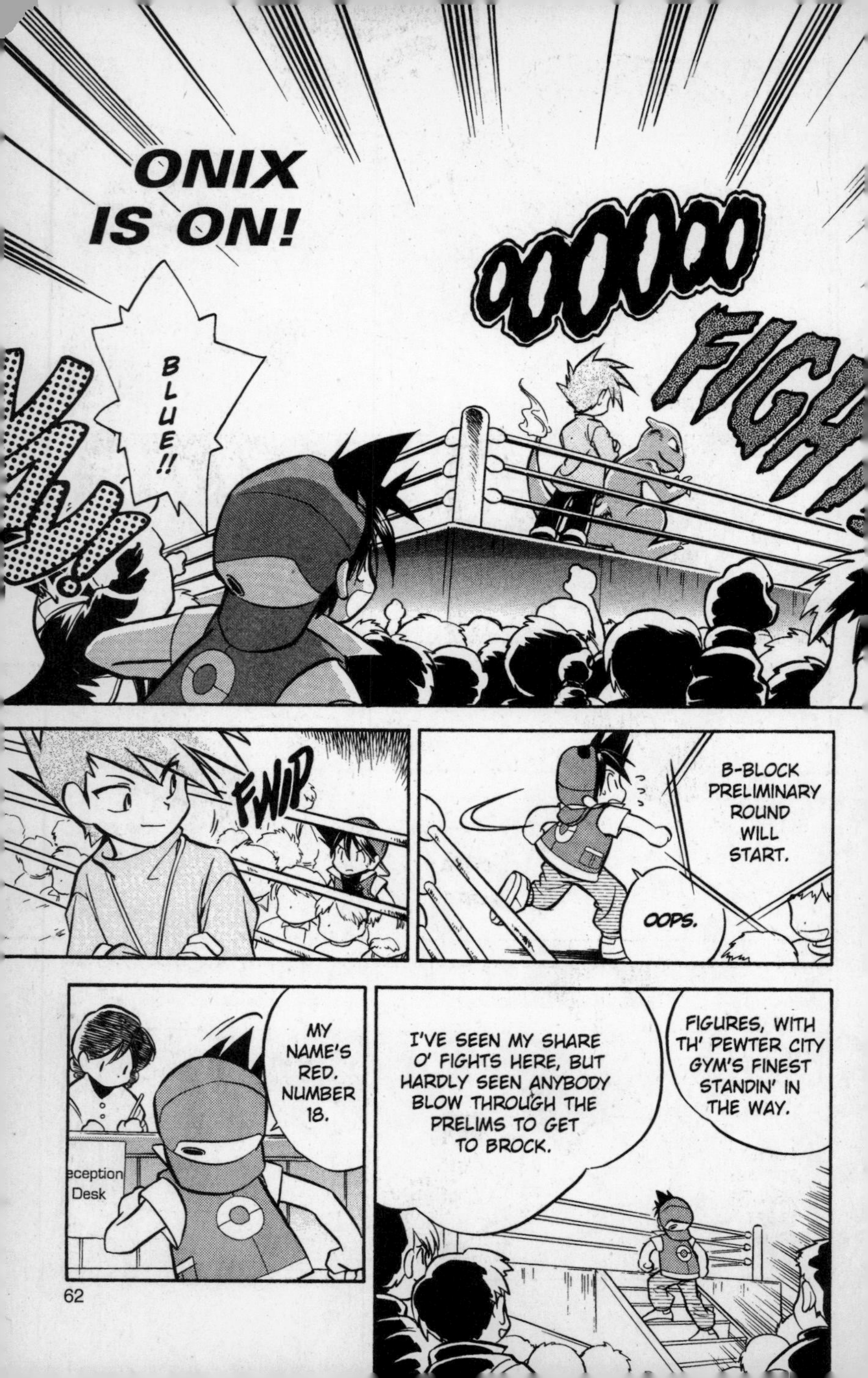
ONIX IS ON!
OOOOOO
FIGH...!
BLUE!!
FWIP
B-BLOCK PRELIMINARY ROUND WILL START.
OOPS.
MY NAME'S RED. NUMBER 18.
eception Desk
I'VE SEEN MY SHARE O' FIGHTS HERE, BUT HARDLY SEEN ANYBODY BLOW THROUGH THE PRELIMS TO GET TO BROCK.
FIGURES, WITH TH' PEWTER CITY GYM'S FINEST STANDIN' IN THE WAY.

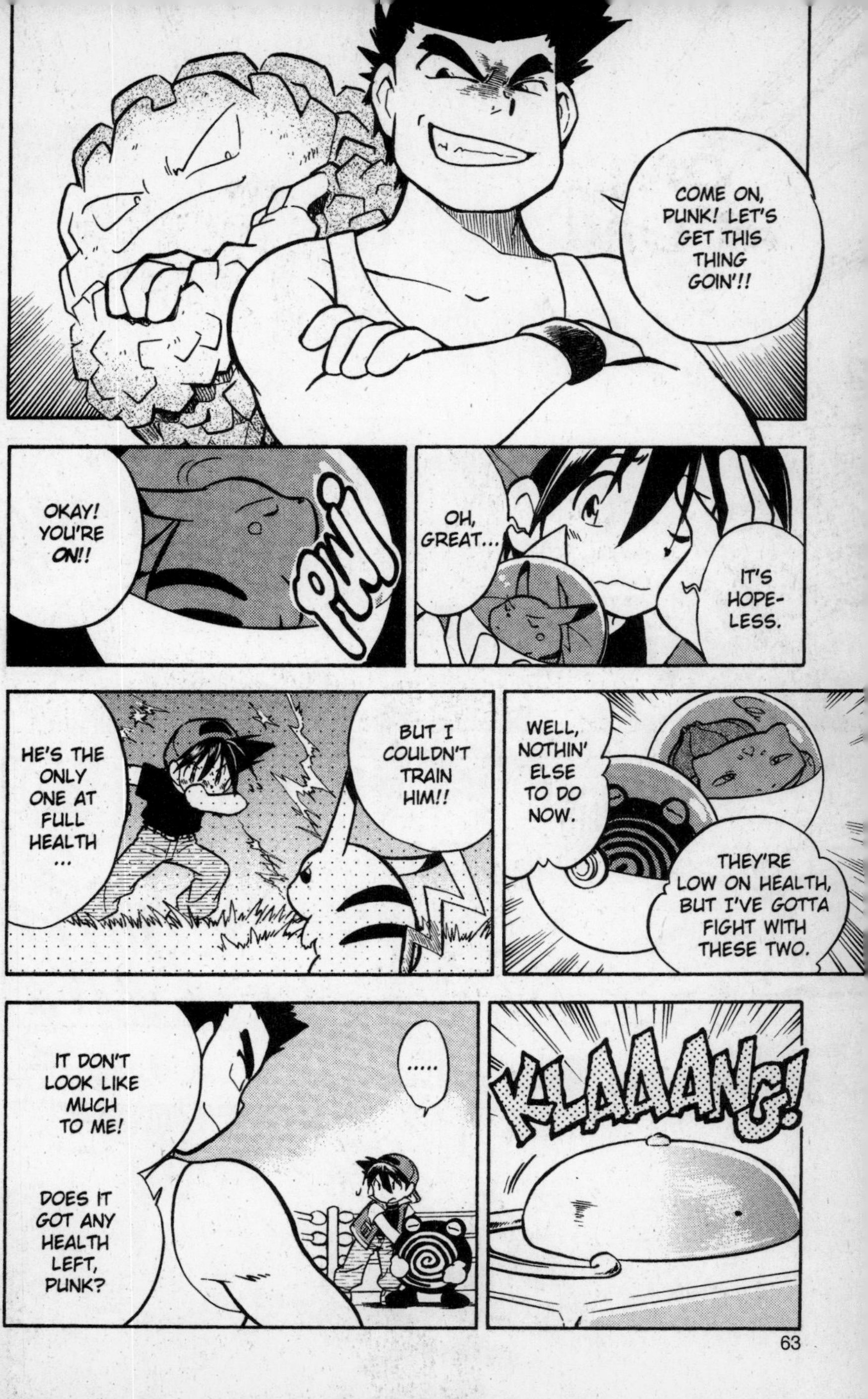
COME ON, PUNK! LET'S GET THIS THING GOIN'!!
OKAY! YOU'RE ON!!
OH, GREAT...
IT'S HOPE-LESS.
WELL, NOTHIN' ELSE TO DO NOW.
THEY'RE LOW ON HEALTH, BUT I'VE GOTTA FIGHT WITH THESE TWO.
BUT I COULDN'T TRAIN HIM!!
HE'S THE ONLY ONE AT FULL HEALTH ...
KLAAANG!
.....
IT DON'T LOOK LIKE MUCH TO ME!
DOES IT GOT ANY HEALTH LEFT, PUNK?

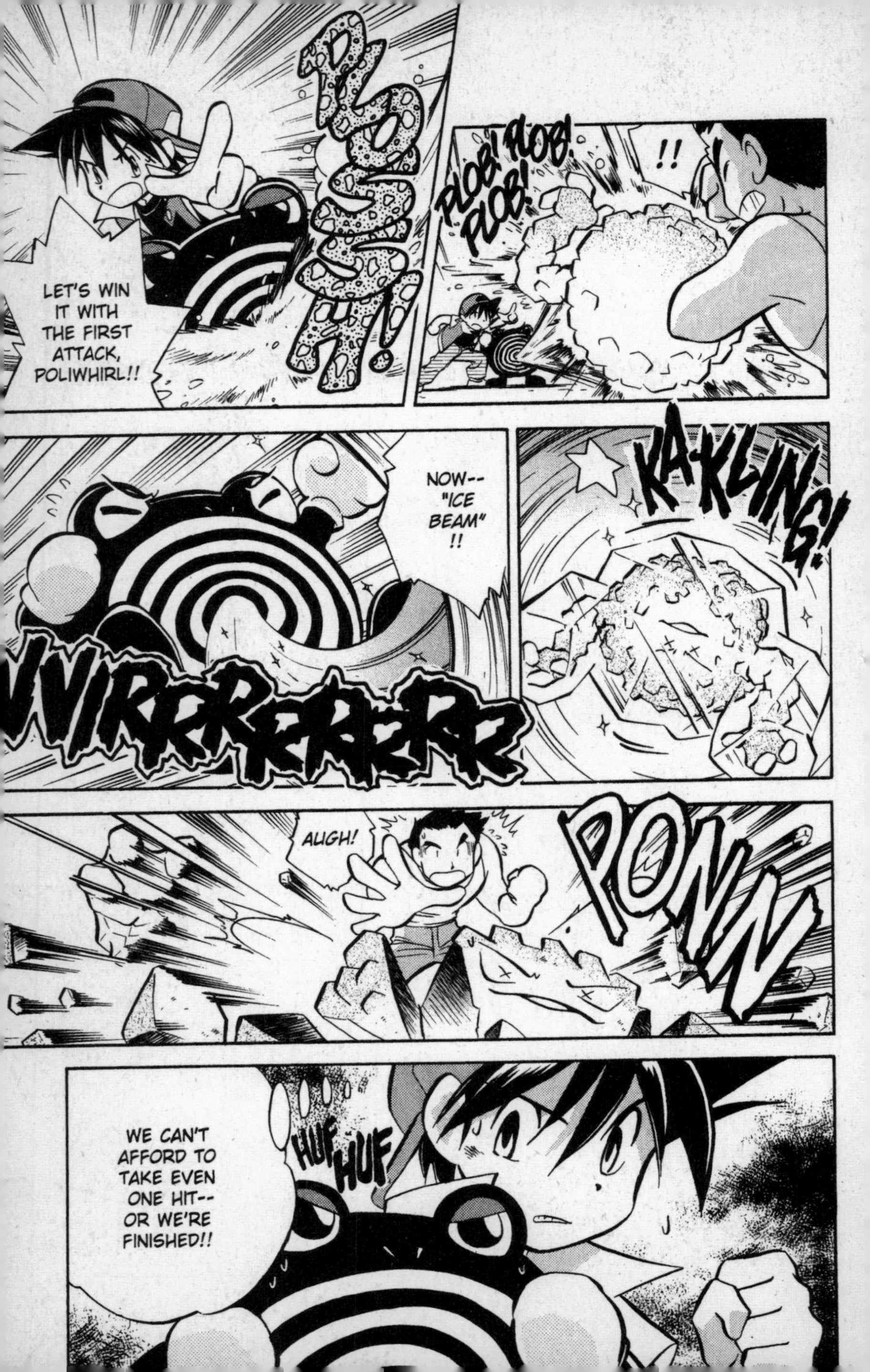

LET'S WIN IT WITH THE FIRST ATTACK, POLIWHIRL!!
PLOB! PLOB! PLOB! PLOB!
!!
NOW-- "ICE BEAM" !!
WRRRRRRRRR
KA-KLING!
AUGH!
PONNN
WE CAN'T AFFORD TO TAKE EVEN ONE HIT-- OR WE'RE FINISHED!!
HUF HUF

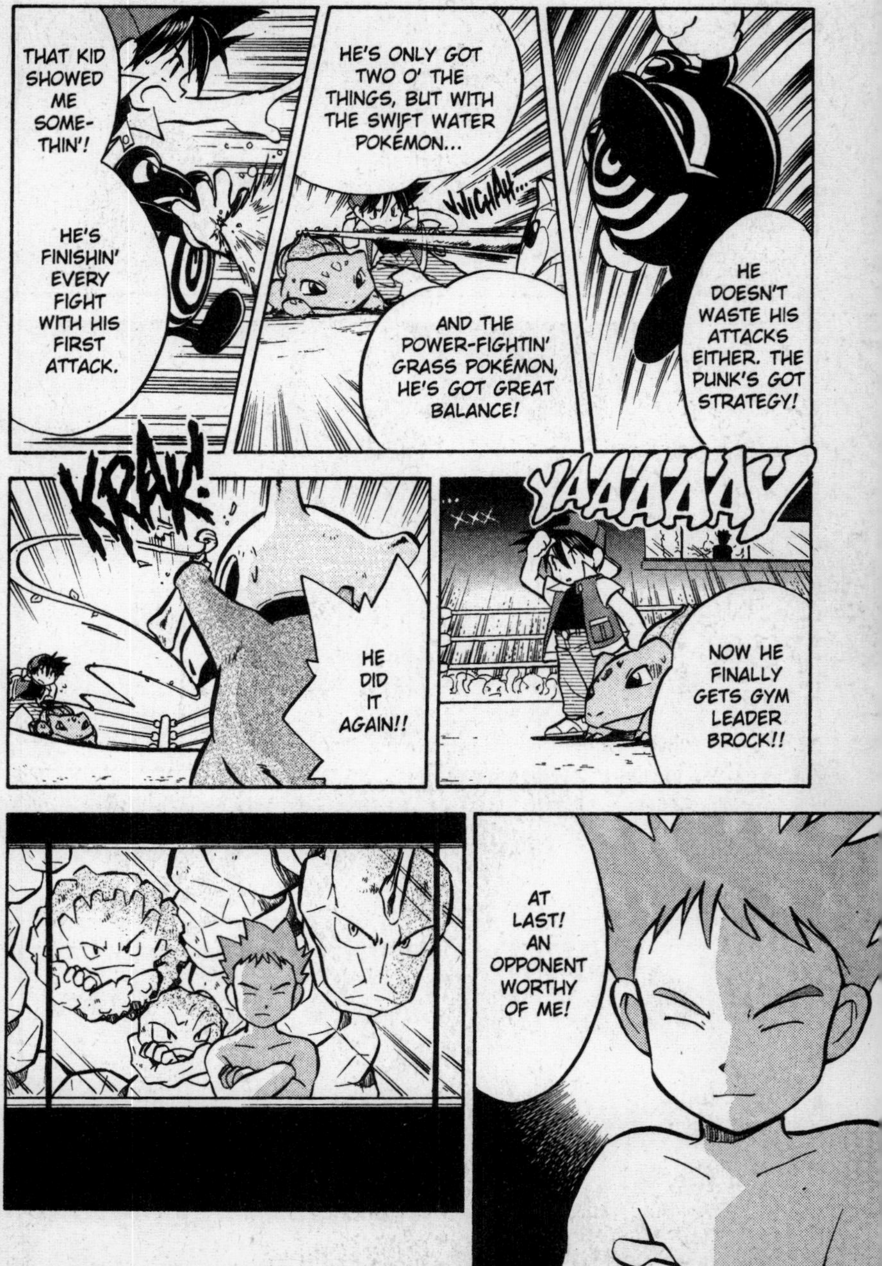
THAT KID SHOWED ME SOME-THIN'!
HE'S FINISHIN' EVERY FIGHT WITH HIS FIRST ATTACK.
HE'S ONLY GOT TWO O' THE THINGS, BUT WITH THE SWIFT WATER POKÉMON...
AND THE POWER-FIGHTIN' GRASS POKÉMON, HE'S GOT GREAT BALANCE!
HE DOESN'T WASTE HIS ATTACKS EITHER. THE PUNK'S GOT STRATEGY!
KRAK!
HE DID IT AGAIN!!
YAAAAAY
NOW HE FINALLY GETS GYM LEADER BROCK!!
AT LAST! AN OPPONENT WORTHY OF ME!

AT THE GYM'S BACK ENTRANCE.

OH, CMON, PIKA-CHU.

POLIWHIRL AND BULBASAUR ARE POOPED.

IF YOU'LL JUST DO IT THIS TIME... PLEASE!!

OKAY?

PWI!

WELL... WE'RE UP.

ZH ZH ZH

KLAAAANG!

NKH

HUH?

SHHHHHH

Pru!

!?

.....

WHERE'S YOUR FAMOUS FIRST ATTACK, BOY!?

THEN I'D BETTER GO FIRST!

ROCK THROW!

DNNK

DNN DNN

CHWIP!

GONG!

CHWIP!

BONG

GONG!

CHWIP!

GONN

NG!

OH, NO!

THE POKÉMON TOOK THE FULL BRUNT OF THE ATTACK!

LOOKS LIKE THIS IS THE END!

CHRRRRR

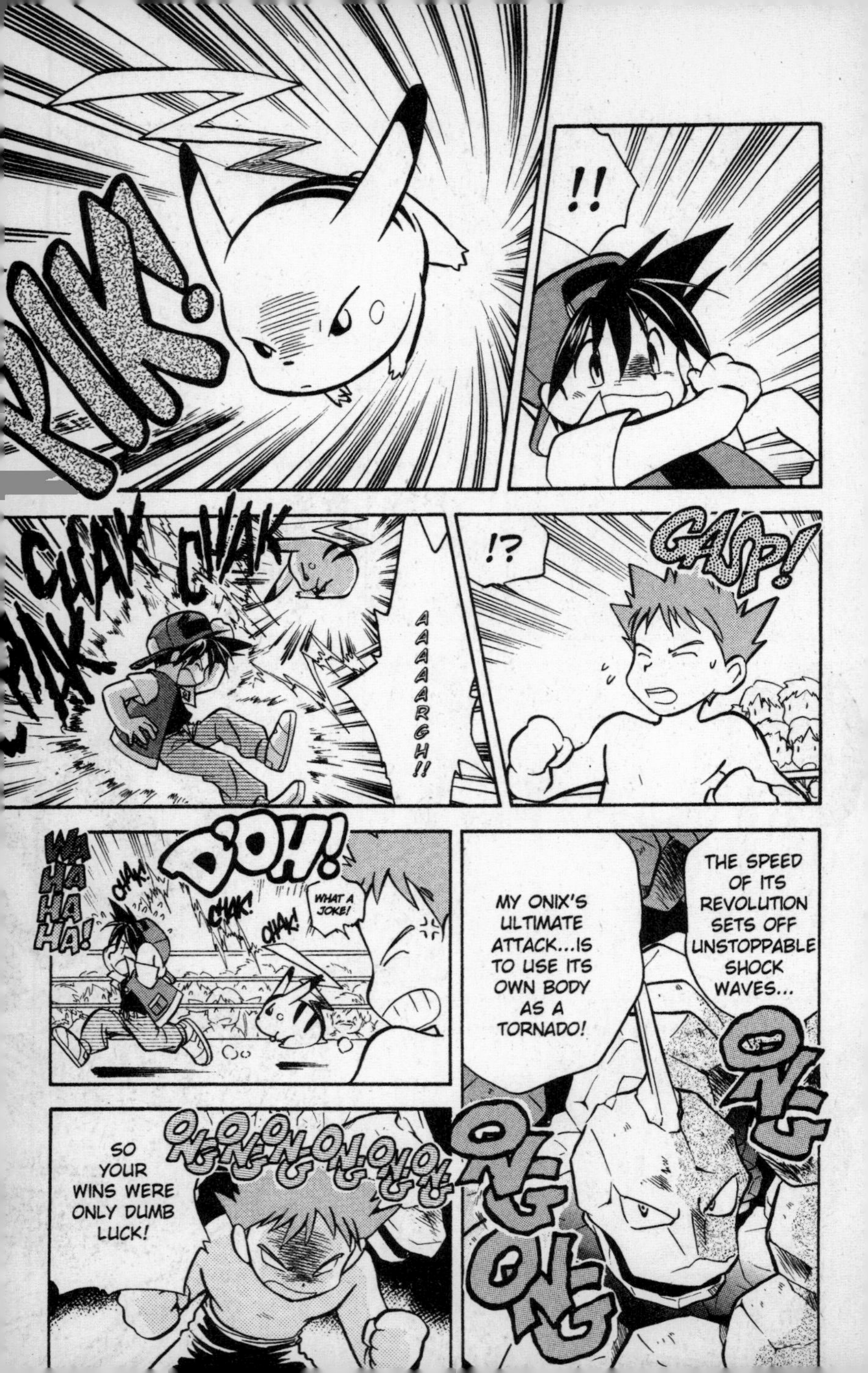

!!
CHAK CHAK
AAAAAARGH!!
!?
GASP!
WAHAHAHAHA!
DOH!
CHAK!
CHAK!
CHAK!
WHAT A JOKE!
MY ONIX'S ULTIMATE ATTACK...IS TO USE ITS OWN BODY AS A TORNADO!
THE SPEED OF ITS REVOLUTION SETS OFF UNSTOPPABLE SHOCK WAVES...
ONG
SO YOUR WINS WERE ONLY DUMB LUCK!
ONGONGONGONGONGONGONG
ONG ONG ONG

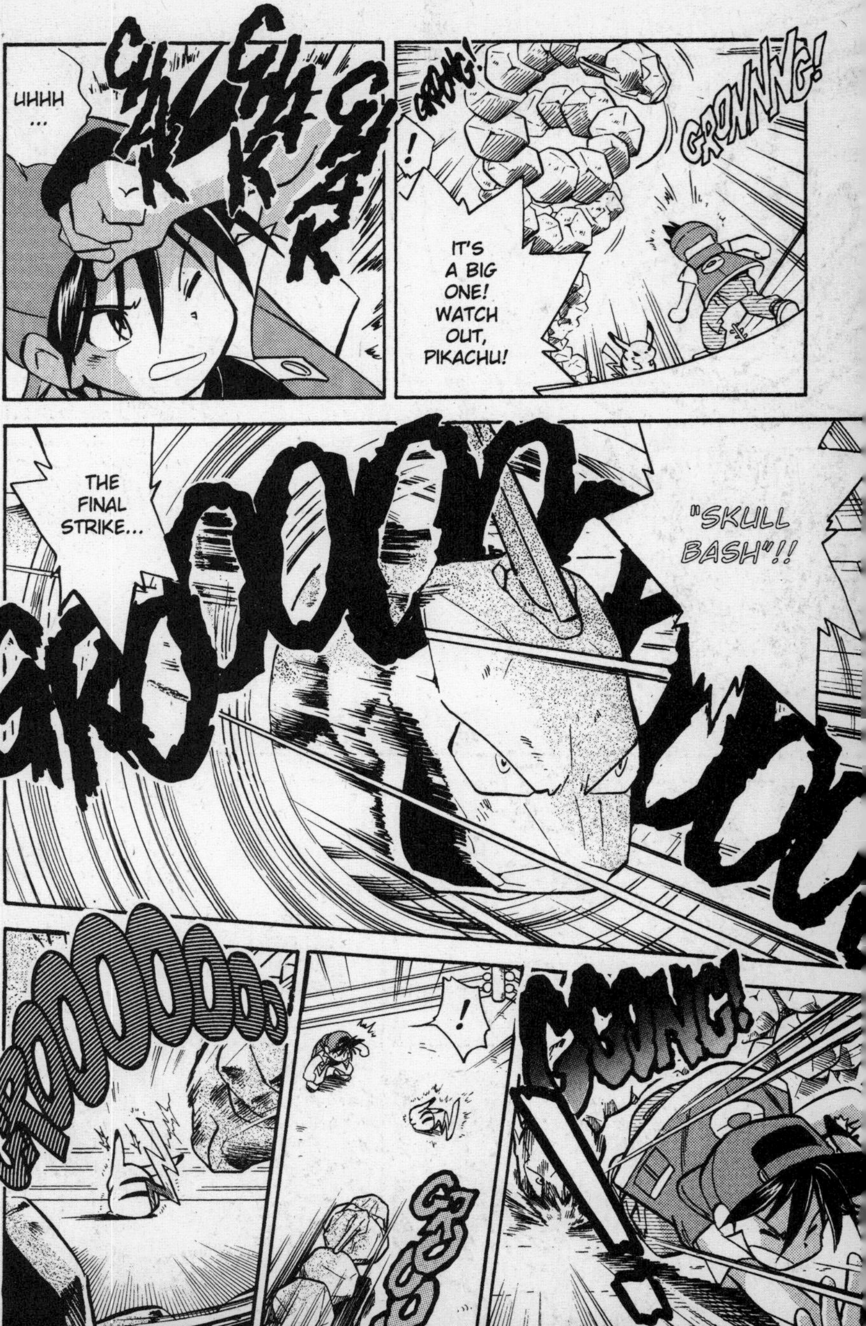

GRONNNG!
GRONG!
!
IT'S A BIG ONE! WATCH OUT, PIKACHU!
UHHH ...
"SKULL BASH"!!
THE FINAL STRIKE...
GEONG!
!

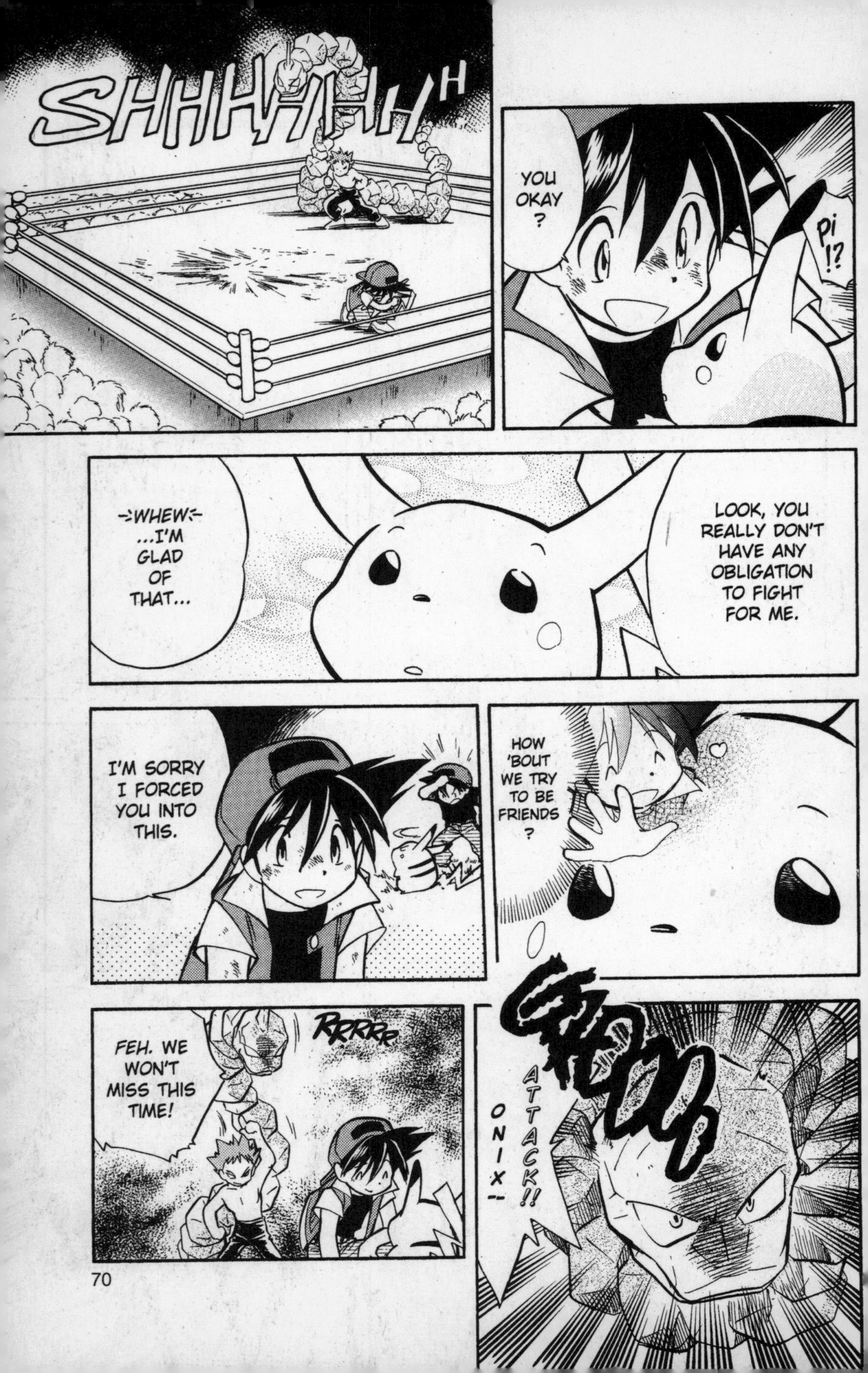
SHHHHHHH
YOU OKAY ?
pi !?
-WHEW- ...I'M GLAD OF THAT...
LOOK, YOU REALLY DON'T HAVE ANY OBLIGATION TO FIGHT FOR ME.
I'M SORRY I FORCED YOU INTO THIS.
HOW 'BOUT WE TRY TO BE FRIENDS ?
FEH. WE WON'T MISS THIS TIME!
RRRRR
ONIX-
ATTACK!!

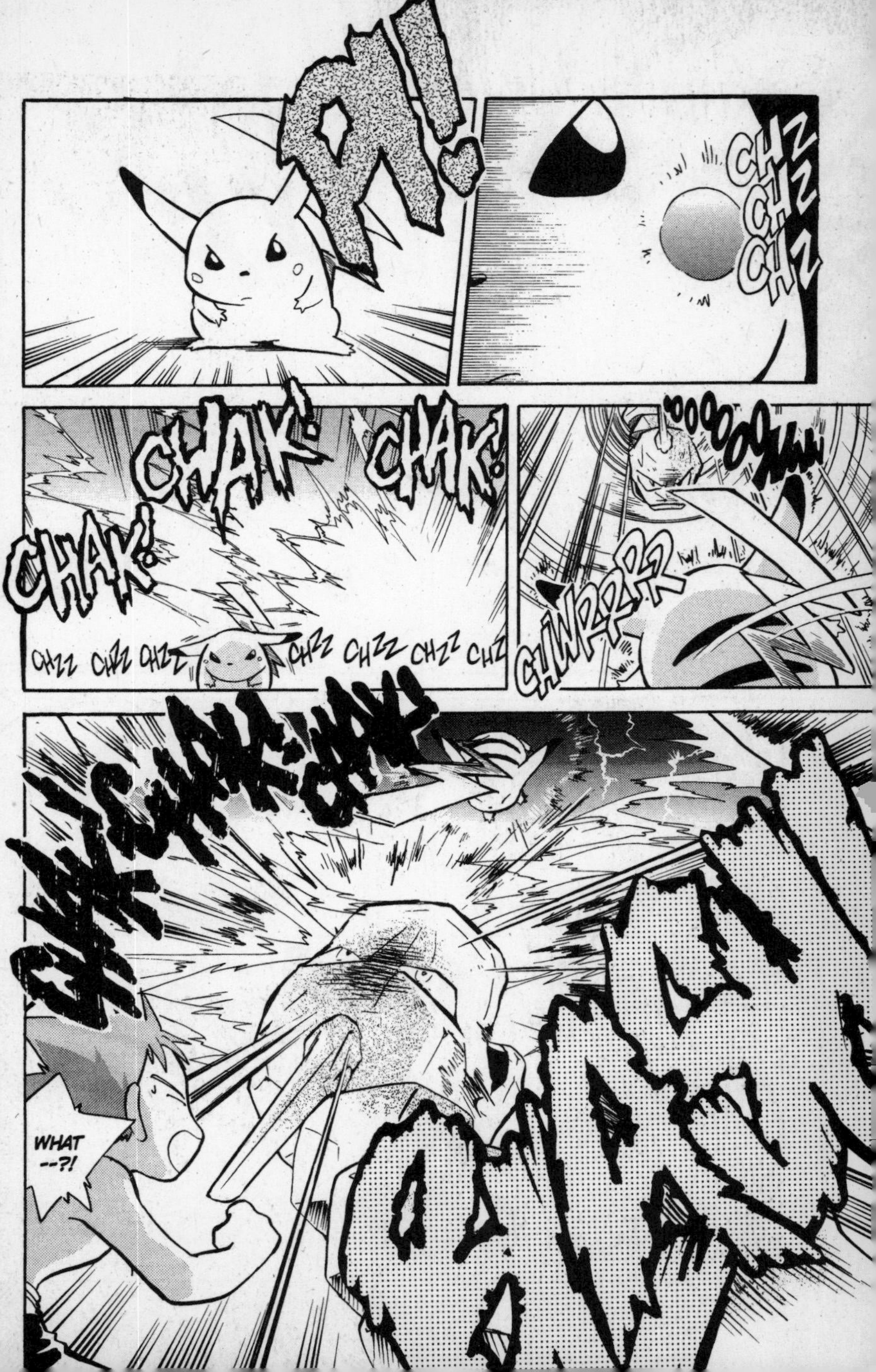
CHZ CHZ CHZ CHZ
CHAK! CHAK! CHAK!
CHZZ CHZZ CHZZ CHZZ CHZZ CHZZ CHZ
WHAT --?!

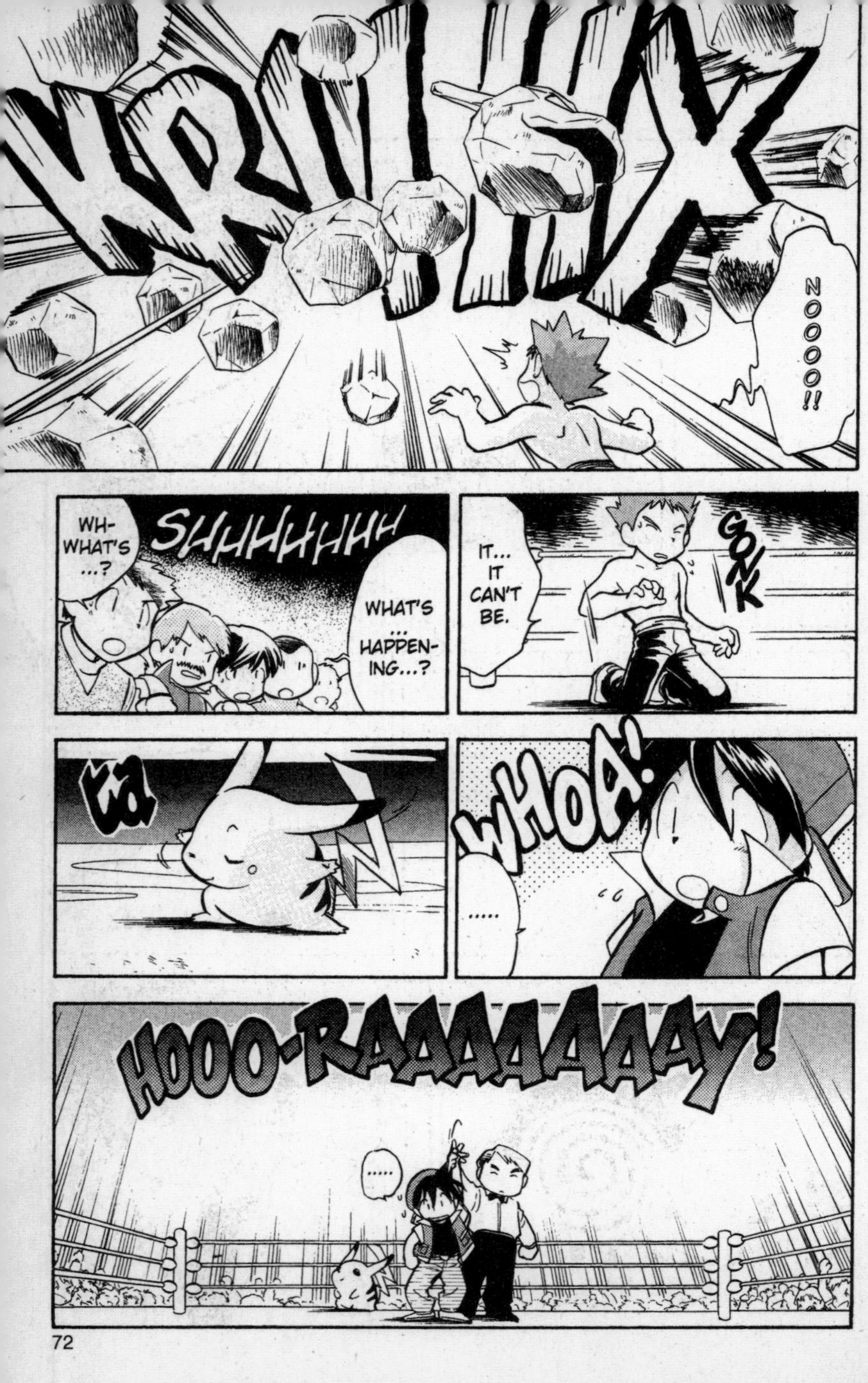
KRUUSSH
NOOOOO!!
WH-WHAT'S ...?
SHHHHHHHH
WHAT'S ... HAPPEN-ING...?
IT... IT CAN'T BE.
GONK
ta
WHOA!
.....
HOOO-RAAAAAAAY!
.....

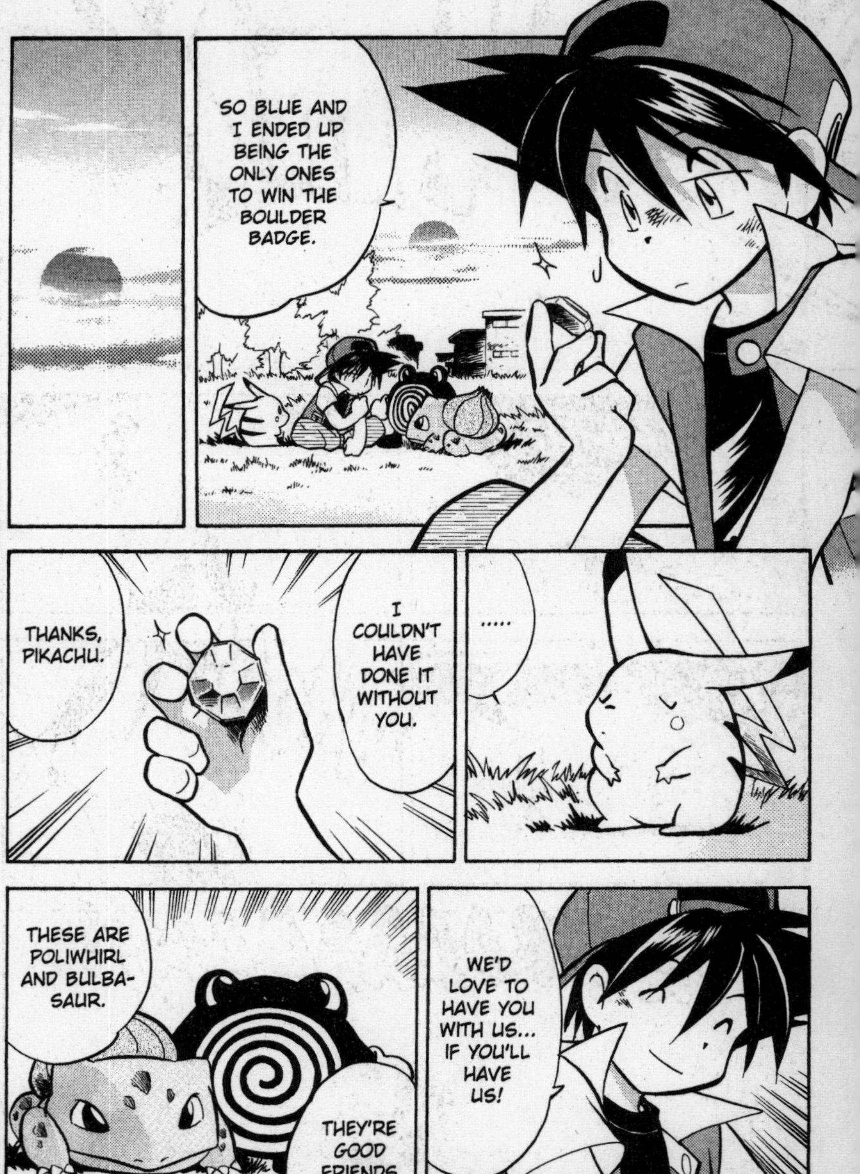
SO BLUE AND I ENDED UP BEING THE ONLY ONES TO WIN THE BOULDER BADGE.
THANKS, PIKACHU.
I COULDN'T HAVE DONE IT WITHOUT YOU.
.....
THESE ARE POLIWHIRL AND BULBA-SAUR.
THEY'RE GOOD FRIENDS OF MINE.
WE'D LOVE TO HAVE YOU WITH US... IF YOU'LL HAVE US!

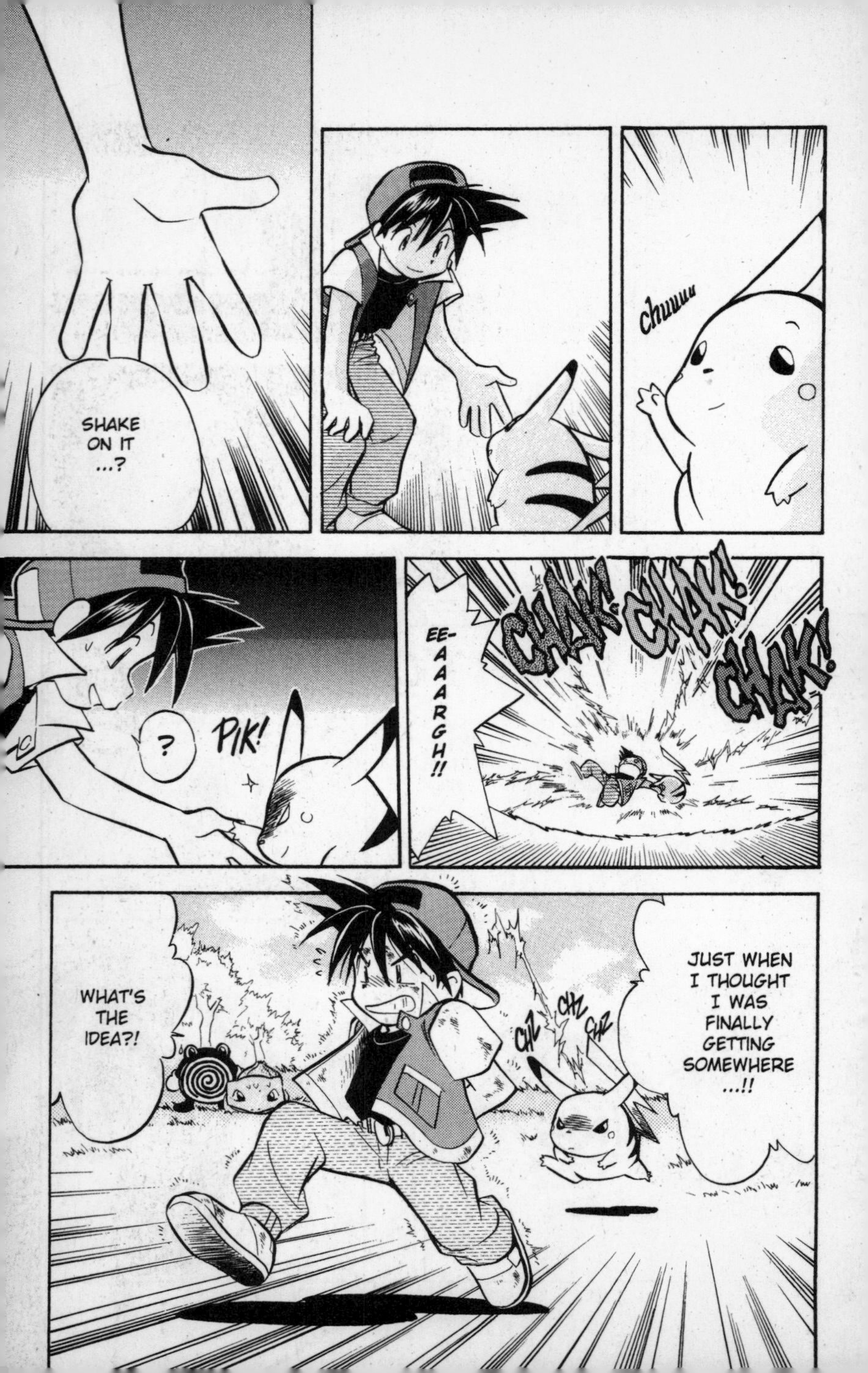
SHAKE ON IT ...?
chuuuu
?
PIK!
EE-AAAARGH!!
CHAK! CHAK! CHAK!
JUST WHEN I THOUGHT I WAS FINALLY GETTING SOMEWHERE ...!!
CHZ CHZ CHZ
WHAT'S THE IDEA?!

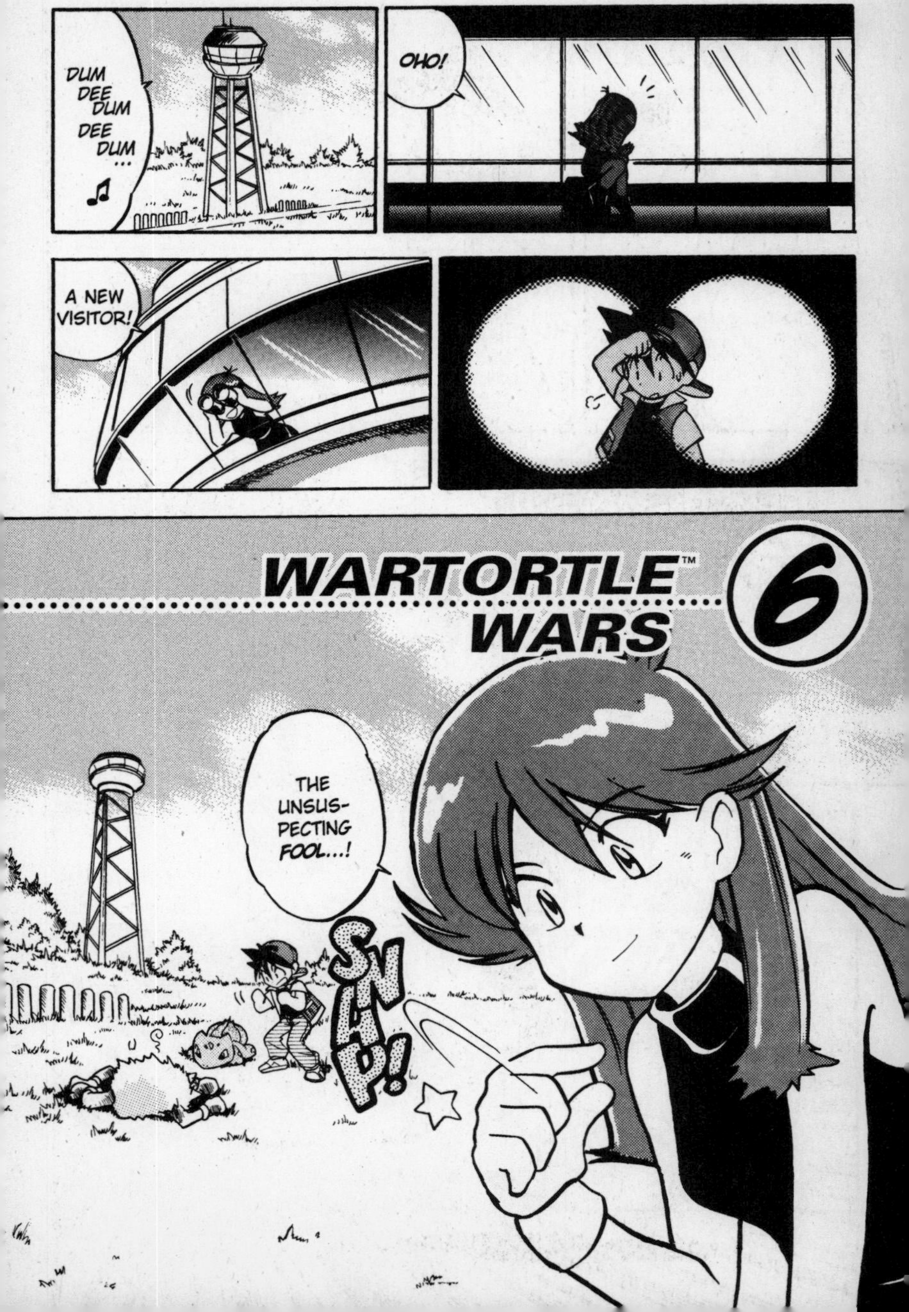
DUM DEE DUM DEE DUM ...
OHO!
A NEW VISITOR!
WARTORTLE™ WARS
6
THE UNSUS-PECTING FOOL...!
SNAP!

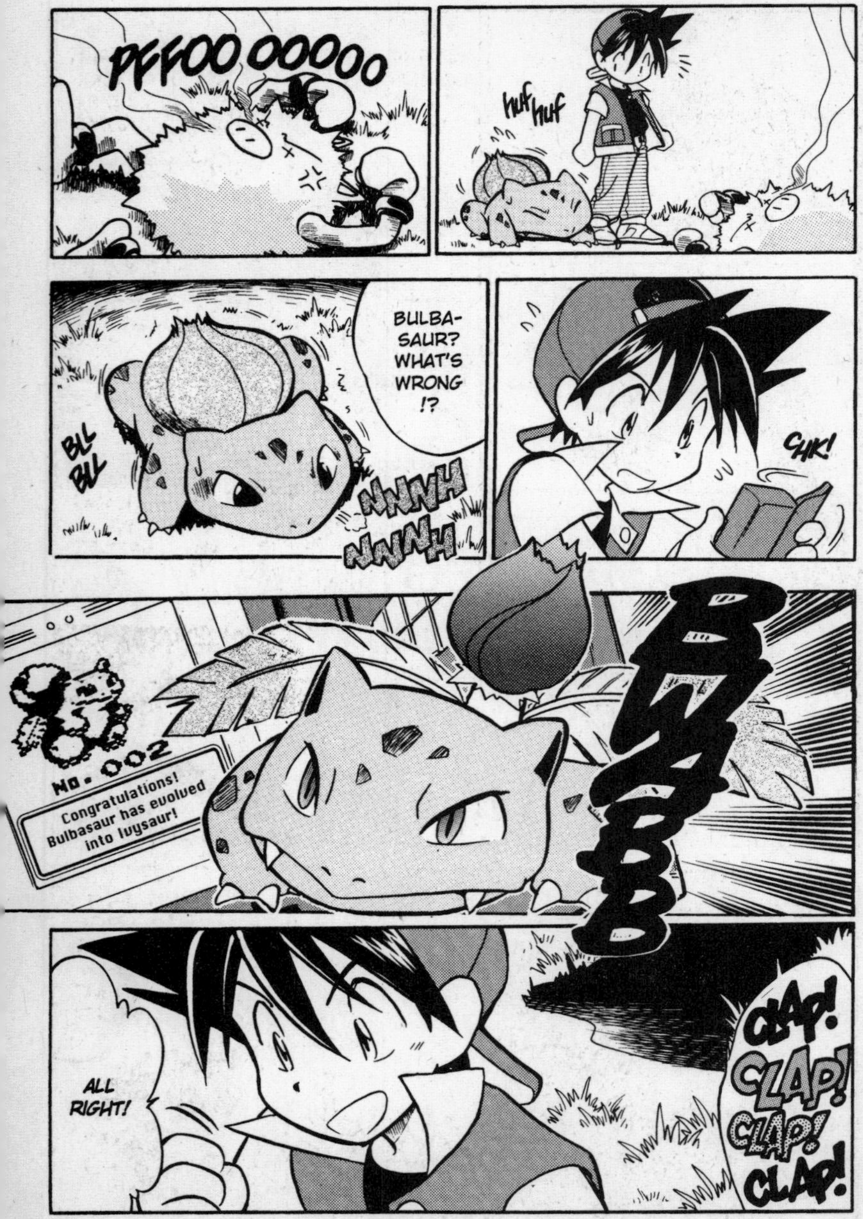
PFFOO OOOOO
huf huf
BLL BLL
BULBA-SAUR? WHAT'S WRONG !?
NNNH NNNH
CHK!
NO. 002
Congratulations! Bulbasaur has evolved into Ivysaur!
ALL RIGHT!
CLAP! CLAP! CLAP! CLAP!

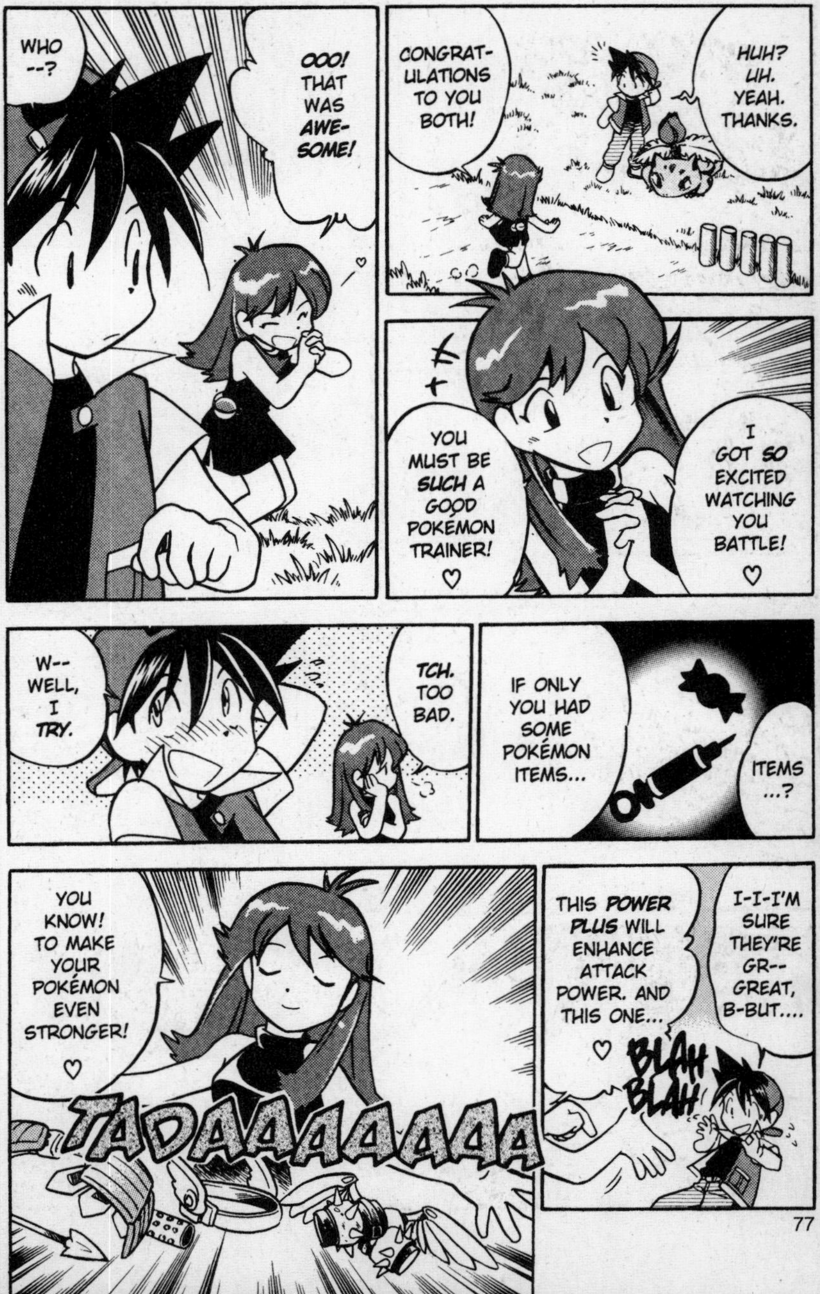

WHO --?
OOO! THAT WAS AWESOME!
CONGRATULATIONS TO YOU BOTH!
HUH? UH. YEAH. THANKS.
YOU MUST BE SUCH A GOOD POKÉMON TRAINER! ♡
I GOT SO EXCITED WATCHING YOU BATTLE! ♡
W-- WELL, I TRY.
TCH. TOO BAD.
IF ONLY YOU HAD SOME POKÉMON ITEMS...
ITEMS ...?
YOU KNOW! TO MAKE YOUR POKÉMON EVEN STRONGER! ♡
TADAAAAAAAAA
THIS POWER PLUS WILL ENHANCE ATTACK POWER. AND THIS ONE... ♡
BLAH BLAH
I-I-I'M SURE THEY'RE GR-- GREAT, B-BUT....

YOU DON'T WANT MY ITEMS?

.....

GUUUUP?

OF ...OF COURSE I DO, BUT...

OH, THANK YOU SO MUCH! THAT'LL BE ₽ 6000. ♡

SKWEEZ

WOW! SHE REALLY LIKED ME! I COULD TELL!

hmph

AND SHE SAYS SHE'S MY AGE!

WORKING FOR HERSELF, TOO--SHE MUST BE REALLY MATURE!

SFF SFF

PIIIIIIIIN

SHFA

ANOTHER ONE!

NOW'S MY CHANCE TO TEST THESE ITEMS!

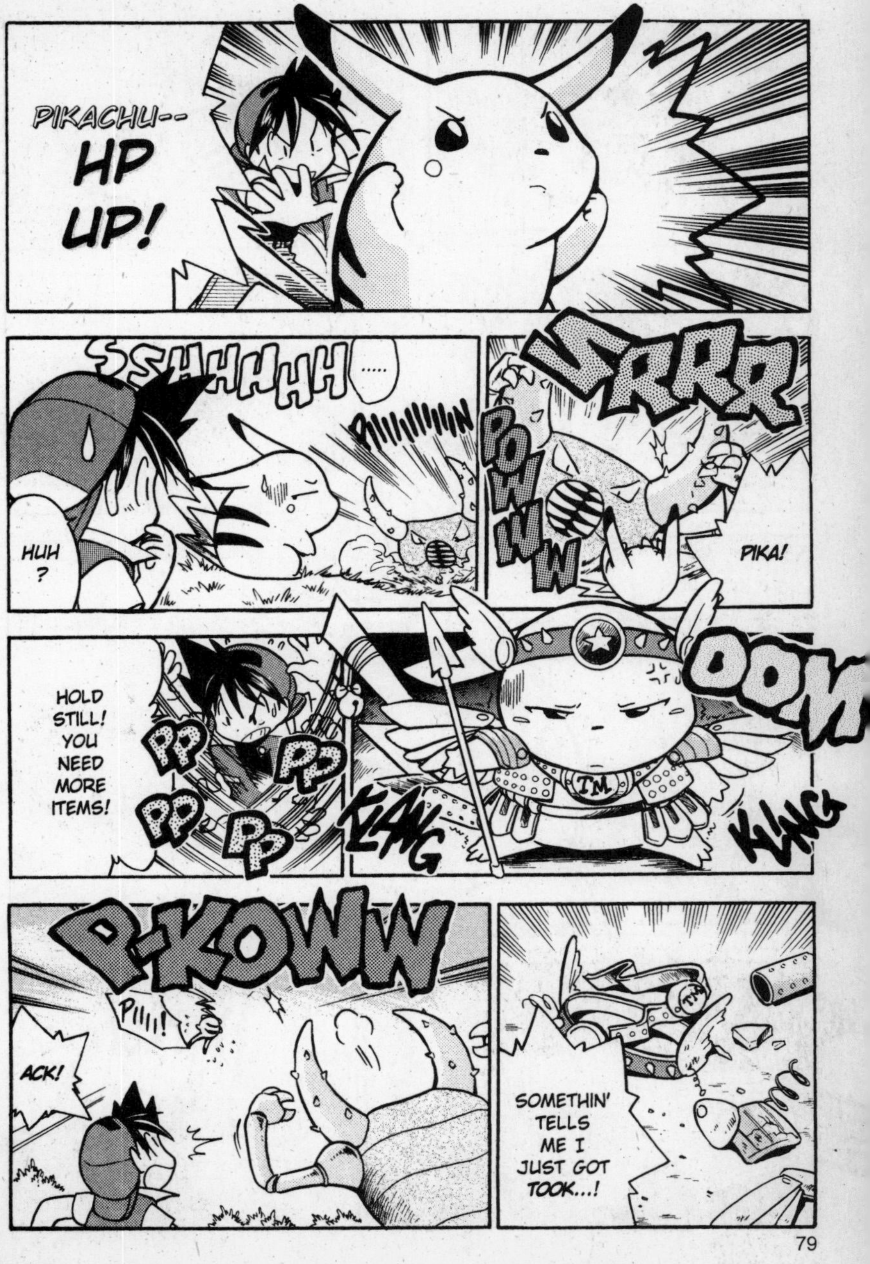
PIKACHU--
HP UP!
SHHHHHH
.....
HUH?
PIIIIIIIN
SRRR
POWWW
PIKA!
HOLD STILL! YOU NEED MORE ITEMS!
PP
PP
PP
PP
KLANG
OOM
KLING
P-KOWW
PIII!
ACK!
SOMETHIN' TELLS ME I JUST GOT TOOK...!

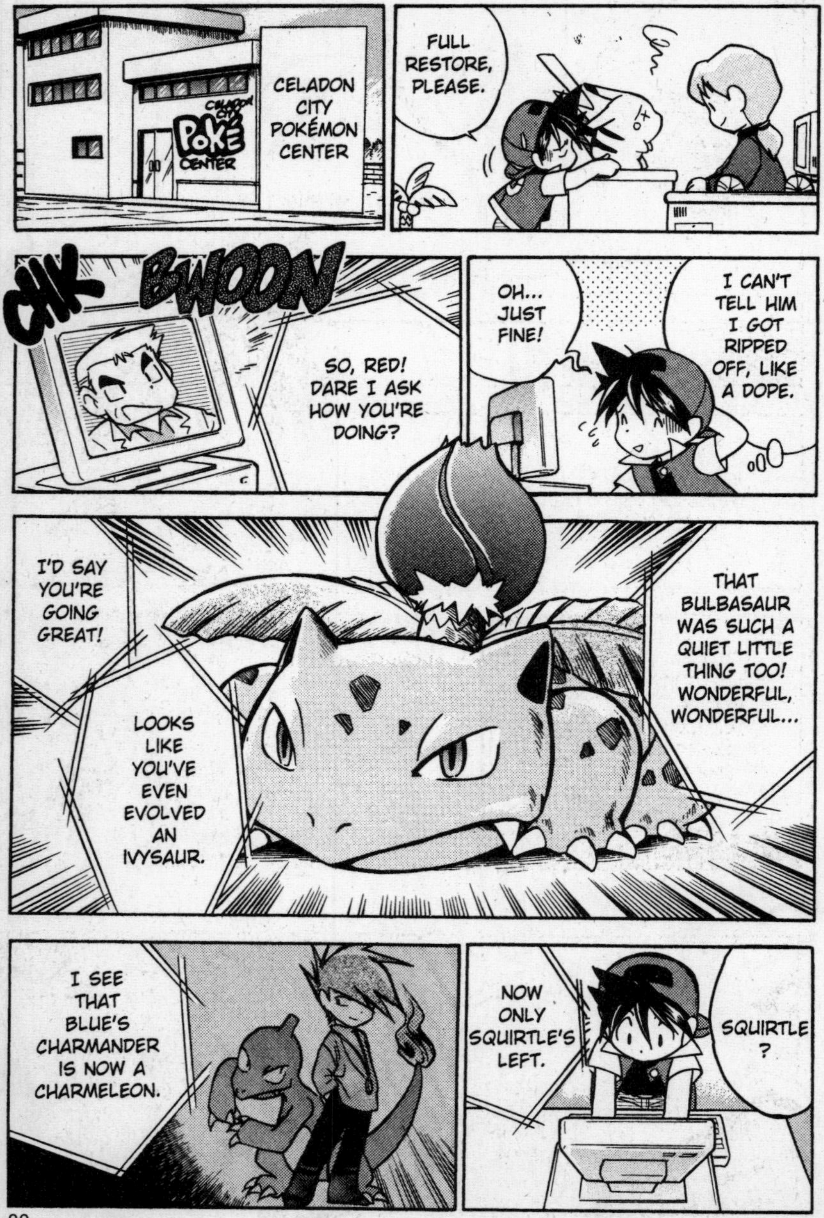
CELADON CITY POKÉMON CENTER
CELADON CITY POKÉ CENTER
FULL RESTORE, PLEASE.
CHK
BWOON
SO, RED! DARE I ASK HOW YOU'RE DOING?
OH... JUST FINE!
I CAN'T TELL HIM I GOT RIPPED OFF, LIKE A DOPE.
I'D SAY YOU'RE GOING GREAT!
LOOKS LIKE YOU'VE EVEN EVOLVED AN IVYSAUR.
THAT BULBASAUR WAS SUCH A QUIET LITTLE THING TOO! WONDERFUL, WONDERFUL...
I SEE THAT BLUE'S CHARMANDER IS NOW A CHARMELEON.
NOW ONLY SQUIRTLE'S LEFT.
SQUIRTLE?

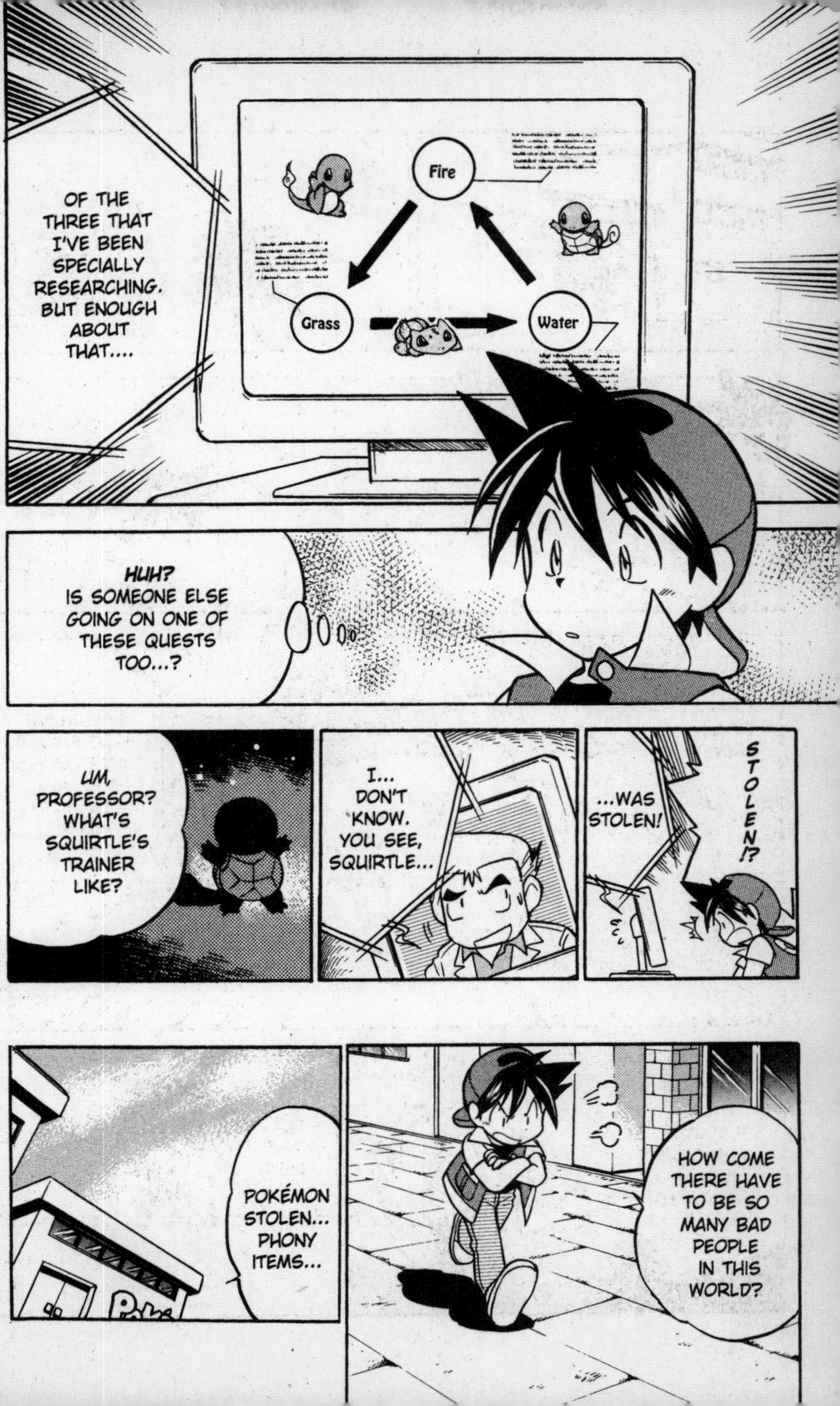
OF THE THREE THAT I'VE BEEN SPECIALLY RESEARCHING. BUT ENOUGH ABOUT THAT....
Fire
Grass
Water
HUH? IS SOMEONE ELSE GOING ON ONE OF THESE QUESTS TOO...?
UM, PROFESSOR? WHAT'S SQUIRTLE'S TRAINER LIKE?
I... DON'T KNOW. YOU SEE, SQUIRTLE...
...WAS STOLEN!
STOLEN!?
POKÉMON STOLEN... PHONY ITEMS...
HOW COME THERE HAVE TO BE SO MANY BAD PEOPLE IN THIS WORLD?

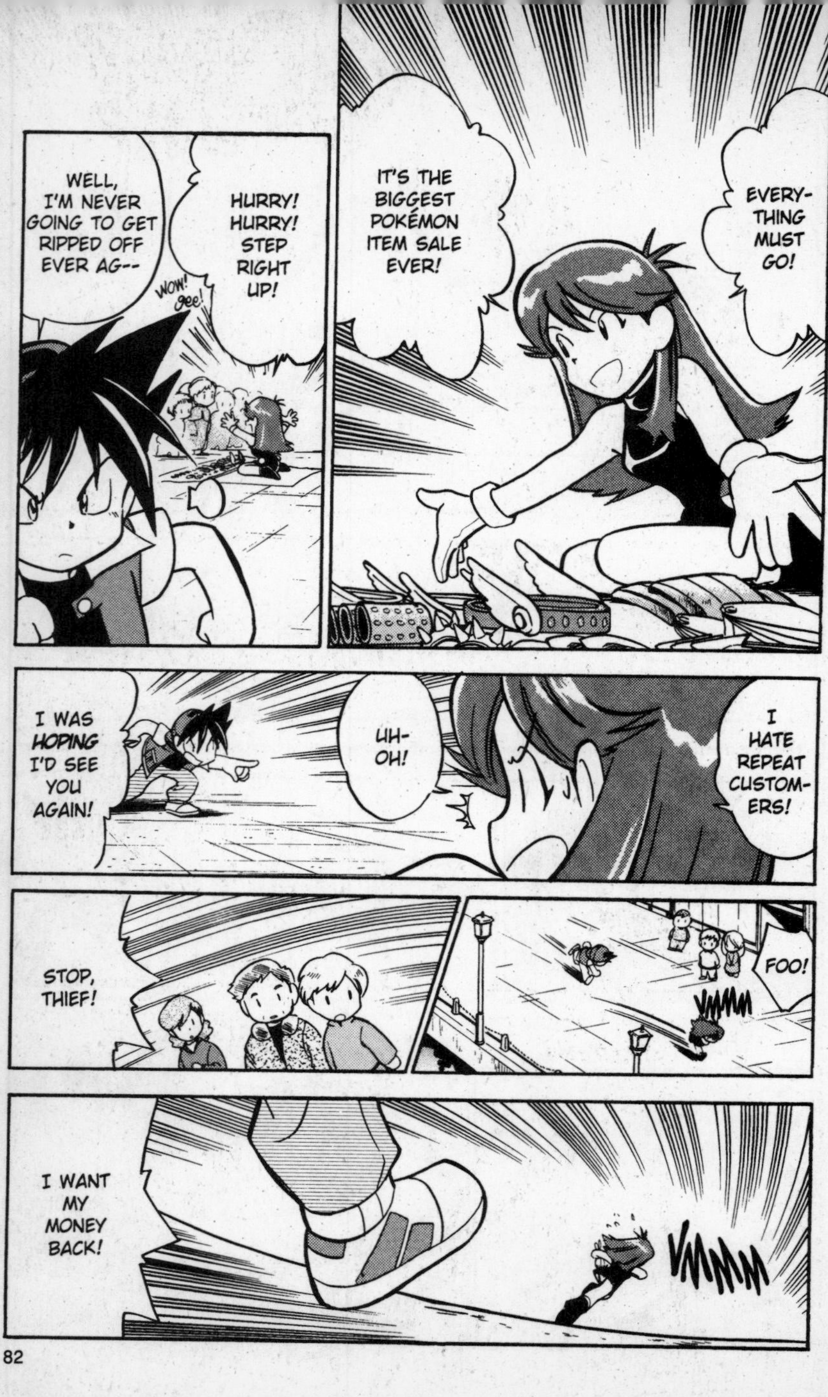

WELL, I'M NEVER GOING TO GET RIPPED OFF EVER AG--
HURRY! HURRY! STEP RIGHT UP!
WOW!
gee!
IT'S THE BIGGEST POKÉMON ITEM SALE EVER!
EVERY-THING MUST GO!
I WAS HOPING I'D SEE YOU AGAIN!
UH-OH!
I HATE REPEAT CUSTOM-ERS!
STOP, THIEF!
FOO!
VMMM
I WANT MY MONEY BACK!
VMMM

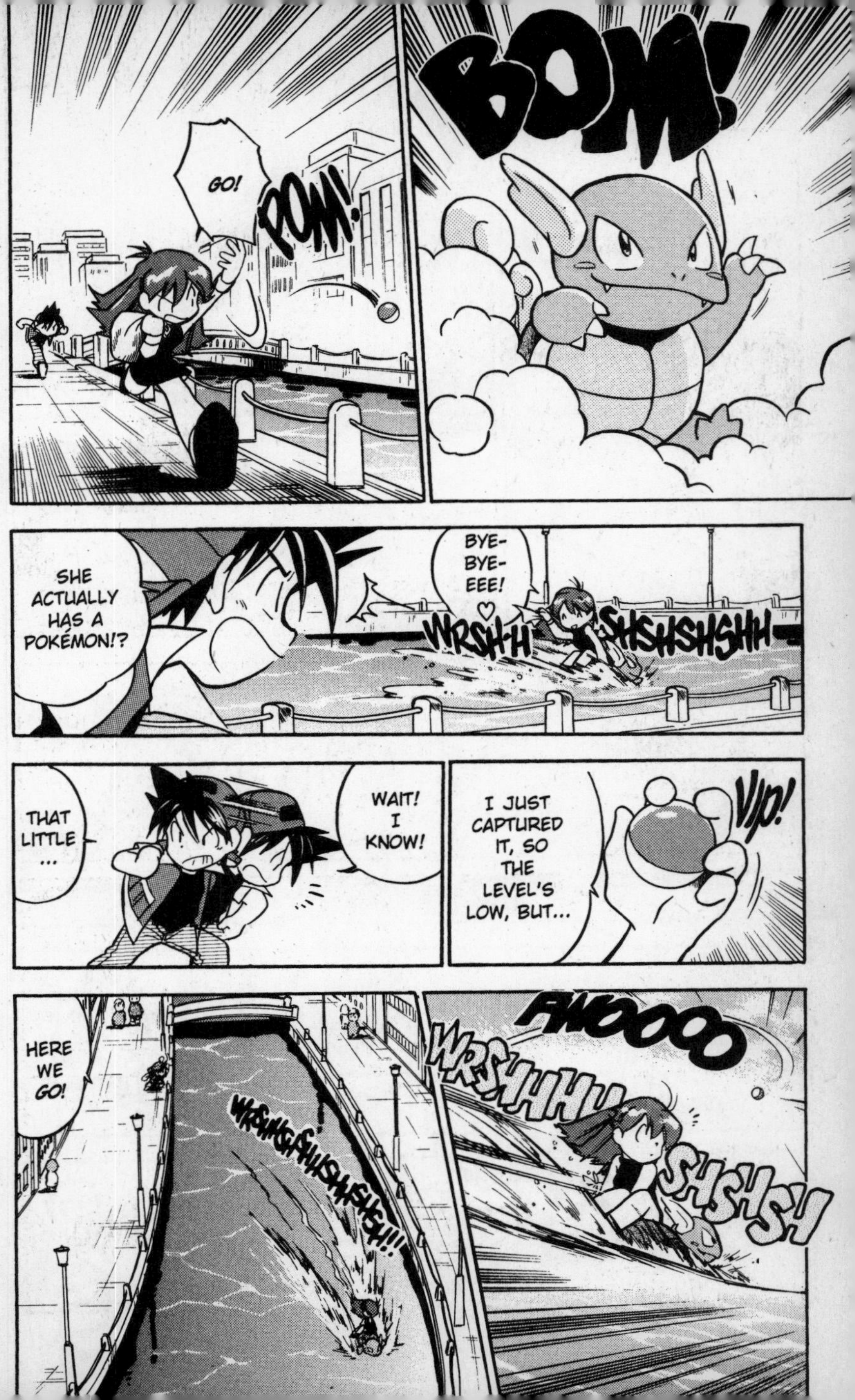
GO!
POM!
BOM!
SHE ACTUALLY HAS A POKÉMON!?
BYE-BYE-EEE! ♡
WRSH-H
SHSHSHSHH
WAIT! I KNOW!
THAT LITTLE ...
I JUST CAPTURED IT, SO THE LEVEL'S LOW, BUT...
VIP!
HERE WE GO!
FWOOOO
WRSHHHH
SHSHSH
WRSHGSHHSHSHSHSHSH!!!

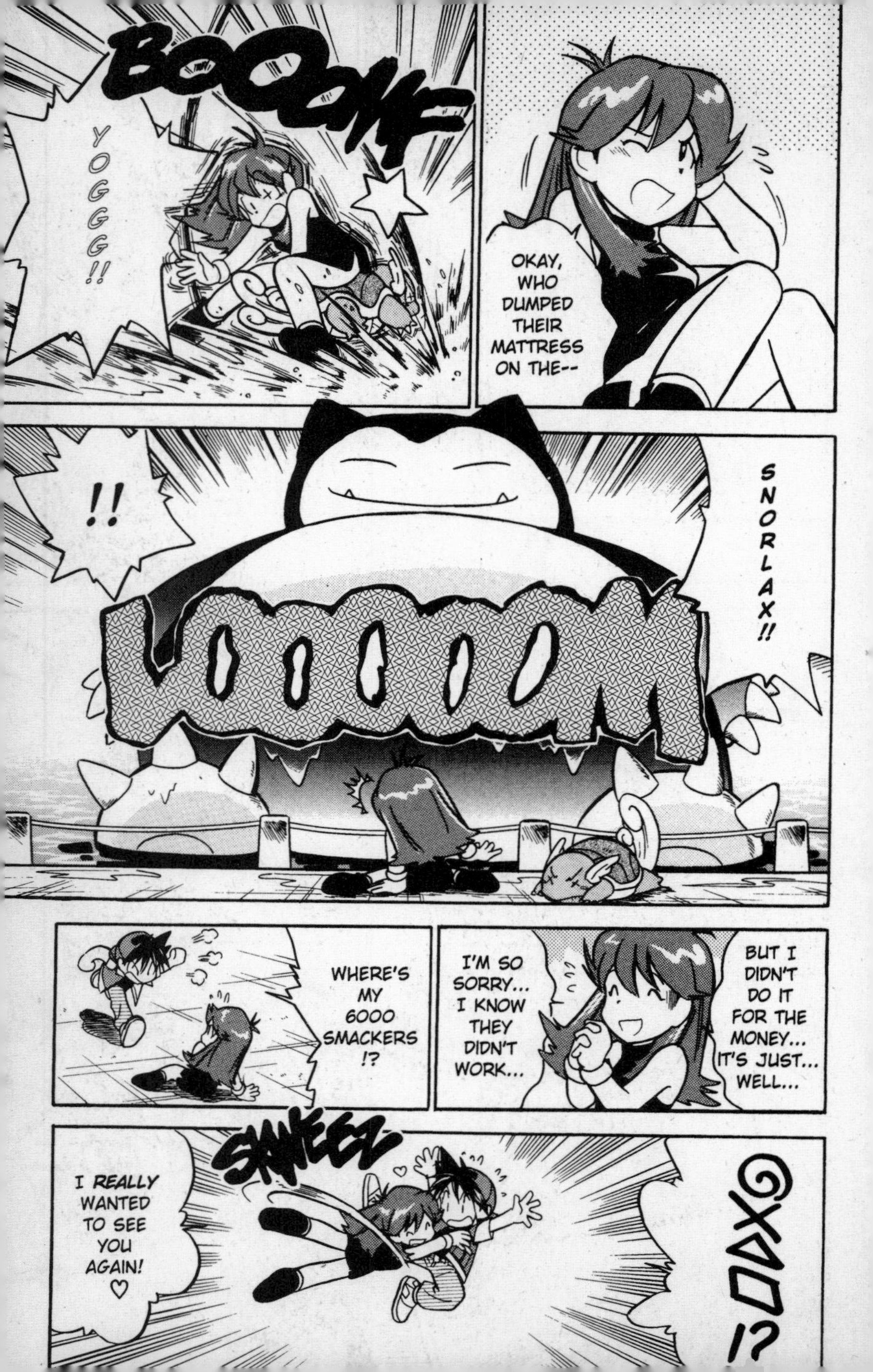
BOOOMF
YOGGG!!
OKAY, WHO DUMPED THEIR MATTRESS ON THE--
SNORLAX!!
!!
VOOOOOM
WHERE'S MY 6000 SMACKERS !?
I'M SO SORRY... I KNOW THEY DIDN'T WORK...
BUT I DIDN'T DO IT FOR THE MONEY... IT'S JUST... WELL...
SWEEEZ
I REALLY WANTED TO SEE YOU AGAIN! ♡
!?

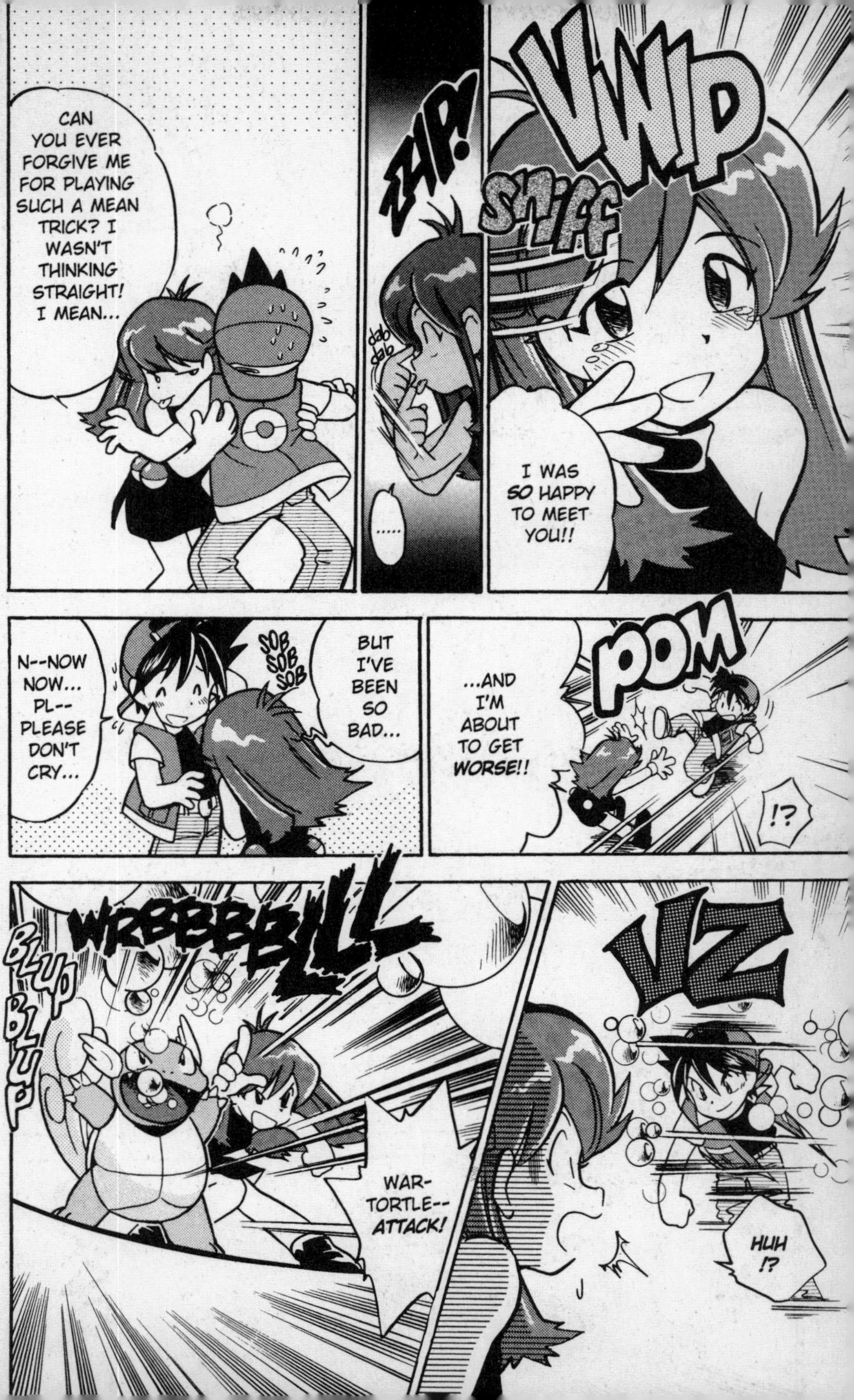
CAN YOU EVER FORGIVE ME FOR PLAYING SUCH A MEAN TRICK? I WASN'T THINKING STRAIGHT! I MEAN...
ZIP!
dab dab
......
VWIP
SNIFF
I WAS SO HAPPY TO MEET YOU!!
N--NOW NOW... PL--PLEASE DON'T CRY...
SOB SOB SOB
BUT I'VE BEEN SO BAD...
...AND I'M ABOUT TO GET WORSE!!
POM
!?
BLUP BLUP
WRBBBBLL
WAR-TORTLE--ATTACK!
VZ
HUH!?

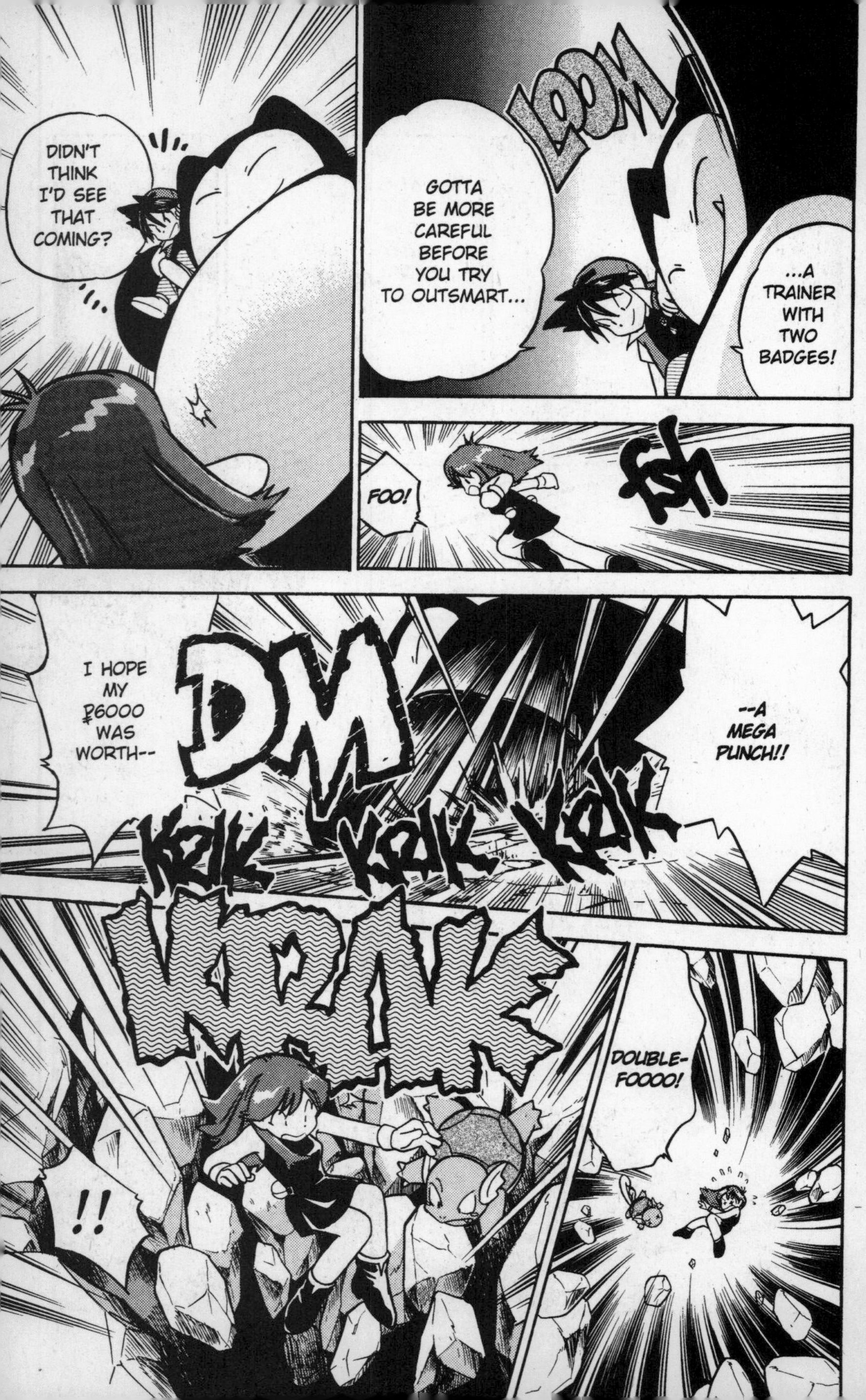
DIDN'T THINK I'D SEE THAT COMING?
LOOM
GOTTA BE MORE CAREFUL BEFORE YOU TRY TO OUTSMART...
...A TRAINER WITH TWO BADGES!
FOO!
fsh
I HOPE MY ₽6000 WAS WORTH--
DM
--A MEGA PUNCH!!
KRIK KRAK KRAK
KRAK
DOUBLE-FOOOO!
!!

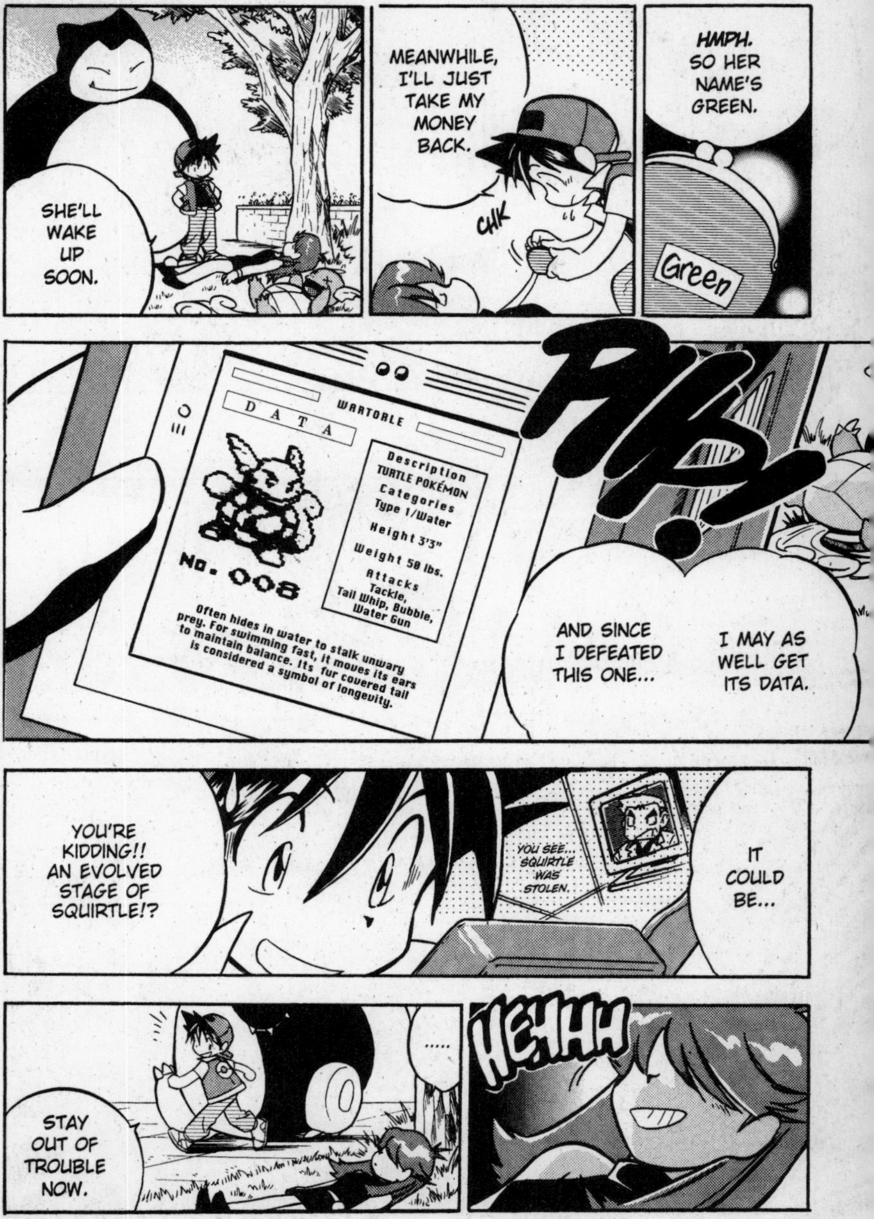
SHE'LL WAKE UP SOON.
MEANWHILE, I'LL JUST TAKE MY MONEY BACK.
CHK
HMPH. SO HER NAME'S GREEN.
Green
WARTORLE
DATA
No. 008
Description
TURTLE POKÉMON
Categories
Type 1/Water
Height 3'3"
Weight 50 lbs.
Attacks
Tackle, Tail Whip, Bubble, Water Gun
Often hides in water to stalk unwary prey. For swimming fast, it moves its ears to maintain balance. Its fur covered tail is considered a symbol of longevity.
PIKY!
AND SINCE I DEFEATED THIS ONE...
I MAY AS WELL GET ITS DATA.
YOU'RE KIDDING!! AN EVOLVED STAGE OF SQUIRTLE!?
YOU SEE... SQUIRTLE WAS STOLEN.
IT COULD BE...
STAY OUT OF TROUBLE NOW.
.....
HEHHH

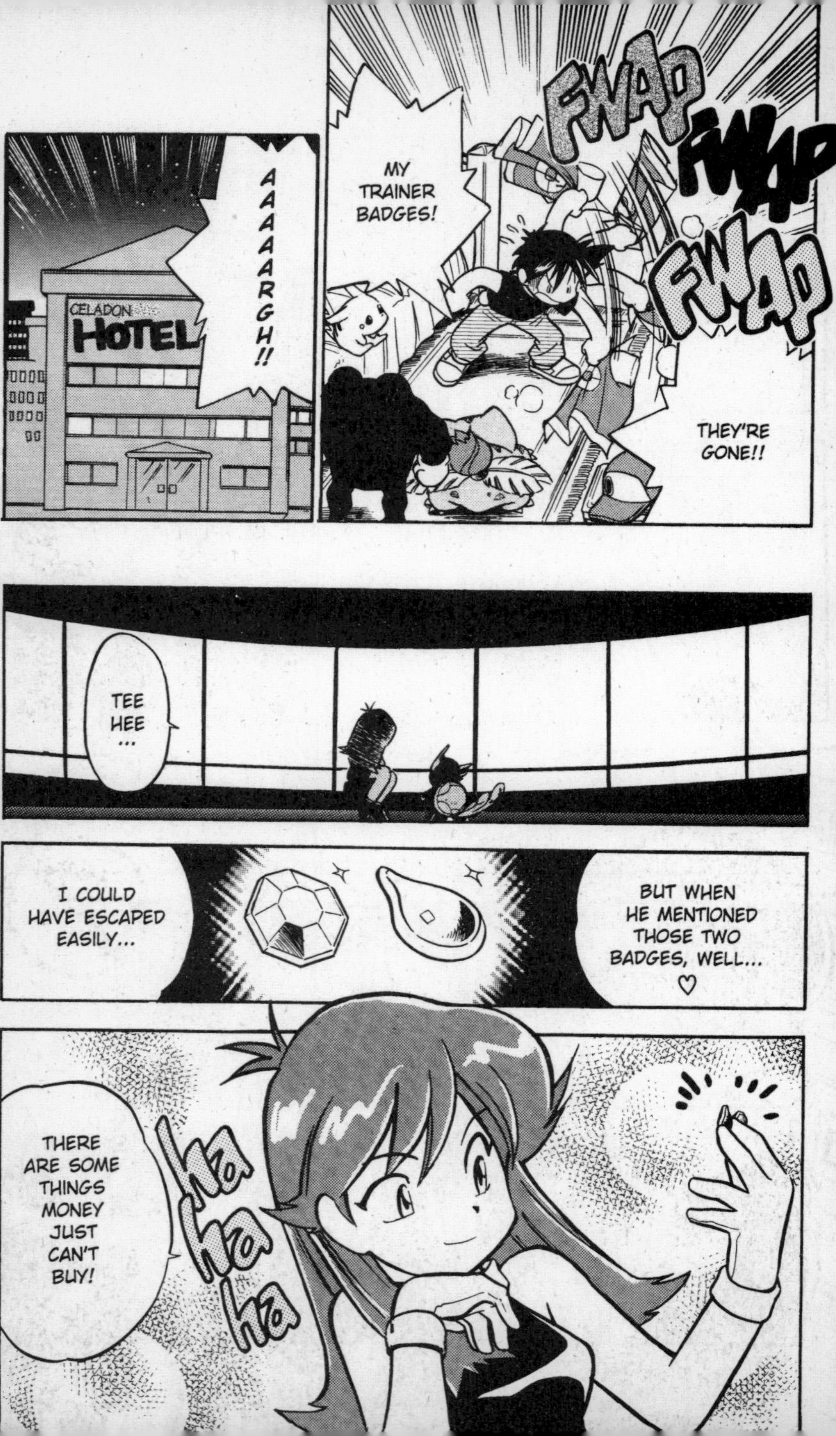
CELADON HOTEL
AAAAAARGH!!
MY TRAINER BADGES!
FWAP FWAP FWAP
THEY'RE GONE!!
TEE HEE...
I COULD HAVE ESCAPED EASILY...
BUT WHEN HE MENTIONED THOSE TWO BADGES, WELL... ♡
THERE ARE SOME THINGS MONEY JUST CAN'T BUY!
ha ha ha

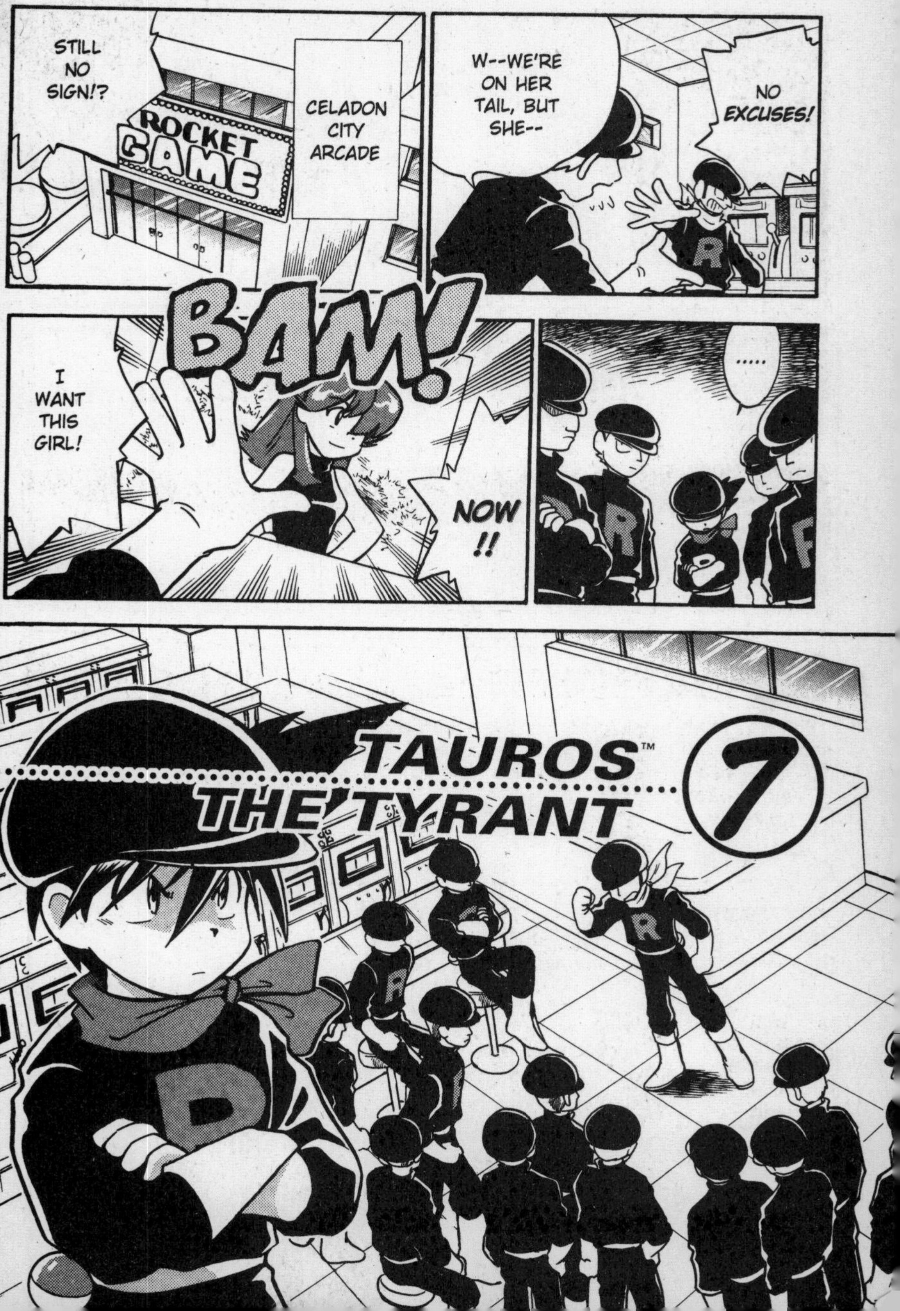
STILL NO SIGN!?
CELADON CITY ARCADE
ROCKET GAME
W--WE'RE ON HER TAIL, BUT SHE--
NO EXCUSES!
BAM!
I WANT THIS GIRL!
NOW !!
.....
TAUROS™ THE TYRANT
7

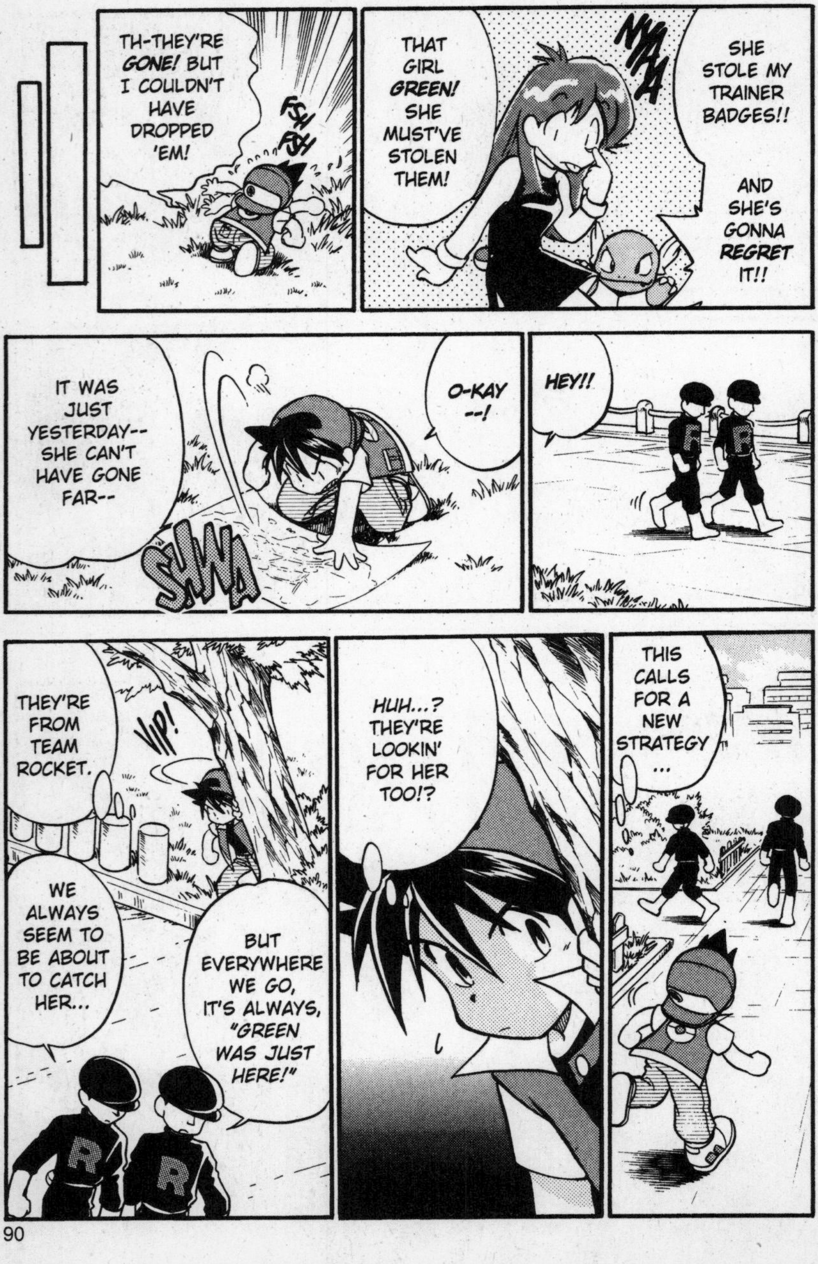
TH-THEY'RE GONE! BUT I COULDN'T HAVE DROPPED 'EM!
FSH FSH
THAT GIRL GREEN! SHE MUST'VE STOLEN THEM!
NYAA
SHE STOLE MY TRAINER BADGES!!
AND SHE'S GONNA REGRET IT!!
IT WAS JUST YESTERDAY-- SHE CAN'T HAVE GONE FAR--
SHWA
O-KAY --!
HEY!!
THEY'RE FROM TEAM ROCKET.
VIP!
WE ALWAYS SEEM TO BE ABOUT TO CATCH HER...
BUT EVERYWHERE WE GO, IT'S ALWAYS, "GREEN WAS JUST HERE!"
HUH...? THEY'RE LOOKIN' FOR HER TOO!?
THIS CALLS FOR A NEW STRATEGY...

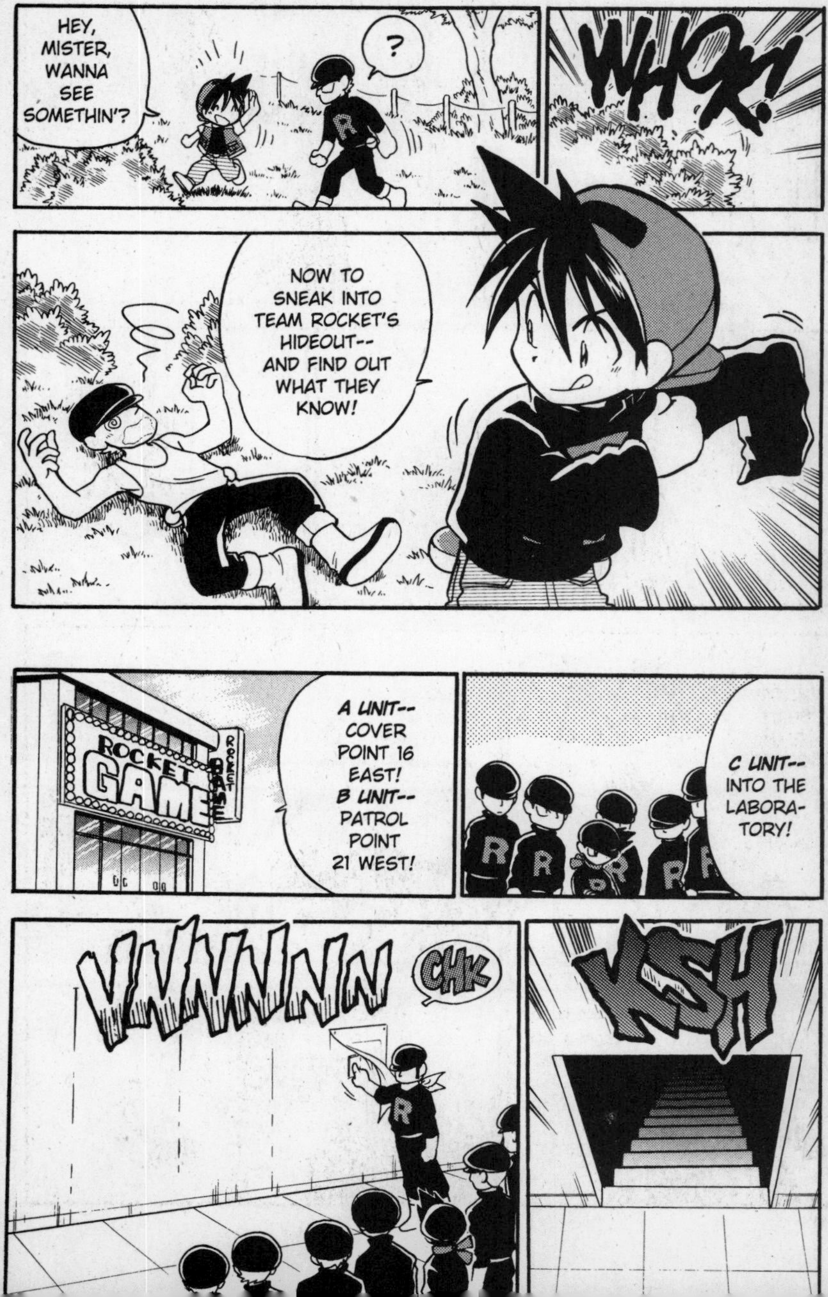
HEY, MISTER, WANNA SEE SOMETHIN'?
?
WHOOM!
NOW TO SNEAK INTO TEAM ROCKET'S HIDEOUT-- AND FIND OUT WHAT THEY KNOW!
ROCKET GAME
ROCKET GAME
A UNIT-- COVER POINT 16 EAST! B UNIT-- PATROL POINT 21 WEST!
C UNIT-- INTO THE LABORA-TORY!
VWWNNN
CHK
KSH

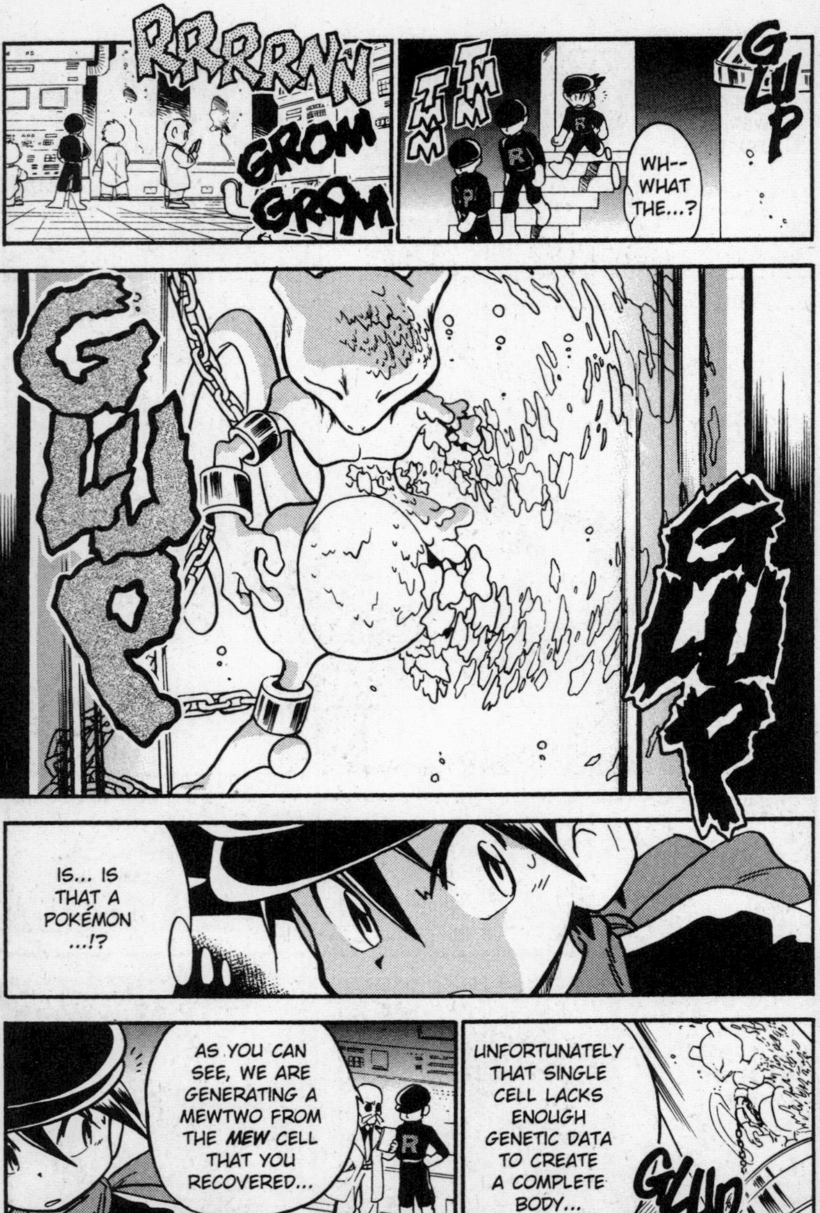
RRRRNN
GROM GROM
TMMM TMMM
WH-- WHAT THE...?
GLUP
GLUP
IS... IS THAT A POKÉMON ...!?
AS YOU CAN SEE, WE ARE GENERATING A MEWTWO FROM THE *MEW* CELL THAT YOU RECOVERED...
UNFORTUNATELY THAT SINGLE CELL LACKS ENOUGH GENETIC DATA TO CREATE A COMPLETE BODY...
GLUP

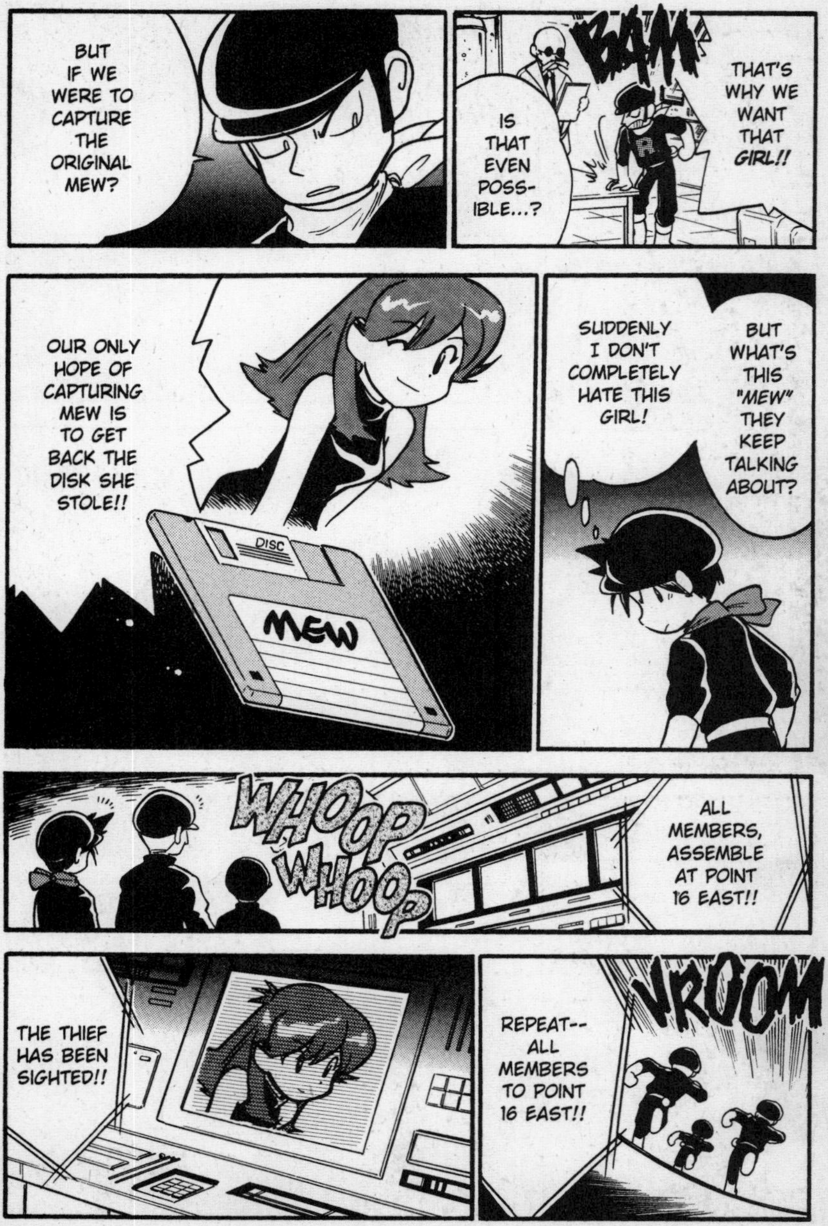
BUT IF WE WERE TO CAPTURE THE ORIGINAL MEW?
IS THAT EVEN POSS-IBLE...?
BAM
THAT'S WHY WE WANT THAT GIRL!!
OUR ONLY HOPE OF CAPTURING MEW IS TO GET BACK THE DISK SHE STOLE!!
DISC
MEW
SUDDENLY I DON'T COMPLETELY HATE THIS GIRL!
BUT WHAT'S THIS "MEW" THEY KEEP TALKING ABOUT?
WHOOP WHOOP
ALL MEMBERS, ASSEMBLE AT POINT 16 EAST!!
THE THIEF HAS BEEN SIGHTED!!
REPEAT--ALL MEMBERS TO POINT 16 EAST!!
VROOM

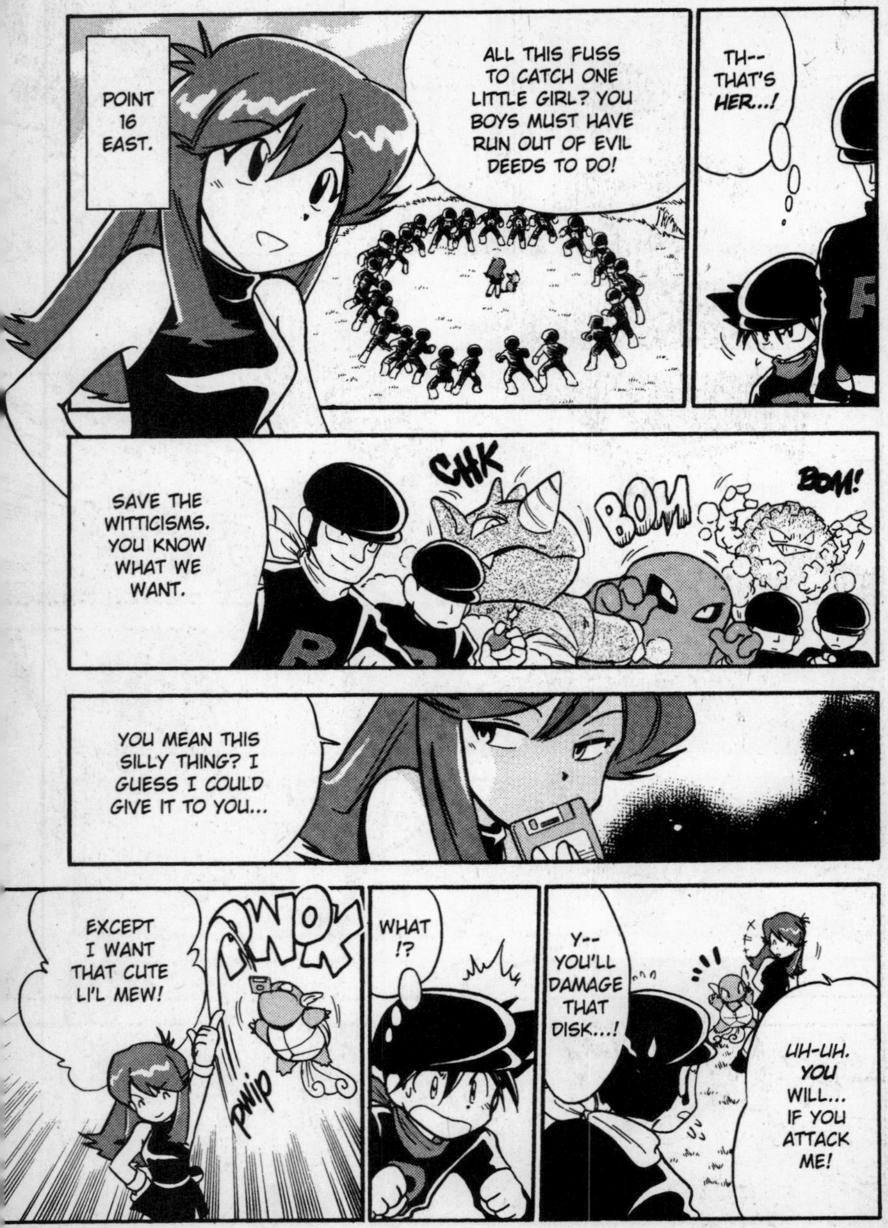
POINT 16 EAST.
ALL THIS FUSS TO CATCH ONE LITTLE GIRL? YOU BOYS MUST HAVE RUN OUT OF EVIL DEEDS TO DO!
TH-- THAT'S HER...!
SAVE THE WITTICISMS. YOU KNOW WHAT WE WANT.
CHK
BOM
BOM!
YOU MEAN THIS SILLY THING? I GUESS I COULD GIVE IT TO YOU...
EXCEPT I WANT THAT CUTE LI'L MEW!
PWIP
WHAT !?
Y-- YOU'LL DAMAGE THAT DISK...!
UH-UH. YOU WILL... IF YOU ATTACK ME!

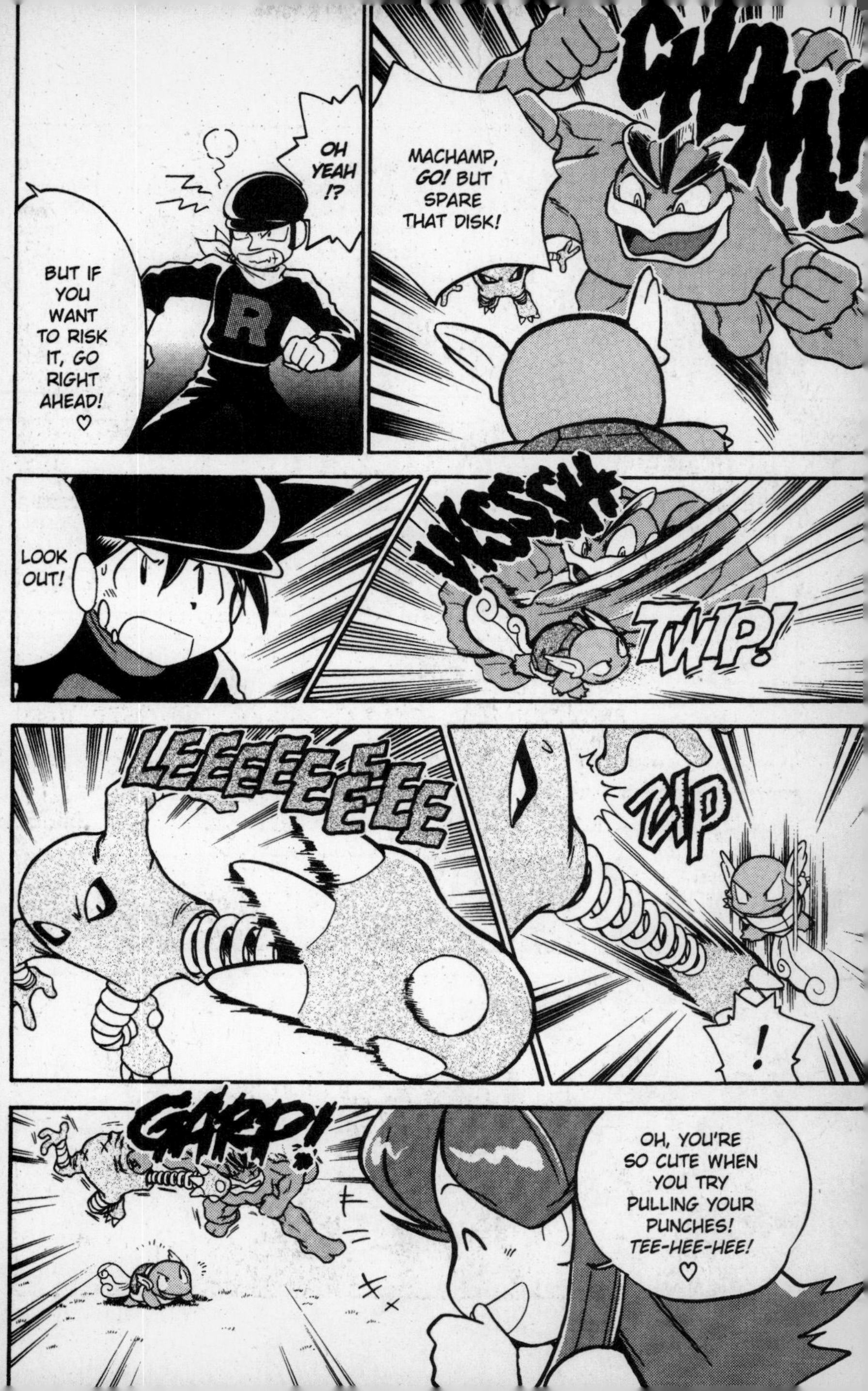
BUT IF YOU WANT TO RISK IT, GO RIGHT AHEAD! ♡
OH YEAH !?
MACHAMP, GO! BUT SPARE THAT DISK!
CHOMP!
LOOK OUT!
WSSH
TWIP!
LEEEEEEEEEEE
ZIP
!
GARP!
OH, YOU'RE SO CUTE WHEN YOU TRY PULLING YOUR PUNCHES! TEE-HEE-HEE! ♡

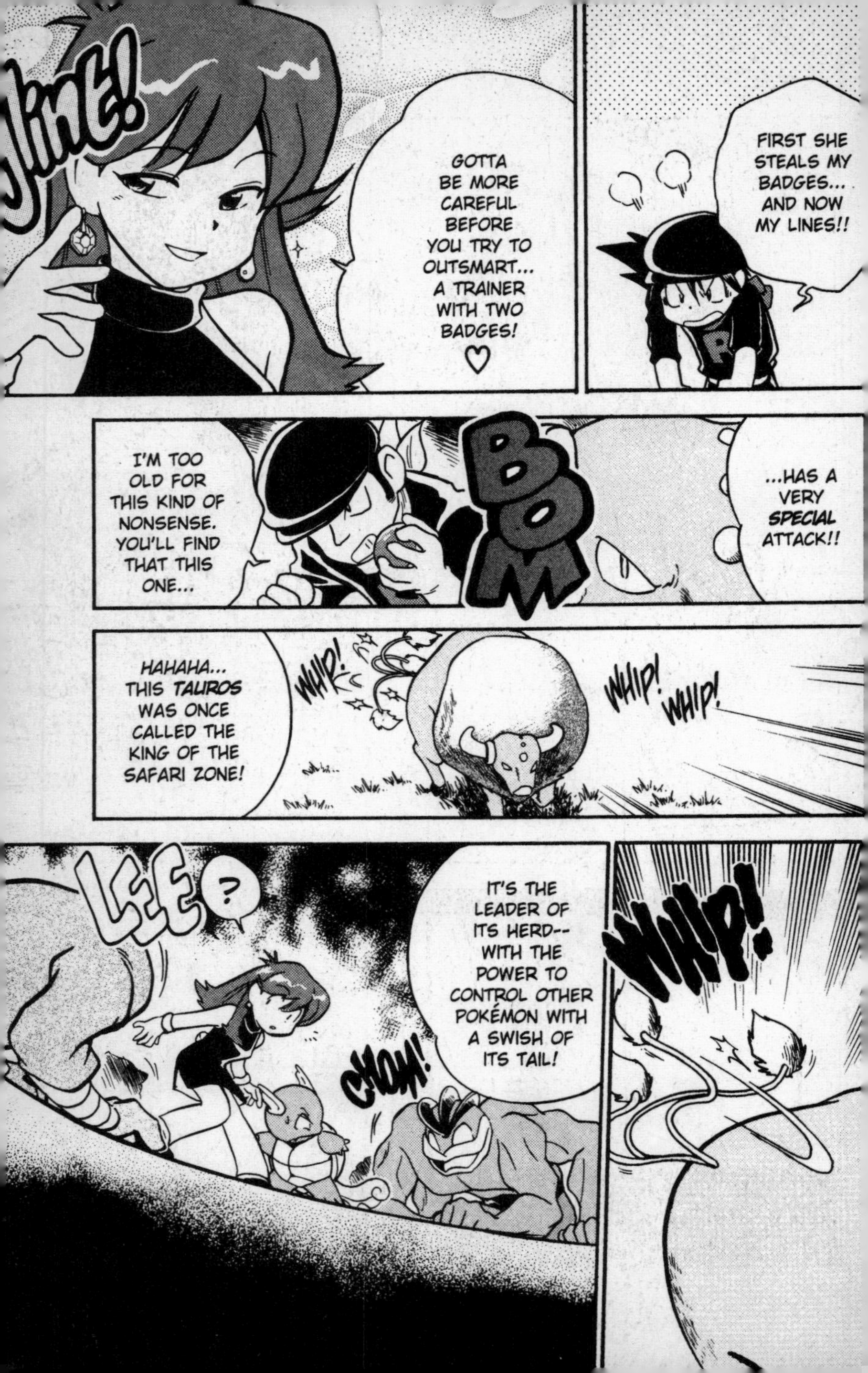
GOTTA BE MORE CAREFUL BEFORE YOU TRY TO OUTSMART... A TRAINER WITH TWO BADGES! ♡
FIRST SHE STEALS MY BADGES... AND NOW MY LINES!!
I'M TOO OLD FOR THIS KIND OF NONSENSE. YOU'LL FIND THAT THIS ONE...
...HAS A VERY *SPECIAL* ATTACK!!
*HAHAHA... THIS **TAUROS** WAS ONCE CALLED THE KING OF THE SAFARI ZONE!*
WHIP!
WHIP!
WHIP!
LEE
?
IT'S THE LEADER OF ITS HERD--WITH THE POWER TO CONTROL OTHER POKÉMON WITH A SWISH OF ITS TAIL!
CHOM!
WHIP!

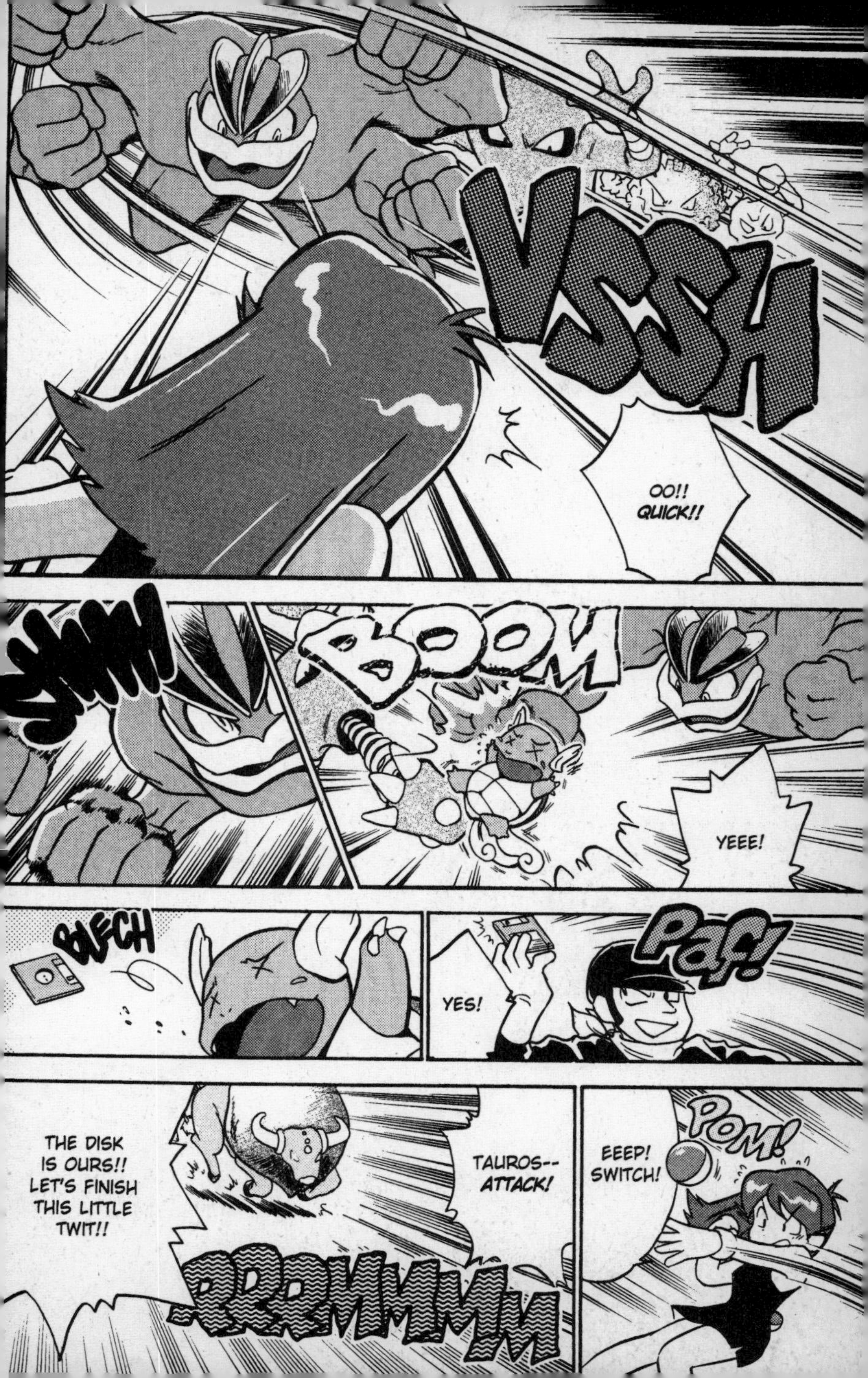
VSSH
OO!! QUICK!!
BOOM
YEEE!
BLECH
YES!
PAF!
THE DISK IS OURS!! LET'S FINISH THIS LITTLE TWIT!!
TAUROS-- ATTACK!
EEEP! SWITCH!
POM!

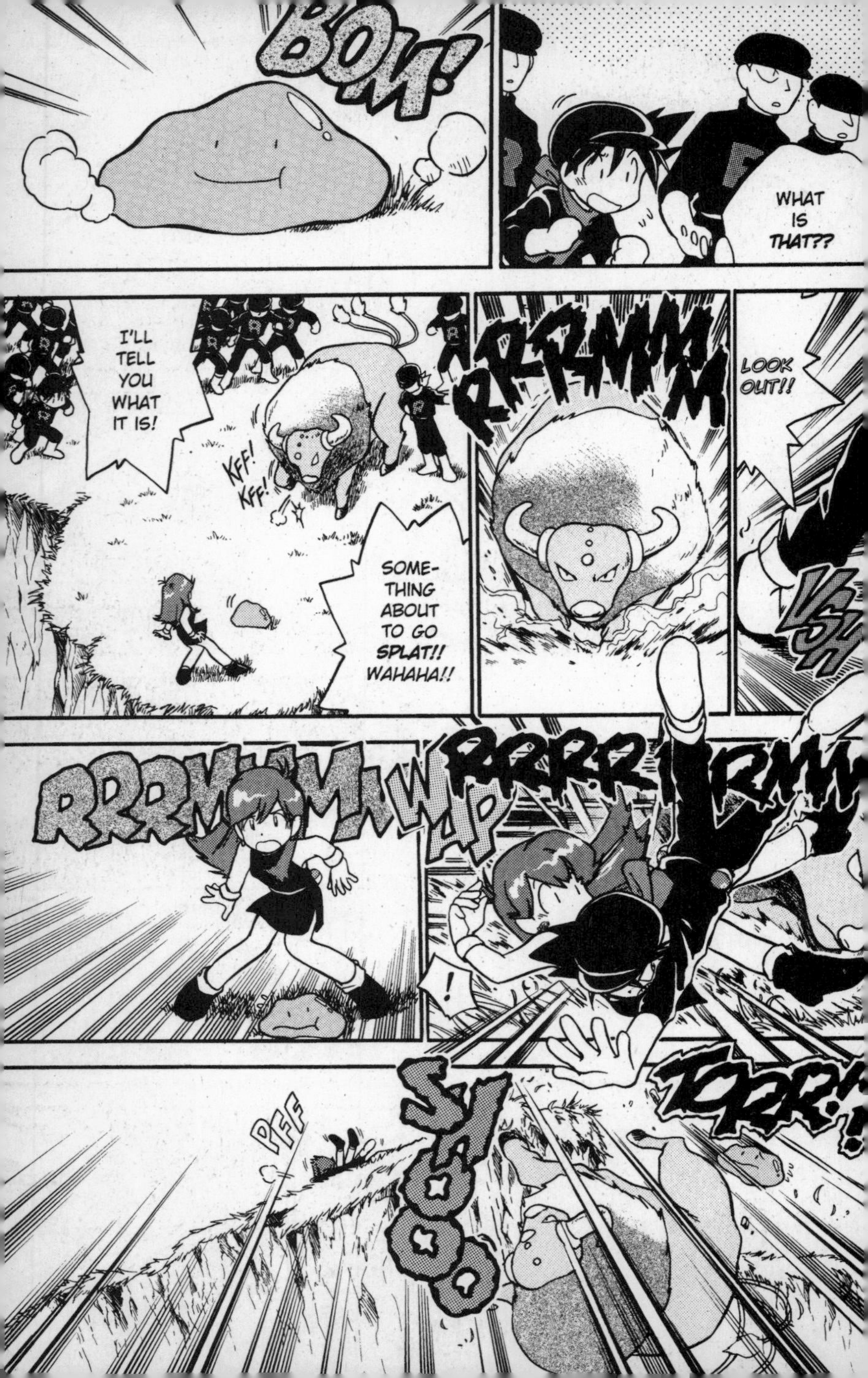
BOM!
WHAT IS THAT??
I'LL TELL YOU WHAT IT IS!
KFF! KFF!
SOME-THING ABOUT TO GO SPLAT!! WAHAHA!!
RRRMMM
LOOK OUT!!
VSH
RRRR
!
PFF
SHOOO
TORR!

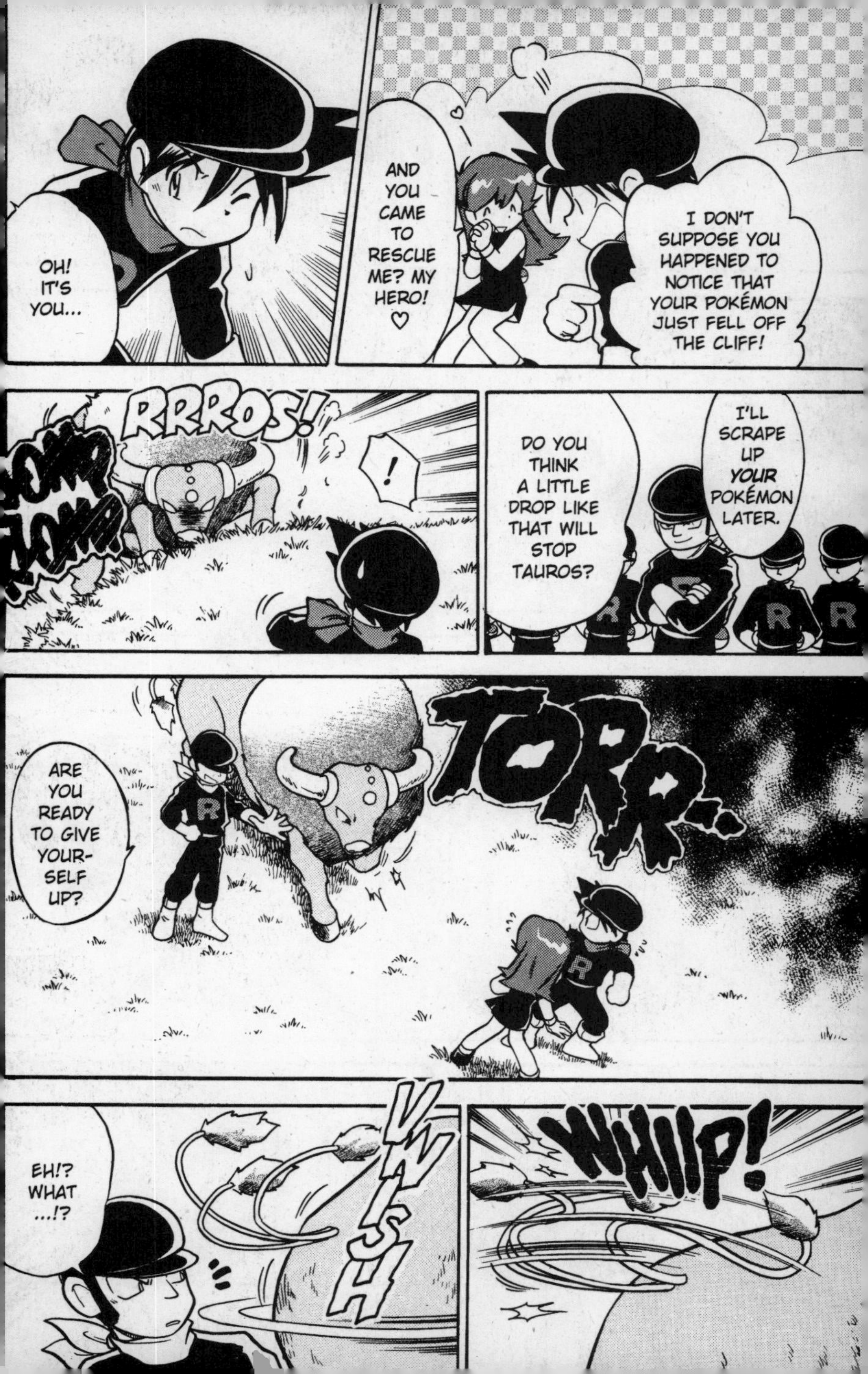

I DON'T SUPPOSE YOU HAPPENED TO NOTICE THAT YOUR POKÉMON JUST FELL OFF THE CLIFF!
AND YOU CAME TO RESCUE ME? MY HERO! ♡
OH! IT'S YOU...
I'LL SCRAPE UP *YOUR* POKÉMON LATER.
DO YOU THINK A LITTLE DROP LIKE THAT WILL STOP TAUROS?
!
RRROS!
STOMP STOMP
TORR..
ARE YOU READY TO GIVE YOUR-SELF UP?
WHIIP!
VWISH
EH!? WHAT ...!?

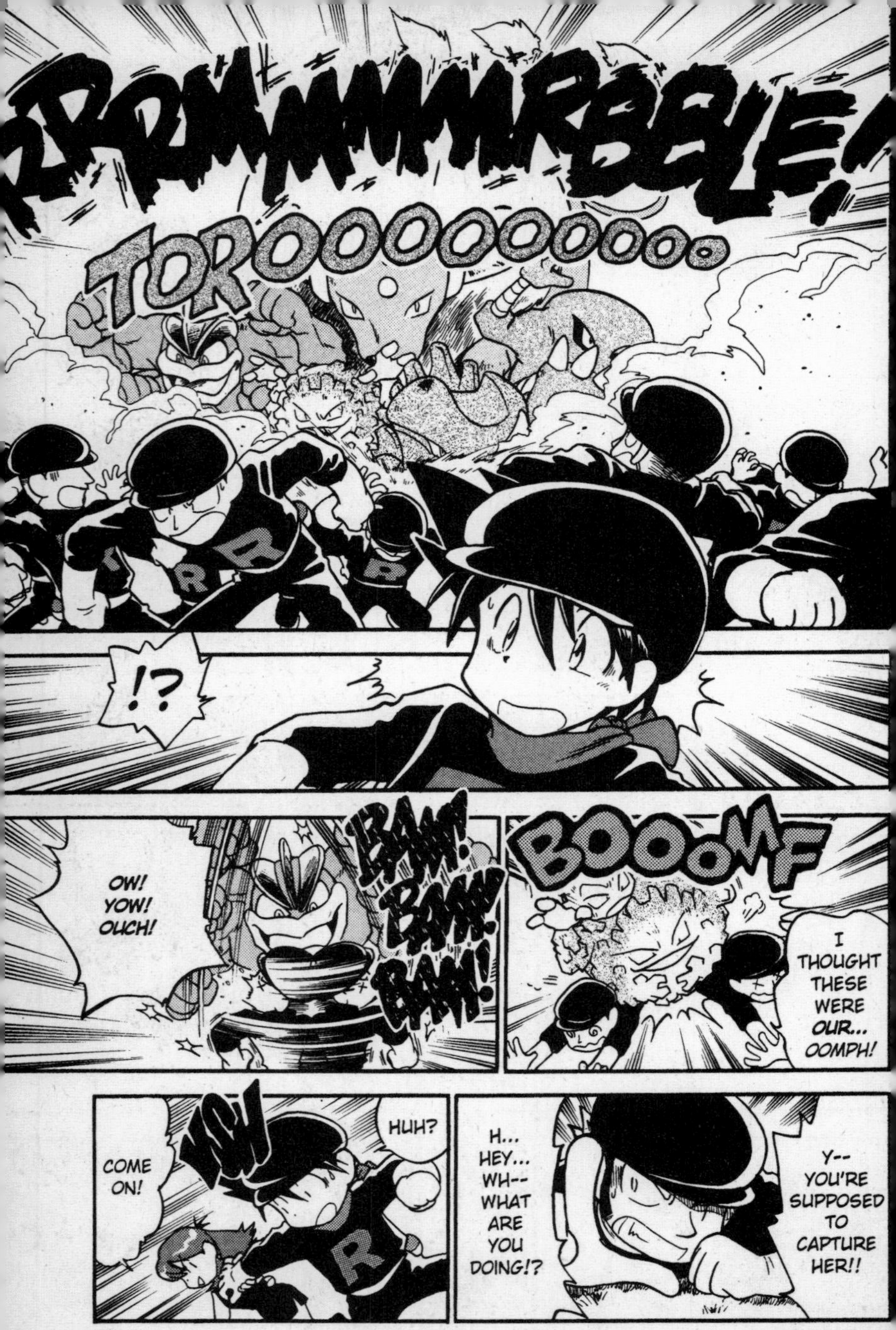
TOROOOOOOOOO
!?
OW! YOW! OUCH!
BAM! BAM! BAM!
BOOOMF
I THOUGHT THESE WERE OUR... OOMPH!
COME ON!
HUH?
H... HEY... WH-- WHAT ARE YOU DOING!?
Y-- YOU'RE SUPPOSED TO CAPTURE HER!!

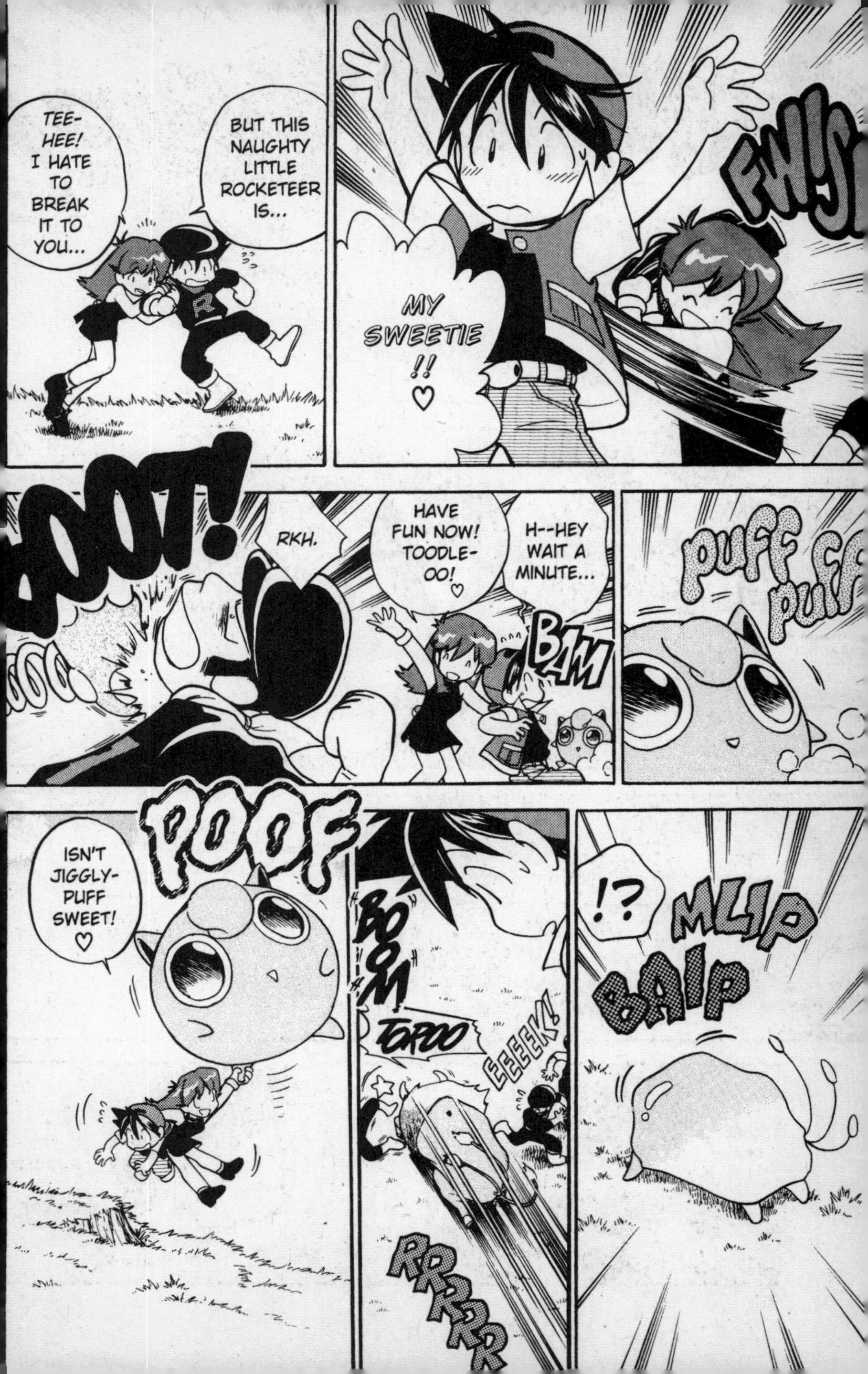
TEE-HEE! I HATE TO BREAK IT TO YOU...
BUT THIS NAUGHTY LITTLE ROCKETEER IS...
MY SWEETIE!! ♡
FWISH
RKH.
HAVE FUN NOW! TOODLE-OO! ♡
H--HEY WAIT A MINUTE...
BAM
puff puff
ISN'T JIGGLY-PUFF SWEET! ♡
POOF
BOOM
TOROO
EEEEK!
RRRRRR
!?
MLIP
BAIP

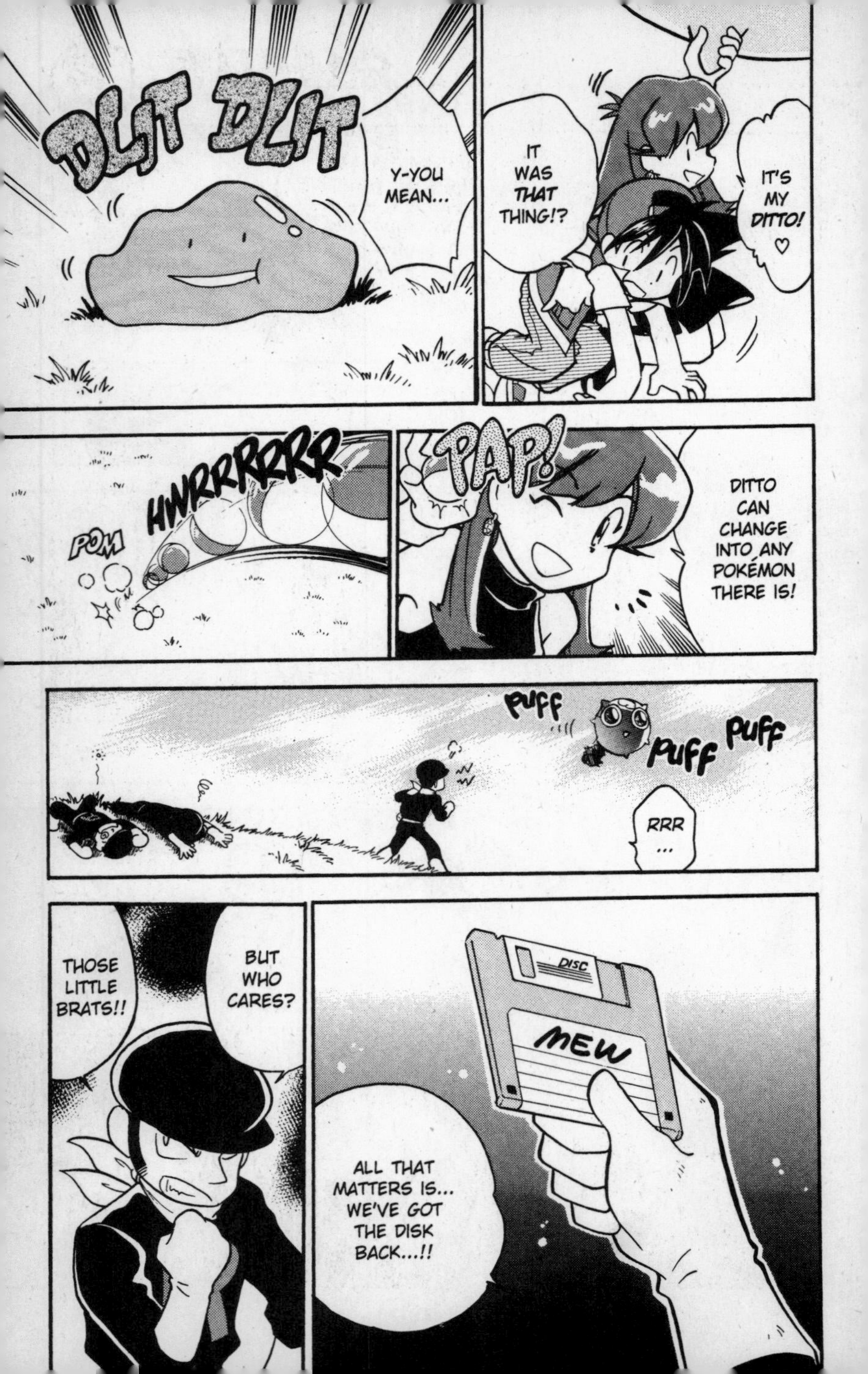
DLIT DLIT
Y-YOU MEAN...
IT WAS THAT THING!?
IT'S MY DITTO! ♡
HWRRRRRR
POM
PAP!
DITTO CAN CHANGE INTO ANY POKÉMON THERE IS!
PUFF
PUFF
PUFF
RRR ...
THOSE LITTLE BRATS!!
BUT WHO CARES?
DISC
MEW
ALL THAT MATTERS IS... WE'VE GOT THE DISK BACK...!!

CHAPTER 8

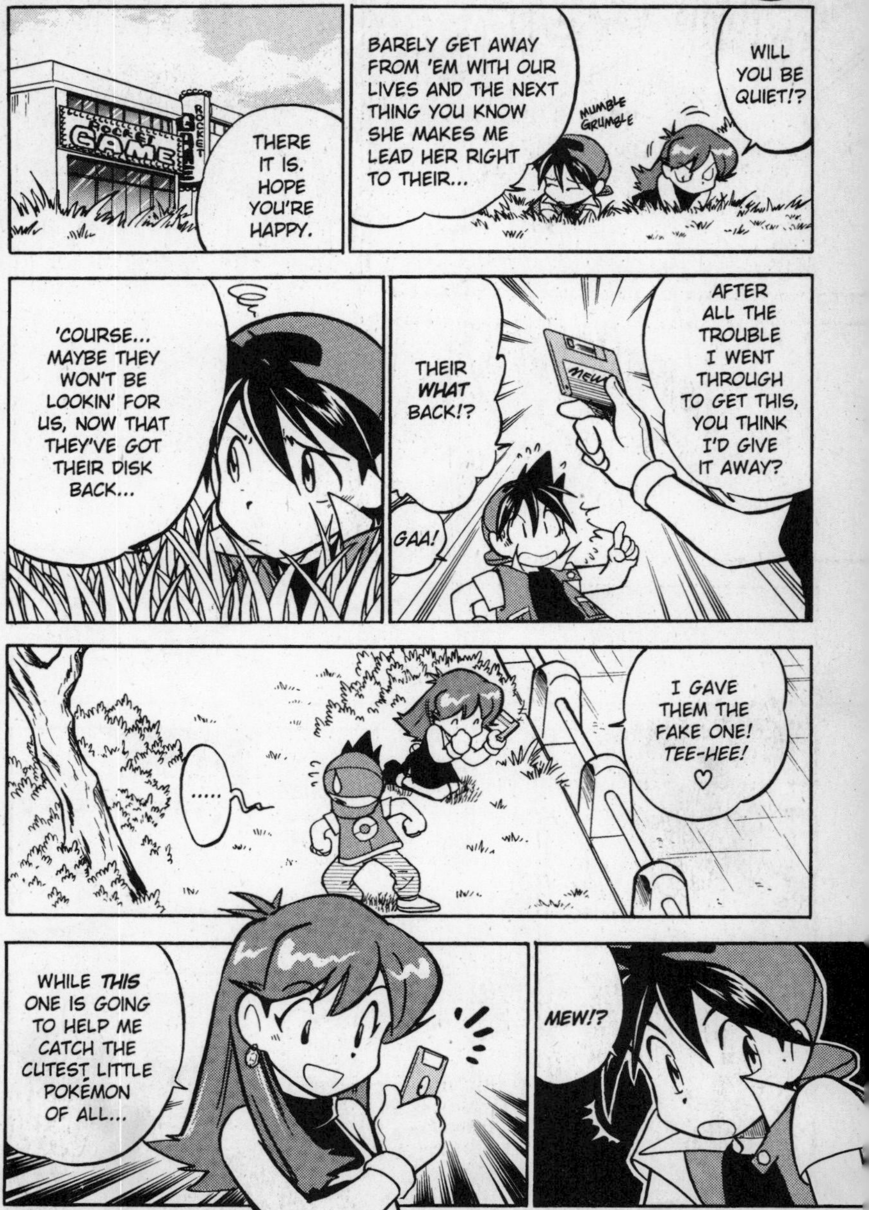

ROCKET GAME
ROCKET
THERE IT IS. HOPE YOU'RE HAPPY.
BARELY GET AWAY FROM 'EM WITH OUR LIVES AND THE NEXT THING YOU KNOW SHE MAKES ME LEAD HER RIGHT TO THEIR...
MUMBLE GRUMBLE
WILL YOU BE QUIET!?
'COURSE... MAYBE THEY WON'T BE LOOKIN' FOR US, NOW THAT THEY'VE GOT THEIR DISK BACK...
THEIR *WHAT* BACK!?
GAA!
MEW
AFTER ALL THE TROUBLE I WENT THROUGH TO GET THIS, YOU THINK I'D GIVE IT AWAY?
......
I GAVE THEM THE FAKE ONE! TEE-HEE! ♡
WHILE *THIS* ONE IS GOING TO HELP ME CATCH THE CUTEST LITTLE POKÉMON OF ALL...
MEW!?

THE JYNX™ JINX

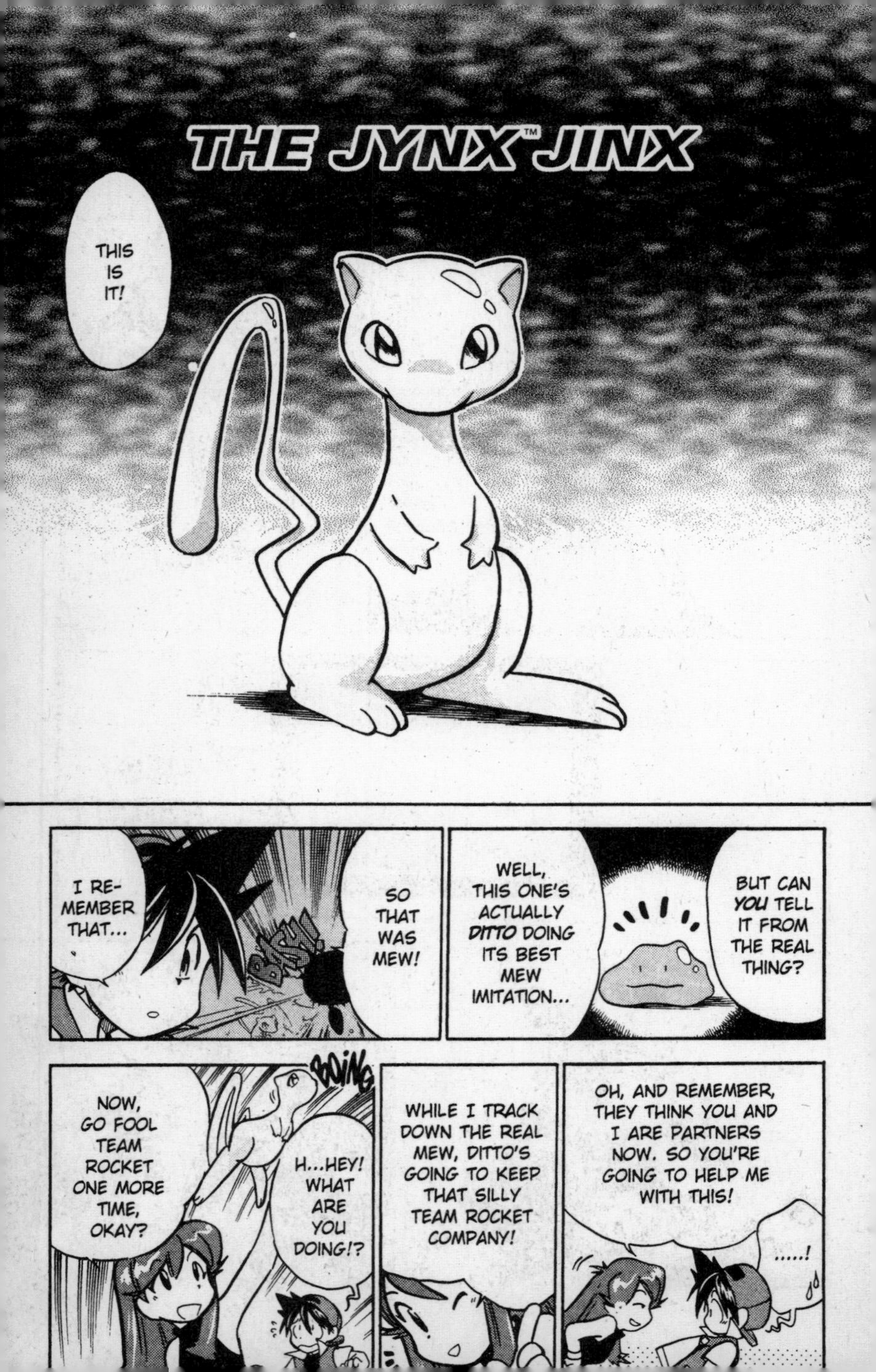
THIS IS IT!
I RE-MEMBER THAT...
SO THAT WAS MEW!
BASH
WELL, THIS ONE'S ACTUALLY *DITTO* DOING ITS BEST MEW IMITATION...
BUT CAN *YOU* TELL IT FROM THE REAL THING?
NOW, GO FOOL TEAM ROCKET ONE MORE TIME, OKAY?
BOING
H...HEY! WHAT ARE YOU DOING!?
WHILE I TRACK DOWN THE REAL MEW, DITTO'S GOING TO KEEP THAT SILLY TEAM ROCKET COMPANY!
OH, AND REMEMBER, THEY THINK YOU AND I ARE PARTNERS NOW. SO YOU'RE GOING TO HELP ME WITH THIS!
.....!

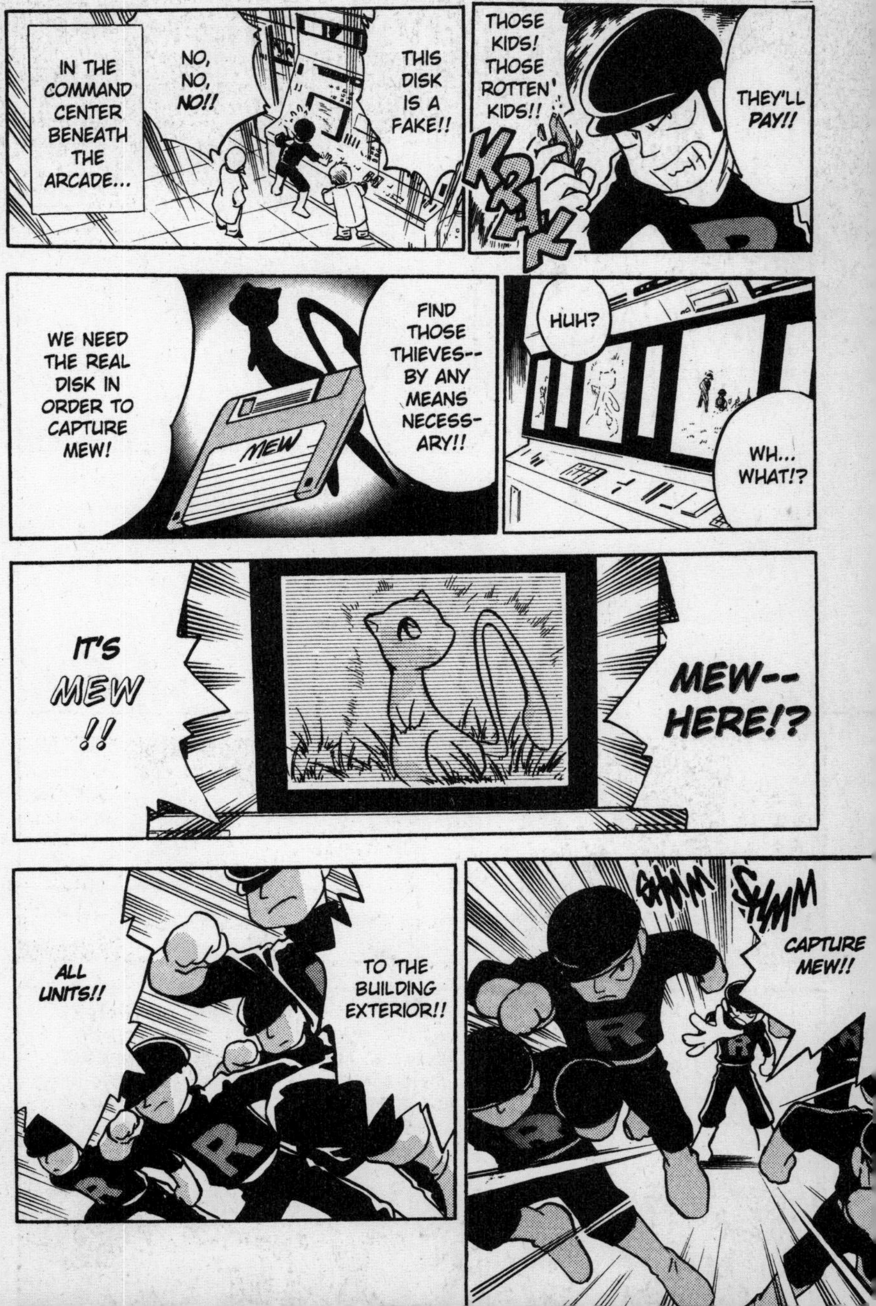
IN THE COMMAND CENTER BENEATH THE ARCADE...
NO, NO, NO!!
THIS DISK IS A FAKE!!
THOSE KIDS! THOSE ROTTEN KIDS!!
KRAK
THEY'LL PAY!!
WE NEED THE REAL DISK IN ORDER TO CAPTURE MEW!
MEW
FIND THOSE THIEVES--BY ANY MEANS NECESSARY!!
HUH?
WH... WHAT!?
IT'S MEW!!
MEW--HERE!?
ALL UNITS!!
TO THE BUILDING EXTERIOR!!
SHMM SHMM
CAPTURE MEW!!

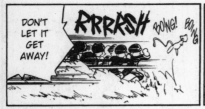

DON'T LET IT GET AWAY!
RRRRSH
BOING!
BOING
THINK DITTO CAN KEEP 'EM FOOLED?
GAME
RRRRSH
BOING!
BOING!
OH, SURE...
UNTIL THEY FIGURE OUT THAT DITTO HAS NO IDEA WHAT MEW'S POWERS ARE SUPPOSED TO BE!
KLONG
WHAT'S THAT?
I CALL IT A MEW-VIEW.
PSYCHIC POKÉMON EMIT CERTAIN BRAINWAVE PATTERNS WHEN THEY USE PSYCHO-KINESIS...
...AND EACH POKÉMON'S PATTERN IS UNIQUE.
CHK
SO BY KEYING THE DISK TO MEW'S PSYCHIC PATTERNS...
I SHOULD BE ABLE TO ZERO IN ON...
YEE-UP! PSYCHIC ACTIVITY IN THE SOUTH-EAST!
WE'LL BE ON IT BEFORE TEAM ROCKET FINISHES PLAYING CATCH THE BOUNCING DITTO!

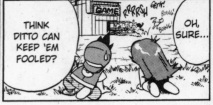

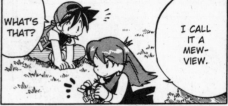

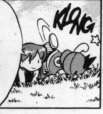

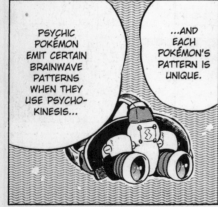

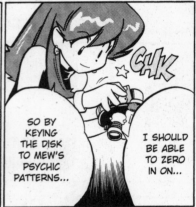

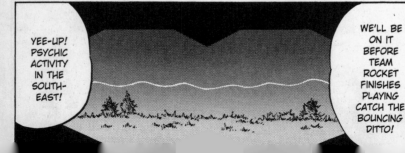

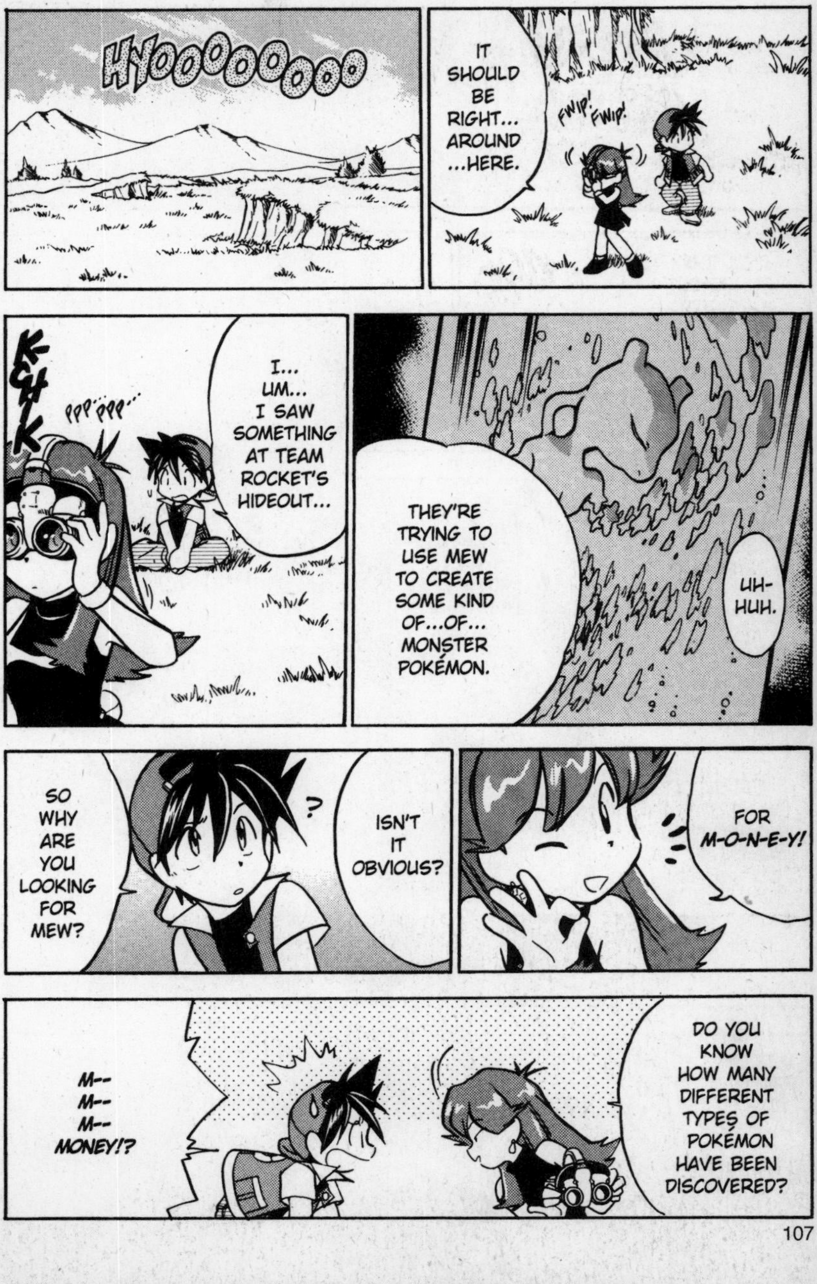
HYOOOOOOOOO
IT SHOULD BE RIGHT... AROUND ...HERE.
FWIP! FWIP!
KCHIK
PPP... PPP...
I... UM... I SAW SOMETHING AT TEAM ROCKET'S HIDEOUT...
THEY'RE TRYING TO USE MEW TO CREATE SOME KIND OF...OF... MONSTER POKÉMON.
UH-HUH.
SO WHY ARE YOU LOOKING FOR MEW?
?
ISN'T IT OBVIOUS?
FOR M-O-N-E-Y!
M-- M-- M-- MONEY!?
DO YOU KNOW HOW MANY DIFFERENT TYPES OF POKÉMON HAVE BEEN DISCOVERED?

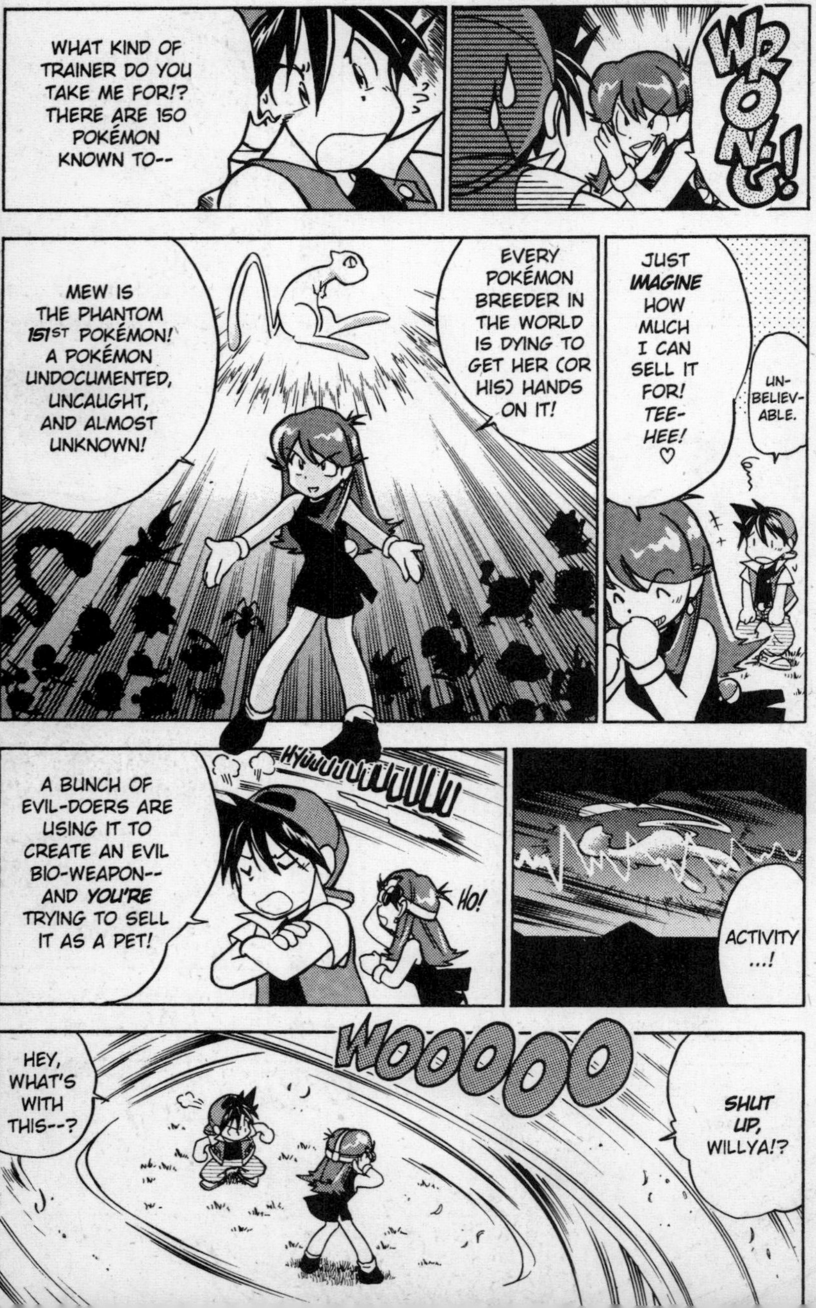

WHAT KIND OF TRAINER DO YOU TAKE ME FOR!? THERE ARE 150 POKÉMON KNOWN TO--
WRONG!
MEW IS THE PHANTOM 151ST POKÉMON! A POKÉMON UNDOCUMENTED, UNCAUGHT, AND ALMOST UNKNOWN!
EVERY POKÉMON BREEDER IN THE WORLD IS DYING TO GET HER (OR HIS) HANDS ON IT!
JUST IMAGINE HOW MUCH I CAN SELL IT FOR! TEE-HEE! ♡
UN-BELIEV-ABLE.
A BUNCH OF EVIL-DOERS ARE USING IT TO CREATE AN EVIL BIO-WEAPON-- AND YOU'RE TRYING TO SELL IT AS A PET!
HO!
ACTIVITY ...!
WOOOOO
HEY, WHAT'S WITH THIS--?
SHUT UP, WILLYA!?

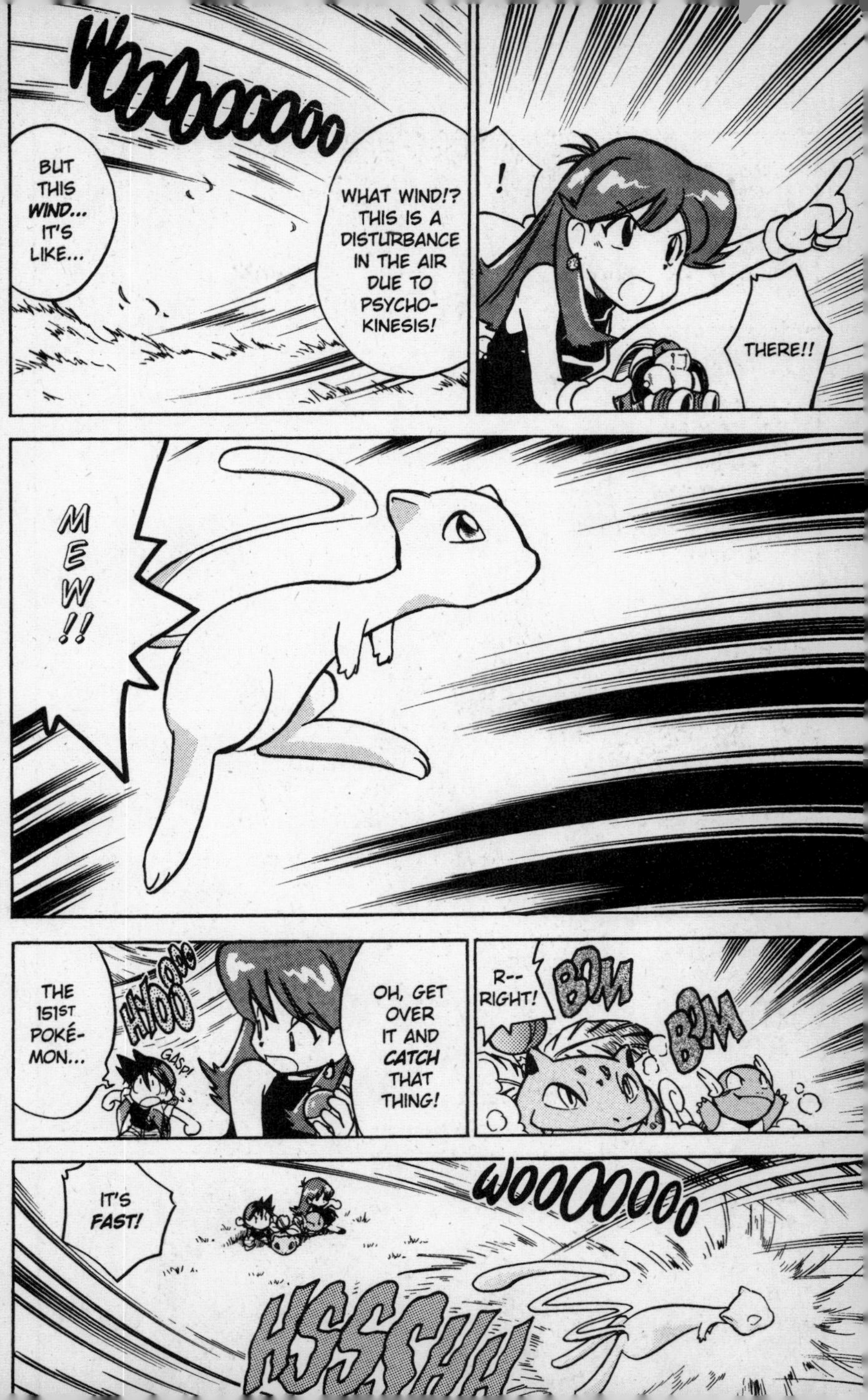
WOOOOOOOOO
BUT THIS WIND... IT'S LIKE...
WHAT WIND!? THIS IS A DISTURBANCE IN THE AIR DUE TO PSYCHO-KINESIS!
!
THERE!!
MEW!!
THE 151ST POKÉ-MON...
HWOOOO
GASP!
OH, GET OVER IT AND CATCH THAT THING!
R-- RIGHT!
BOM
BOM
IT'S FAST!
WOOOOOOOO
HSSCHH

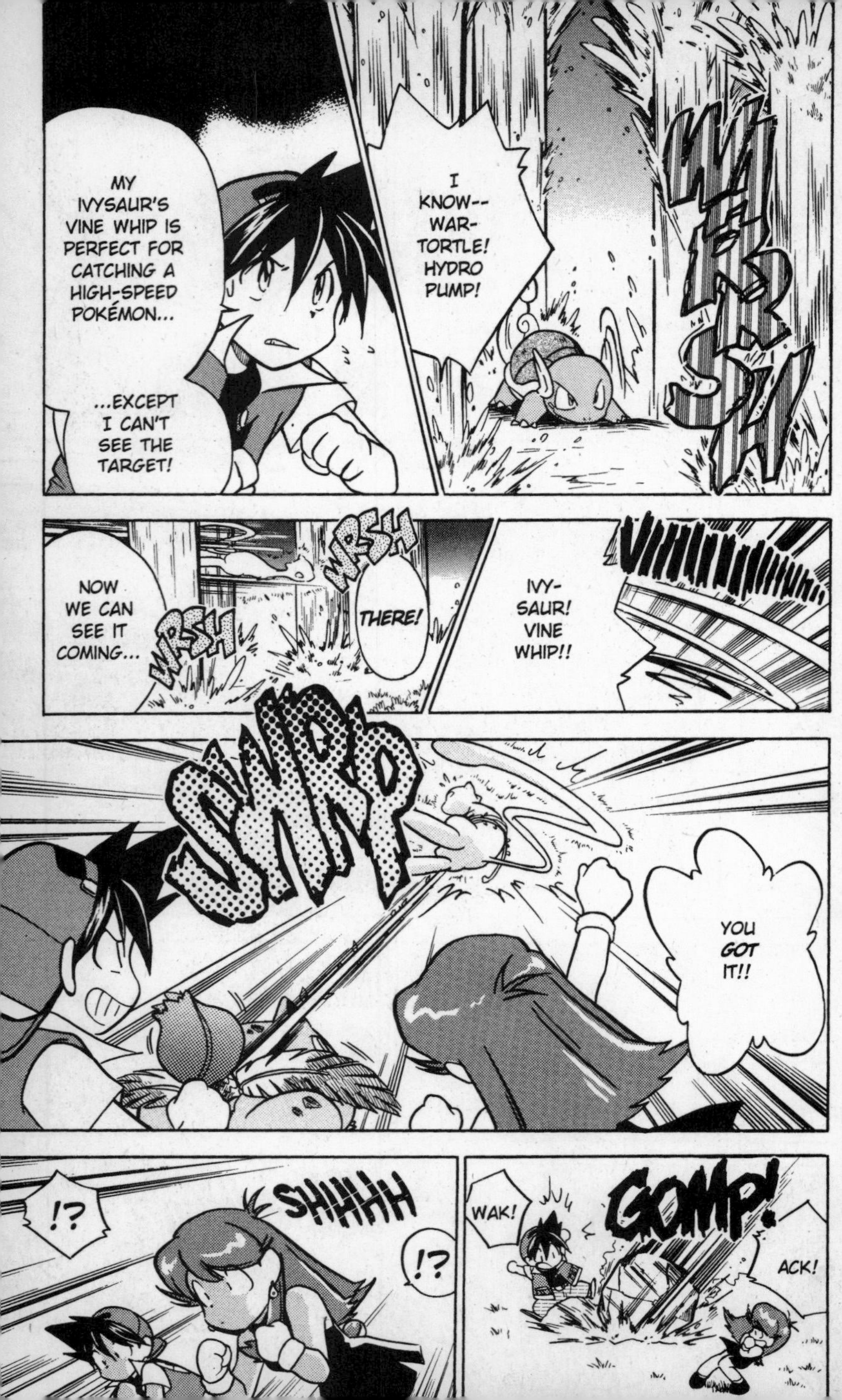
MY IVYSAUR'S VINE WHIP IS PERFECT FOR CATCHING A HIGH-SPEED POKÉMON...
...EXCEPT I CAN'T SEE THE TARGET!
I KNOW-- WAR-TORTLE! HYDRO PUMP!
NOW WE CAN SEE IT COMING...
WRSH
WRSH
THERE!
IVY-SAUR! VINE WHIP!!
YOU GOT IT!!
!?
SHHHH
!?
WAK!
GOMP!
ACK!

DID YOU REALLY THINK YOU COULD GET AWAY WITH IT!?

UH-OH. LOOKS LIKE THEY CAUGHT ON!

FWIP

DT!

JYNX, ATTACK! PSY-BEAM!

JJJJJJJJ

mewww

TNG

JNG

M-- MEW'S ABOUT TO ESCAPE...!

I'LL KEEP THESE GUYS OCCUPIED!

YOU TAKE MEW-- AND GET OUT!

REALLY ...?

IF MEW ENDS UP IN THEIR HANDS...

JIII

UGH...

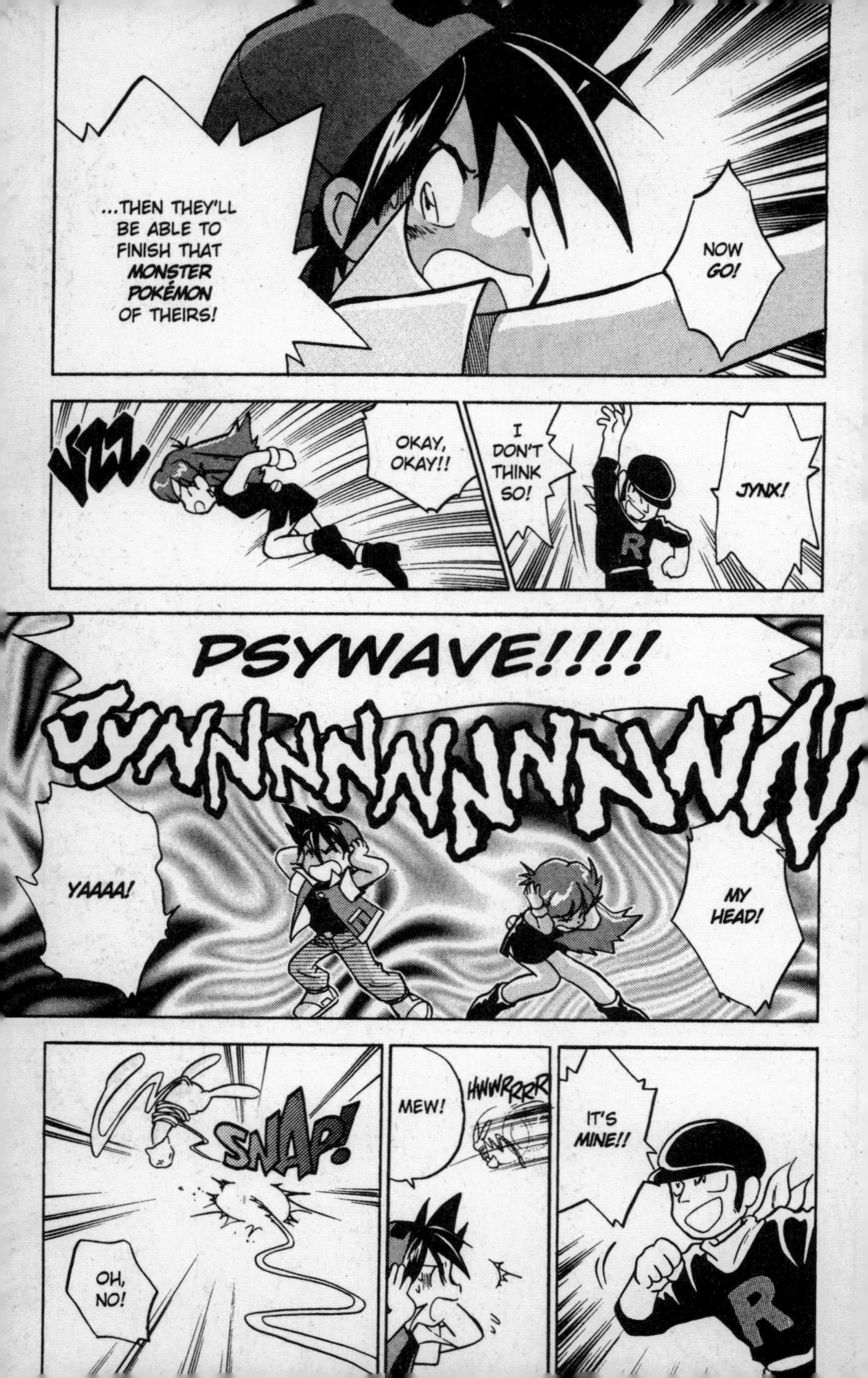
...THEN THEY'LL BE ABLE TO FINISH THAT MONSTER POKÉMON OF THEIRS!
NOW GO!
VZZZ
OKAY, OKAY!!
I DON'T THINK SO!
JYNX!
PSYWAVE!!!!
JYNNNNWNNNWN
YAAAA!
MY HEAD!
SNAP!
OH, NO!
MEW!
HWWRRRR
IT'S MINE!!

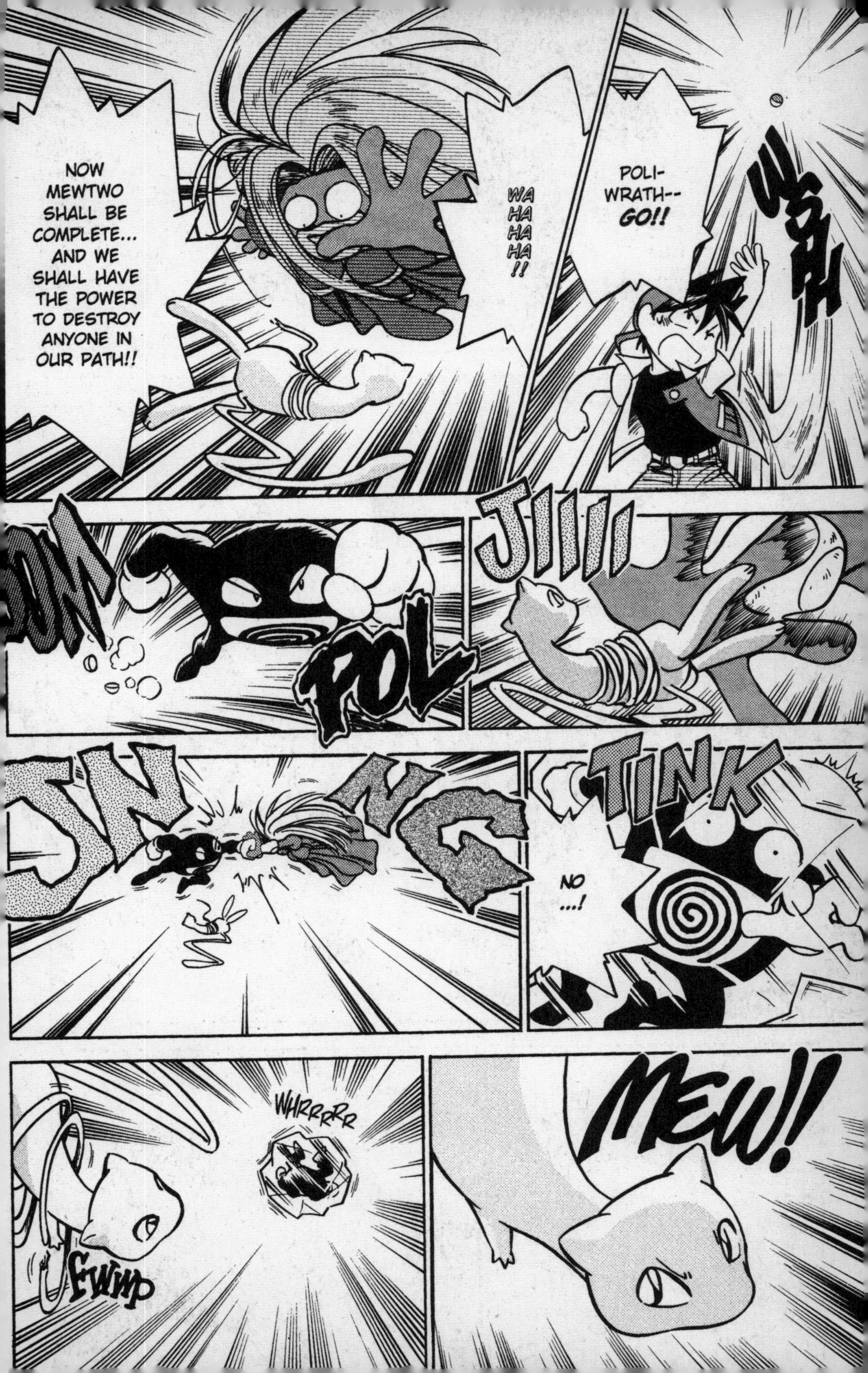
NOW MEWTWO SHALL BE COMPLETE... AND WE SHALL HAVE THE POWER TO DESTROY ANYONE IN OUR PATH!!
WA HA HA HA HA !!
POLI-WRATH-- GO!!
WSHH
POL
JIIII
NG
TINK
NO ...!
WHRRRRR
FWMP
MEW!!

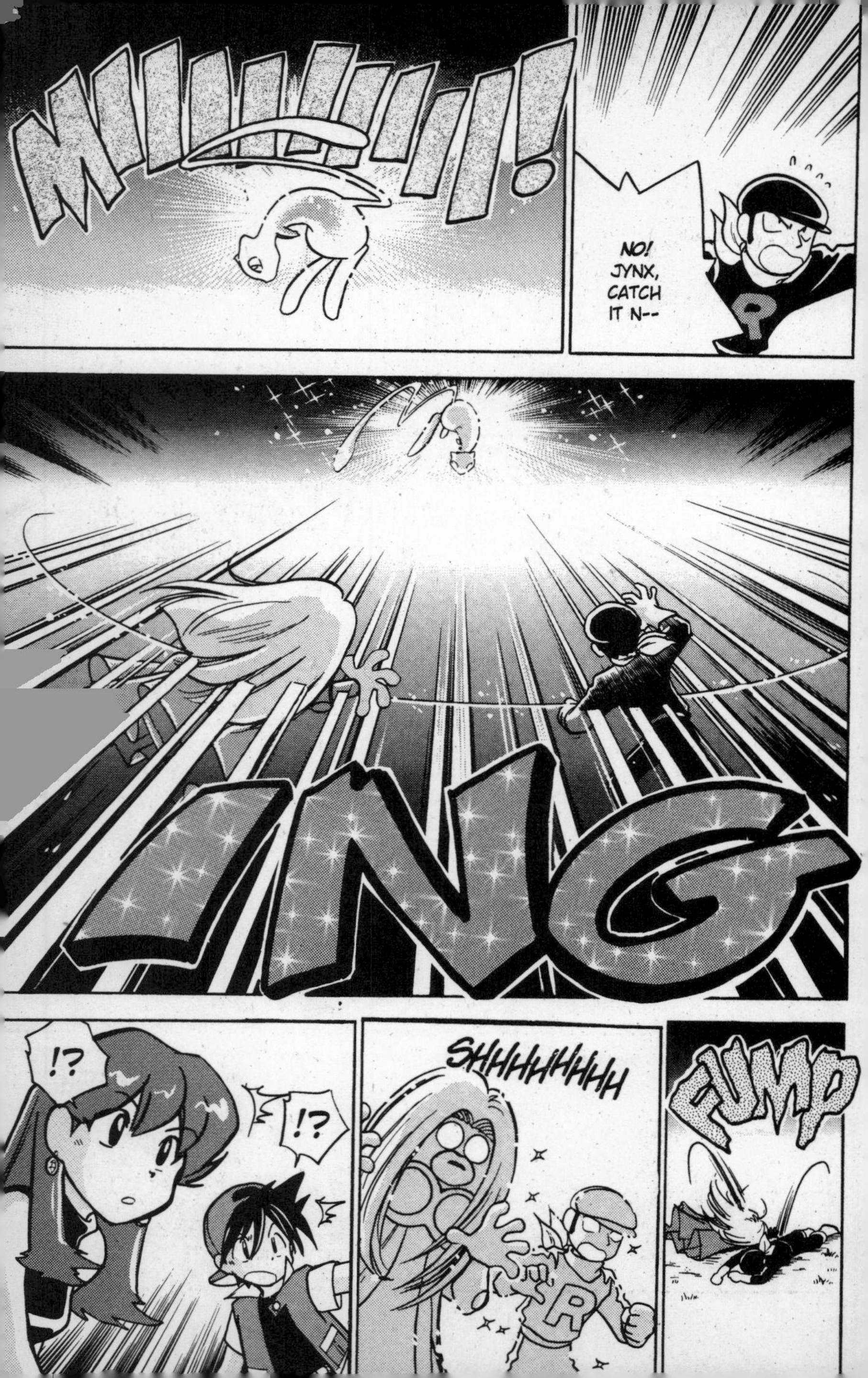
MIIIIIIIII!
NO! JYNX, CATCH IT N--
ING
!?
!?
SHHHHHHHHH
FUMP

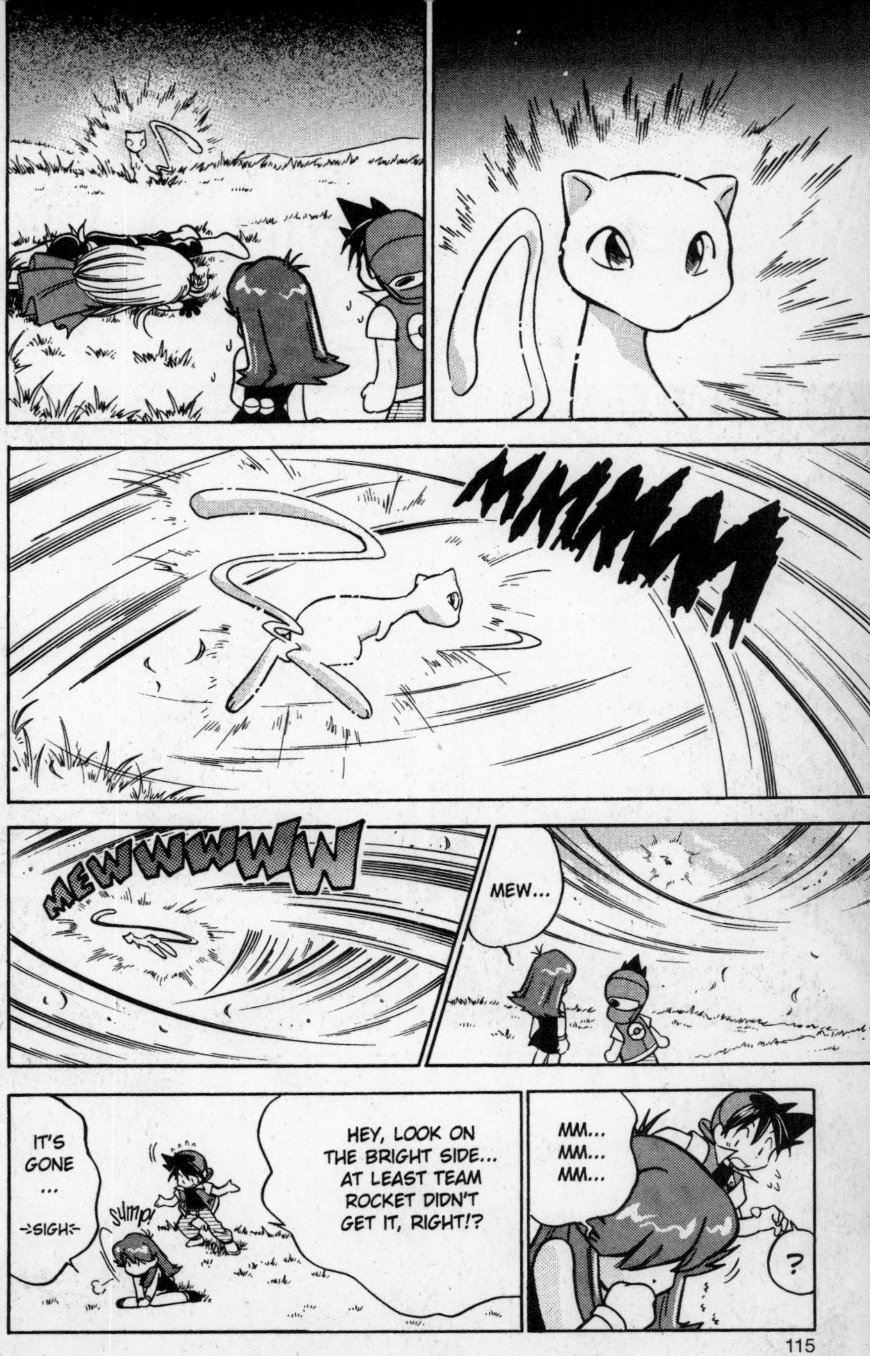
MMMMM
MEWWWWWW
MEW...
IT'S GONE ...
-SIGH-
SLUMP!
HEY, LOOK ON THE BRIGHT SIDE... AT LEAST TEAM ROCKET DIDN'T GET IT, RIGHT!?
MM... MM... MM...
?

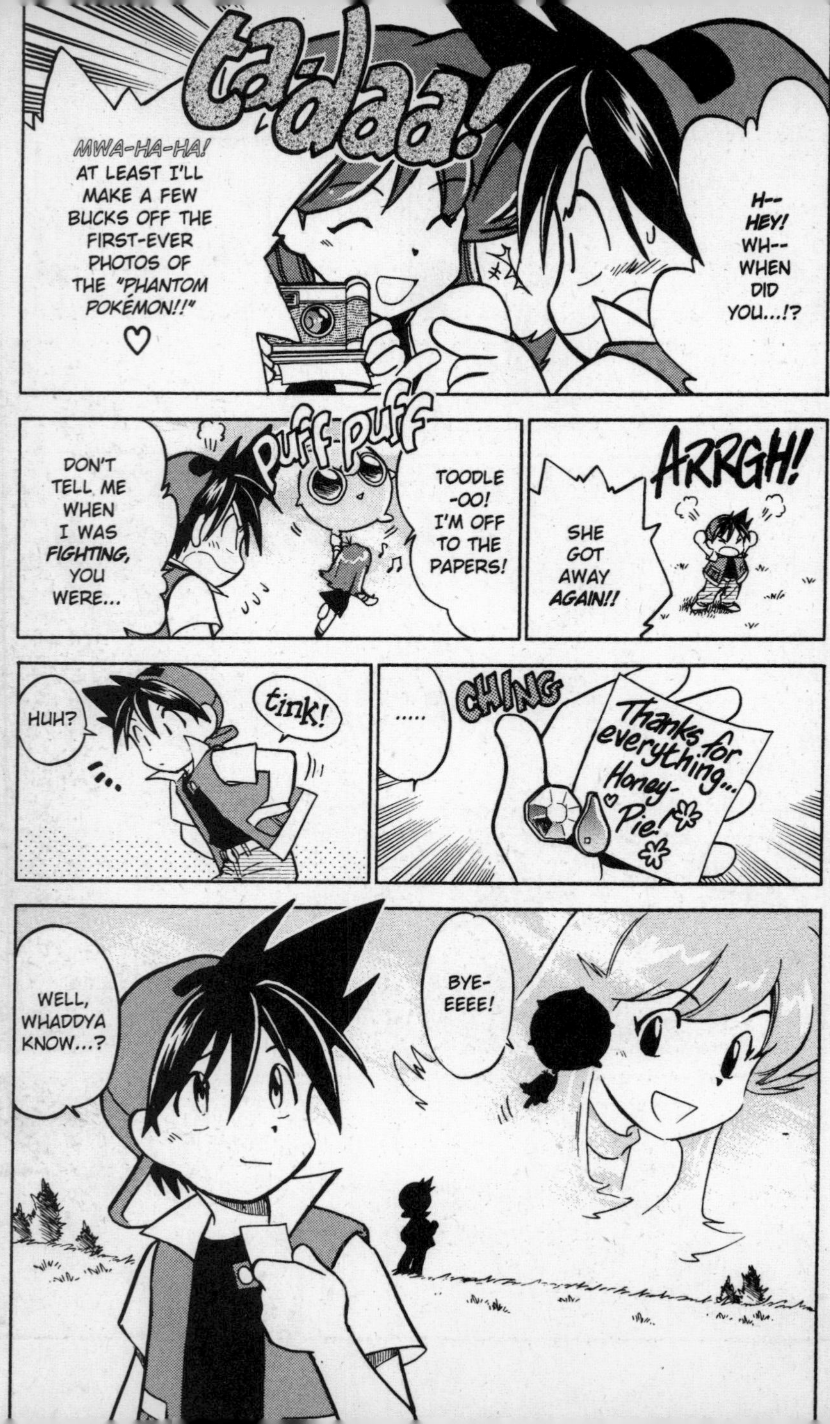

ta-daa!
MWA-HA-HA! AT LEAST I'LL MAKE A FEW BUCKS OFF THE FIRST-EVER PHOTOS OF THE "PHANTOM POKÉMON!!" ♡
H-- HEY! WH-- WHEN DID YOU...!?
DON'T TELL ME WHEN I WAS FIGHTING, YOU WERE...
puff-puff
TOODLE -OO! I'M OFF TO THE PAPERS!
ARRGH!
SHE GOT AWAY AGAIN!!
HUH?
tink!
.....
CHING
Thanks for everything... Honey-Pie!
WELL, WHADDYA KNOW...?
BYE-EEEE!

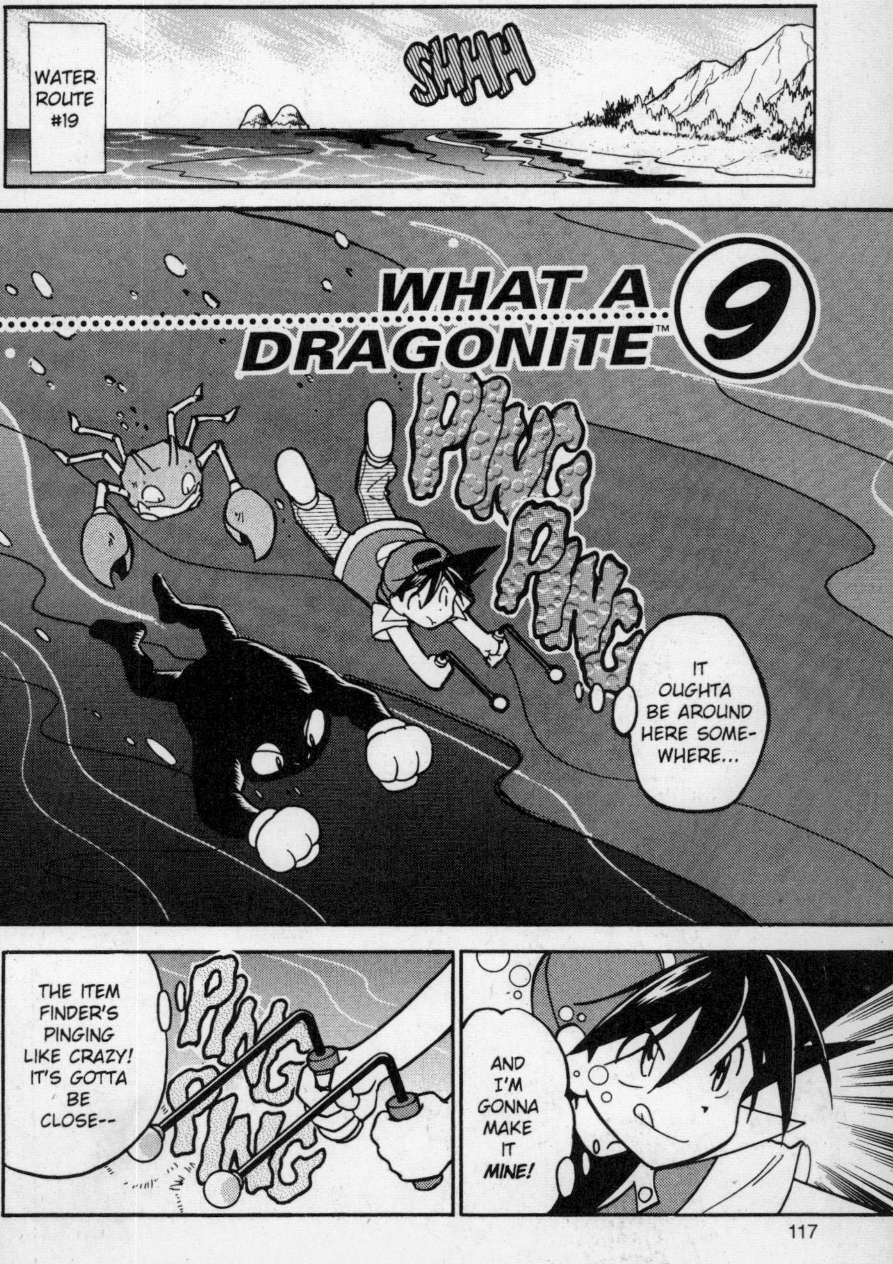
WATER ROUTE #19
SHHH
WHAT A DRAGONITE™ 9
PING PING
IT OUGHTA BE AROUND HERE SOME-WHERE...
THE ITEM FINDER'S PINGING LIKE CRAZY! IT'S GOTTA BE CLOSE--
PING PING
AND I'M GONNA MAKE IT *MINE!*

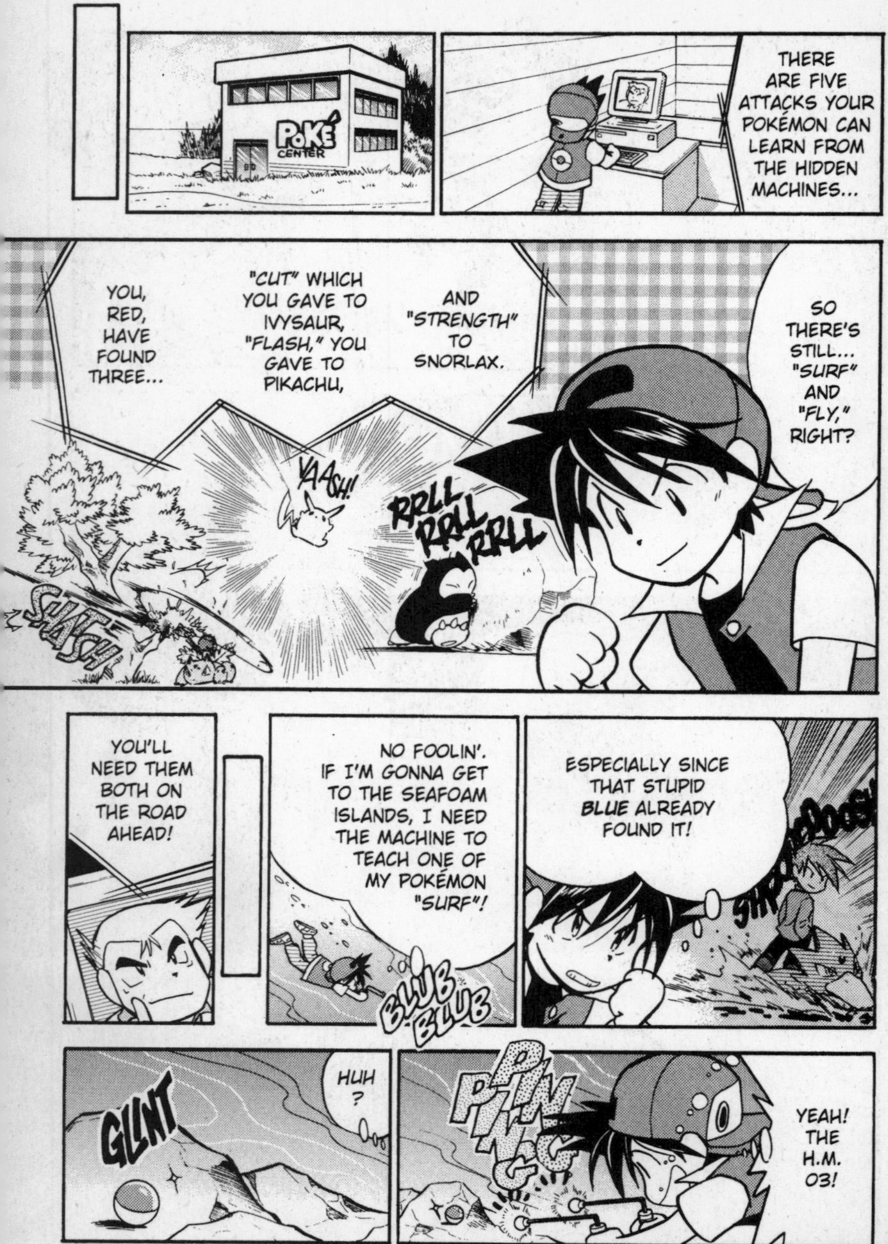
THERE ARE FIVE ATTACKS YOUR POKÉMON CAN LEARN FROM THE HIDDEN MACHINES...
YOU, RED, HAVE FOUND THREE...
"CUT" WHICH YOU GAVE TO IVYSAUR, "FLASH," YOU GAVE TO PIKACHU,
AND "STRENGTH" TO SNORLAX.
SO THERE'S STILL... "SURF" AND "FLY," RIGHT?
YAASH!
RRLL RRLL RRLL
SHASH
YOU'LL NEED THEM BOTH ON THE ROAD AHEAD!
NO FOOLIN'. IF I'M GONNA GET TO THE SEAFOAM ISLANDS, I NEED THE MACHINE TO TEACH ONE OF MY POKÉMON "SURF"!
BLUB BLUB
ESPECIALLY SINCE THAT STUPID BLUE ALREADY FOUND IT!
GLINT
HUH ?
PING
YEAH! THE H.M. 03!

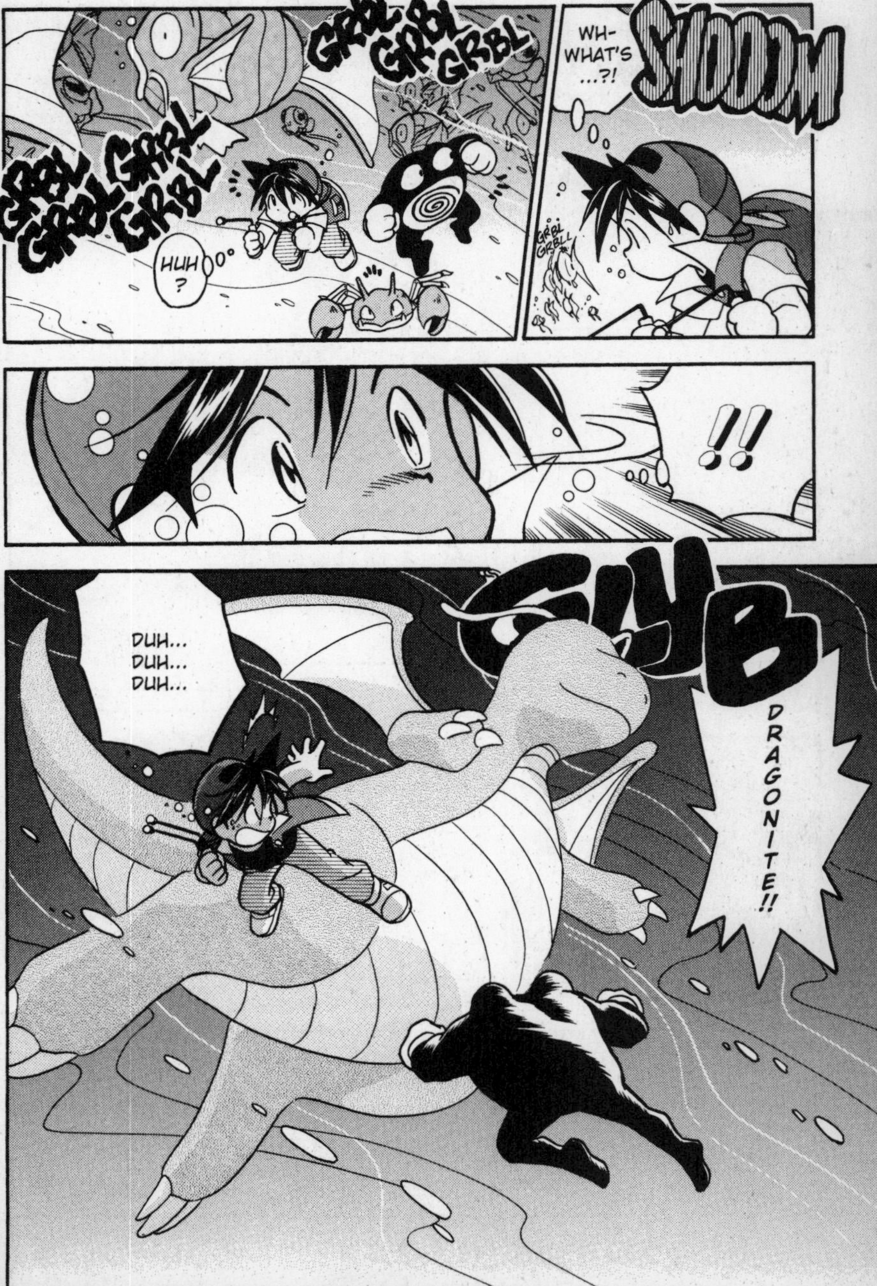
SHOOOM
WH- WHAT'S ...?!
GRBL GRBLL
GRBL GRBL GRBL
GRBL GRBL GRBL GRBL
HUH ?
!!
GLUB
DUH... DUH... DUH...
DRAGONITE!!

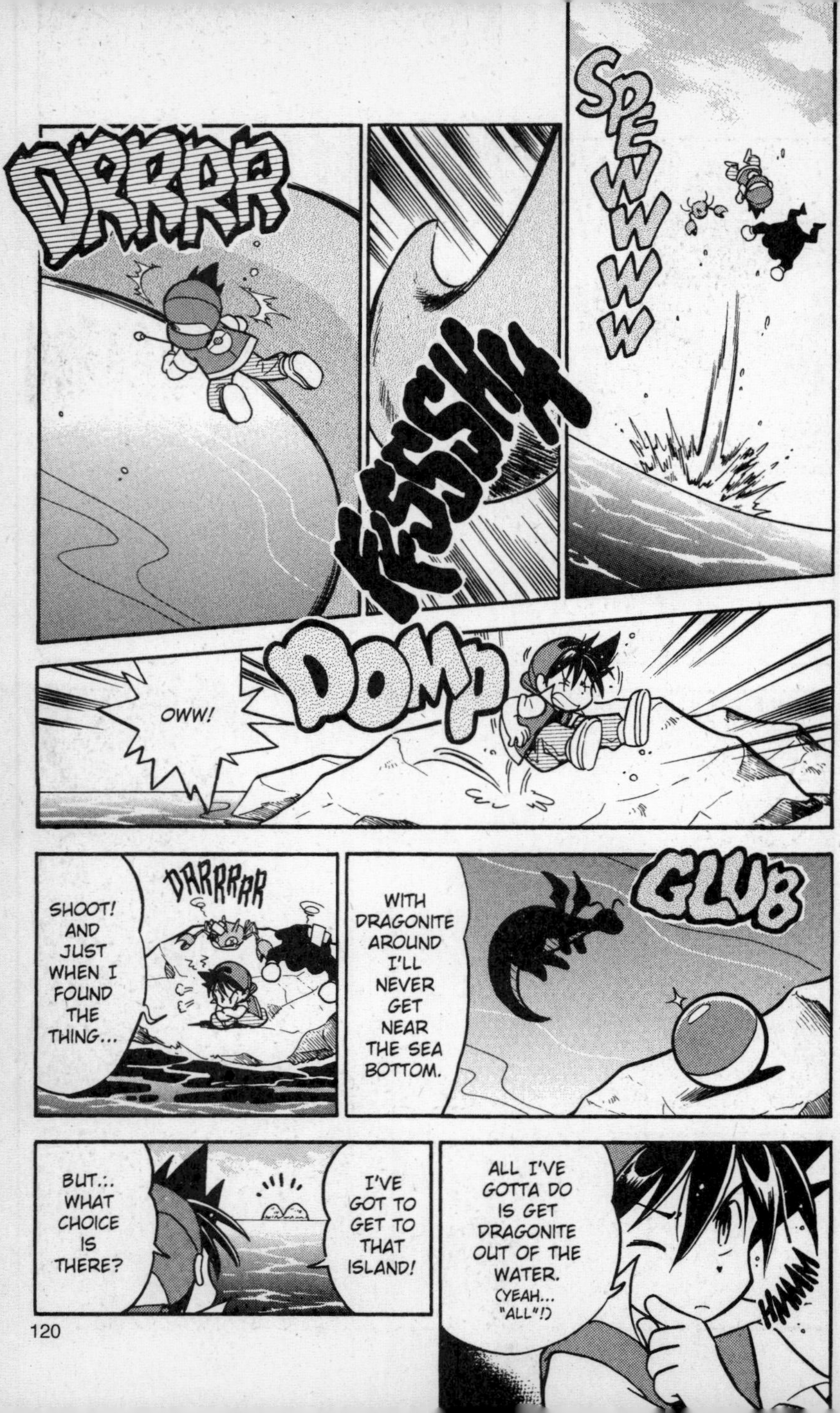
DRRRR
KSSSH
SPEWWWWW
DOMP
OWW!
DRRRRRR
SHOOT! AND JUST WHEN I FOUND THE THING...
WITH DRAGONITE AROUND I'LL NEVER GET NEAR THE SEA BOTTOM.
GLUB
BUT... WHAT CHOICE IS THERE?
I'VE GOT TO GET TO THAT ISLAND!
ALL I'VE GOTTA DO IS GET DRAGONITE OUT OF THE WATER. (YEAH... "ALL"!)
HMMM

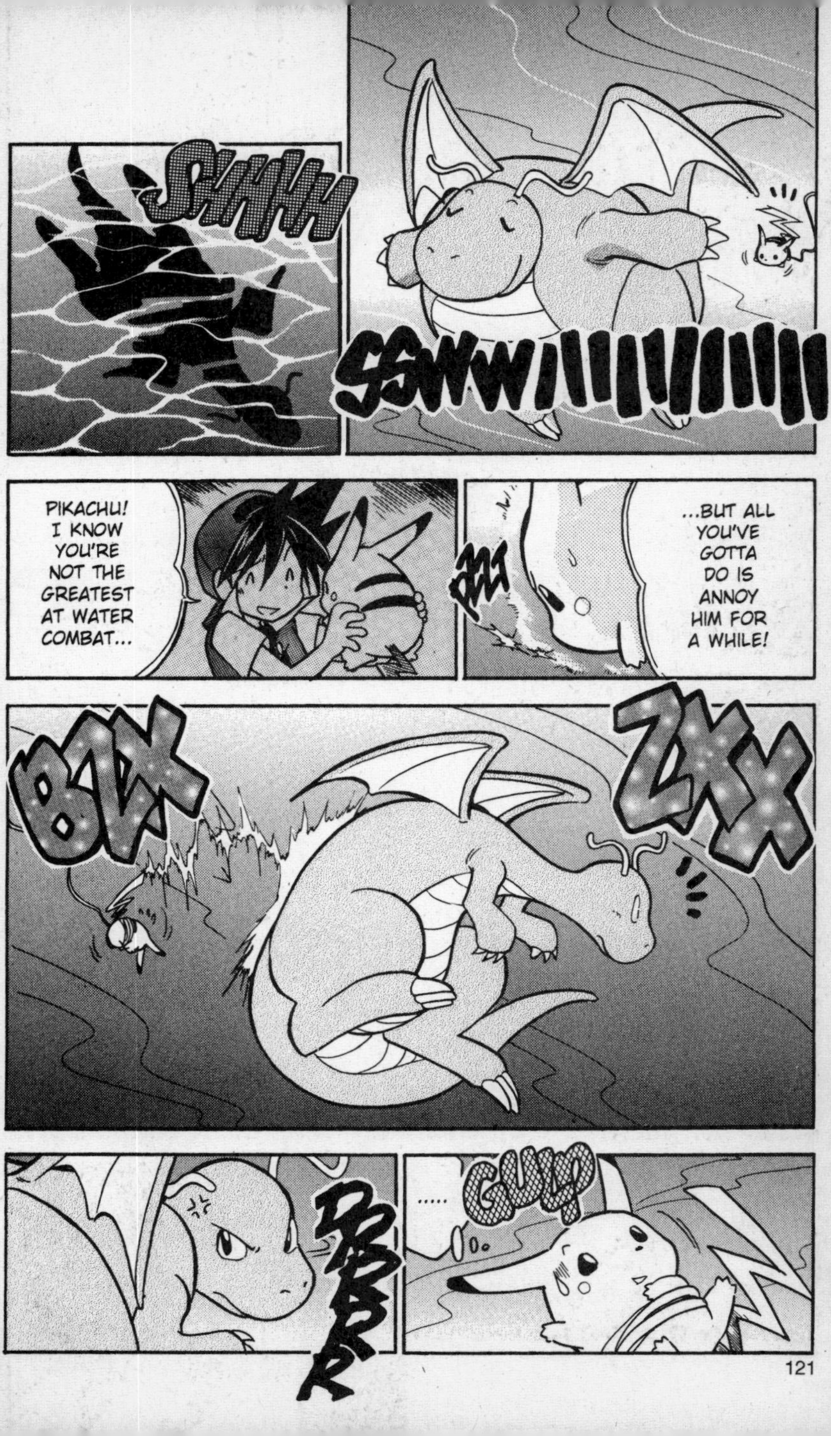
SHHHH
SSWWIIIIIIIIIIIIIII
PIKACHU! I KNOW YOU'RE NOT THE GREATEST AT WATER COMBAT...
...BUT ALL YOU'VE GOTTA DO IS ANNOY HIM FOR A WHILE!
BZZ
ZXX
.....
GULP
DBBRR

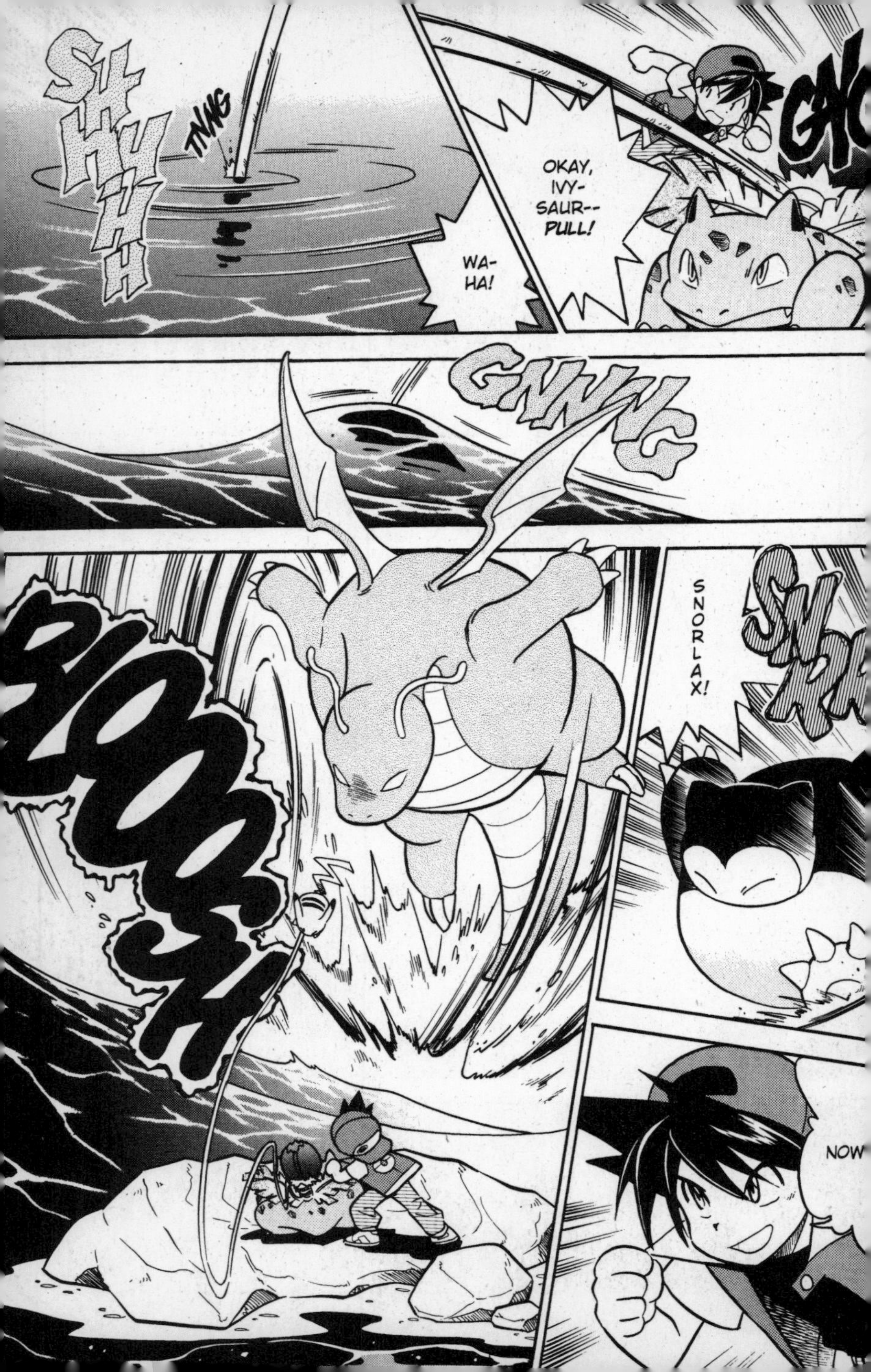

SHHHHHH
TWNG
GAG
OKAY, IVY-SAUR-- PULL!
WA-HA!
GNNNG
SNORLAX!
SHWA
BOOOOSH
NOW

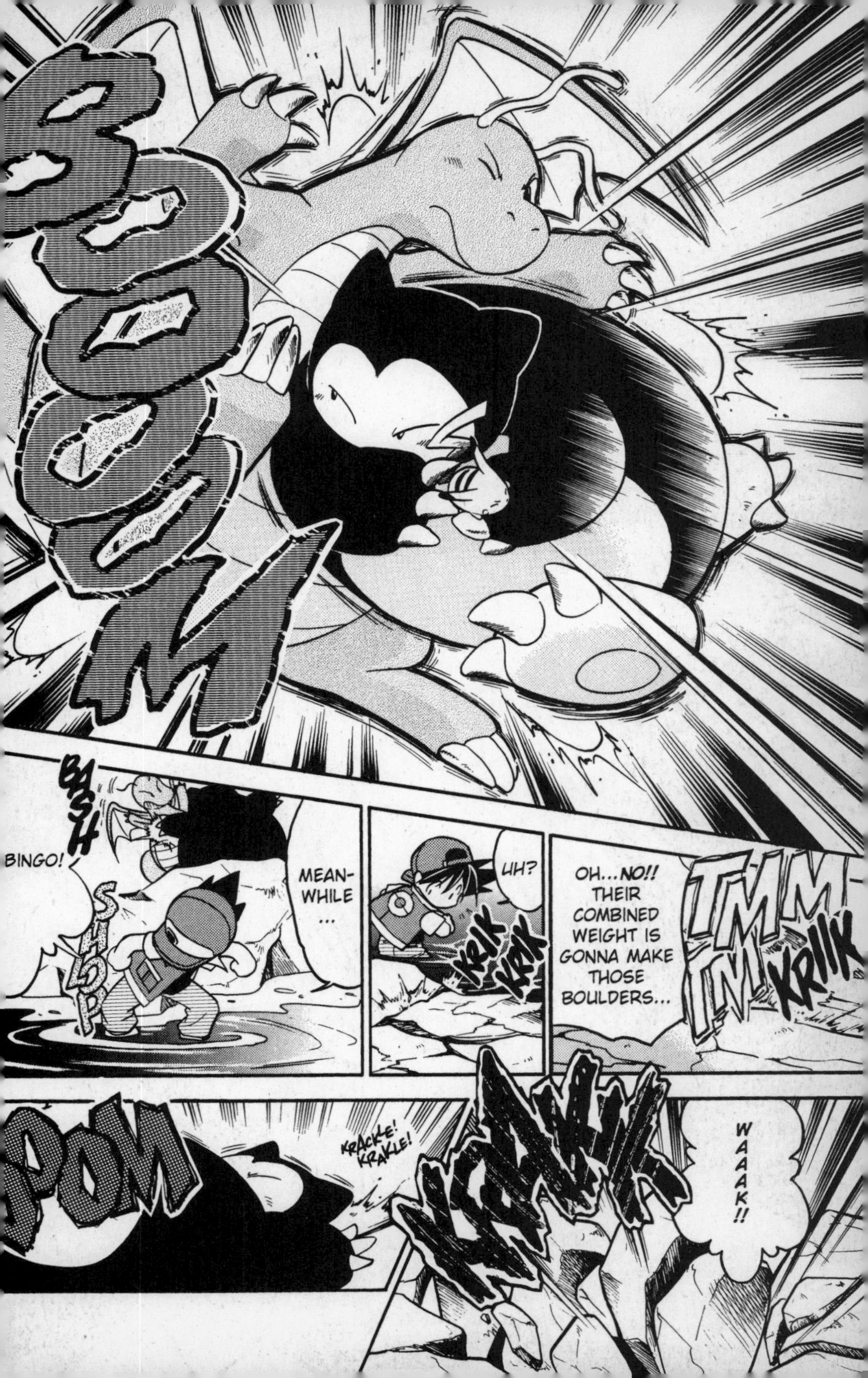
BOOM
BASH
BINGO!
SHLOOP
MEAN-WHILE...
UH?
KRIK KRIK
OH...NO!! THEIR COMBINED WEIGHT IS GONNA MAKE THOSE BOULDERS...
TMMM
KRIIK
POM
KRACKLE! KRAKLE!
WAAAK!!

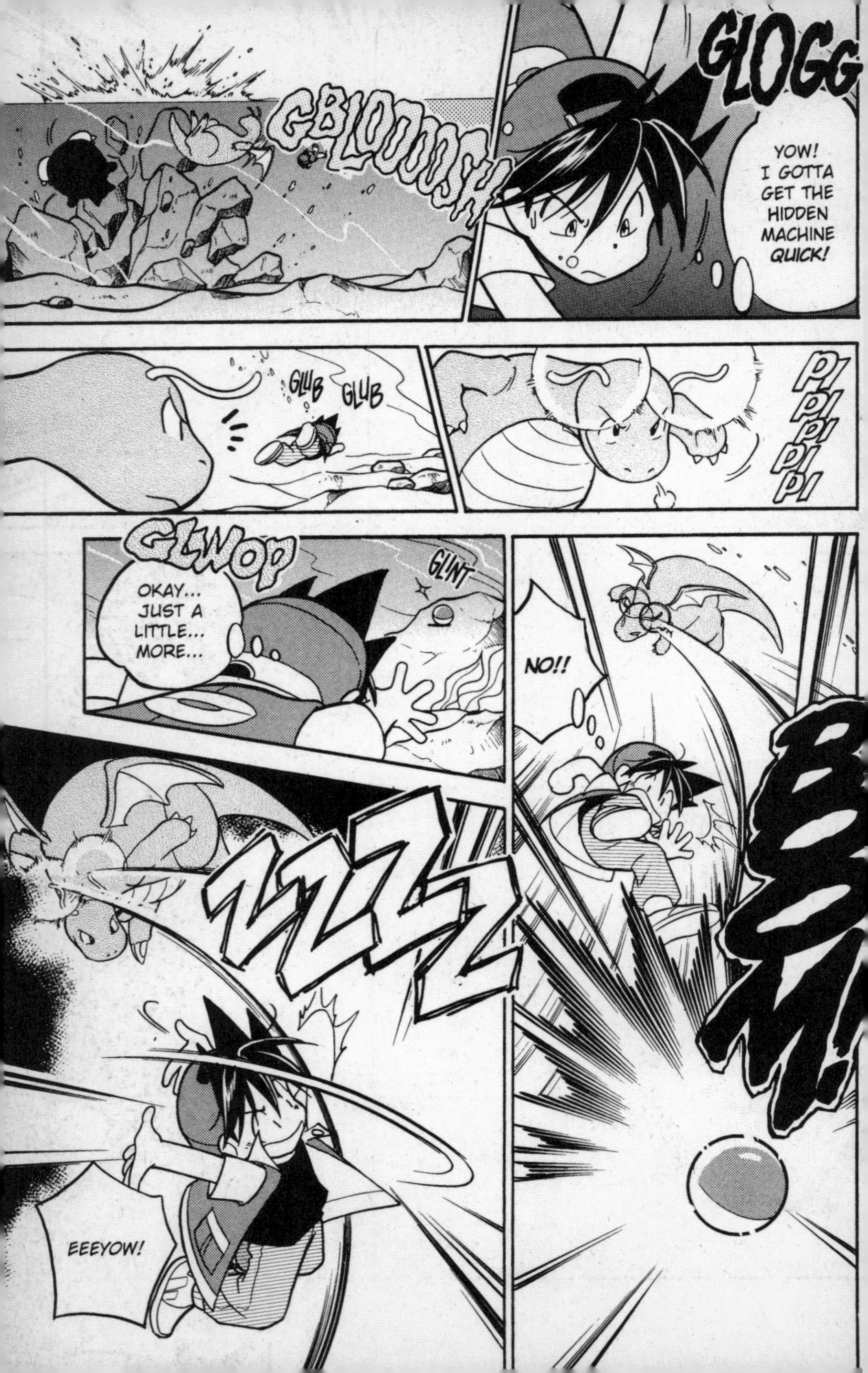
GBLOOOSH
GLOGG
YOW! I GOTTA GET THE HIDDEN MACHINE QUICK!
GLUB
GLUB
PI PI PI PI PI
GLWOP
OKAY... JUST A LITTLE... MORE...
GLINT
NO!!
ZZZZ
EEEYOW!

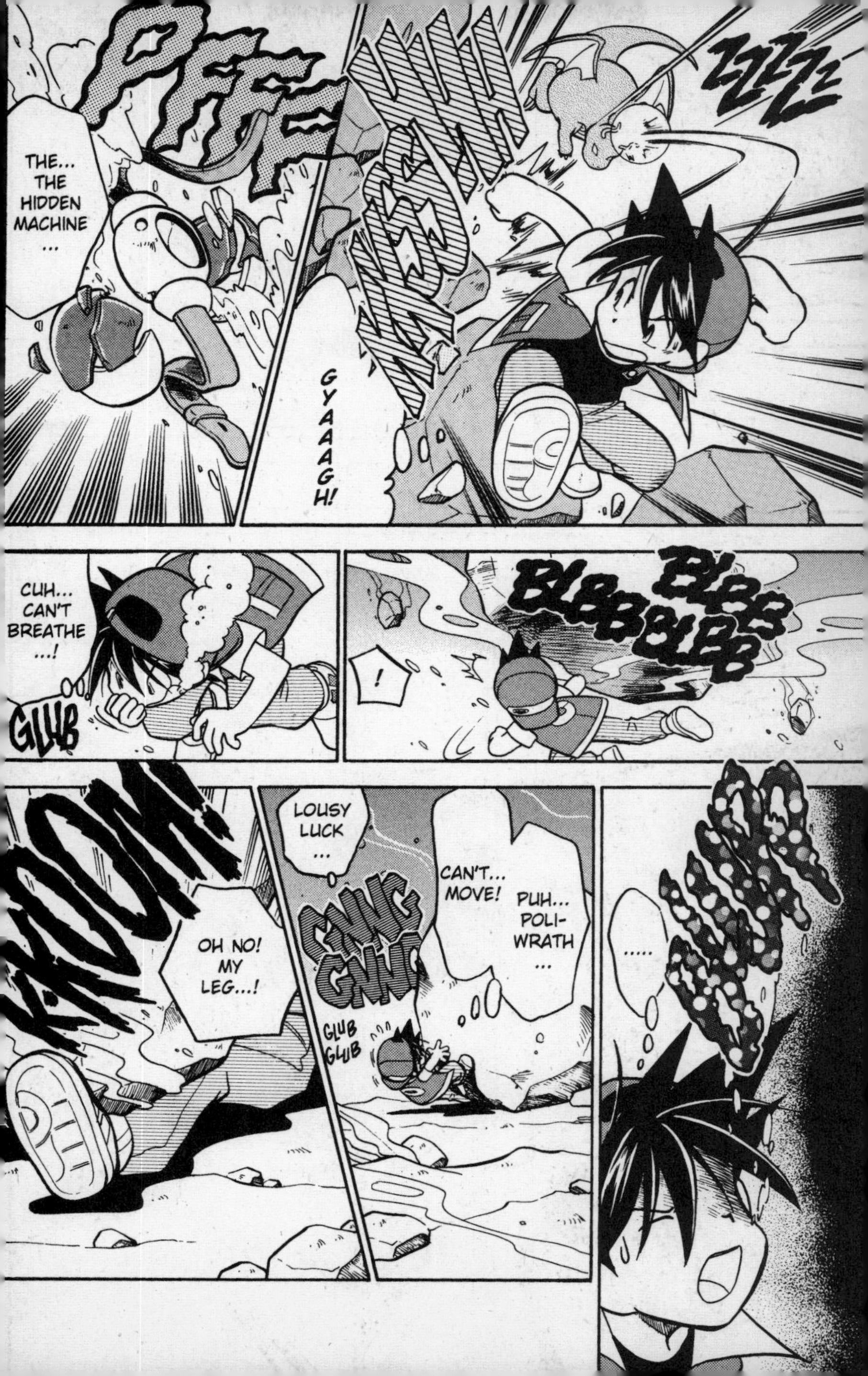
ZZZZZ
PFFF
THE... THE HIDDEN MACHINE ...
GYAAAAGH!
BLBB BLBB BLBB BLBB
!
CUH... CAN'T BREATHE ...!
GLUB
PUH... POLI-WRATH ...
CAN'T... MOVE!
LOUSY LUCK ...
GNNG GNNG
GLUB GLUB
OH NO! MY LEG...!
.....

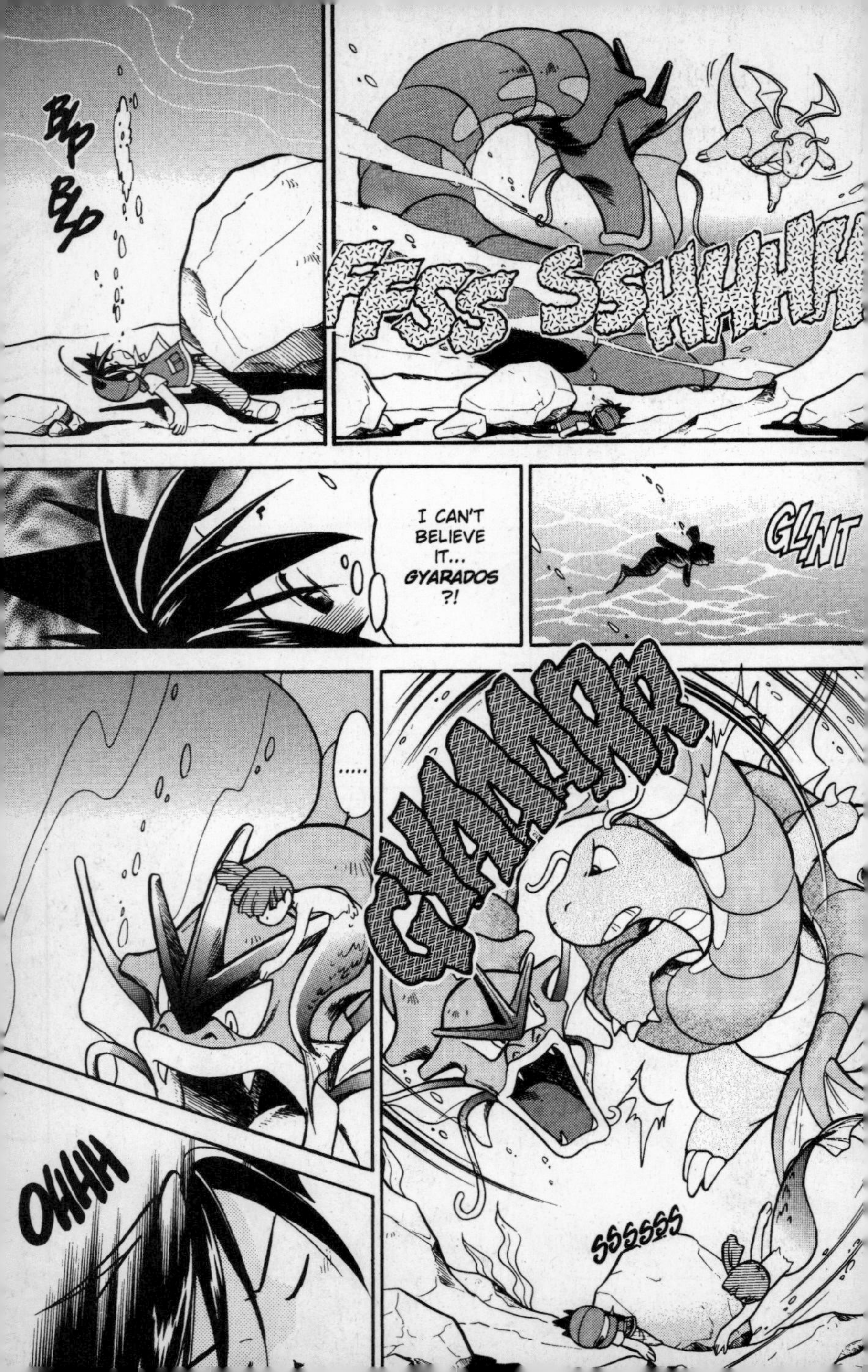
FSSS SSHHHH
BLP BLP
GLINT
I CAN'T BELIEVE IT... GYARADOS ?!
GWAAARR
.....
OHHH
SSSSSS

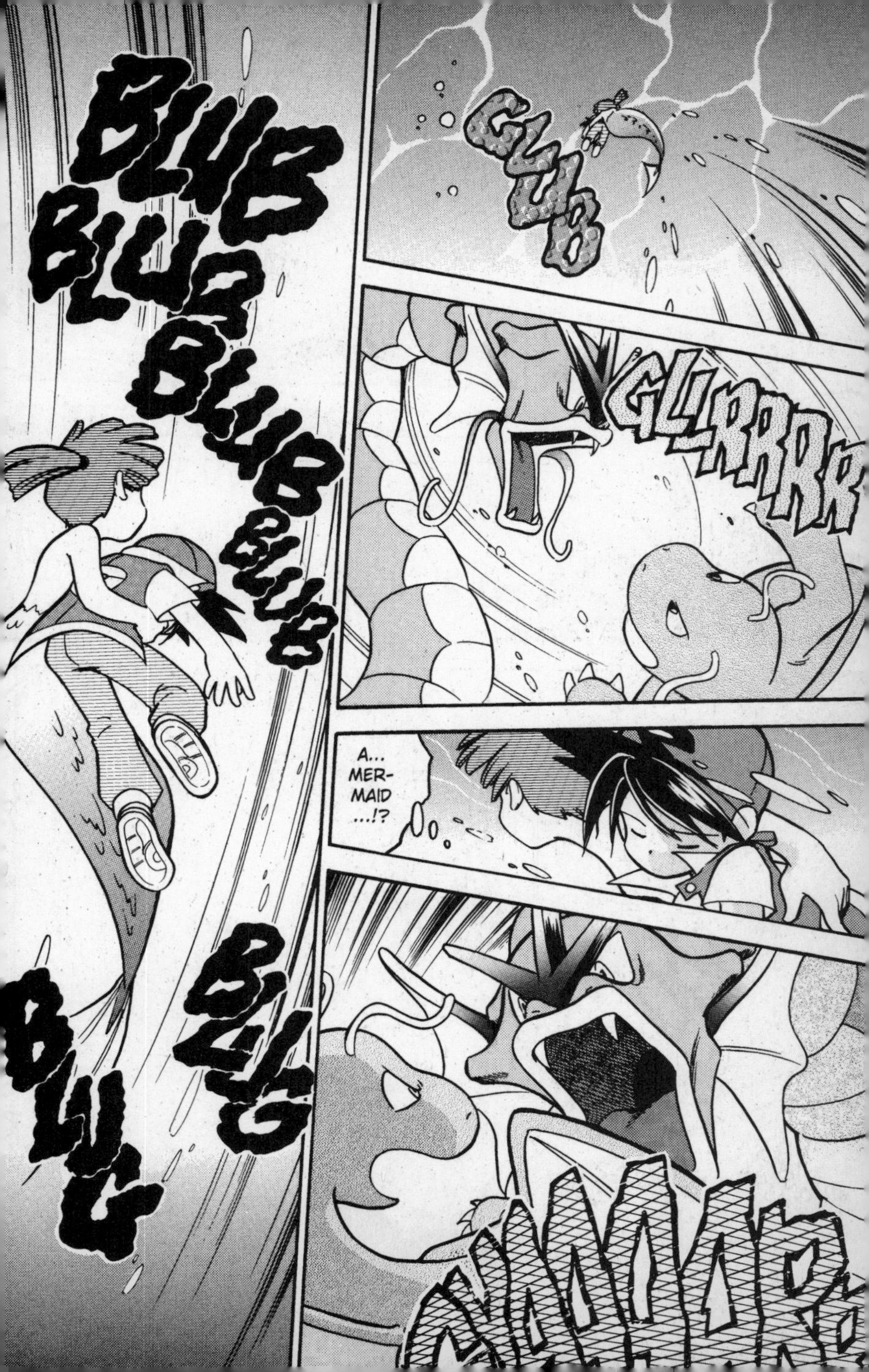
GLUB
GLRRRR
A... MER-MAID ...!?
BLUB BLUB BLUB BLUB BLUB
BLUG BLUG

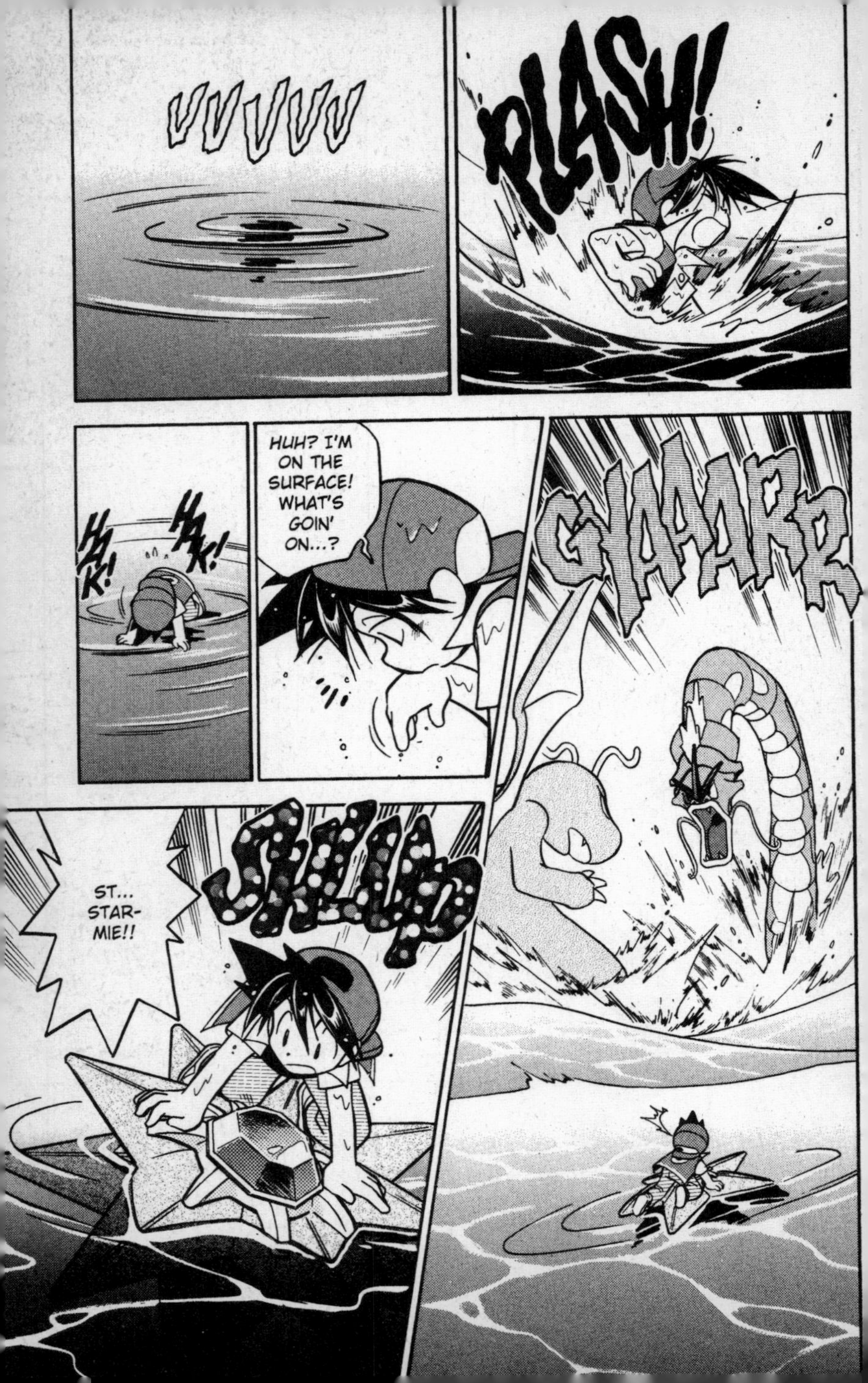
VVVVV
PLASH!
HAK! HAK!
HUH? I'M ON THE SURFACE! WHAT'S GOIN' ON...?
GYAAARR
SHLUP
ST... STAR-MIE!!

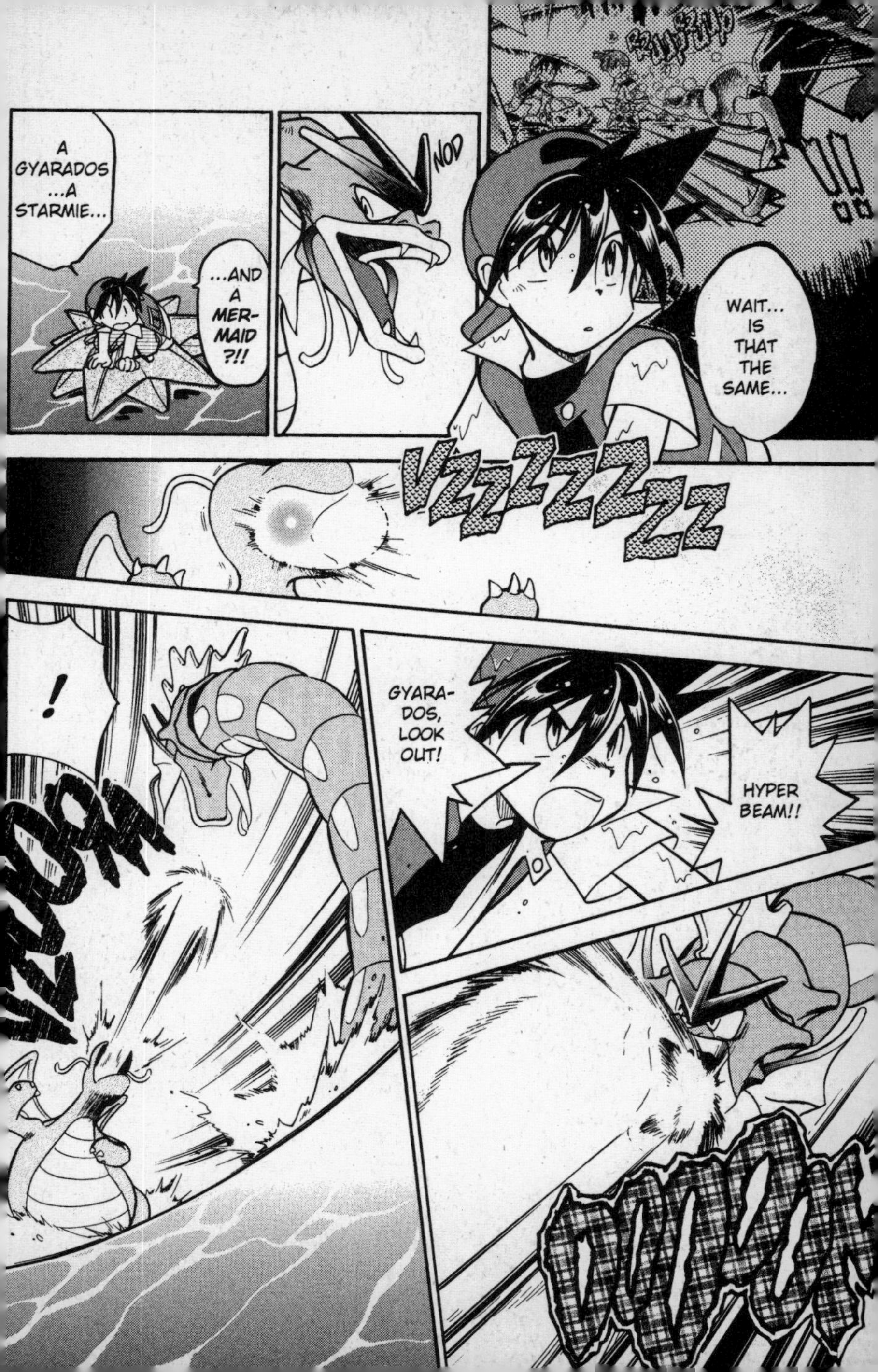

!!
WAIT... IS THAT THE SAME...
NOD
A GYARADOS ...A STARMIE...
...AND A MER-MAID ?!!
VZZZZZZZ
HYPER BEAM!!
GYARA-DOS, LOOK OUT!
!

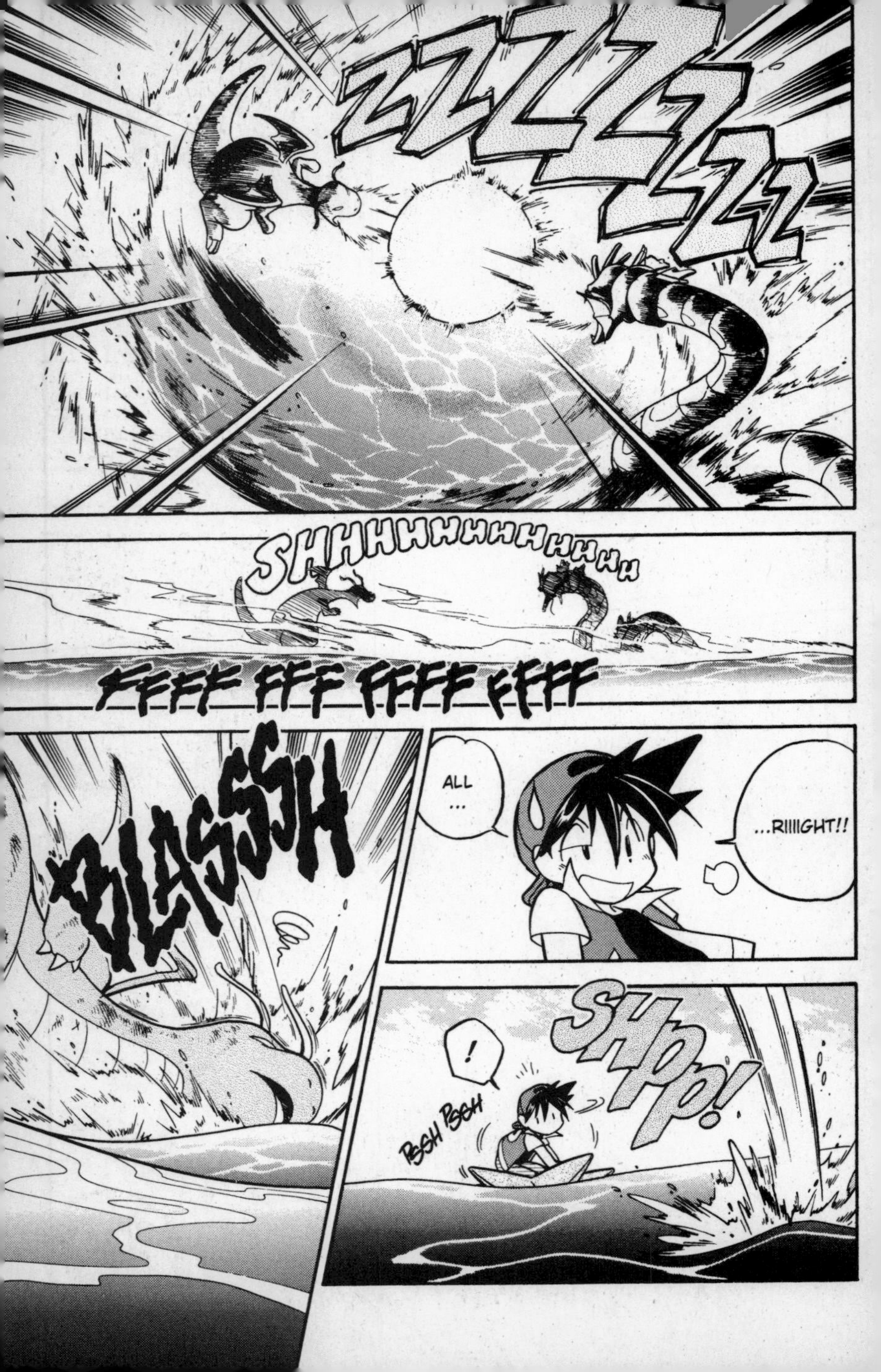
ZZZZZZZ
SHHHHHHHHHHHHH
FFFF FFF FFFF FFFF
ALL ...
...RIIIIGHT!!
BLASSSH
SHPP!
!
PSSH PSSH

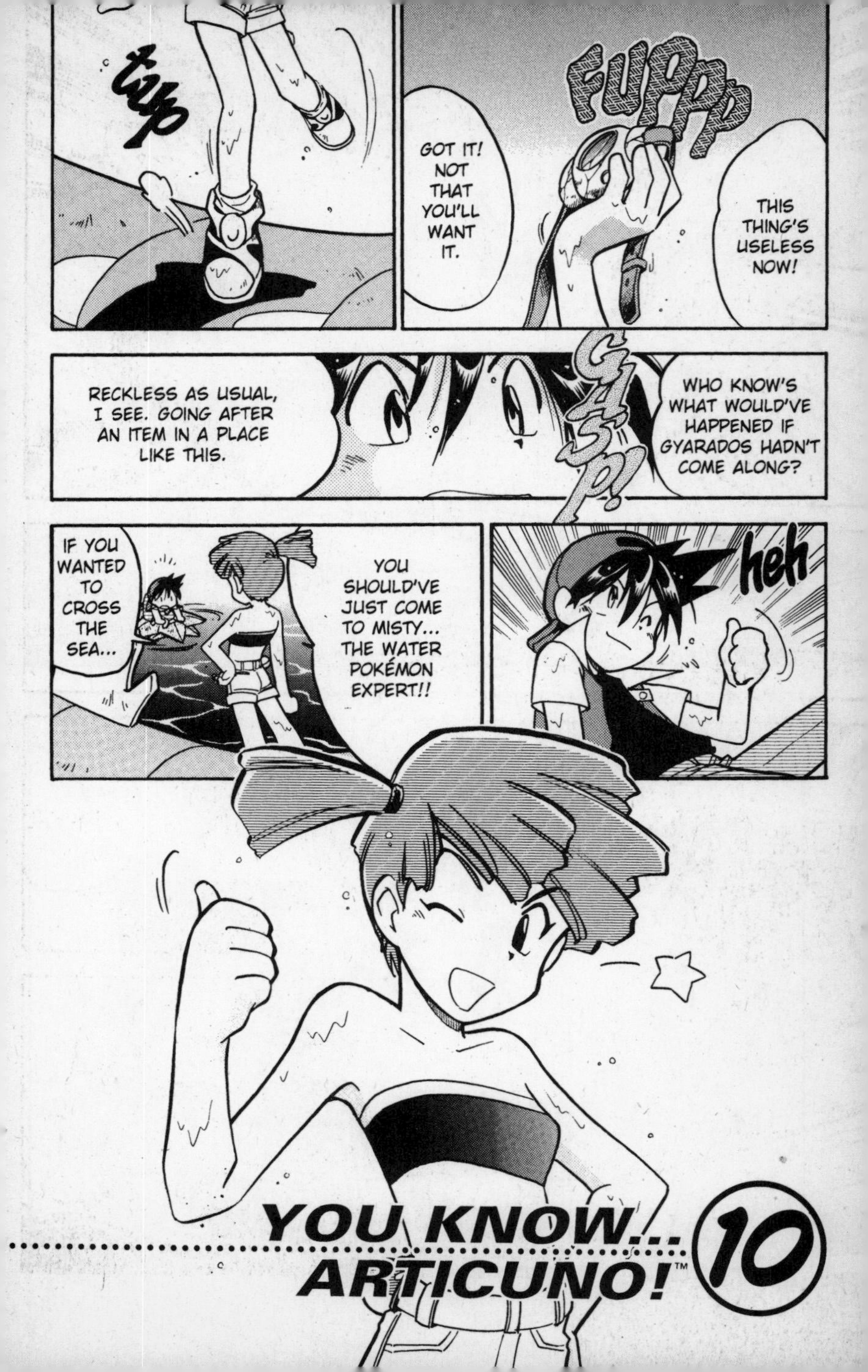
FUPPP
GOT IT! NOT THAT YOU'LL WANT IT.
THIS THING'S USELESS NOW!
RECKLESS AS USUAL, I SEE. GOING AFTER AN ITEM IN A PLACE LIKE THIS.
GASP!
WHO KNOW'S WHAT WOULD'VE HAPPENED IF GYARADOS HADN'T COME ALONG?
IF YOU WANTED TO CROSS THE SEA...
YOU SHOULD'VE JUST COME TO MISTY... THE WATER POKÉMON EXPERT!!
heh
YOU KNOW... ARTICUNO!™
10

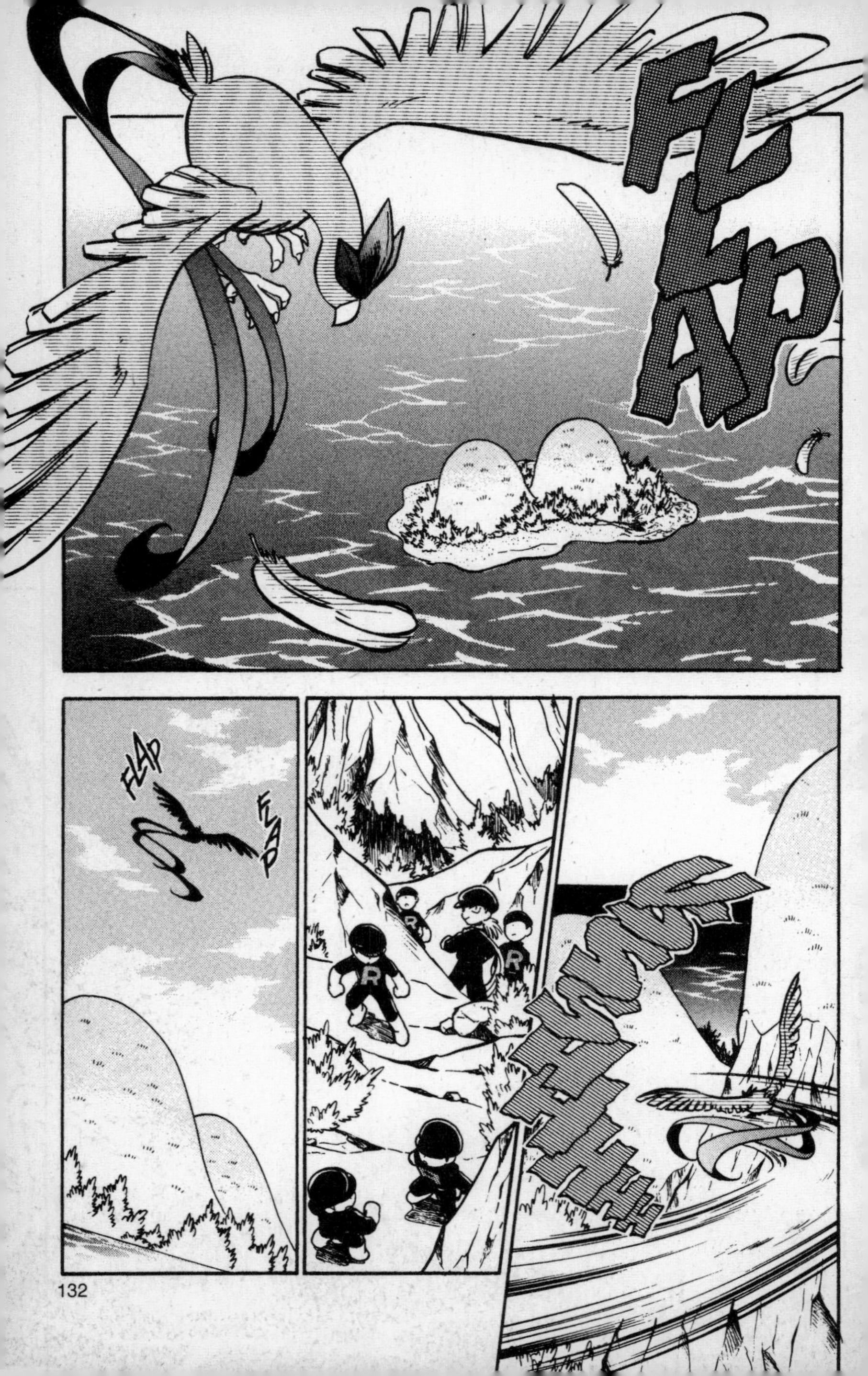
FLAP
FLAP
FLAP

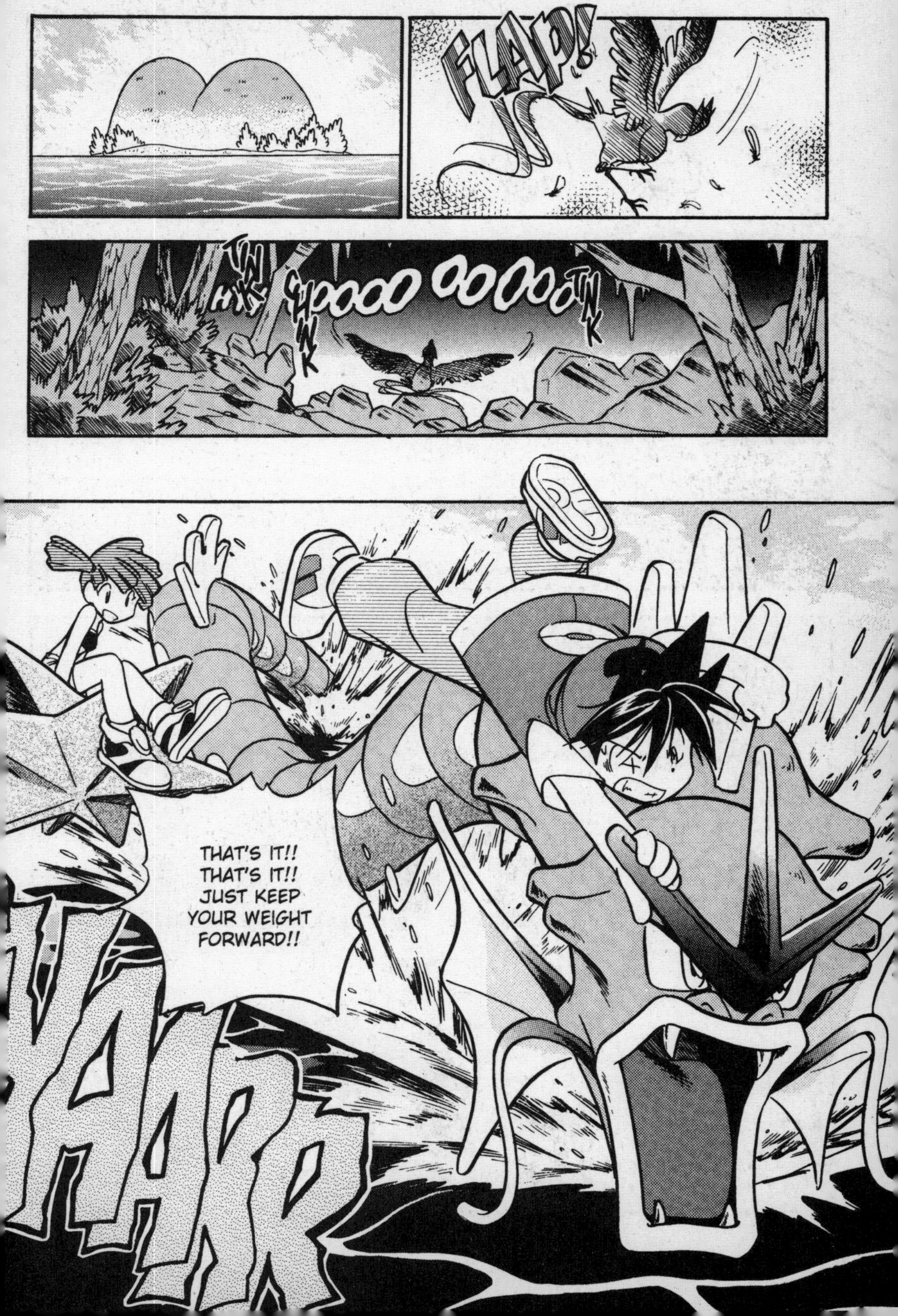
FLAP!
THAT'S IT!! THAT'S IT!! JUST KEEP YOUR WEIGHT FORWARD!!

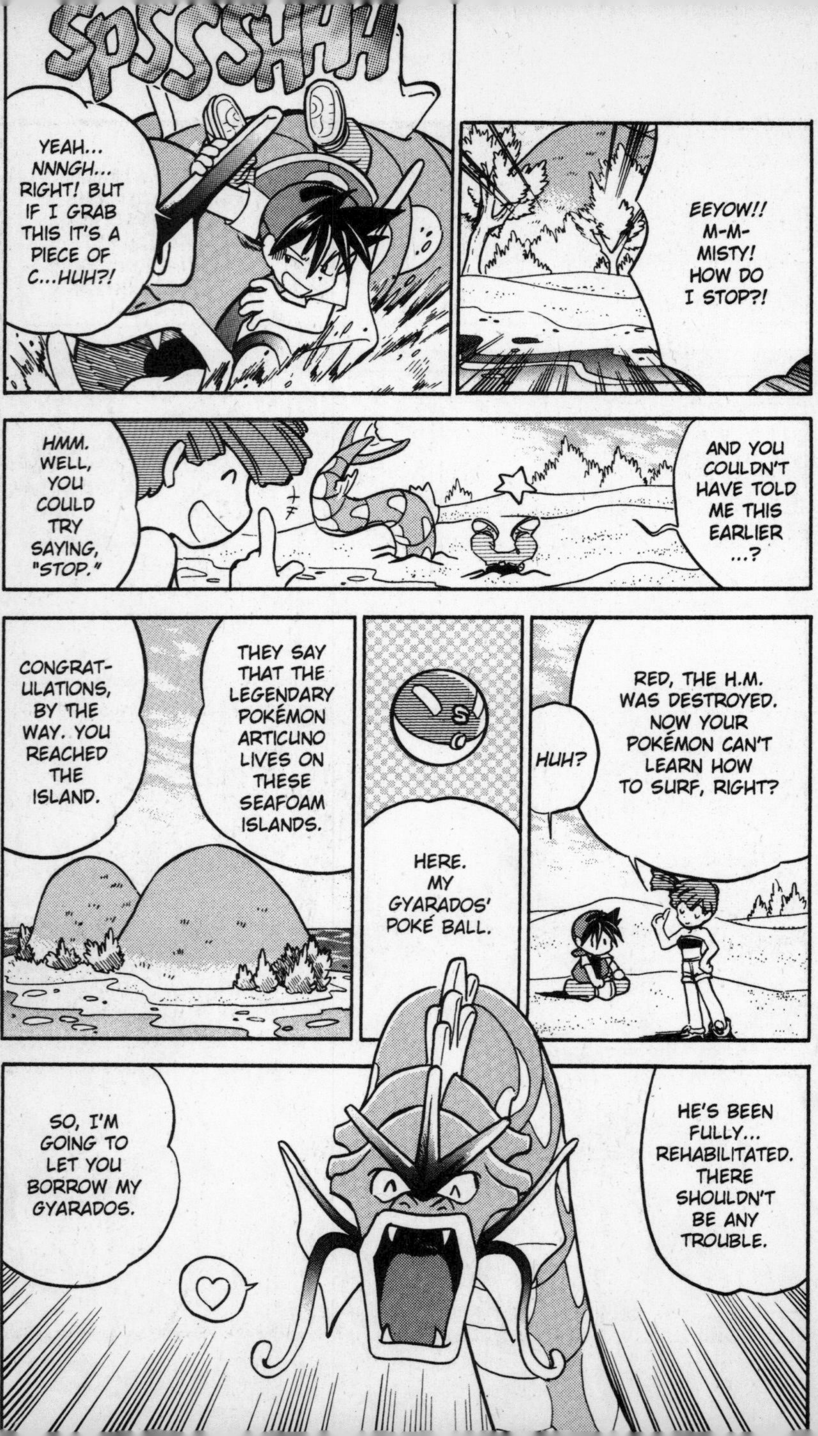
SPSSSHHH
YEAH... NNNGH... RIGHT! BUT IF I GRAB THIS IT'S A PIECE OF C...HUH?!
EEYOW!! M-M-MISTY! HOW DO I STOP?!
HMM. WELL, YOU COULD TRY SAYING, "STOP."
AND YOU COULDN'T HAVE TOLD ME THIS EARLIER ...?
CONGRAT-ULATIONS, BY THE WAY. YOU REACHED THE ISLAND.
THEY SAY THAT THE LEGENDARY POKÉMON ARTICUNO LIVES ON THESE SEAFOAM ISLANDS.
RED, THE H.M. WAS DESTROYED. NOW YOUR POKÉMON CAN'T LEARN HOW TO SURF, RIGHT?
HUH?
HERE. MY GYARADOS' POKÉ BALL.
SO, I'M GOING TO LET YOU BORROW MY GYARADOS.
HE'S BEEN FULLY... REHABILITATED. THERE SHOULDN'T BE ANY TROUBLE.

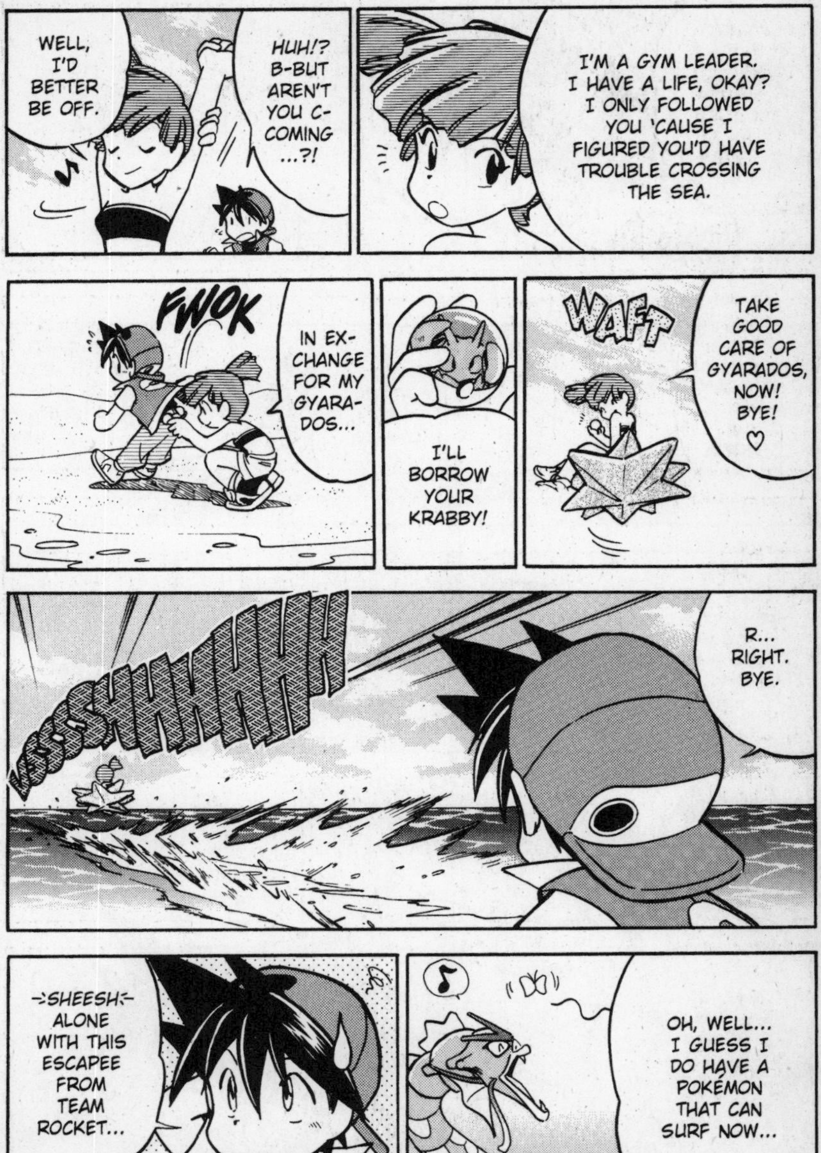
WELL, I'D BETTER BE OFF.
HUH!? B-BUT AREN'T YOU C-COMING ...?!
I'M A GYM LEADER. I HAVE A LIFE, OKAY? I ONLY FOLLOWED YOU 'CAUSE I FIGURED YOU'D HAVE TROUBLE CROSSING THE SEA.
FWOK
IN EX-CHANGE FOR MY GYARA-DOS...
I'LL BORROW YOUR KRABBY!
WAFT
TAKE GOOD CARE OF GYARADOS, NOW! BYE! ♡
WOOSHHHHHH
R... RIGHT. BYE.
-SHEESH- ALONE WITH THIS ESCAPEE FROM TEAM ROCKET...
OH, WELL... I GUESS I DO HAVE A POKÉMON THAT CAN SURF NOW...

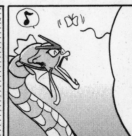

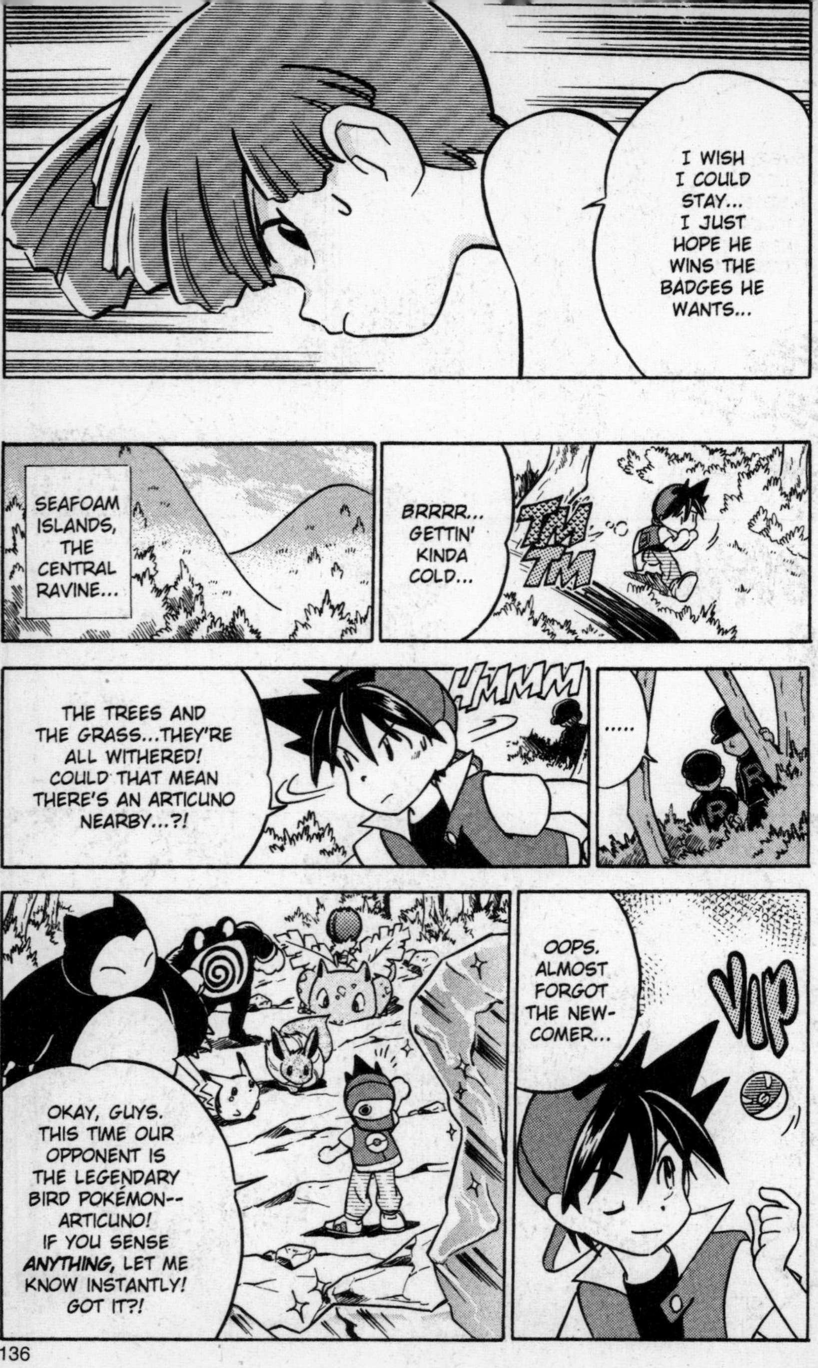
I WISH I COULD STAY... I JUST HOPE HE WINS THE BADGES HE WANTS...
SEAFOAM ISLANDS, THE CENTRAL RAVINE...
BRRRR... GETTIN' KINDA COLD...
TM TM
THE TREES AND THE GRASS...THEY'RE ALL WITHERED! COULD THAT MEAN THERE'S AN ARTICUNO NEARBY...?!
HMMM
.....
OKAY, GUYS. THIS TIME OUR OPPONENT IS THE LEGENDARY BIRD POKÉMON--ARTICUNO! IF YOU SENSE *ANYTHING*, LET ME KNOW INSTANTLY! GOT IT?!
OOPS. ALMOST FORGOT THE NEW-COMER...
VIP

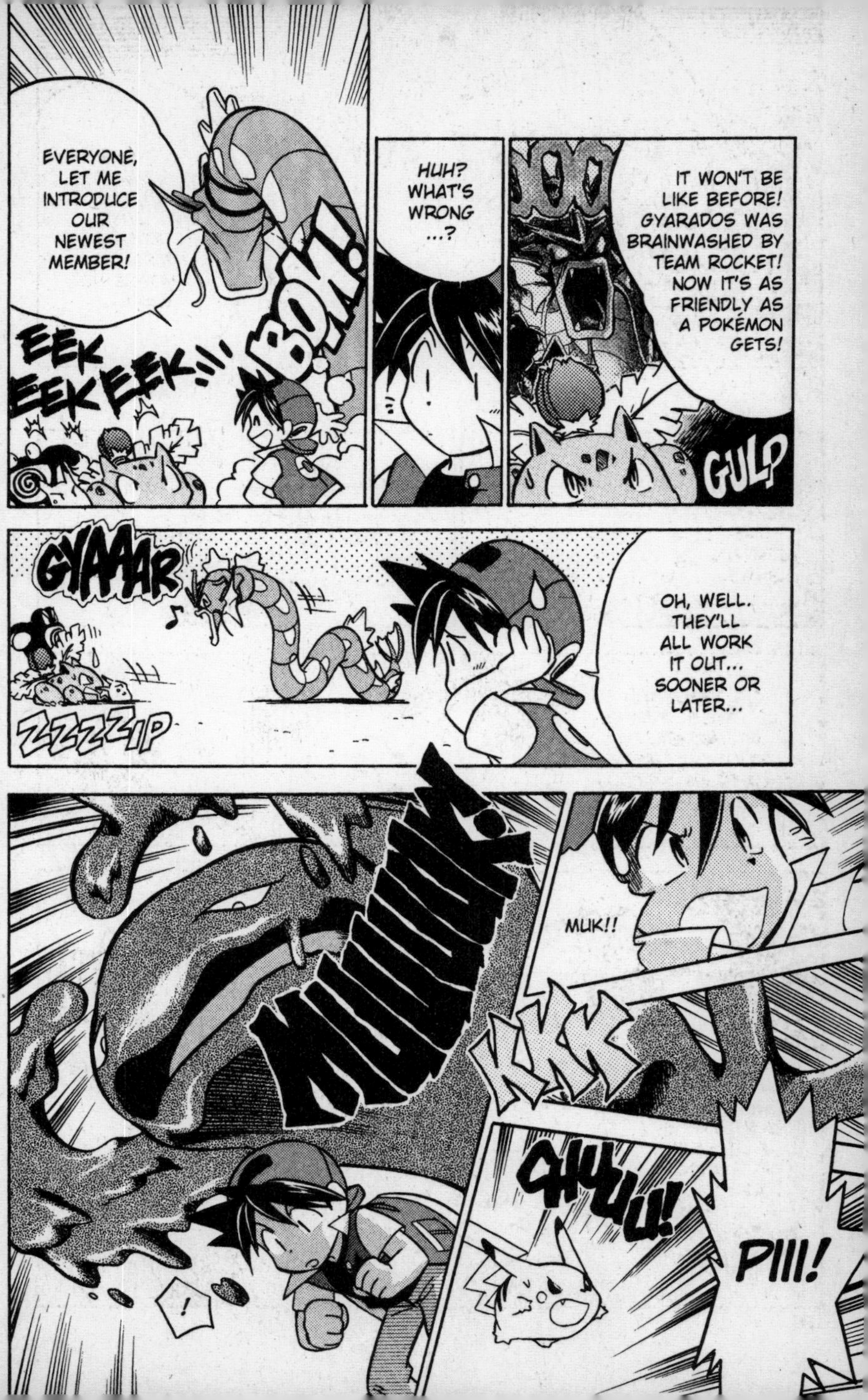
EVERYONE, LET ME INTRODUCE OUR NEWEST MEMBER!
BOAH!!
EEK EEK EEK EEK
HUH? WHAT'S WRONG ...?
IT WON'T BE LIKE BEFORE! GYARADOS WAS BRAINWASHED BY TEAM ROCKET! NOW IT'S AS FRIENDLY AS A POKÉMON GETS!
GULP
GYAAAR
ZZZZZIP
OH, WELL. THEY'LL ALL WORK IT OUT... SOONER OR LATER...
MUUUUK!
MUK!!
KKK
CHUUU!
PIII!

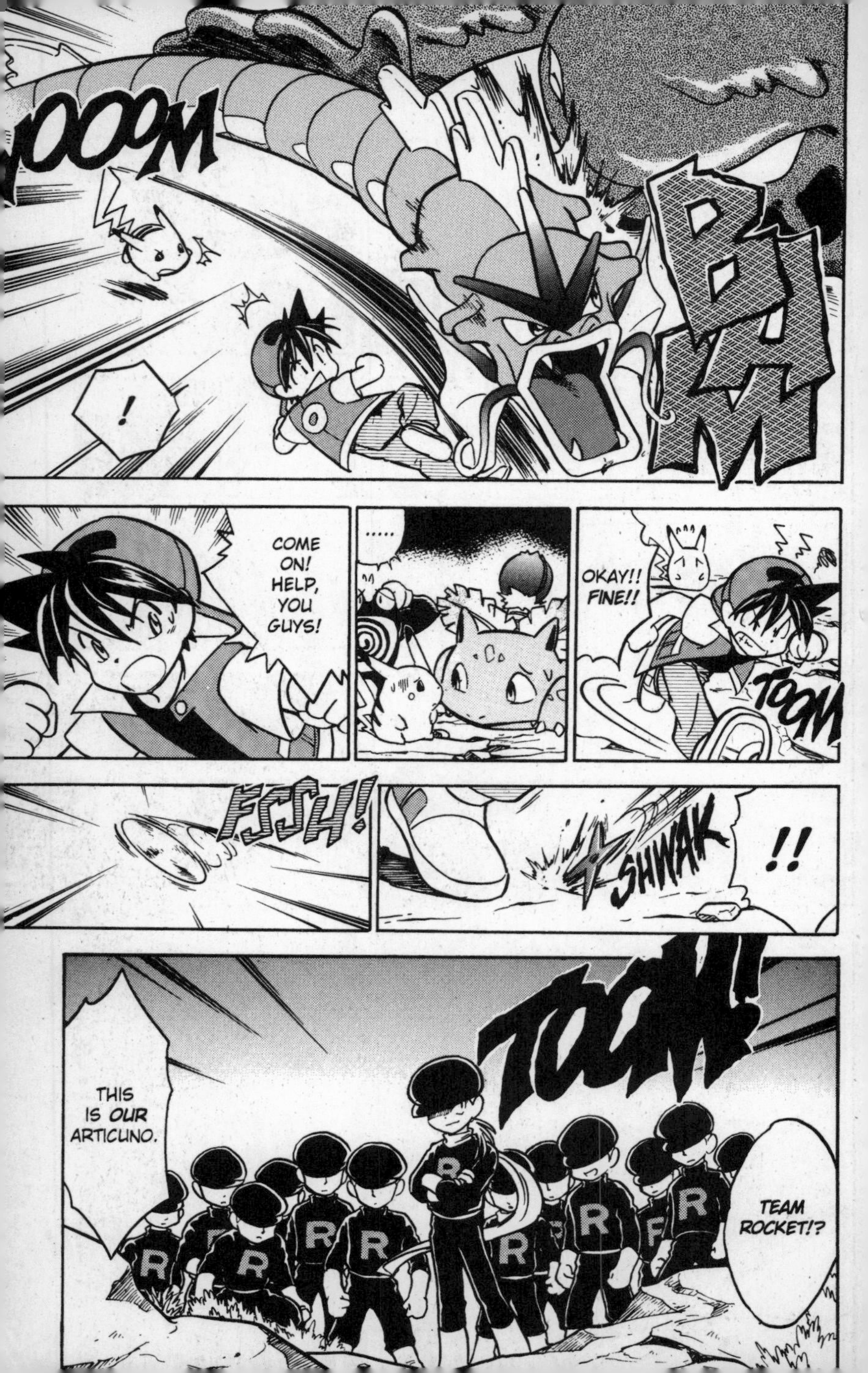
OOOM
BAM
!
COME ON! HELP, YOU GUYS!
.....
OKAY!! FINE!!
TOOM
FSSH!
SHWAK
!!
TOOM!
THIS IS OUR ARTICUNO.
TEAM ROCKET!?

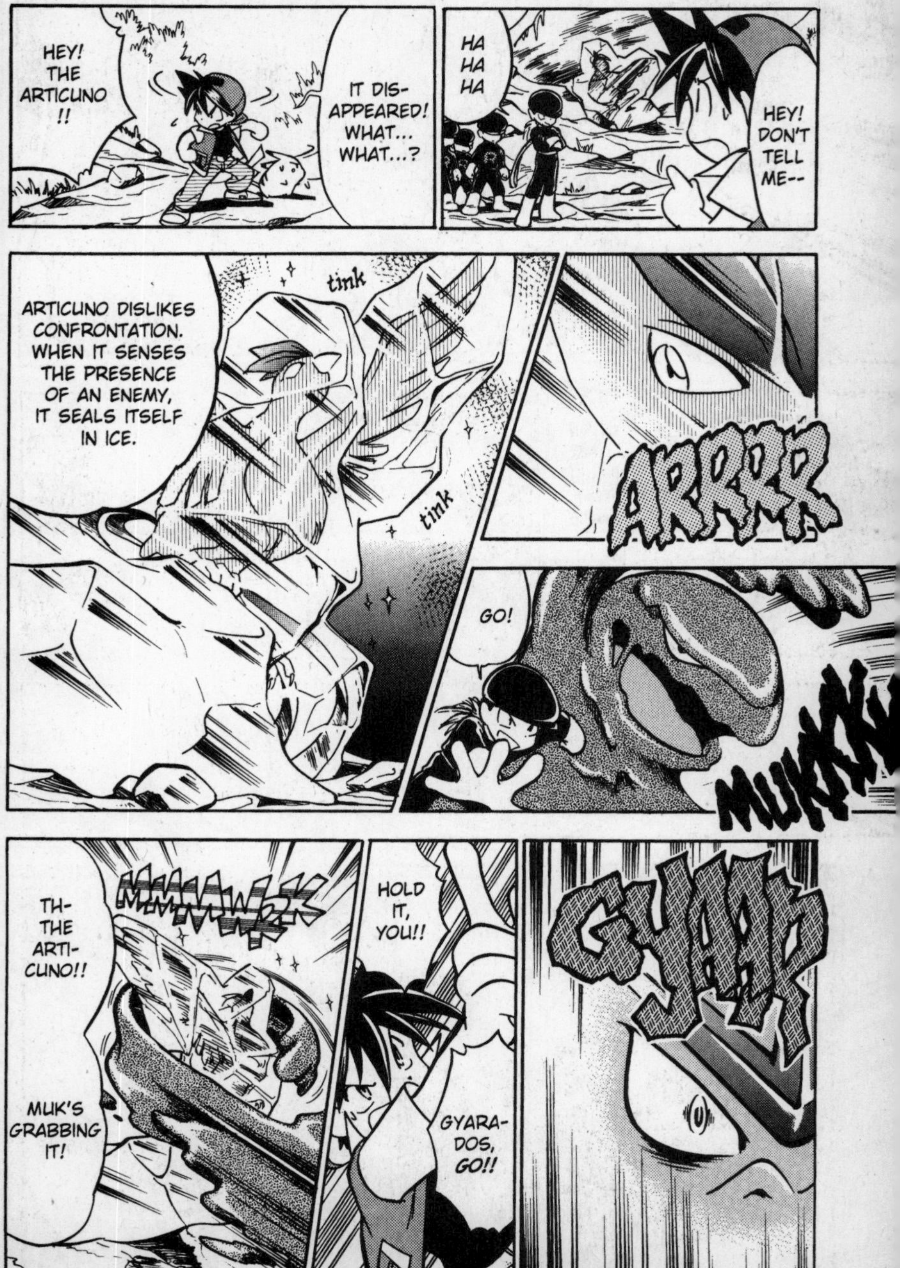
HEY! THE ARTICUNO !!
IT DIS-APPEARED! WHAT... WHAT...?
HA HA HA
HEY! DON'T TELL ME--
ARTICUNO DISLIKES CONFRONTATION. WHEN IT SENSES THE PRESENCE OF AN ENEMY, IT SEALS ITSELF IN ICE.
tink
tink
ARRRR
GO!
TH-THE ARTI-CUNO!!
MUK'S GRABBING IT!
HOLD IT, YOU!!
GYARA-DOS, GO!!
GYAAR

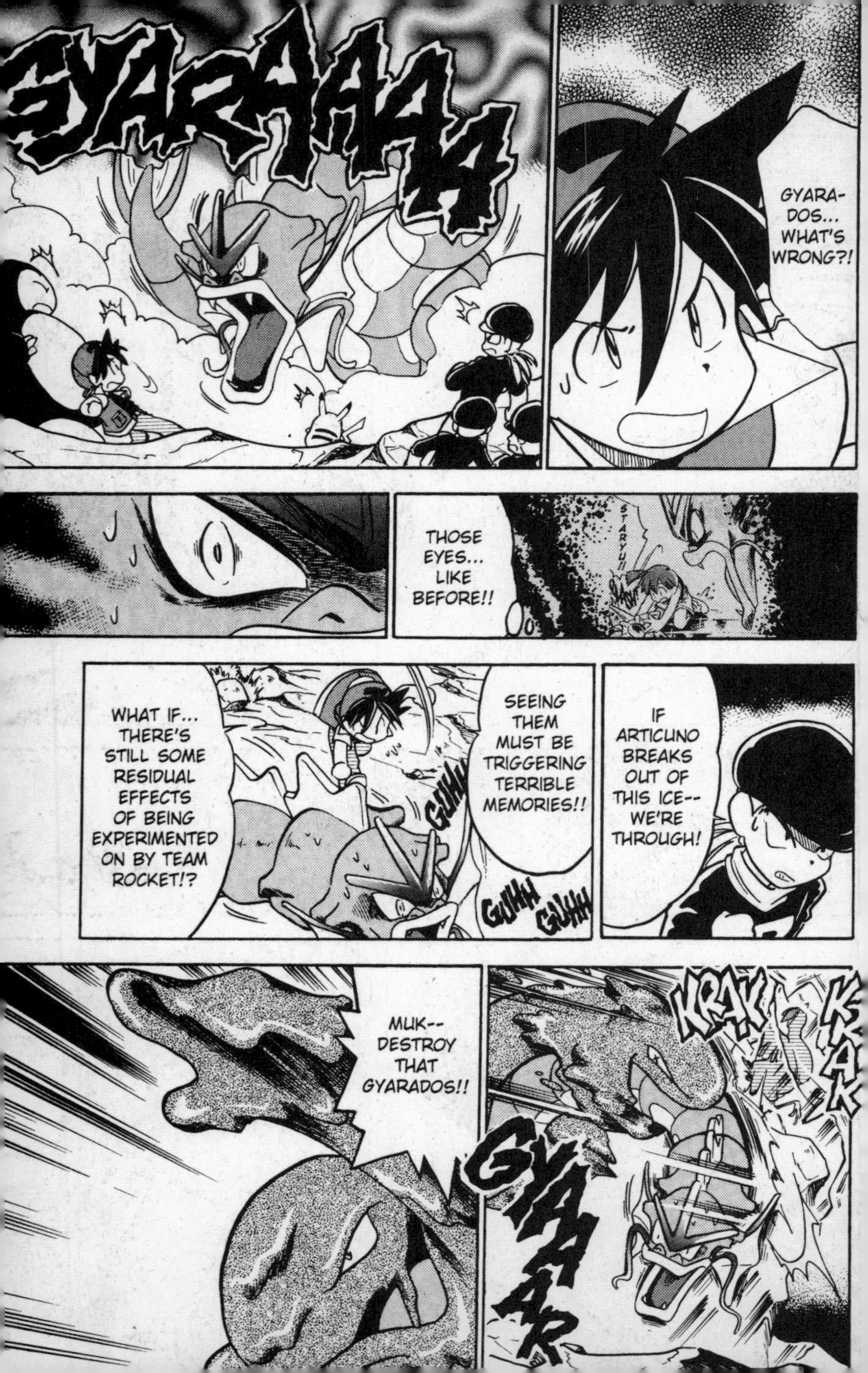
GYARAAAA
GYARA-DOS... WHAT'S WRONG?!
THOSE EYES... LIKE BEFORE!!
WHAT IF... THERE'S STILL SOME RESIDUAL EFFECTS OF BEING EXPERIMENTED ON BY TEAM ROCKET!?
GUHH
SEEING THEM MUST BE TRIGGERING TERRIBLE MEMORIES!!
GUHH GUHH
IF ARTICUNO BREAKS OUT OF THIS ICE-- WE'RE THROUGH!
MUK-- DESTROY THAT GYARADOS!!
KRAK KRAK
GYAAAR

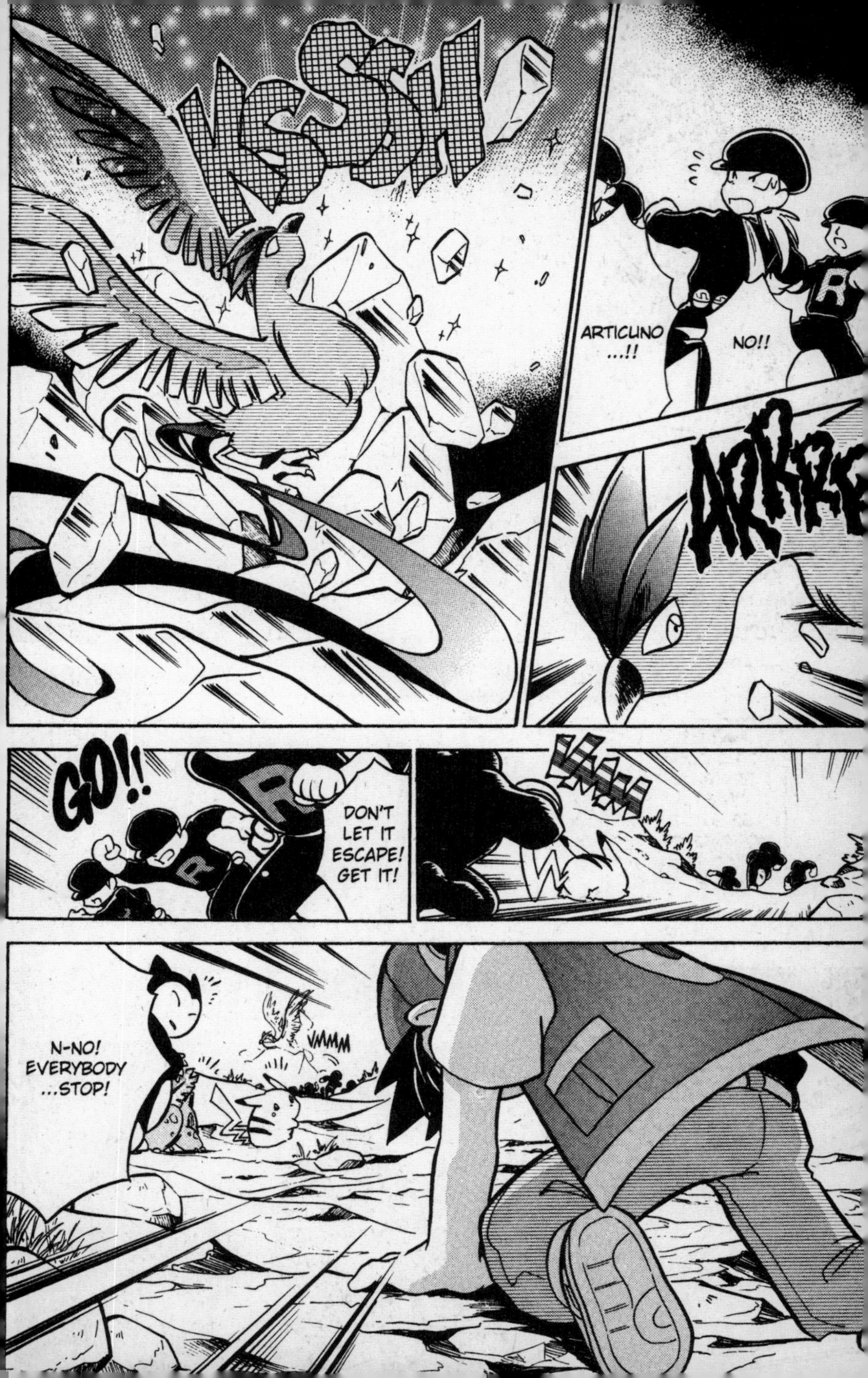
VOSSH
ARTICUNO ...!!
NO!!
ARRRE
GO!!
DON'T LET IT ESCAPE! GET IT!
VMMM
N-NO! EVERYBODY ...STOP!
VMMM

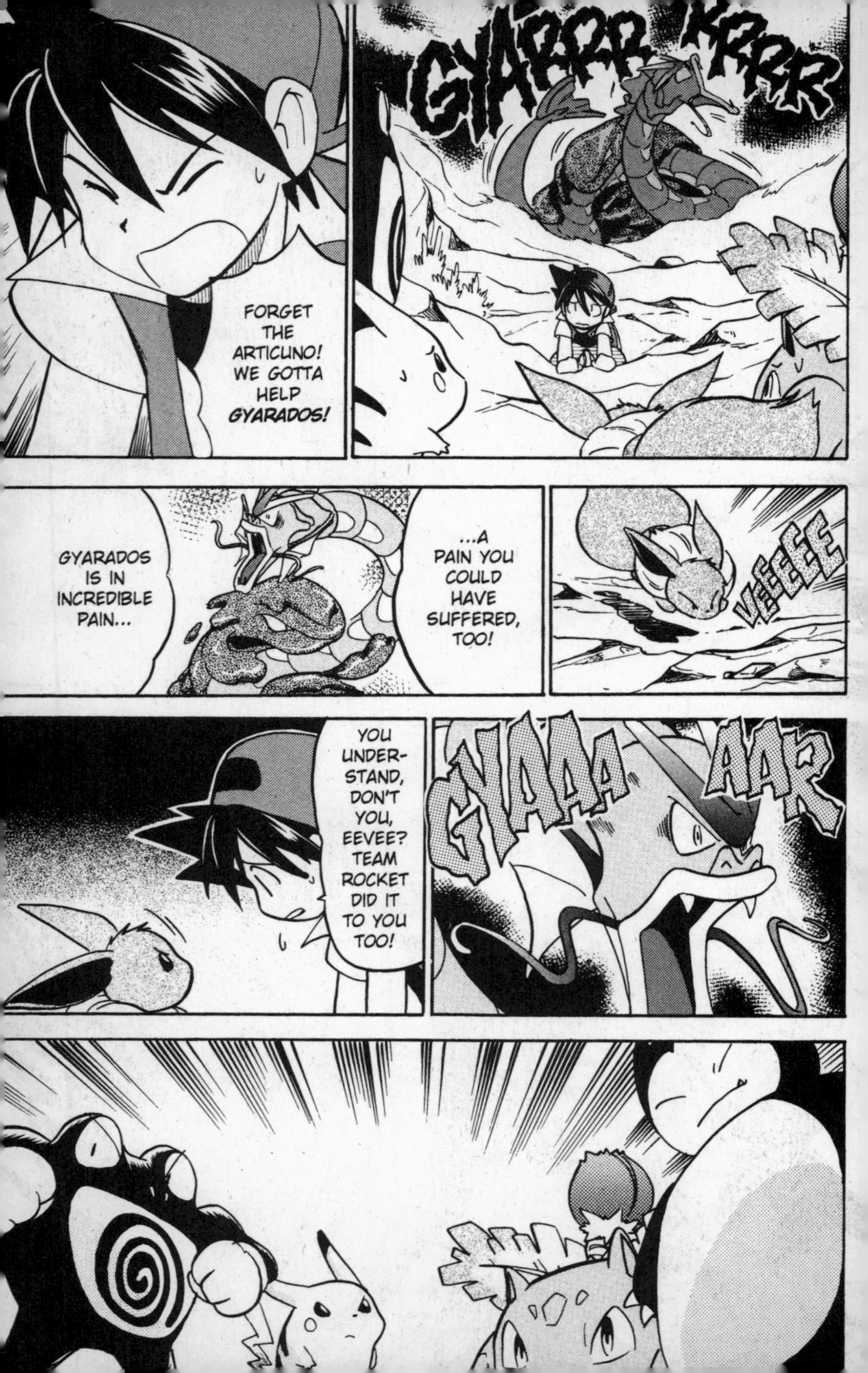

FORGET THE ARTICUNO! WE GOTTA HELP *GYARADOS!*
GYARRR KRRR
GYARADOS IS IN INCREDIBLE PAIN...
...A PAIN YOU COULD HAVE SUFFERED, TOO!
VEEEE
YOU UNDER-STAND, DON'T YOU, EEVEE? TEAM ROCKET DID IT TO YOU TOO!
GYAAAA AAR

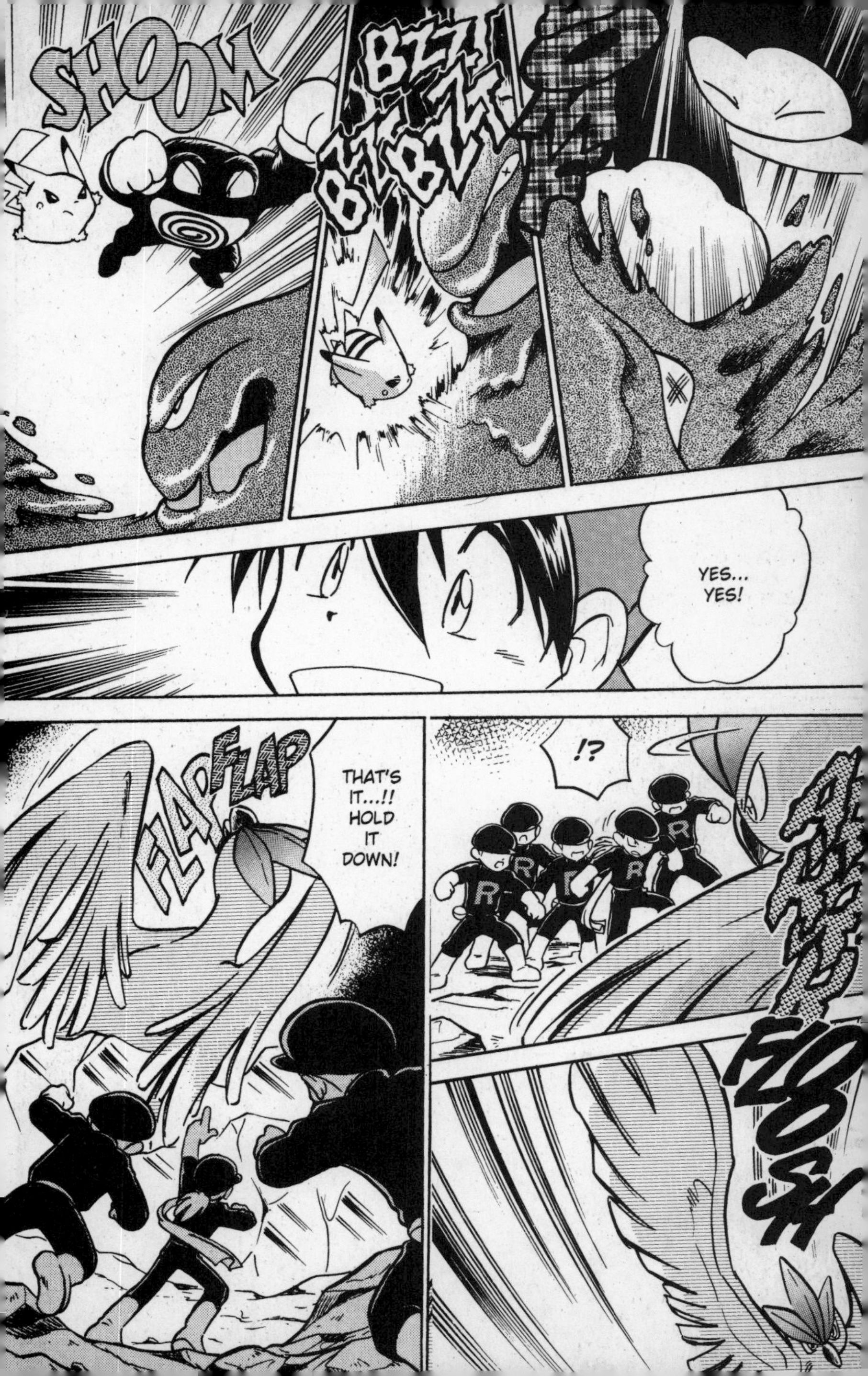
SHOOM
BZZT!
BZZT BZZT
YES... YES!
FLAPFLAP
THAT'S IT...!! HOLD IT DOWN!
!?

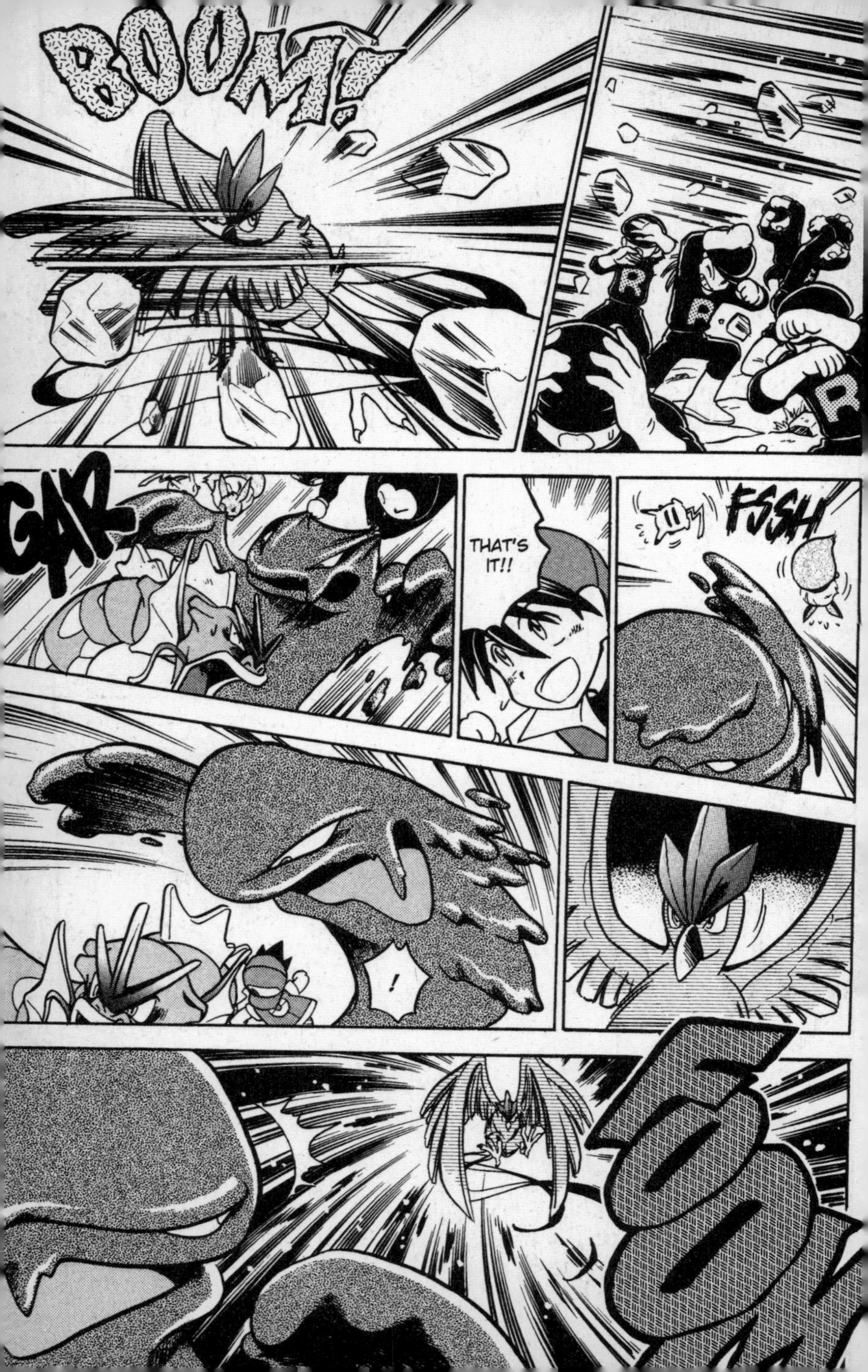
BOOM!
GAR
THAT'S IT!!
FSSH
!

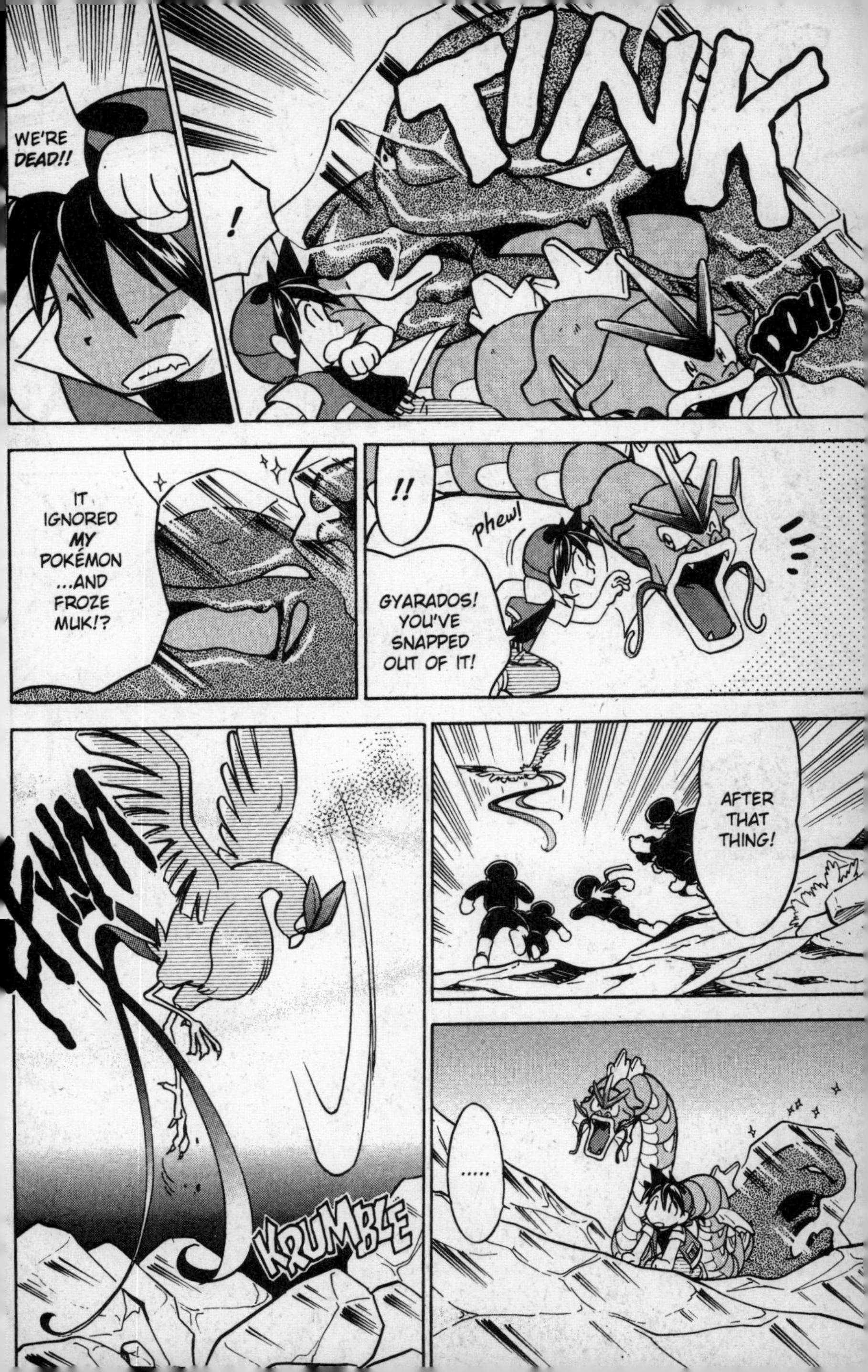
TINK
WE'RE DEAD!!
!
DOH!
IT IGNORED MY POKÉMON ...AND FROZE MUK!?
!!
phew!
GYARADOS! YOU'VE SNAPPED OUT OF IT!
AFTER THAT THING!
KRUMBLE
.....

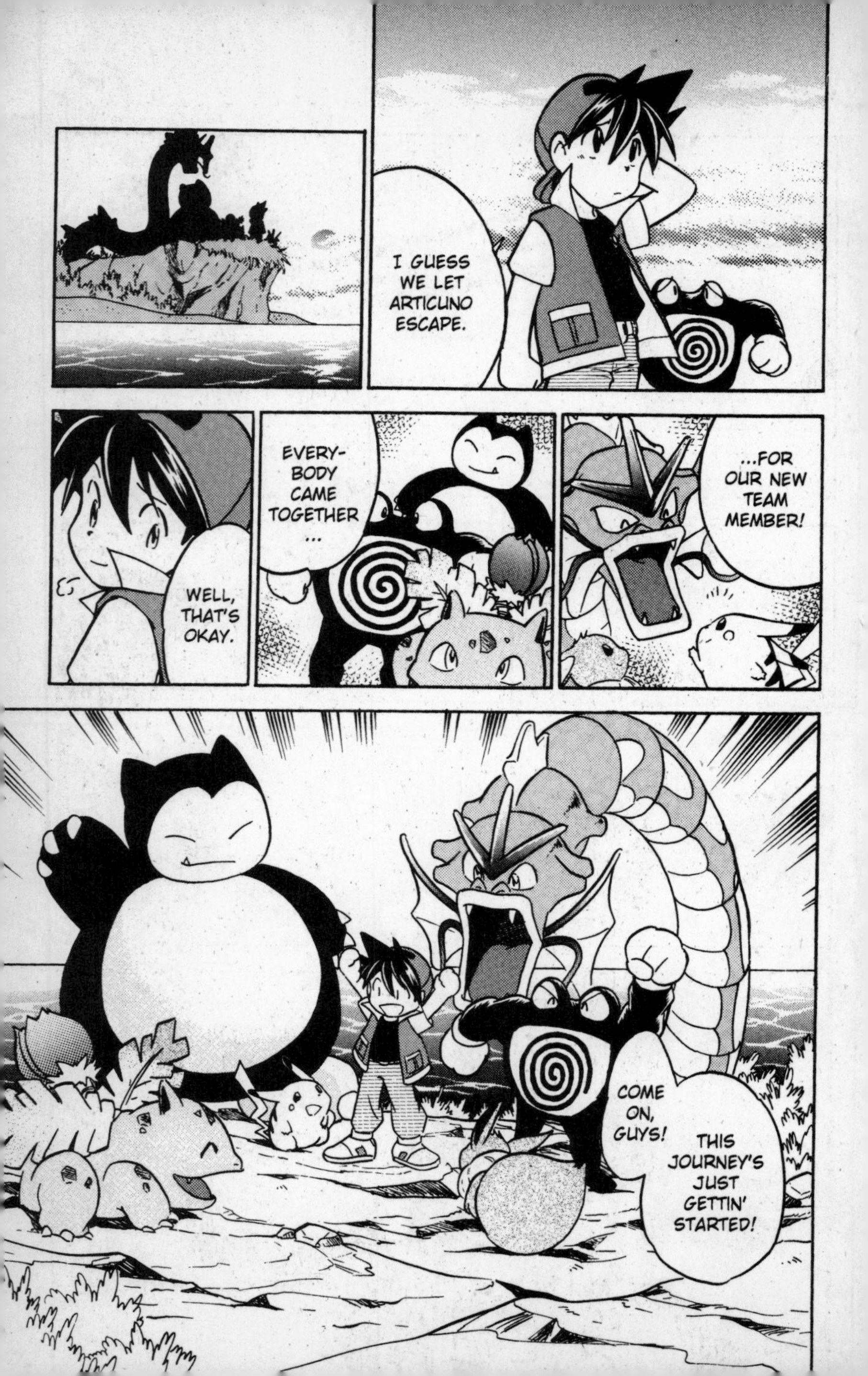
I GUESS WE LET ARTICUNO ESCAPE.
WELL, THAT'S OKAY.
EVERY-BODY CAME TOGETHER ...
...FOR OUR NEW TEAM MEMBER!
COME ON, GUYS!
THIS JOURNEY'S JUST GETTIN' STARTED!

CHAPTER 11

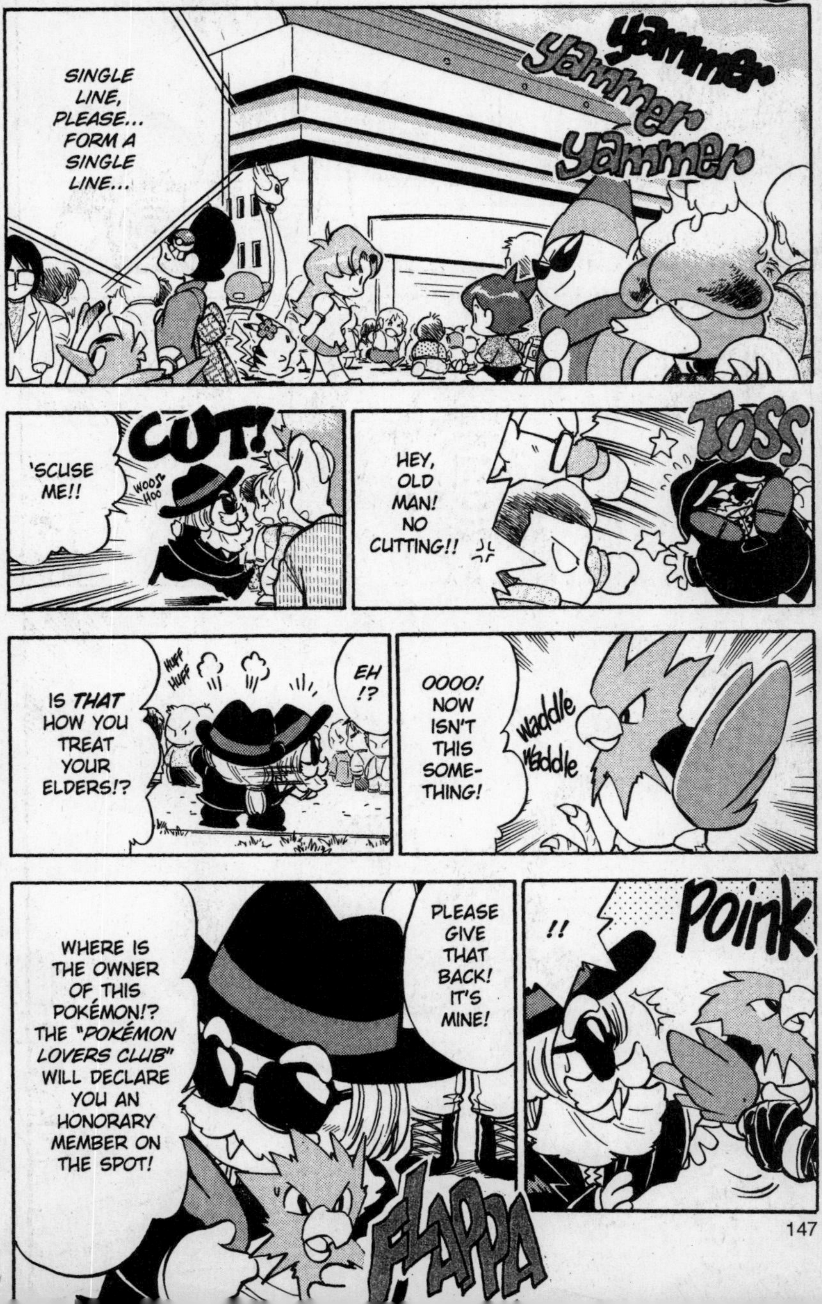

SINGLE LINE, PLEASE... FORM A SINGLE LINE...
yammer yammer yammer
'SCUSE ME!!
CUT!
HEY, OLD MAN! NO CUTTING!!
TOSS
HUFF HUFF
IS *THAT* HOW YOU TREAT YOUR ELDERS!?
EH!?
OOOO! NOW ISN'T THIS SOME-THING!
waddle waddle
WHERE IS THE OWNER OF THIS POKÉMON!? THE *"POKÉMON LOVERS CLUB"* WILL DECLARE YOU AN HONORARY MEMBER ON THE SPOT!
PLEASE GIVE THAT BACK! IT'S MINE!
FLAPPA
!!
Poink

AH... AH...

ONE TO ENTER. REGISTRA... Y-YES SIR.

SHFF SHFF

EXCELLENT. ALL THREE... ARE HERE!!

LEAGUE

RED

GREEN

BLUE

UOOOOOOORA

THE POKÉMON LEAGUE!!

JUST A SPEAROW CARRIER

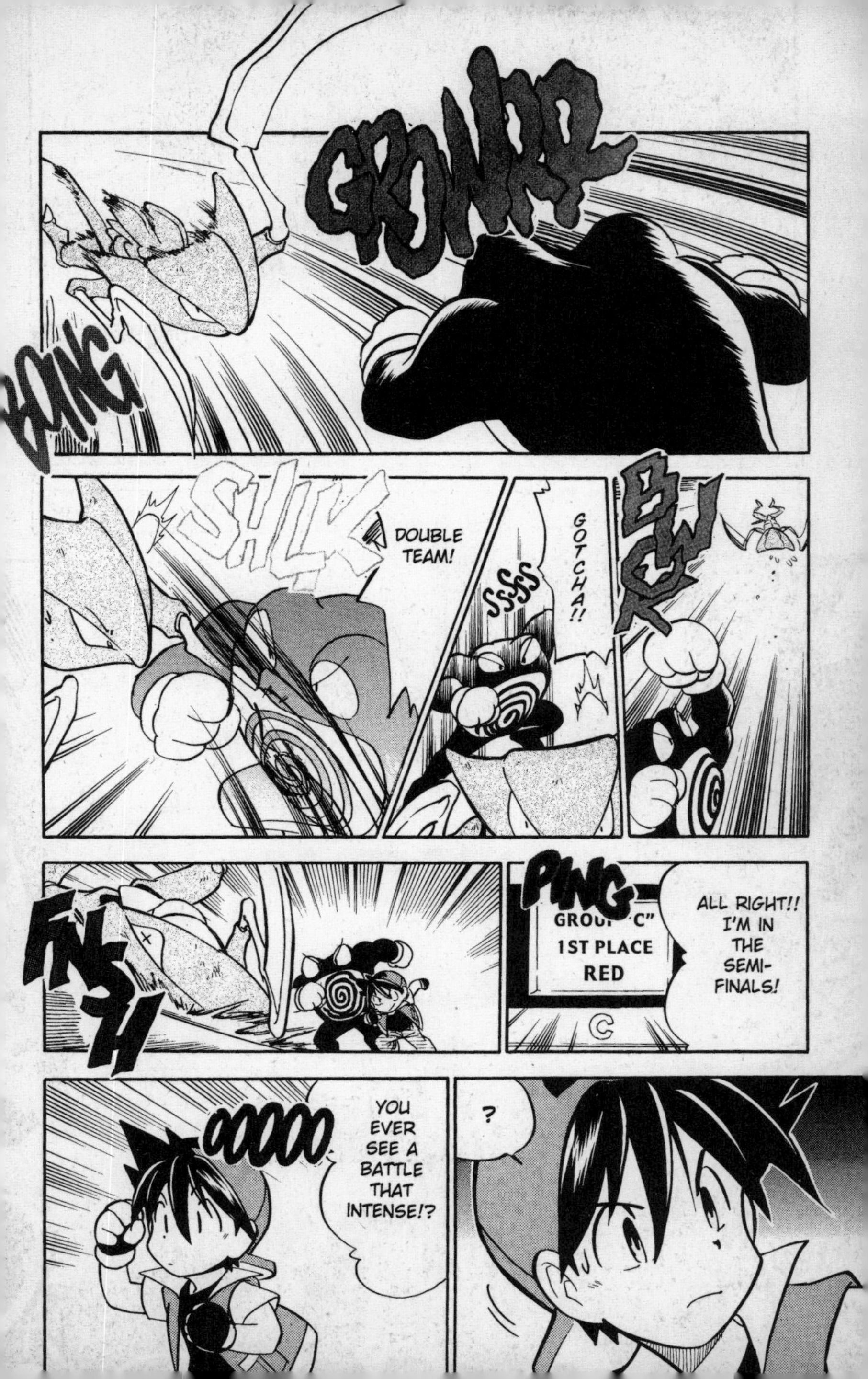
GRONRR
BOING
SHLIK
DOUBLE TEAM!
GOTCHA!!
SSSSS
BWOK
FWASH
PING
GROUP "C" 1ST PLACE RED
ALL RIGHT!! I'M IN THE SEMI-FINALS!
OOOOO
YOU EVER SEE A BATTLE THAT INTENSE!?
?

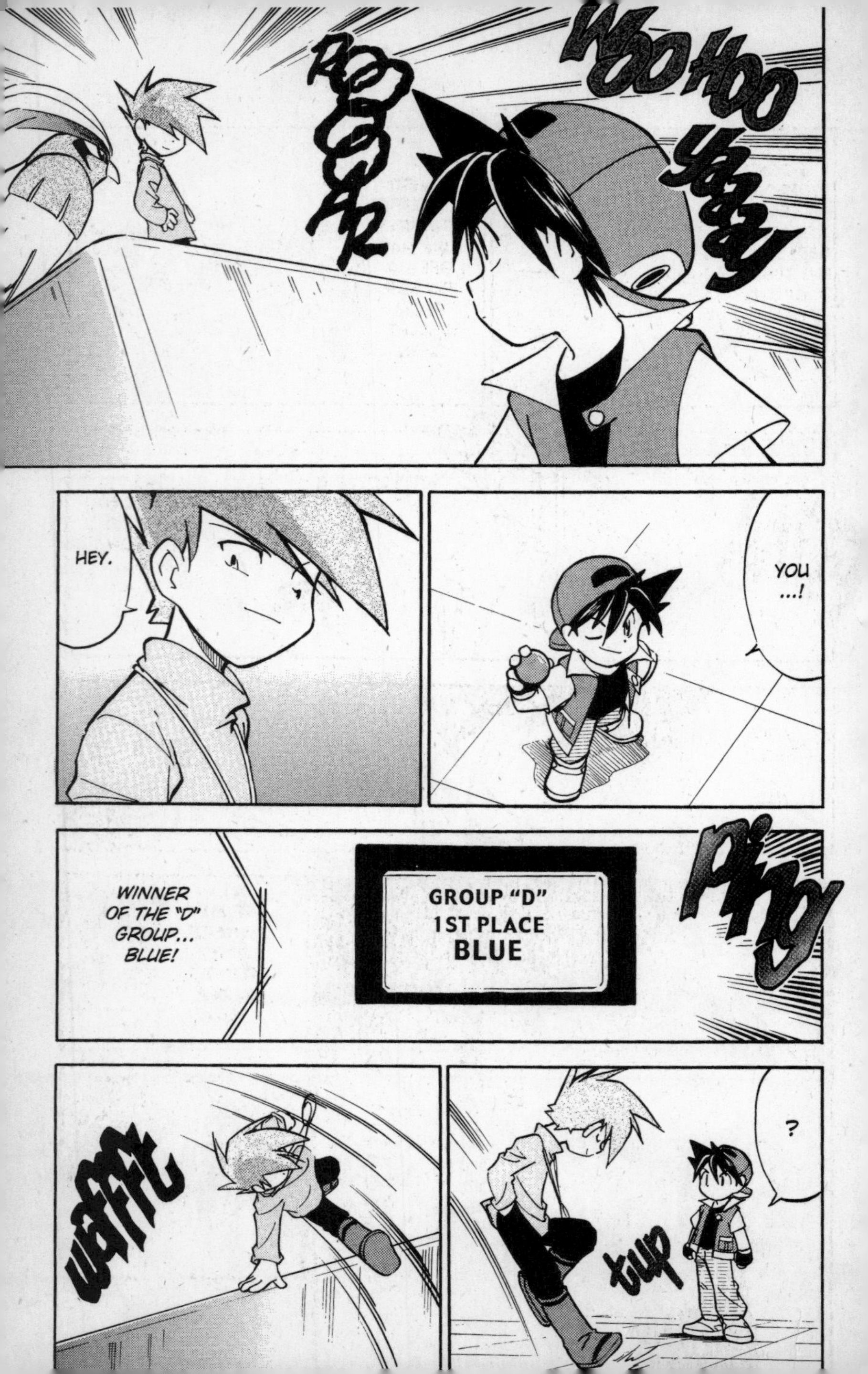
HEY.
YOU ...!
WINNER OF THE "D" GROUP... BLUE!
GROUP "D"
1ST PLACE
BLUE
Ping
?
tup

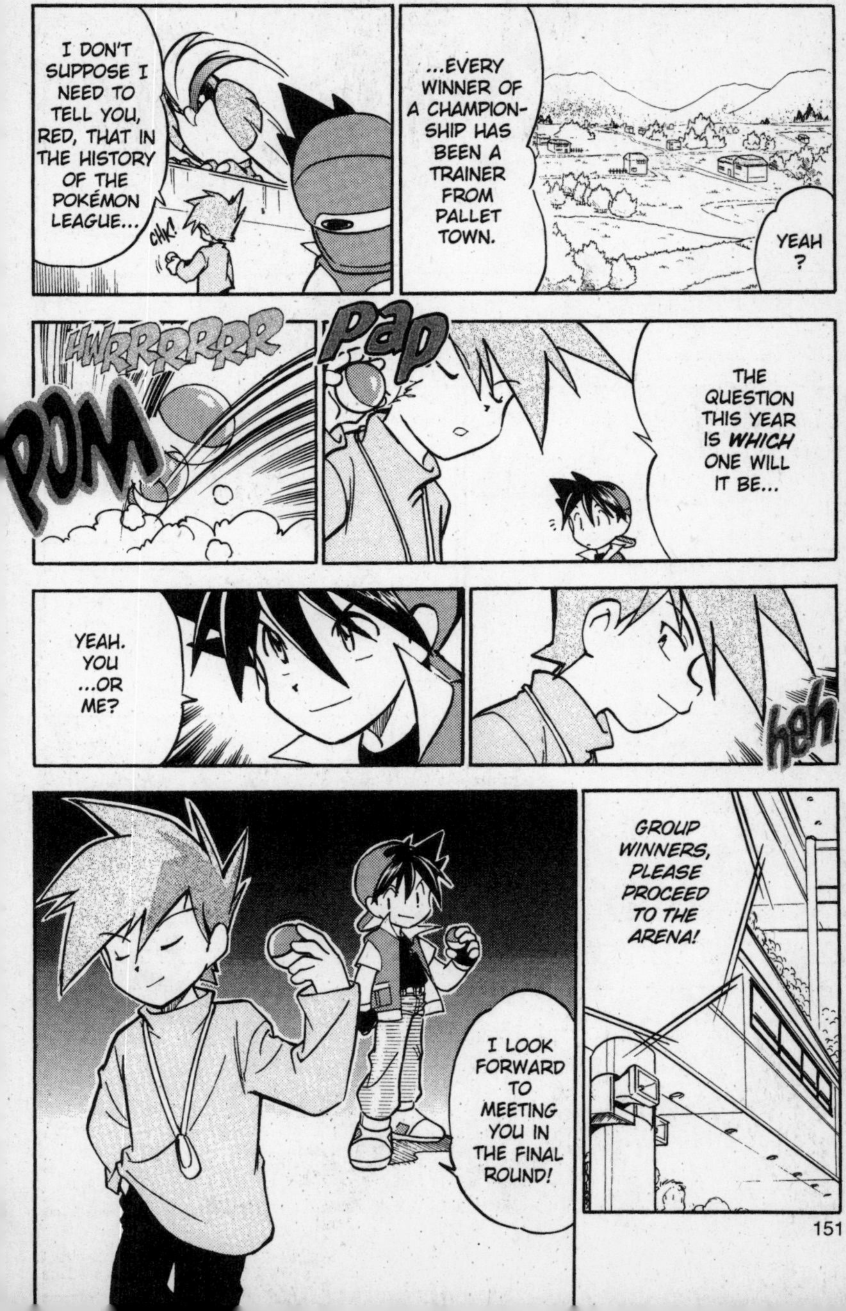

I DON'T SUPPOSE I NEED TO TELL YOU, RED, THAT IN THE HISTORY OF THE POKÉMON LEAGUE...
CHK!
...EVERY WINNER OF A CHAMPIONSHIP HAS BEEN A TRAINER FROM PALLET TOWN.
YEAH?
HWRRRRRRR
POM
PAP
THE QUESTION THIS YEAR IS *WHICH* ONE WILL IT BE...
YEAH. YOU ...OR ME?
heh
GROUP WINNERS, PLEASE PROCEED TO THE ARENA!
I LOOK FORWARD TO MEETING YOU IN THE FINAL ROUND!

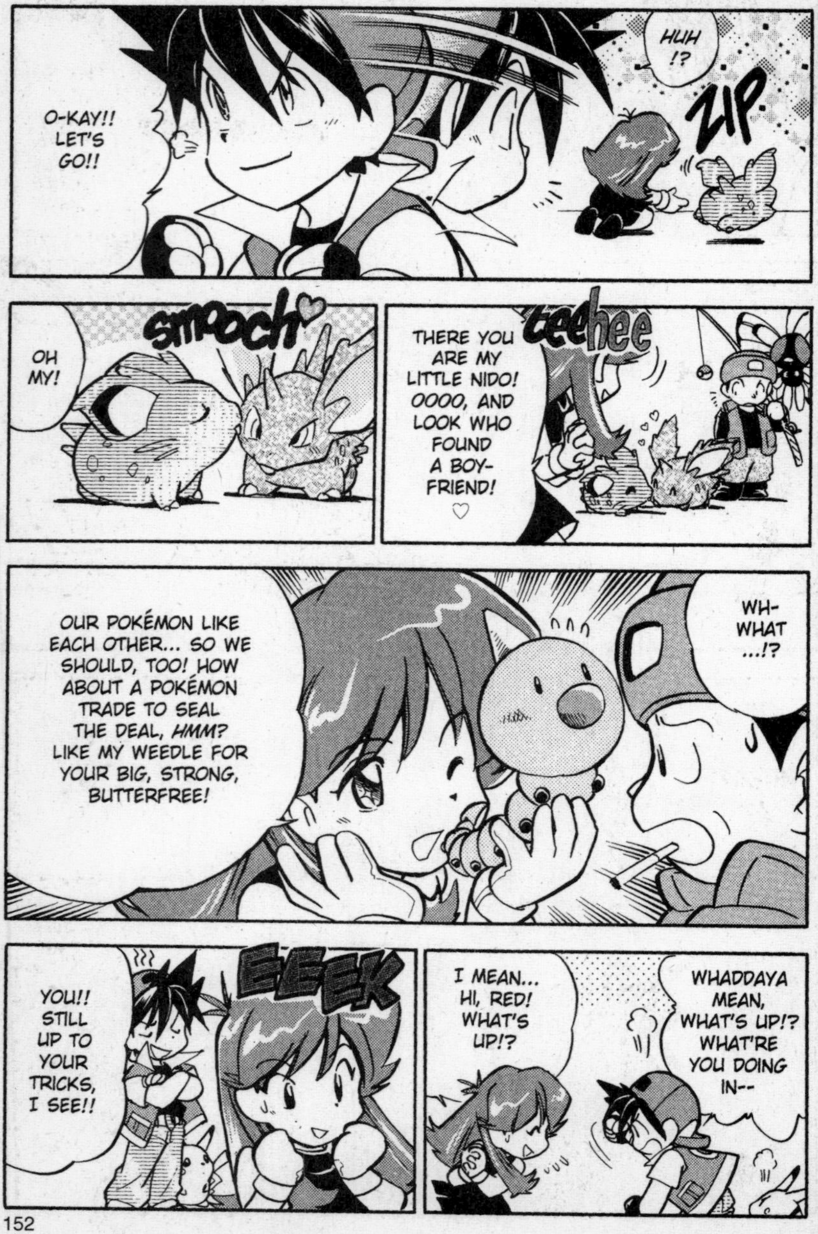
O-KAY!! LET'S GO!!
HUH !?
ZIP
OH MY!
SMOOCH
TEEHEE
THERE YOU ARE MY LITTLE NIDO! OOOO, AND LOOK WHO FOUND A BOY-FRIEND!
OUR POKÉMON LIKE EACH OTHER... SO WE SHOULD, TOO! HOW ABOUT A POKÉMON TRADE TO SEAL THE DEAL, HMM? LIKE MY WEEDLE FOR YOUR BIG, STRONG, BUTTERFREE!
WH-WHAT ...!?
YOU!! STILL UP TO YOUR TRICKS, I SEE!!
EEEK
I MEAN... HI, RED! WHAT'S UP!?
WHADDAYA MEAN, WHAT'S UP!? WHAT'RE YOU DOING IN--

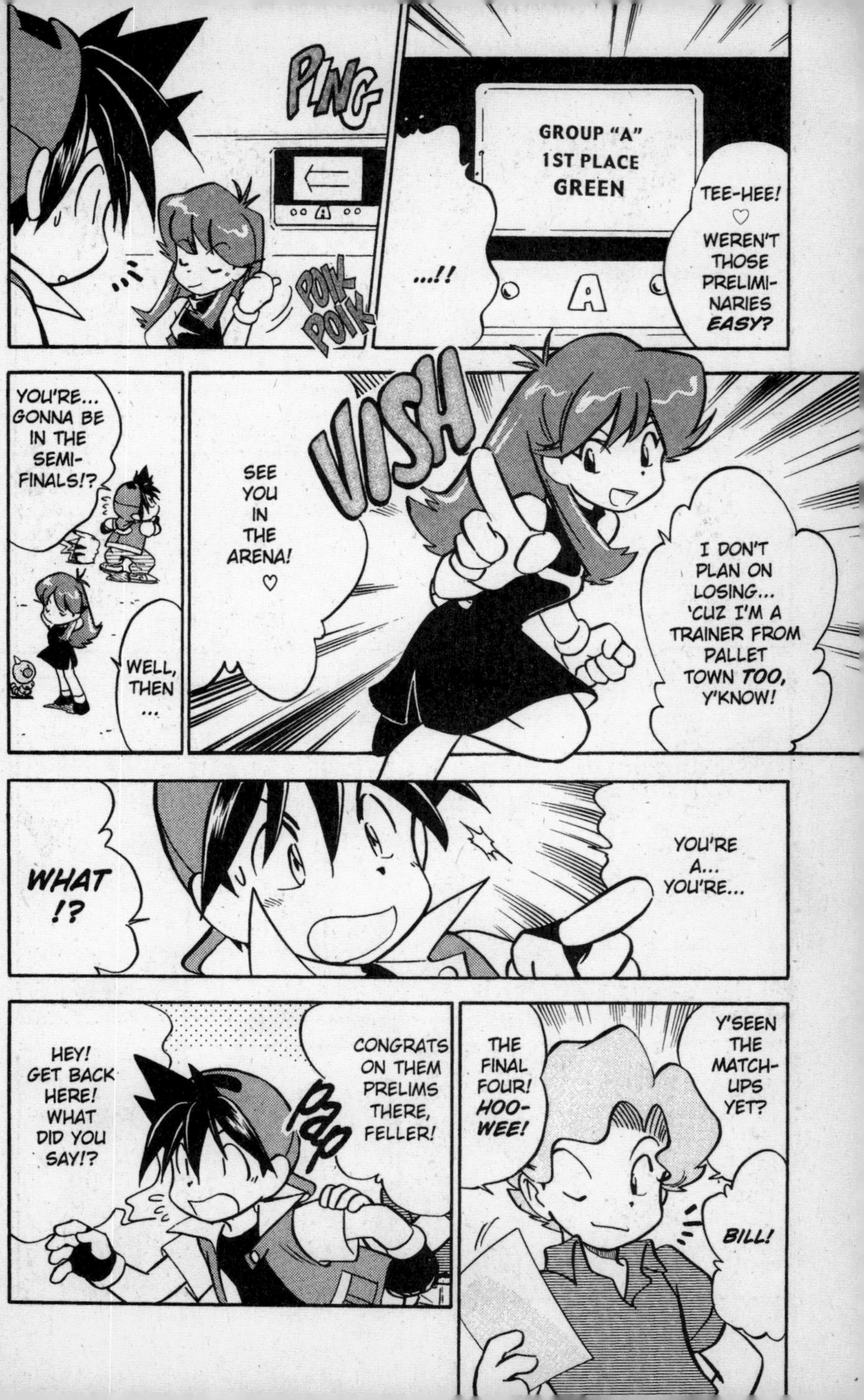

PING
POIK POIK
...!!
GROUP "A"
1ST PLACE
GREEN
TEE-HEE! ♡ WEREN'T THOSE PRELIMINARIES EASY?
YOU'RE... GONNA BE IN THE SEMI-FINALS!?
WELL, THEN ...
I DON'T PLAN ON LOSING... 'CUZ I'M A TRAINER FROM PALLET TOWN TOO, Y'KNOW!
VISH
SEE YOU IN THE ARENA! ♡
YOU'RE A... YOU'RE...
WHAT !?
HEY! GET BACK HERE! WHAT DID YOU SAY!?
PAP
CONGRATS ON THEM PRELIMS THERE, FELLER!
BILL!
THE FINAL FOUR! HOO-WEE!
Y'SEEN THE MATCH-UPS YET?

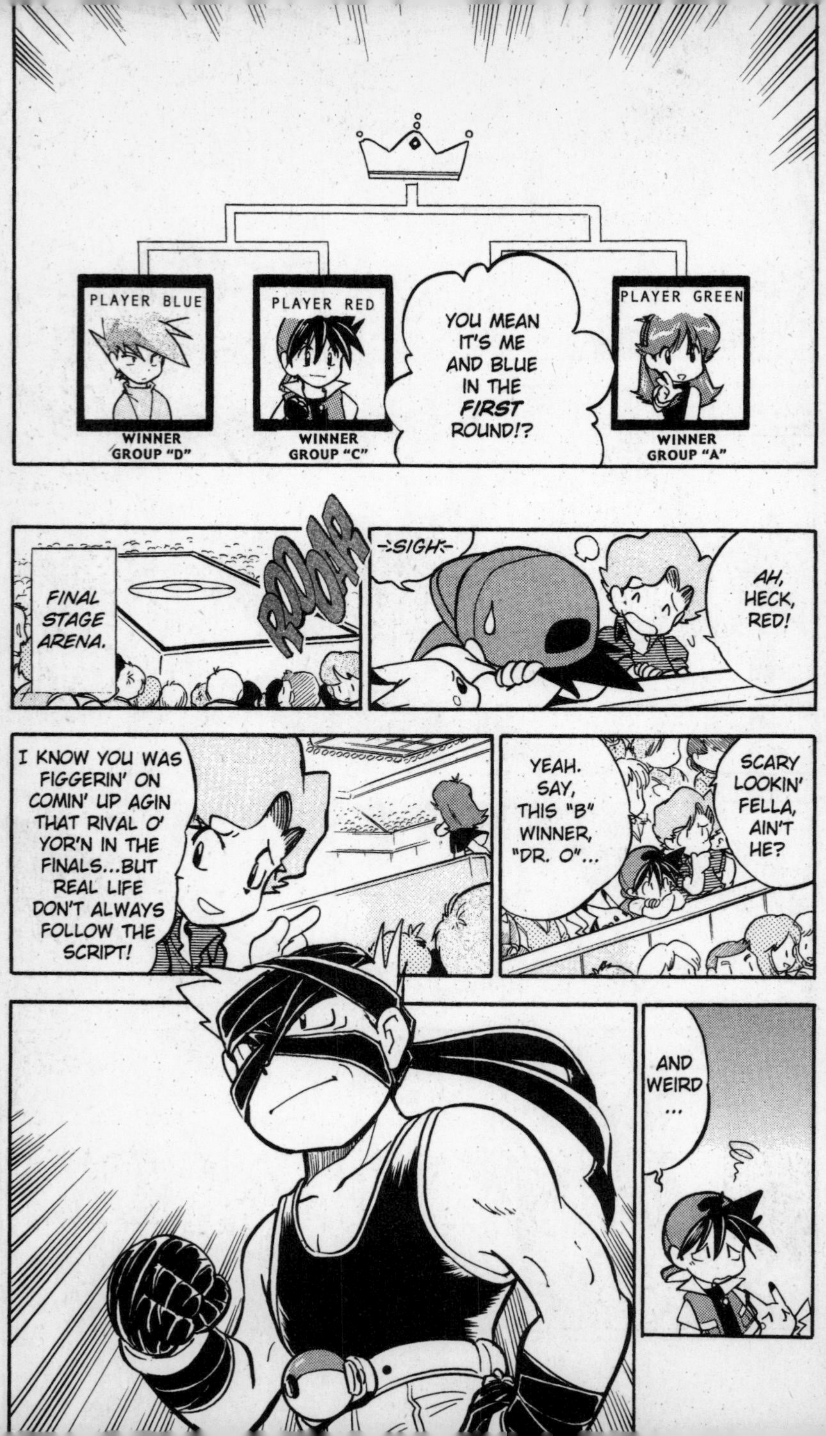
PLAYER BLUE
WINNER GROUP "D"
PLAYER RED
WINNER GROUP "C"
YOU MEAN IT'S ME AND BLUE IN THE FIRST ROUND!?
PLAYER GREEN
WINNER GROUP "A"
FINAL STAGE ARENA.
ROOAR
-SIGH-
AH, HECK, RED!
I KNOW YOU WAS FIGGERIN' ON COMIN' UP AGIN THAT RIVAL O' YOR'N IN THE FINALS...BUT REAL LIFE DON'T ALWAYS FOLLOW THE SCRIPT!
SCARY LOOKIN' FELLA, AIN'T HE?
YEAH. SAY, THIS "B" WINNER, "DR. O"...
AND WEIRD ...

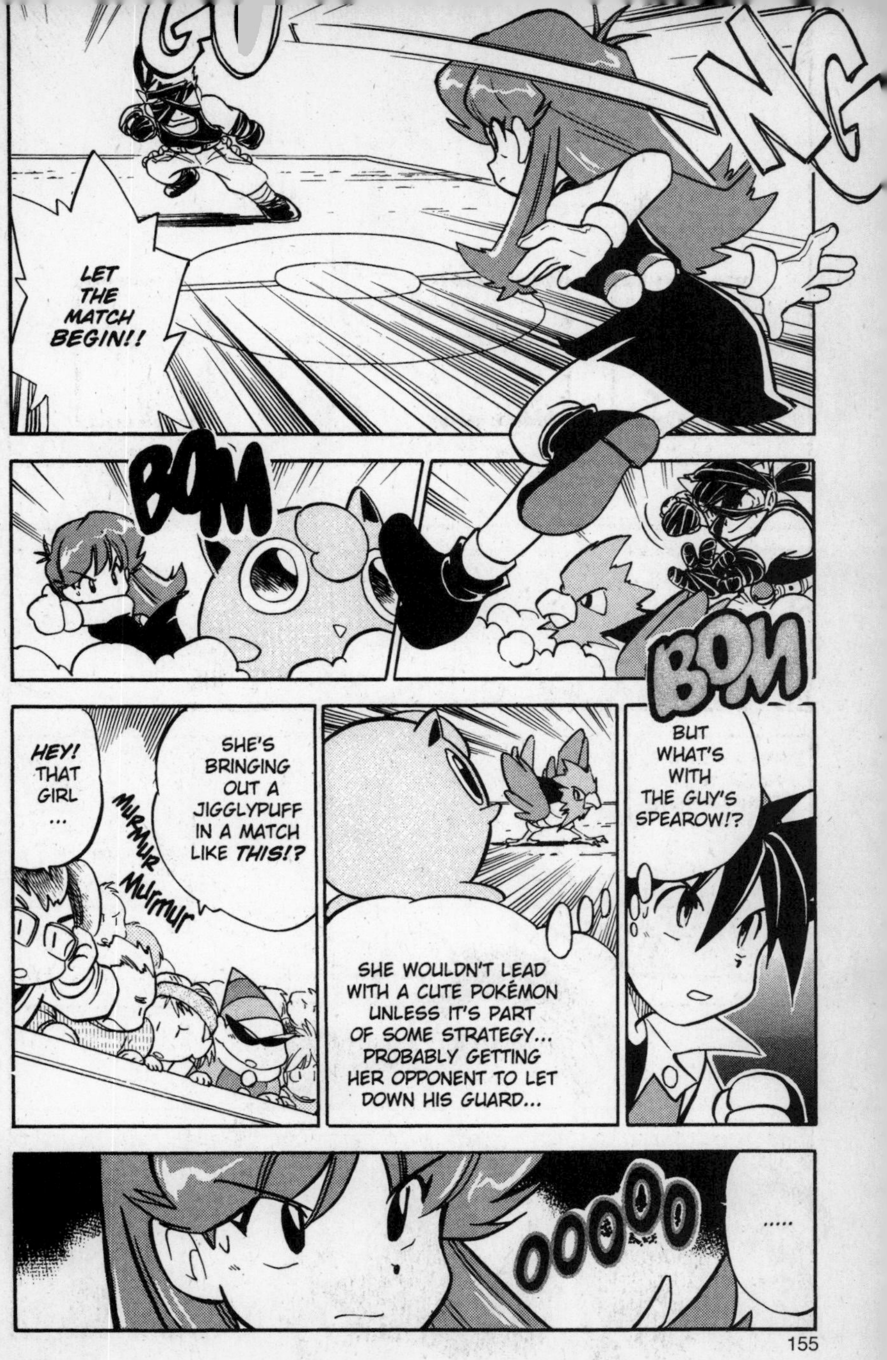
GO
NNG
LET THE MATCH BEGIN!!
BOM
BOM
HEY! THAT GIRL ...
MURMUR MURMUR
SHE'S BRINGING OUT A JIGGLYPUFF IN A MATCH LIKE THIS!?
SHE WOULDN'T LEAD WITH A CUTE POKÉMON UNLESS IT'S PART OF SOME STRATEGY... PROBABLY GETTING HER OPPONENT TO LET DOWN HIS GUARD...
BUT WHAT'S WITH THE GUY'S SPEAROW!?
OOOOO
.....

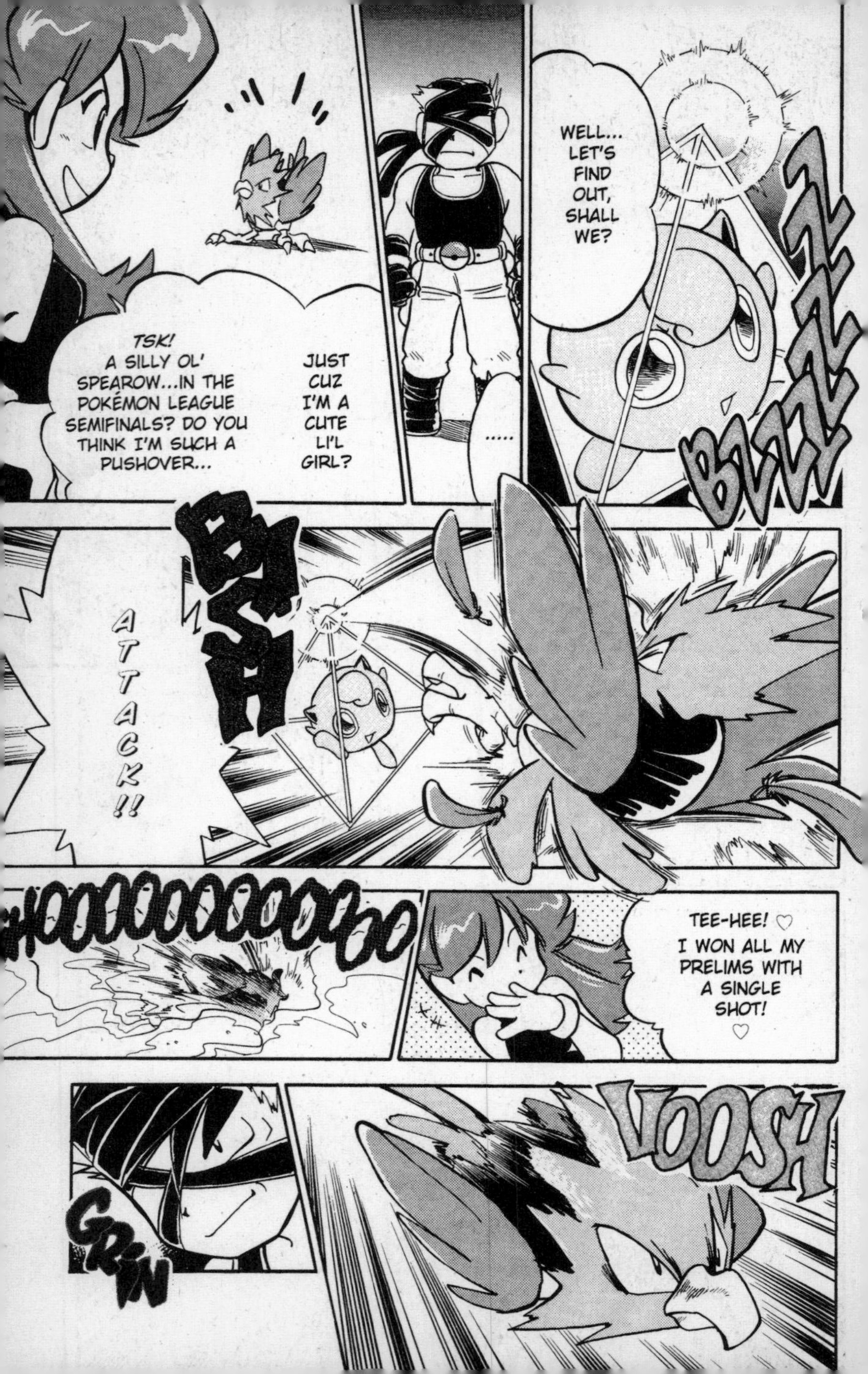
TSK!
A SILLY OL' SPEAROW...IN THE POKÉMON LEAGUE SEMIFINALS? DO YOU THINK I'M SUCH A PUSHOVER...
JUST CUZ I'M A CUTE LI'L GIRL?
.....
WELL... LET'S FIND OUT, SHALL WE?
BZZZZZZ
BASH
ATTACK!!
HOOOOOOOOOOO
TEE-HEE! ♡ I WON ALL MY PRELIMS WITH A SINGLE SHOT! ♡
GRIN
VOOSH

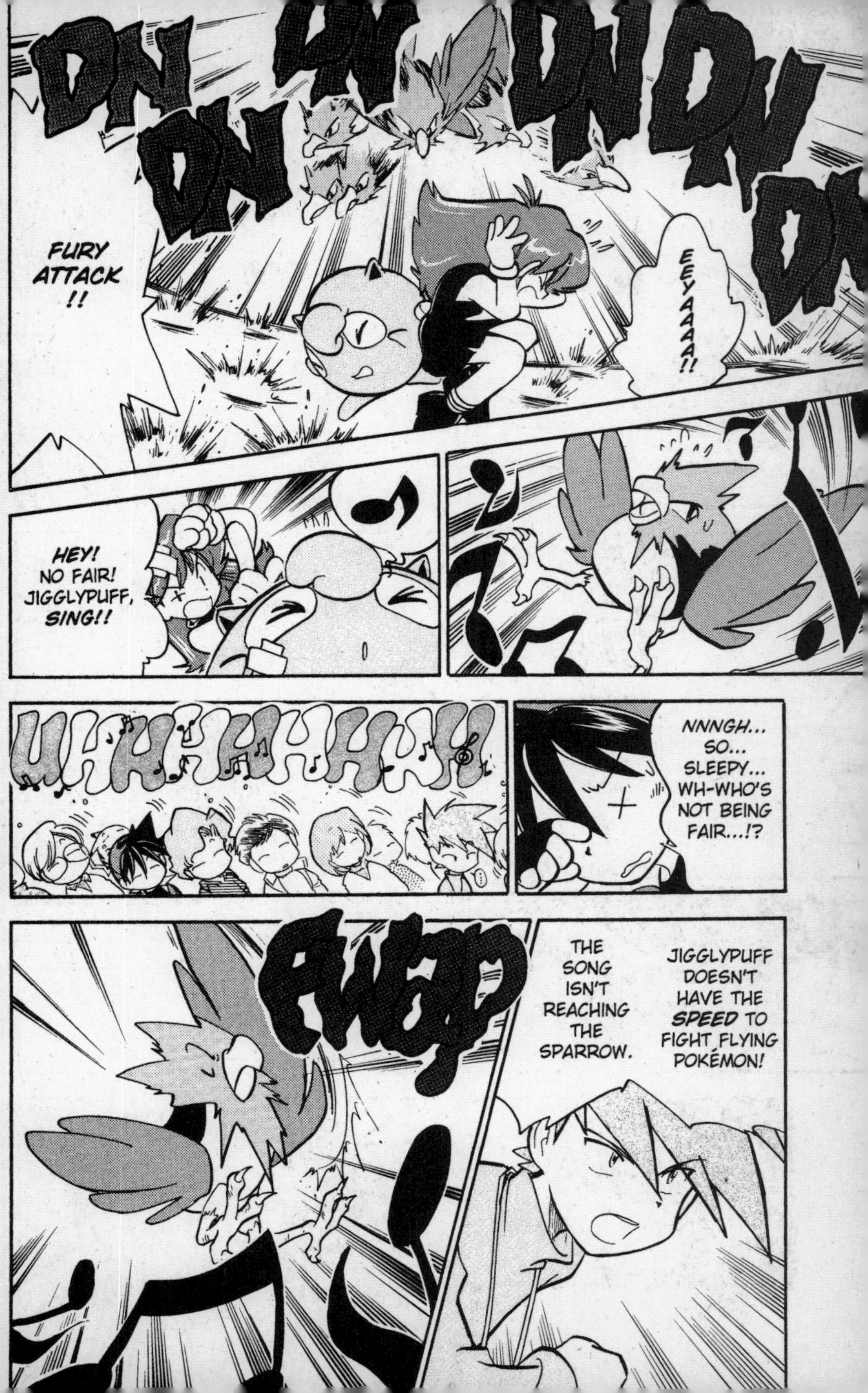
DN DN DN DN DN DN DN DN
FURY ATTACK !!
EEYAAAAA!!
HEY! NO FAIR! JIGGLYPUFF, SING!!
NNNGH... SO... SLEEPY... WH-WHO'S NOT BEING FAIR...!?
THE SONG ISN'T REACHING THE SPARROW.
JIGGLYPUFF DOESN'T HAVE THE SPEED TO FIGHT FLYING POKÉMON!

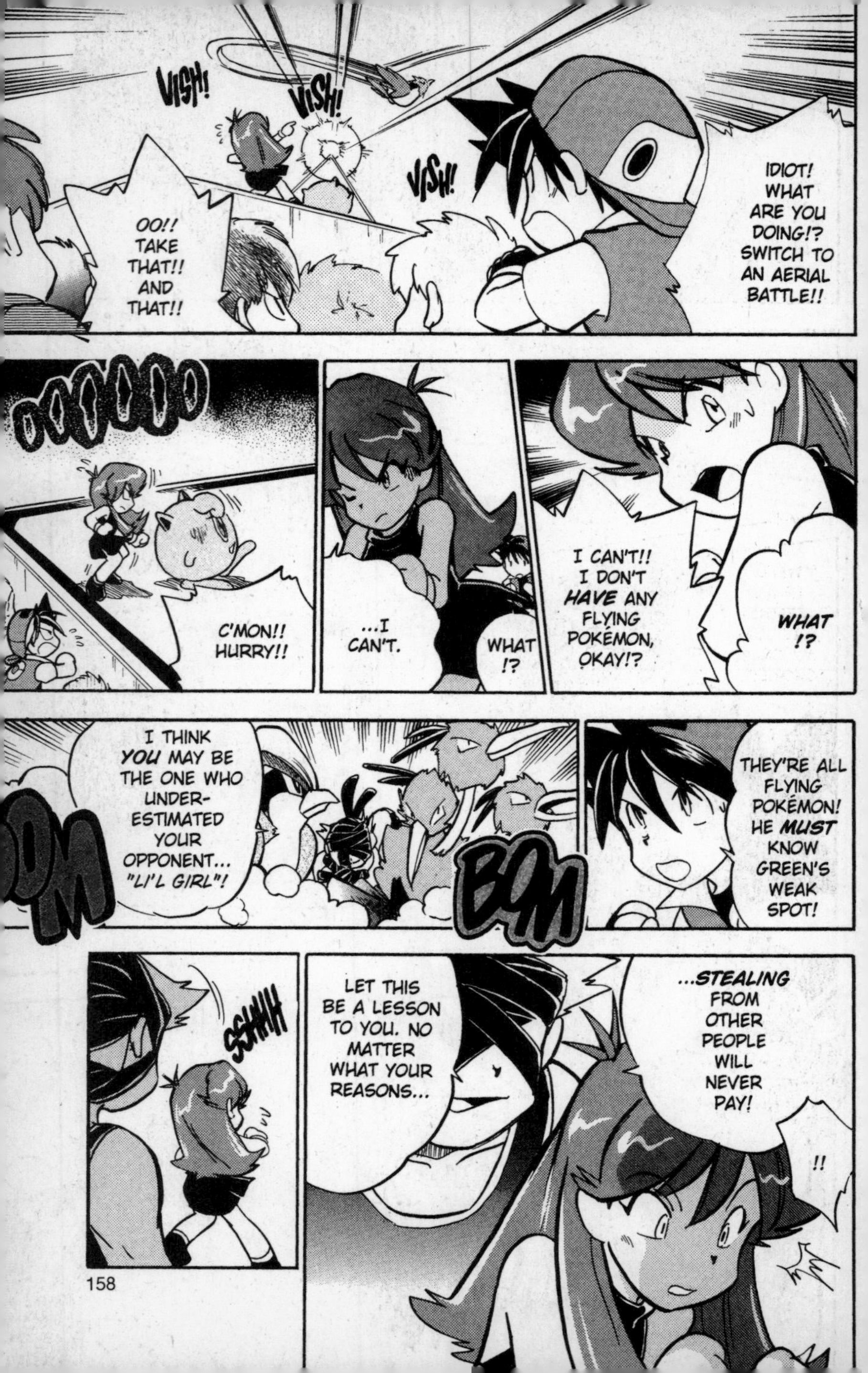
VISH!
VISH!
VISH!
IDIOT! WHAT ARE YOU DOING!? SWITCH TO AN AERIAL BATTLE!!
OO!! TAKE THAT!! AND THAT!!
C'MON!! HURRY!!
...I CAN'T.
WHAT !?
I CAN'T!! I DON'T *HAVE* ANY FLYING POKÉMON, OKAY!?
WHAT !?
I THINK *YOU* MAY BE THE ONE WHO UNDER-ESTIMATED YOUR OPPONENT... "LI'L GIRL"!
BOM
THEY'RE ALL FLYING POKÉMON! HE *MUST* KNOW GREEN'S WEAK SPOT!
SSHHH
LET THIS BE A LESSON TO YOU. NO MATTER WHAT YOUR REASONS...
...*STEALING* FROM OTHER PEOPLE WILL NEVER PAY!
!!

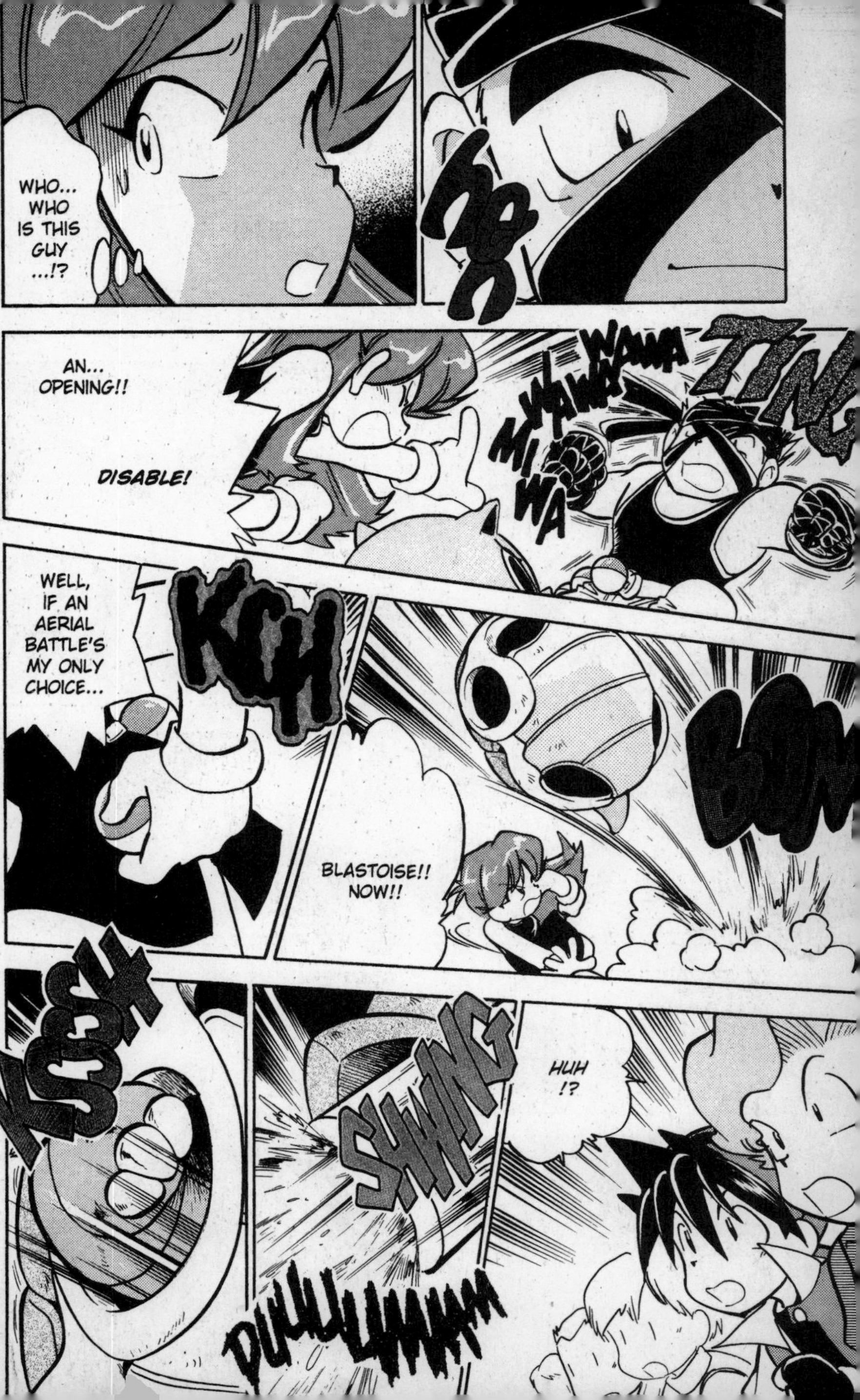
WHO... WHO IS THIS GUY ...!?
AN... OPENING!!
DISABLE!
TING
WELL, IF AN AERIAL BATTLE'S MY ONLY CHOICE...
KCH
BLASTOISE!! NOW!!
SWING
HUH !?

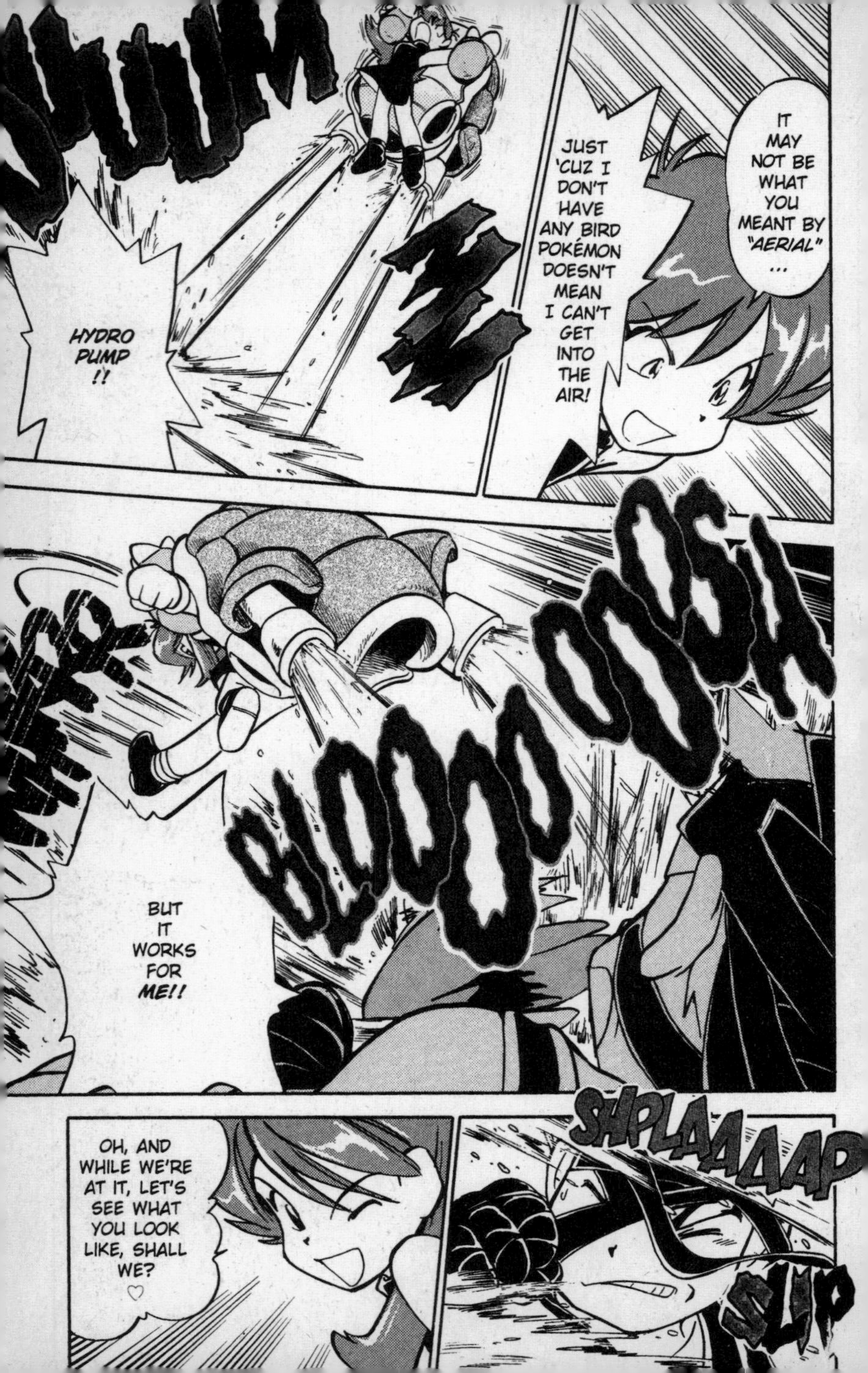
HYDRO PUMP!!
JUST 'CUZ I DON'T HAVE ANY BIRD POKÉMON DOESN'T MEAN I CAN'T GET INTO THE AIR!
IT MAY NOT BE WHAT YOU MEANT BY "AERIAL" ...
BUT IT WORKS FOR ME!!
OH, AND WHILE WE'RE AT IT, LET'S SEE WHAT YOU LOOK LIKE, SHALL WE? ♡
SHPLAAAAAP
SLIP

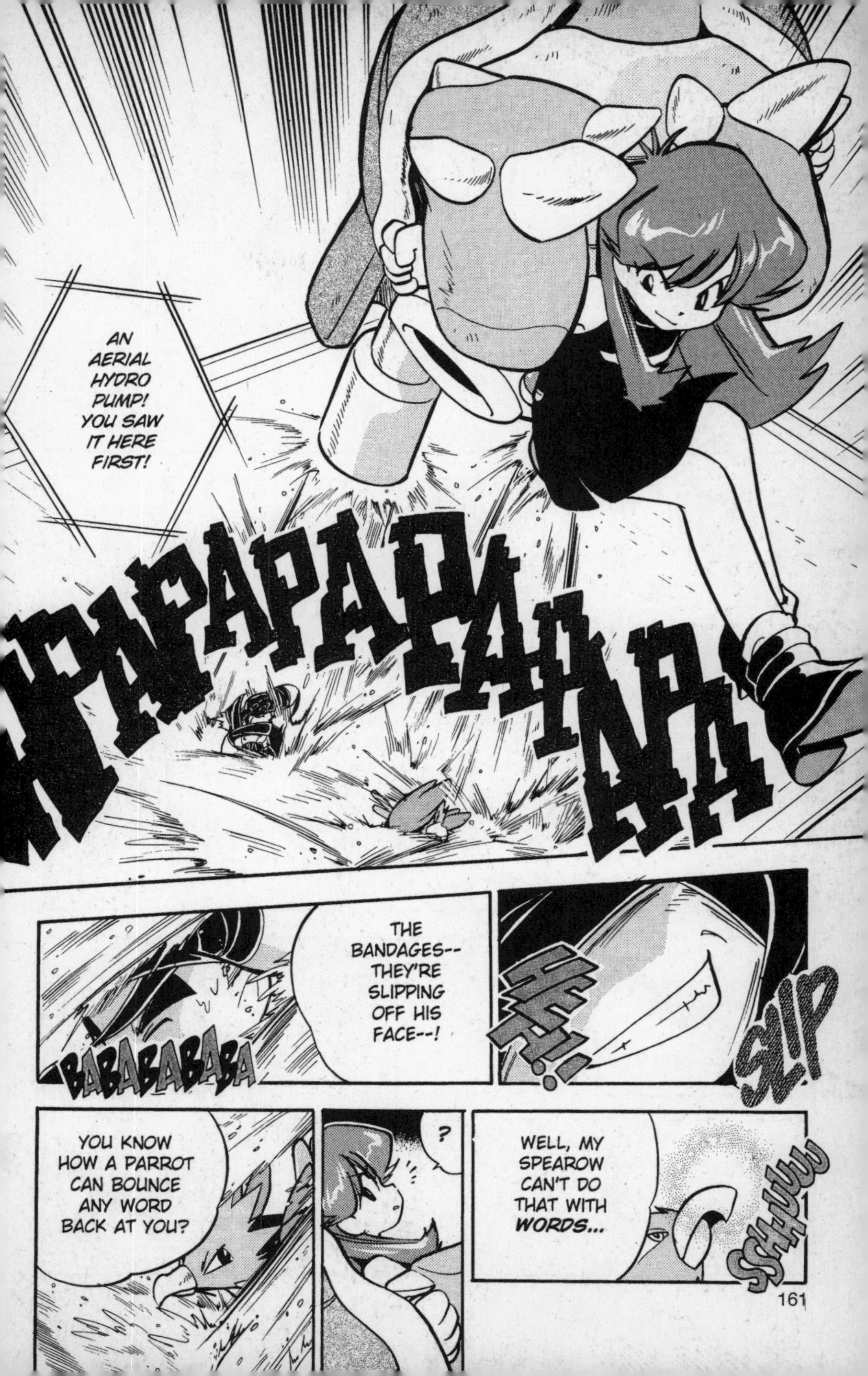
AN AERIAL HYDRO PUMP! YOU SAW IT HERE FIRST!
PAPAPAPAPAPAPA
BABABABABA
THE BANDAGES-- THEY'RE SLIPPING OFF HIS FACE--!
HEH!
SLIP
YOU KNOW HOW A PARROT CAN BOUNCE ANY WORD BACK AT YOU?
?
WELL, MY SPEAROW CAN'T DO THAT WITH ***WORDS...***
SSHUUU

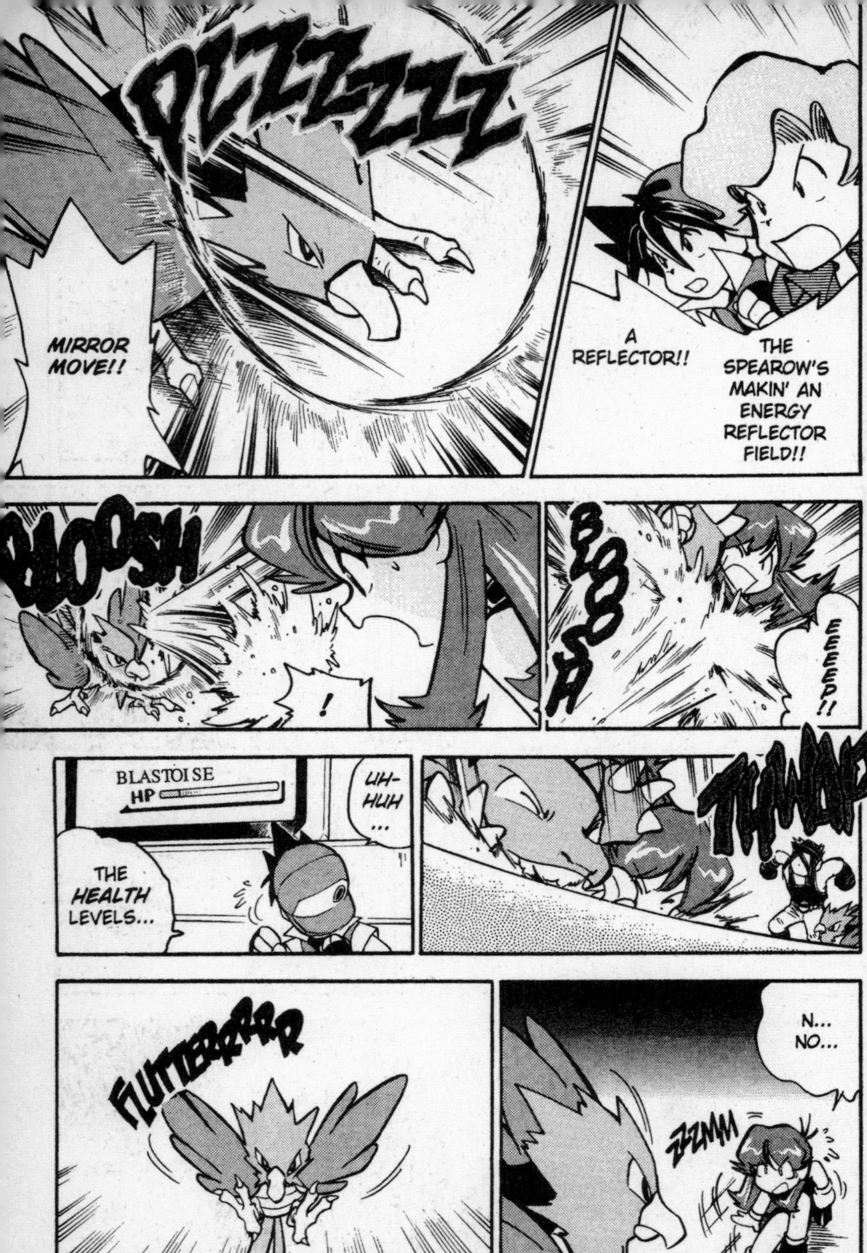
PZZZZZZ
MIRROR MOVE!!
A REFLECTOR!!
THE SPEAROW'S MAKIN' AN ENERGY REFLECTOR FIELD!!
BLOOSH
!
BLOOSH
EEEEEP!!
BLASTOISE
HP
UH-HUH...
THE HEALTH LEVELS...
THWAP
FLUTTERRRR
N... NO...

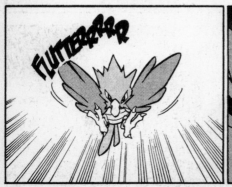

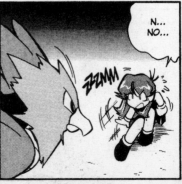

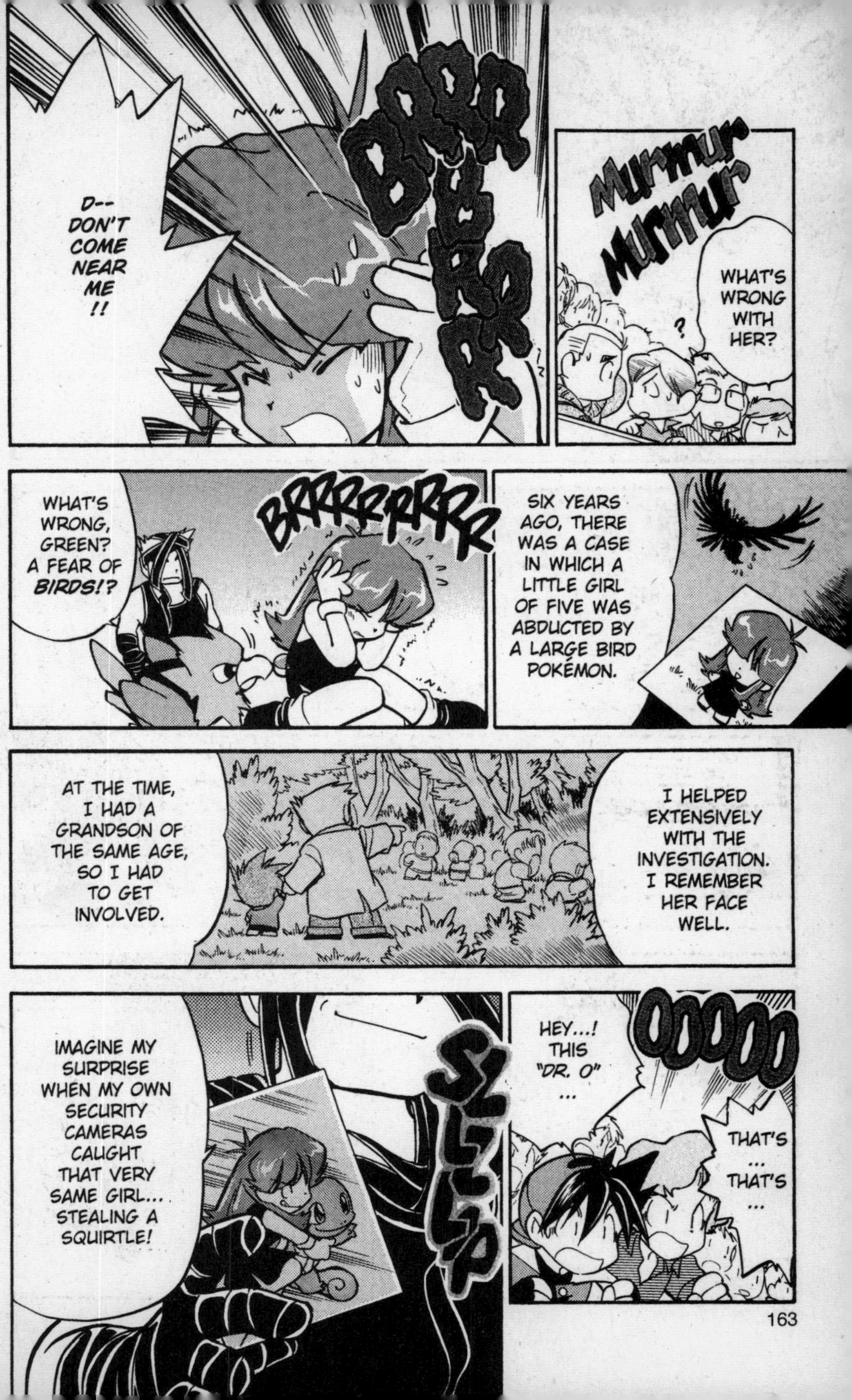
D-- DON'T COME NEAR ME !!
BRRR RRR RR
MURMUR MURMUR
WHAT'S WRONG WITH HER?
WHAT'S WRONG, GREEN? A FEAR OF *BIRDS!?*
BRRRRRRRRR
SIX YEARS AGO, THERE WAS A CASE IN WHICH A LITTLE GIRL OF FIVE WAS ABDUCTED BY A LARGE BIRD POKÉMON.
AT THE TIME, I HAD A GRANDSON OF THE SAME AGE, SO I HAD TO GET INVOLVED.
I HELPED EXTENSIVELY WITH THE INVESTIGATION. I REMEMBER HER FACE WELL.
IMAGINE MY SURPRISE WHEN MY OWN SECURITY CAMERAS CAUGHT THAT VERY SAME GIRL... STEALING A SQUIRTLE!
SLLLLP
OOOOO
HEY...! THIS "DR. O" ...
THAT'S ... THAT'S ...

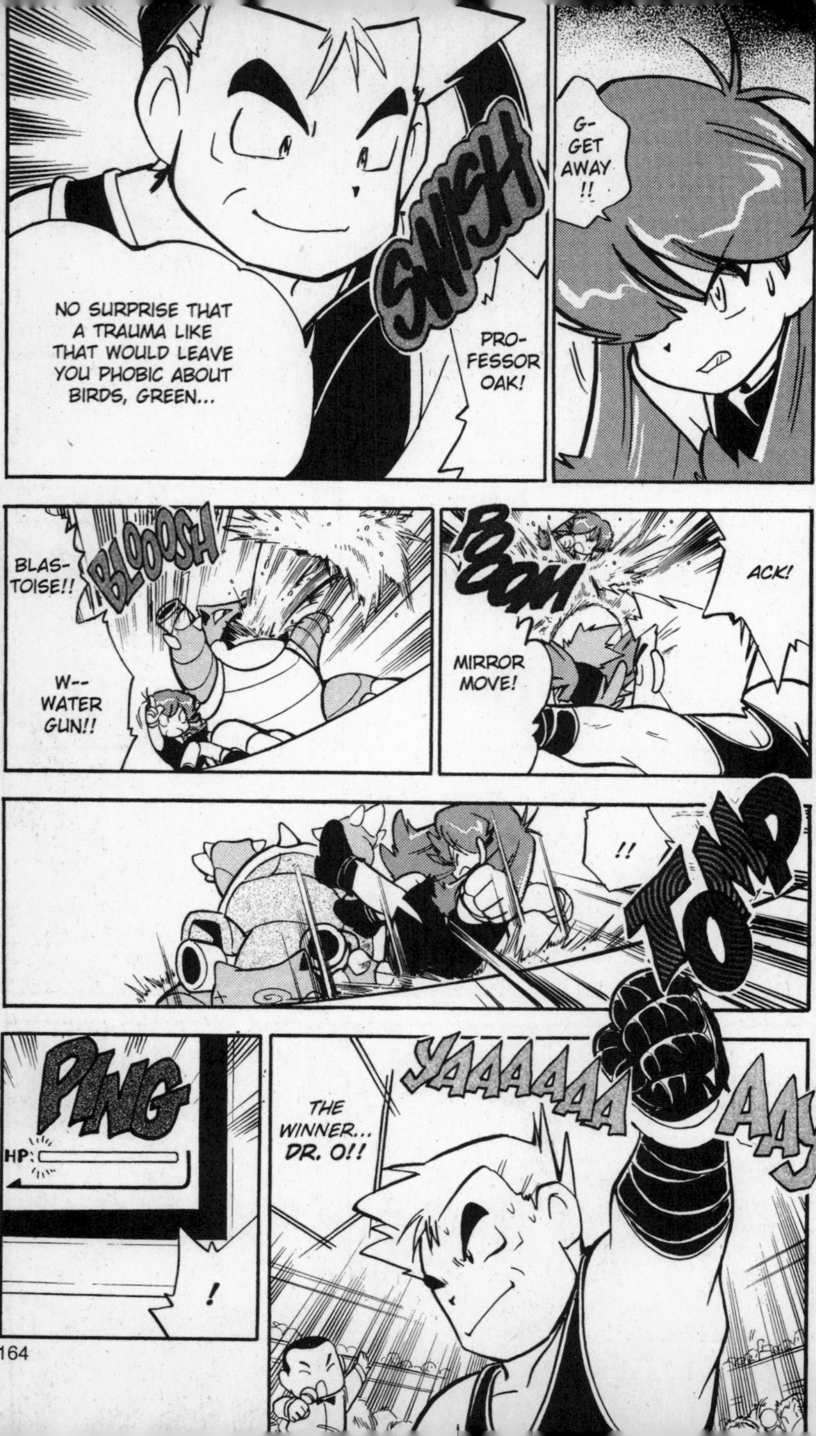
NO SURPRISE THAT A TRAUMA LIKE THAT WOULD LEAVE YOU PHOBIC ABOUT BIRDS, GREEN...
SWISH
PROFESSOR OAK!
G-GET AWAY!!
BLAS-TOISE!!
BLOOOSH
W--WATER GUN!!
BOOOM
ACK!
MIRROR MOVE!
!!
TOMP
PING
HP:
!
YAAAAAAAAAY
THE WINNER... DR. O!!

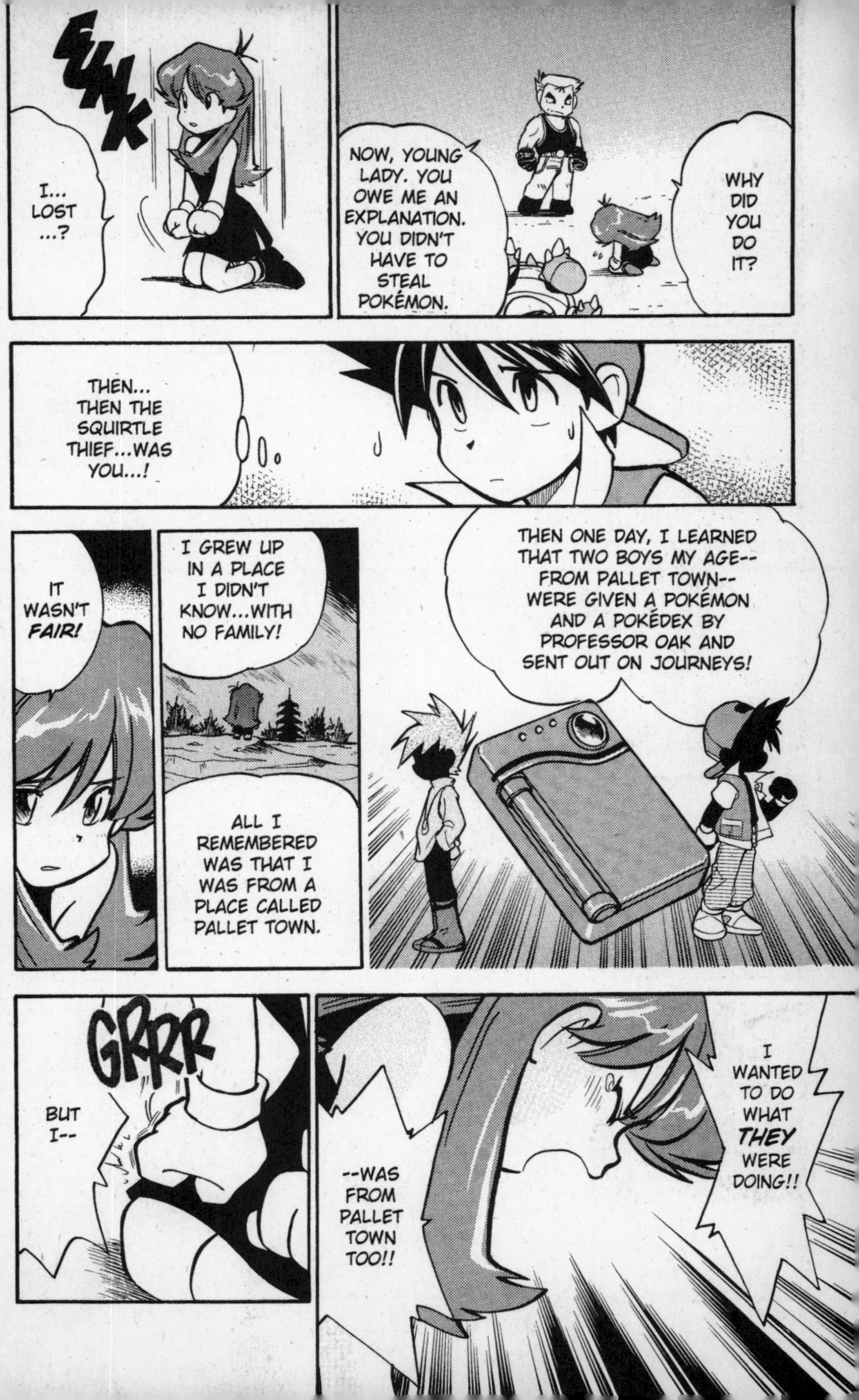
I... LOST ...?
NOW, YOUNG LADY. YOU OWE ME AN EXPLANATION. YOU DIDN'T HAVE TO STEAL POKÉMON.
WHY DID YOU DO IT?
THEN... THEN THE SQUIRTLE THIEF...WAS YOU...!
IT WASN'T *FAIR!*
I GREW UP IN A PLACE I DIDN'T KNOW...WITH NO FAMILY!
ALL I REMEMBERED WAS THAT I WAS FROM A PLACE CALLED PALLET TOWN.
THEN ONE DAY, I LEARNED THAT TWO BOYS MY AGE-- FROM PALLET TOWN-- WERE GIVEN A POKÉMON AND A POKÉDEX BY PROFESSOR OAK AND SENT OUT ON JOURNEYS!
GRRR
BUT I--
--WAS FROM PALLET TOWN TOO!!
I WANTED TO DO WHAT *THEY* WERE DOING!!

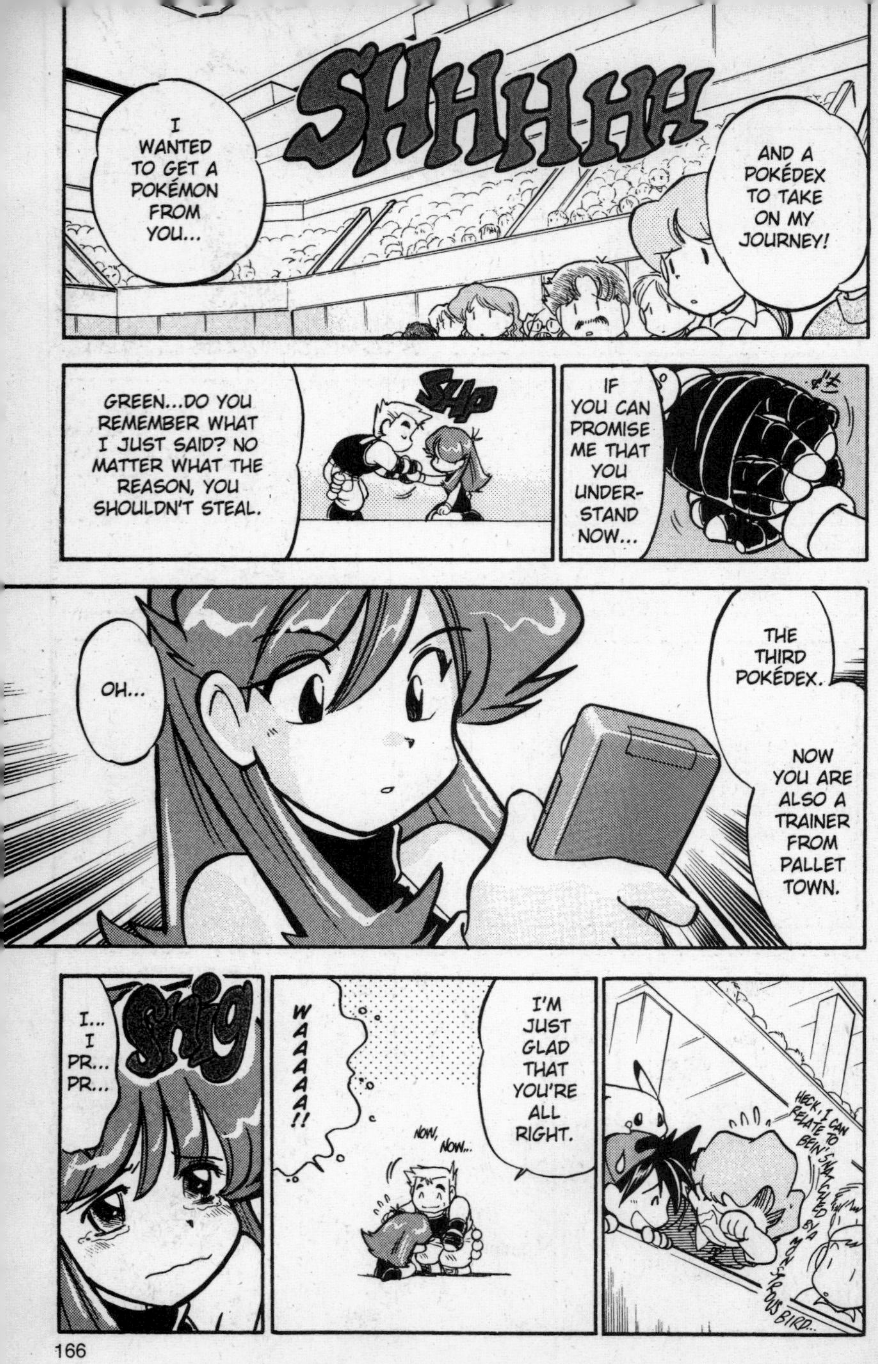
SHHHHH
I WANTED TO GET A POKÉMON FROM YOU...
AND A POKÉDEX TO TAKE ON MY JOURNEY!
SHP
GREEN...DO YOU REMEMBER WHAT I JUST SAID? NO MATTER WHAT THE REASON, YOU SHOULDN'T STEAL.
IF YOU CAN PROMISE ME THAT YOU UNDER-STAND NOW...
THE THIRD POKÉDEX.
NOW YOU ARE ALSO A TRAINER FROM PALLET TOWN.
OH...
SNIG
I... I PR... PR...
WAAAAAA!!
I'M JUST GLAD THAT YOU'RE ALL RIGHT.
NOW, NOW...
HECK, I CAN RELATE TO BEIN' SNATCHED BY A MONSTROUS BIRD...

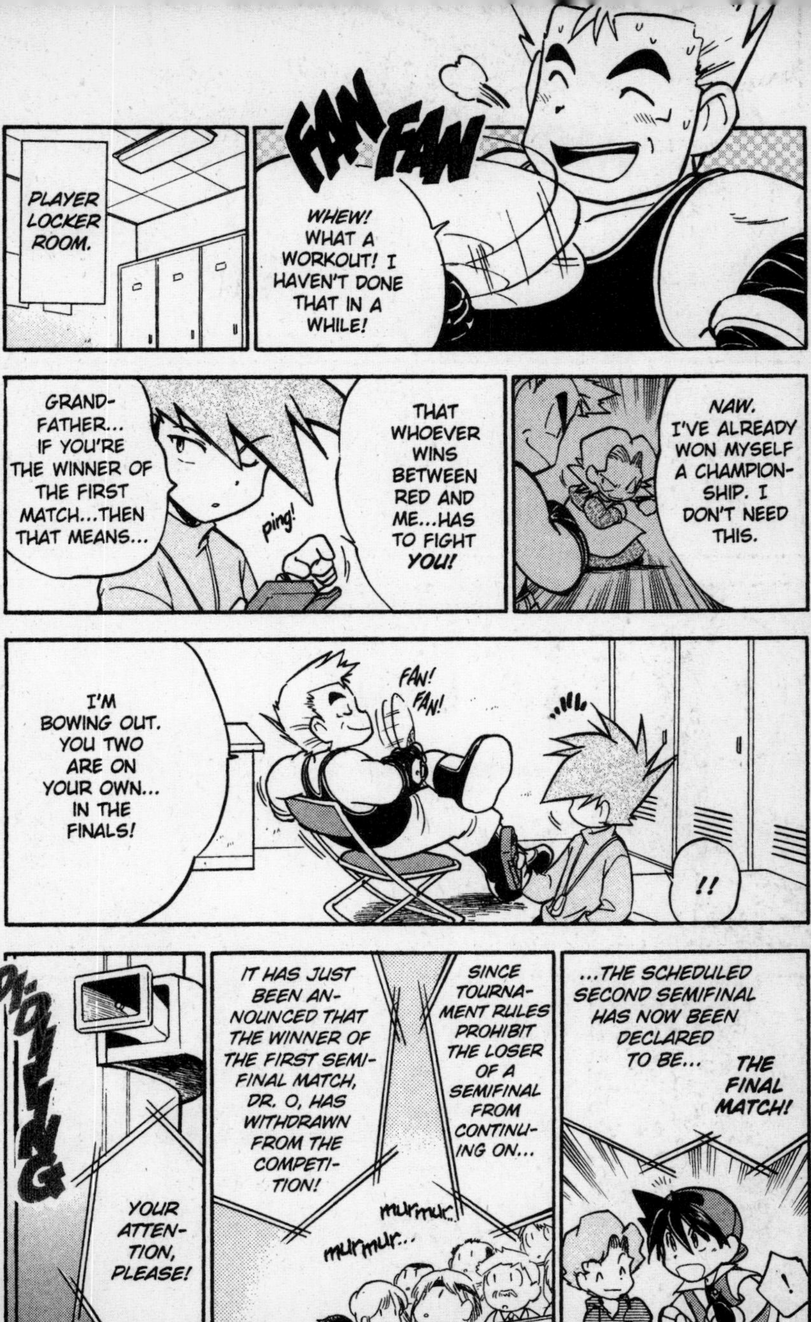
PLAYER LOCKER ROOM.
FAN FAN
WHEW! WHAT A WORKOUT! I HAVEN'T DONE THAT IN A WHILE!
GRAND-FATHER... IF YOU'RE THE WINNER OF THE FIRST MATCH...THEN THAT MEANS...
ping!
THAT WHOEVER WINS BETWEEN RED AND ME...HAS TO FIGHT YOU!
NAW. I'VE ALREADY WON MYSELF A CHAMPION-SHIP. I DON'T NEED THIS.
I'M BOWING OUT. YOU TWO ARE ON YOUR OWN... IN THE FINALS!
FAN! FAN!
!!
YOUR ATTEN-TION, PLEASE!
IT HAS JUST BEEN AN-NOUNCED THAT THE WINNER OF THE FIRST SEMI-FINAL MATCH, DR. O, HAS WITHDRAWN FROM THE COMPETI-TION!
SINCE TOURNA-MENT RULES PROHIBIT THE LOSER OF A SEMIFINAL FROM CONTINU-ING ON...
murmur...
murmur...
...THE SCHEDULED SECOND SEMIFINAL HAS NOW BEEN DECLARED TO BE...
THE FINAL MATCH!
!

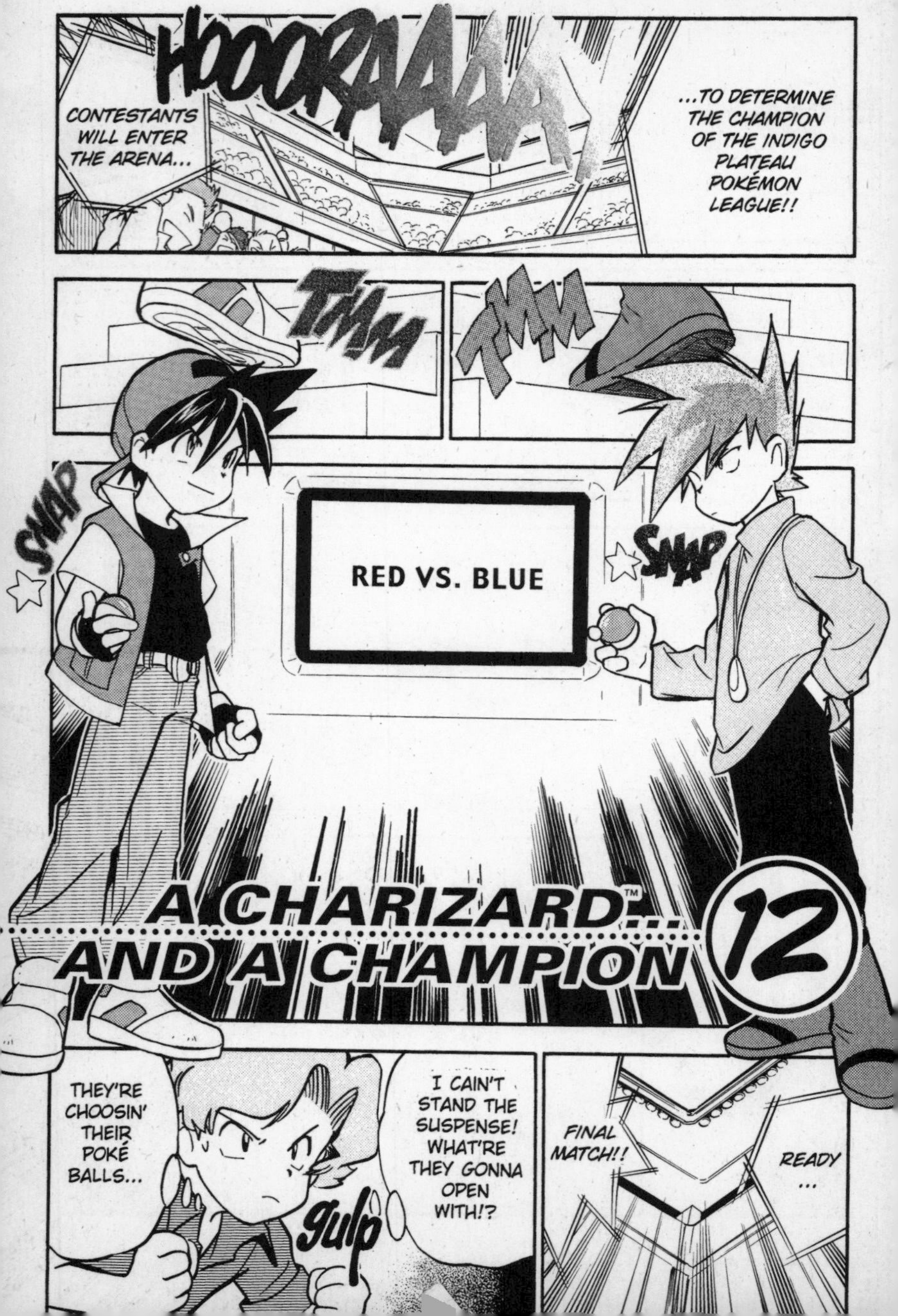
HOOORAAAA
...TO DETERMINE THE CHAMPION OF THE INDIGO PLATEAU POKÉMON LEAGUE!!
CONTESTANTS WILL ENTER THE ARENA...
TMM
TMM
RED VS. BLUE
SNAP
SNAP
A CHARIZARD™... AND A CHAMPION
12
READY ...
FINAL MATCH!!
I CAIN'T STAND THE SUSPENSE! WHAT'RE THEY GONNA OPEN WITH!?
THEY'RE CHOOSIN' THEIR POKÉ BALLS...
gulp

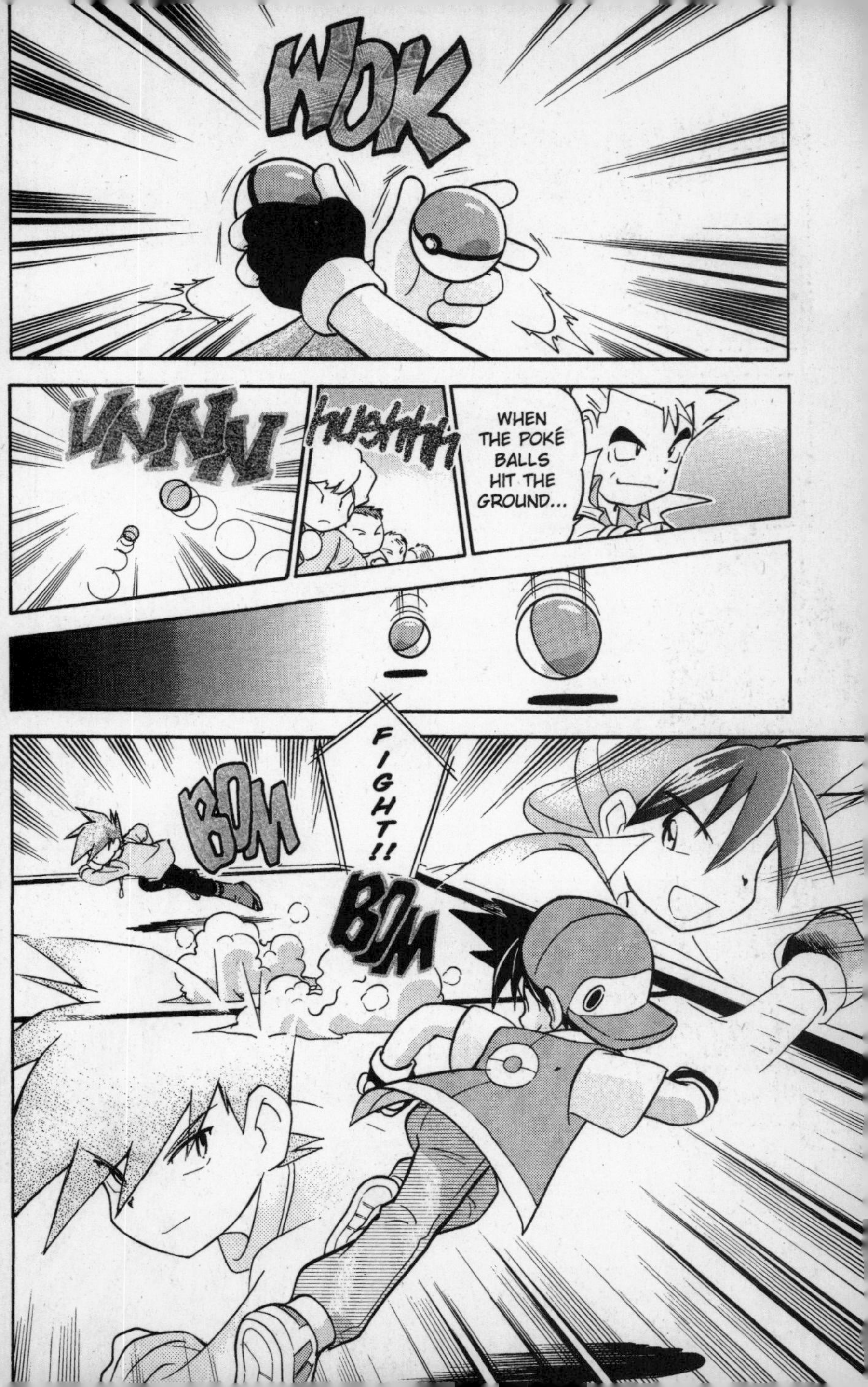
WOK
VNNN
hushhh
WHEN THE POKÉ BALLS HIT THE GROUND...
FIGHT!!
BOM
BOM

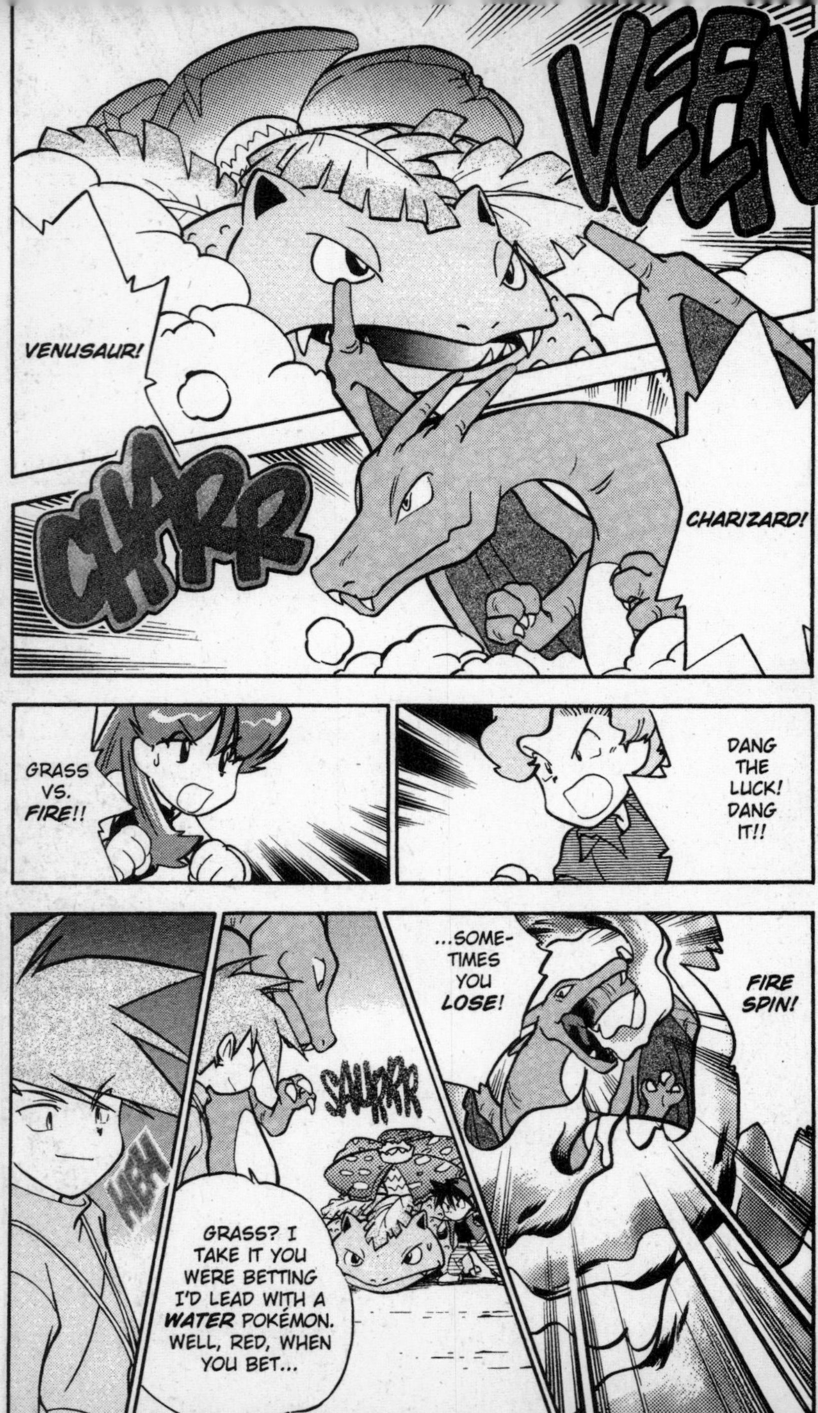
VEEN
VENUSAUR!
CHARR
CHARIZARD!
GRASS VS. FIRE!!
DANG THE LUCK! DANG IT!!
HEH
GRASS? I TAKE IT YOU WERE BETTING I'D LEAD WITH A WATER POKÉMON. WELL, RED, WHEN YOU BET...
SAURRR
...SOMETIMES YOU LOSE!
FIRE SPIN!

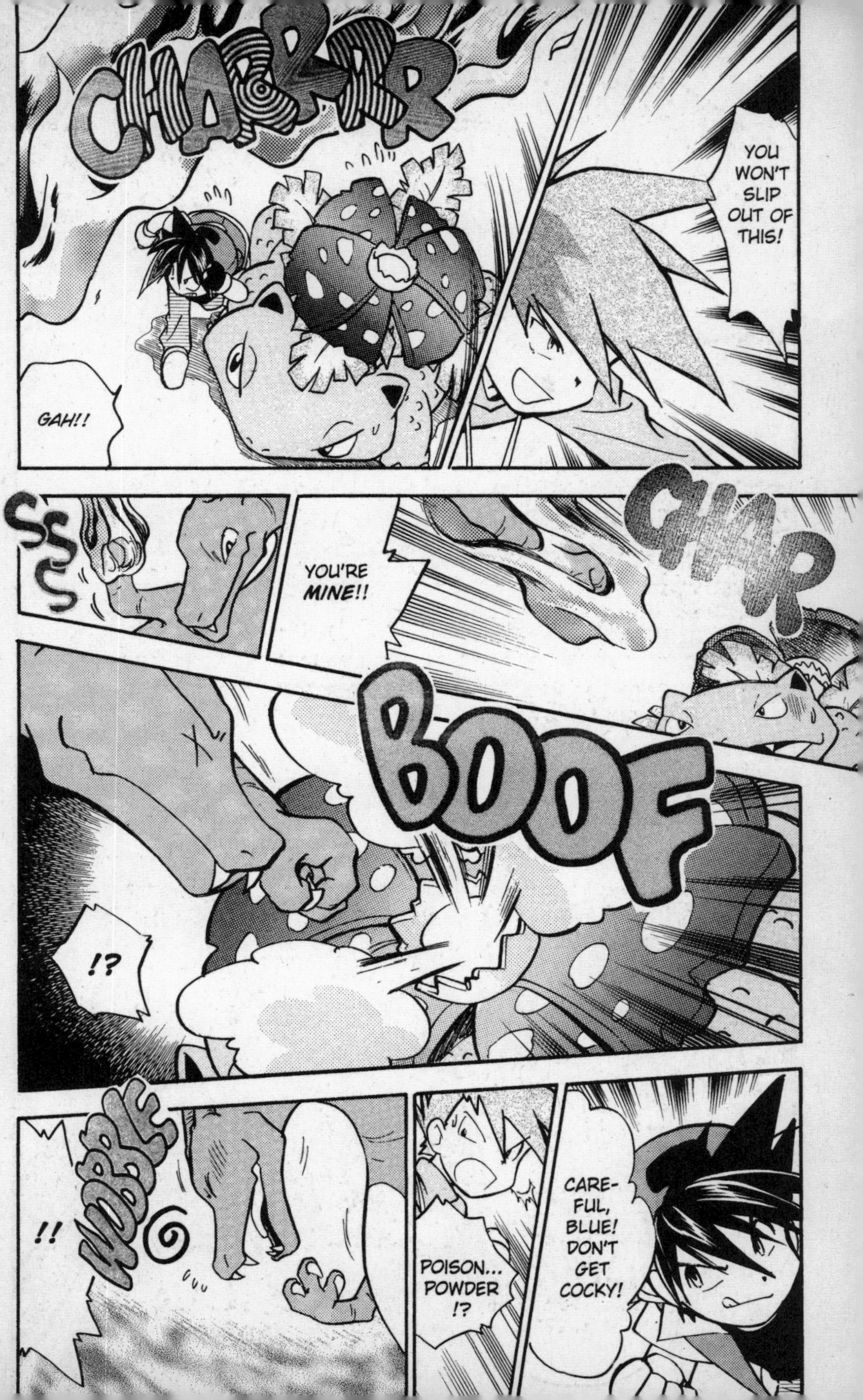
CHARRR
YOU WON'T SLIP OUT OF THIS!
GAH!!
CHAR
YOU'RE MINE!!
SSS
BOOF
!?
CARE-FUL, BLUE! DON'T GET COCKY!
POISON... POWDER !?
!!
WOBBLE

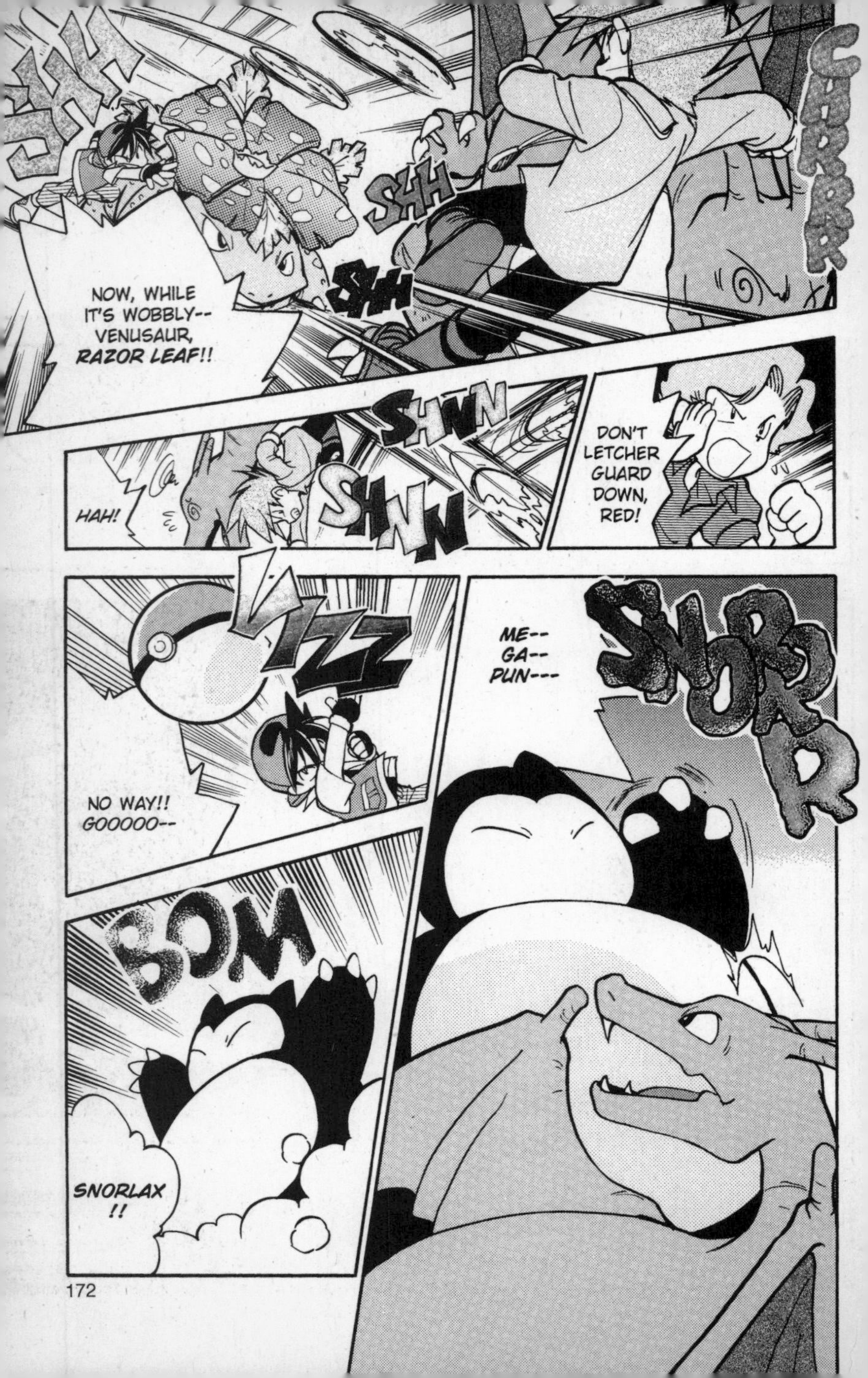
CHRRR
SHH
SHH
NOW, WHILE IT'S WOBBLY-- VENUSAUR, RAZOR LEAF!!
DON'T LETCHER GUARD DOWN, RED!
SHNN
SHNN
HAH!
VIZZ
NO WAY!! GOOOOO--
SNORRR
ME-- GA-- PUN---
BOM
SNORLAX !!

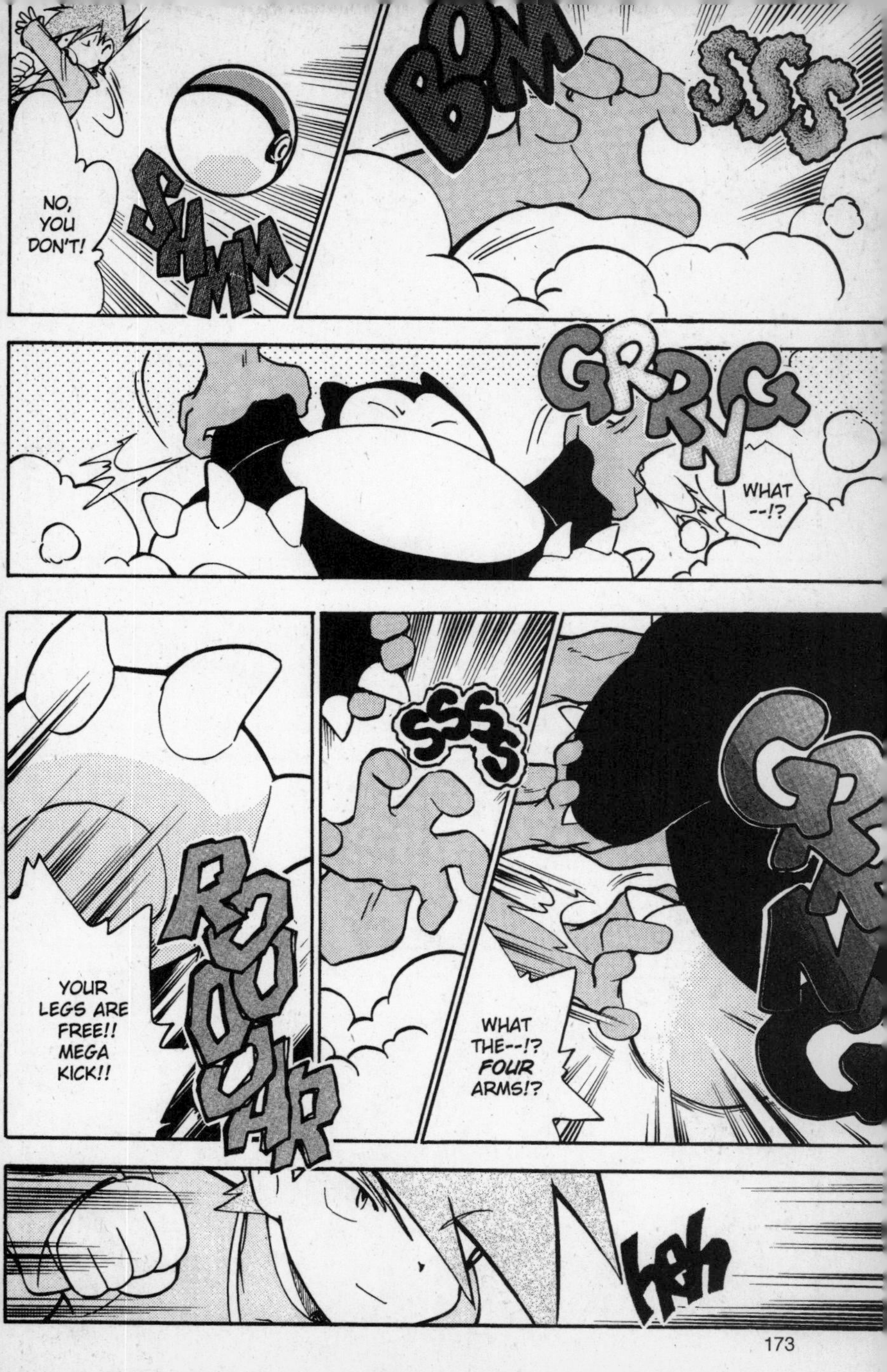
NO, YOU DON'T!
SHMMM
BOOM
SSS
GRRRNG
WHAT --!?
YOUR LEGS ARE FREE!! MEGA KICK!!
ROOOOAR
SSSS
WHAT THE--!? *FOUR* ARMS!?
heh

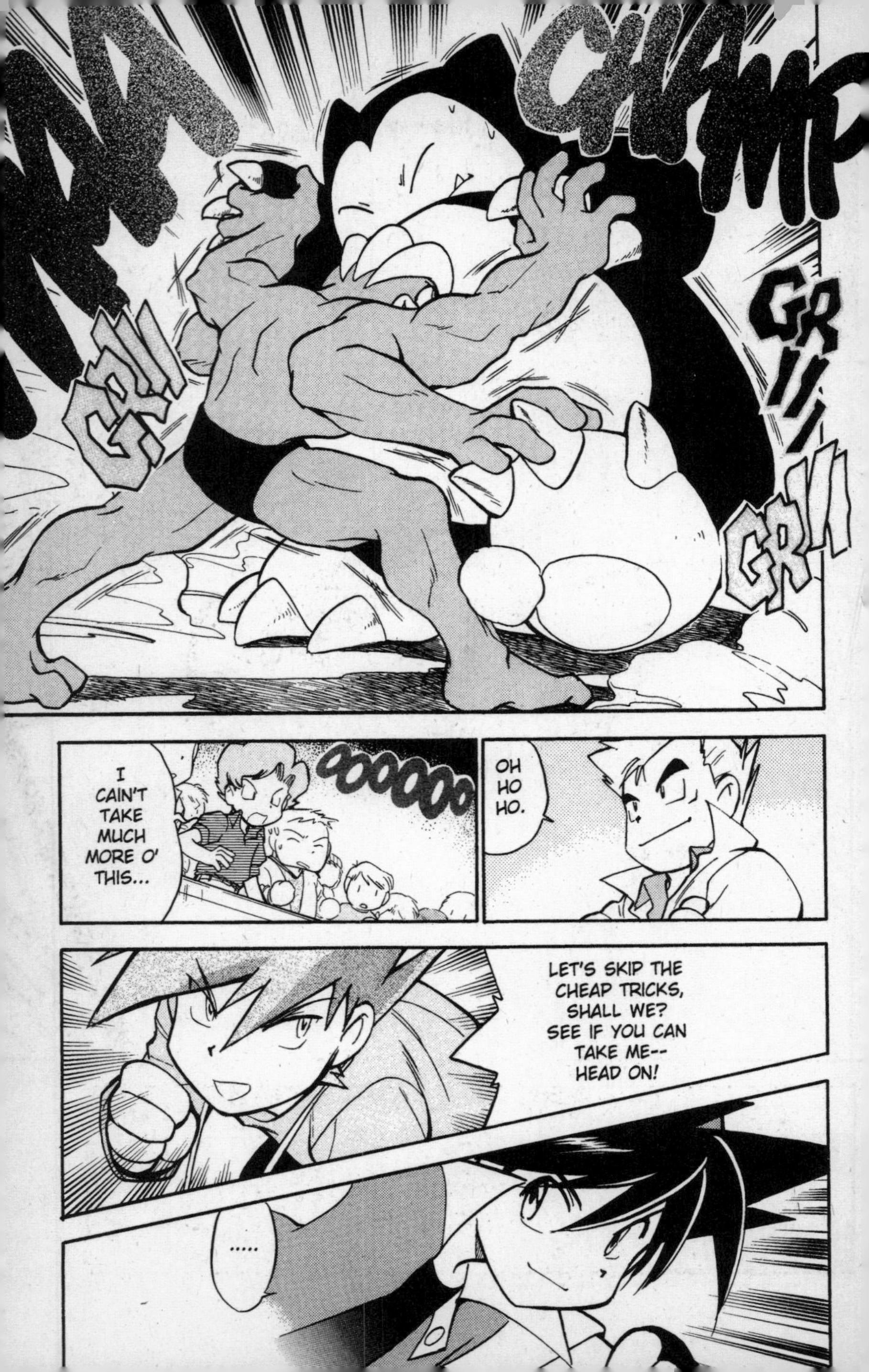

CHAMP
GR
GRI
GRI
I CAIN'T TAKE MUCH MORE O' THIS...
OOOOOOO
OH HO HO.
LET'S SKIP THE CHEAP TRICKS, SHALL WE? SEE IF YOU CAN TAKE ME--HEAD ON!
.....

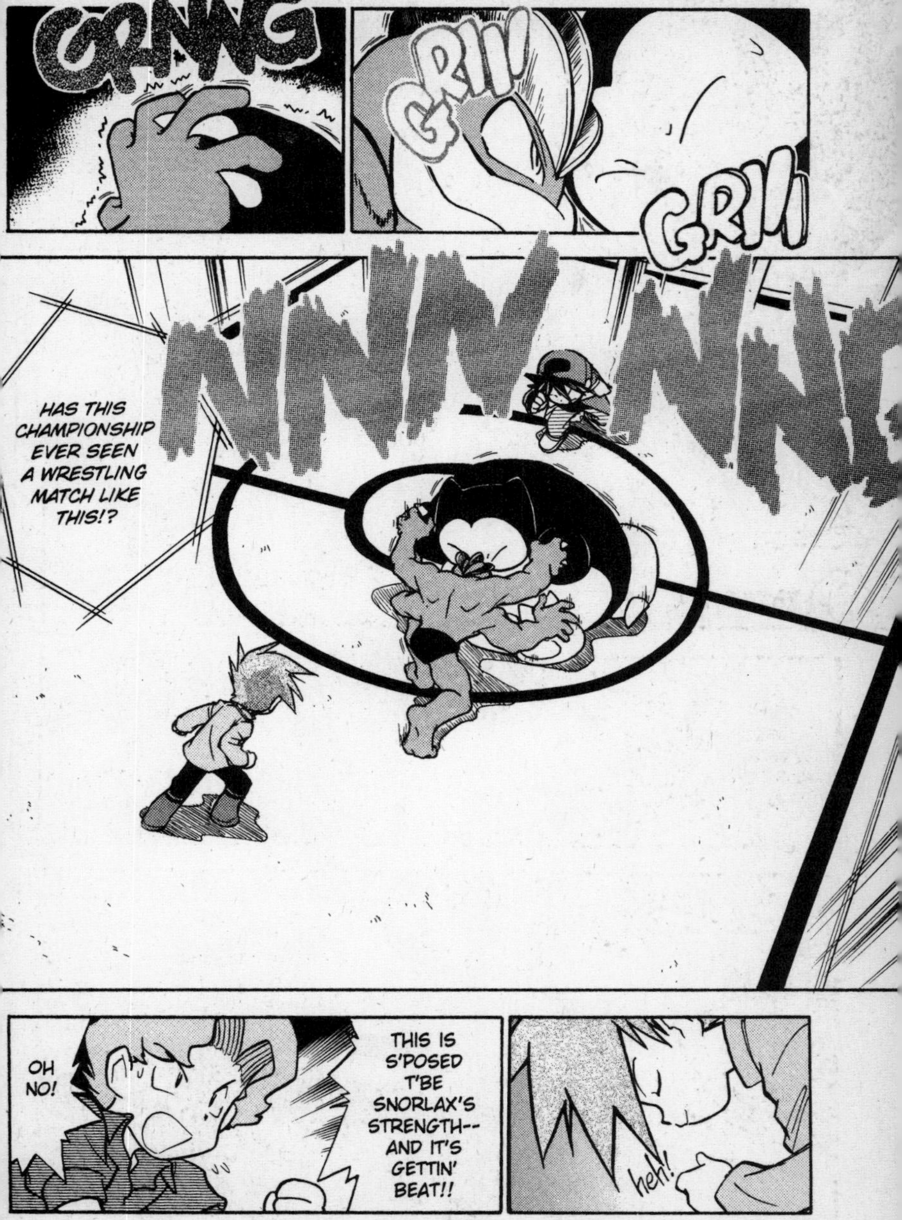
GRNWG
GRII
GRII
NNNNNN
HAS THIS CHAMPIONSHIP EVER SEEN A WRESTLING MATCH LIKE THIS!?
OH NO!
THIS IS S'POSED T'BE SNORLAX'S STRENGTH-- AND IT'S GETTIN' BEAT!!
heh!

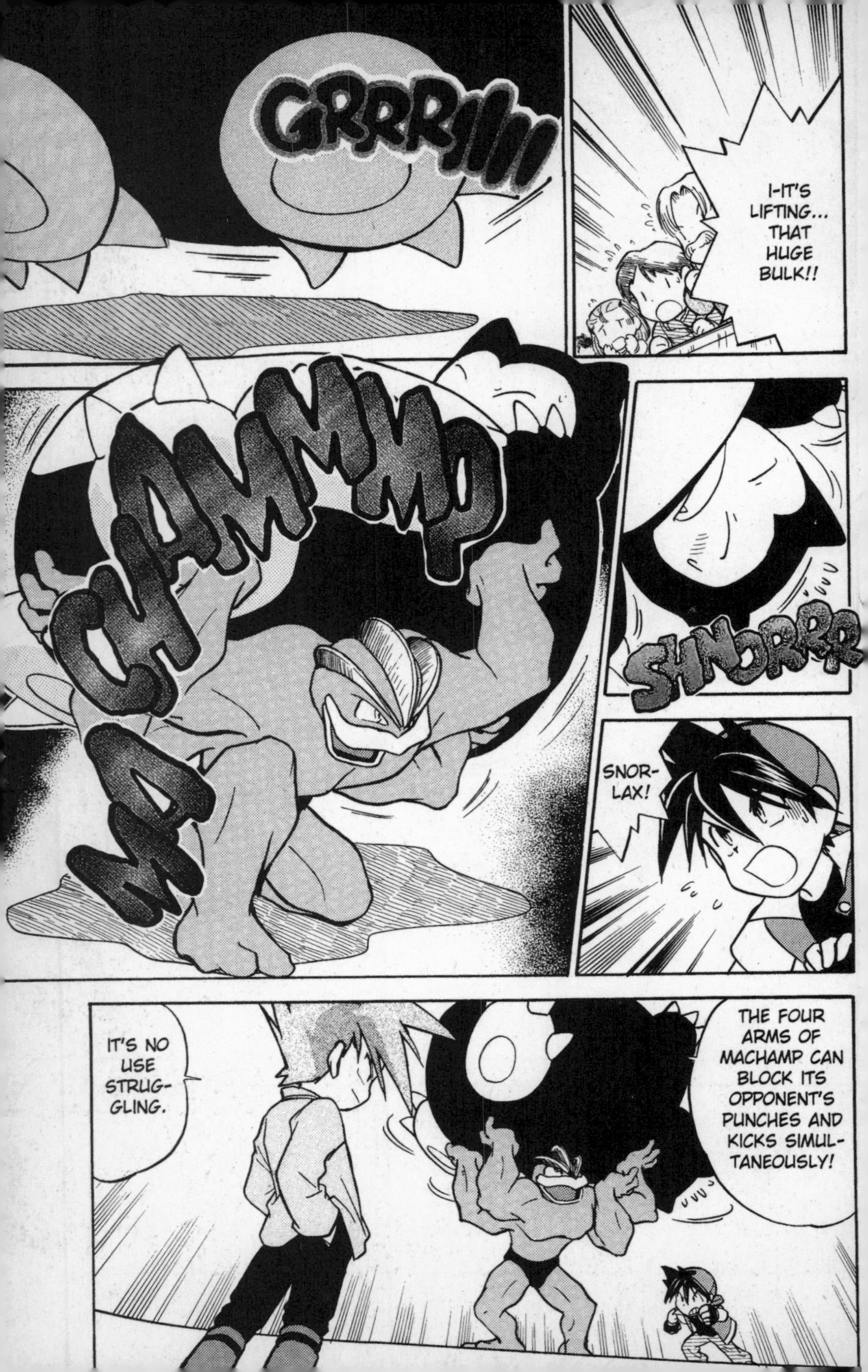
GRRR!!!!
I-IT'S LIFTING... THAT HUGE BULK!!
CHAMMMP
MA
SHNORRR
SNOR-LAX!
IT'S NO USE STRUG-GLING.
THE FOUR ARMS OF MACHAMP CAN BLOCK ITS OPPONENT'S PUNCHES AND KICKS SIMUL-TANEOUSLY!

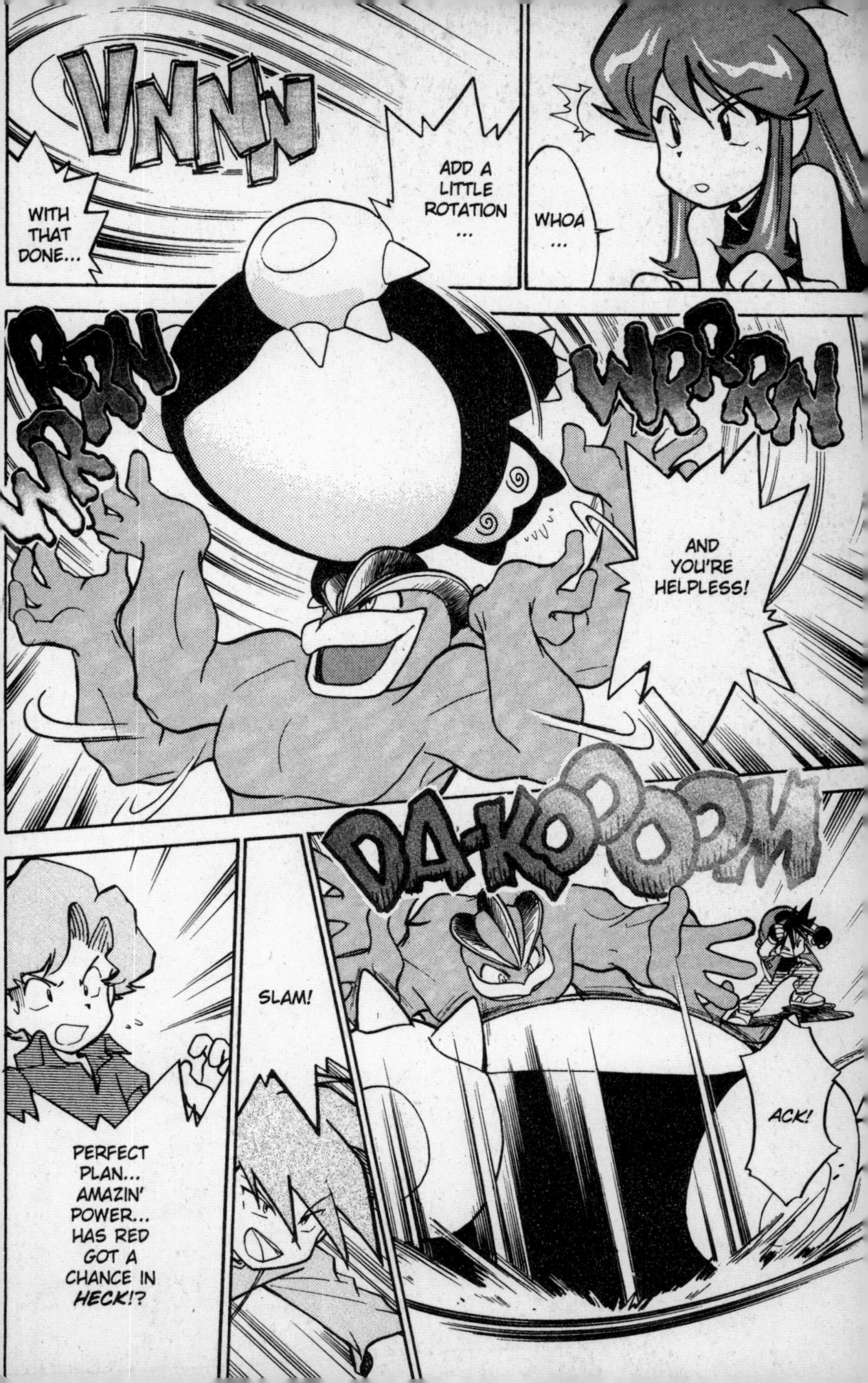

WITH THAT DONE...
ADD A LITTLE ROTATION ...
WHOA ...
AND YOU'RE HELPLESS!
SLAM!
ACK!
PERFECT PLAN... AMAZIN' POWER... HAS RED GOT A CHANCE IN *HECK*!?

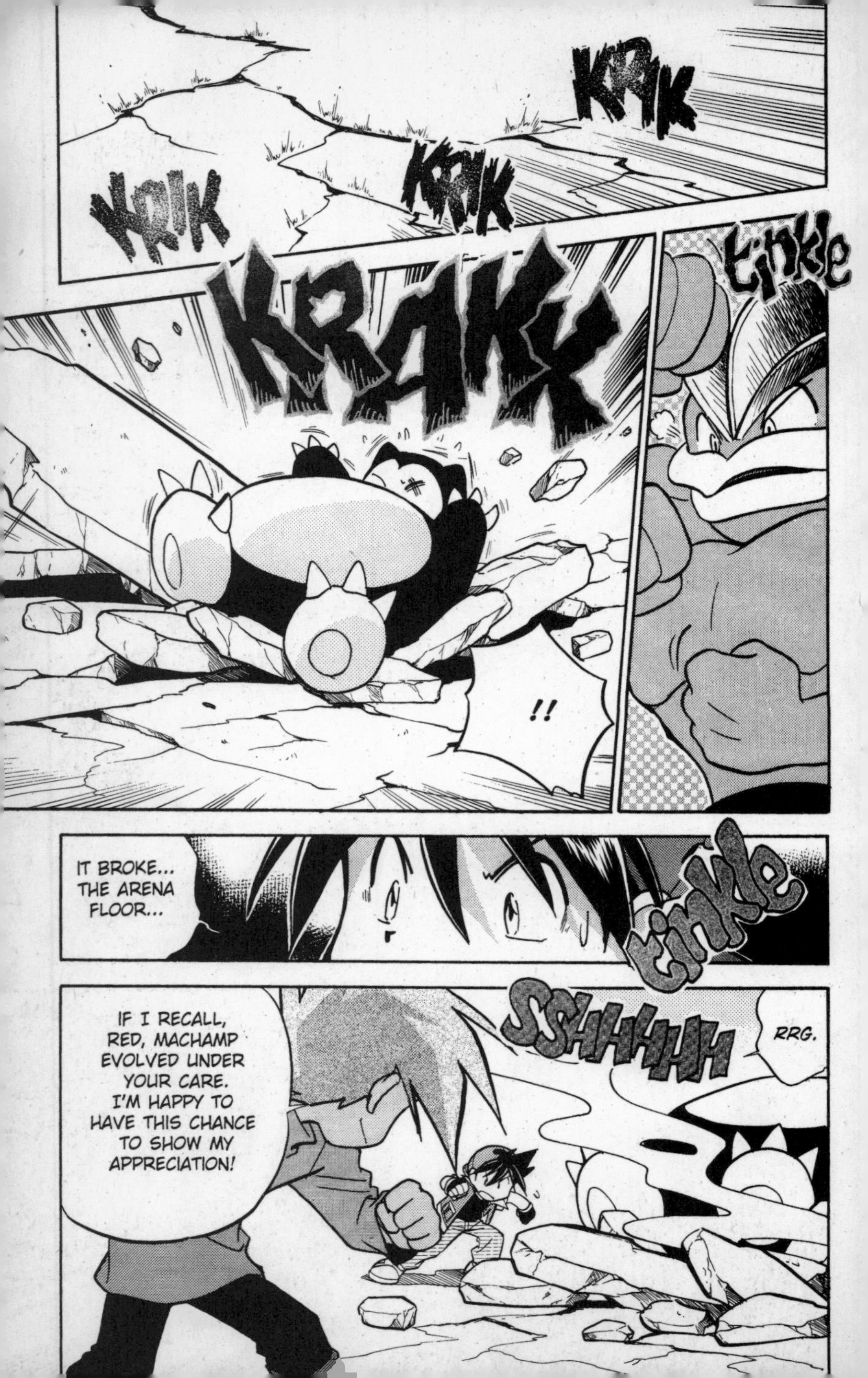
KRIK
KRIK
KRIK
KRAKK
tinkle
!!
IT BROKE... THE ARENA FLOOR...
tinkle
IF I RECALL, RED, MACHAMP EVOLVED UNDER YOUR CARE. I'M HAPPY TO HAVE THIS CHANCE TO SHOW MY APPRECIATION!
SSHHHHH
RRG.

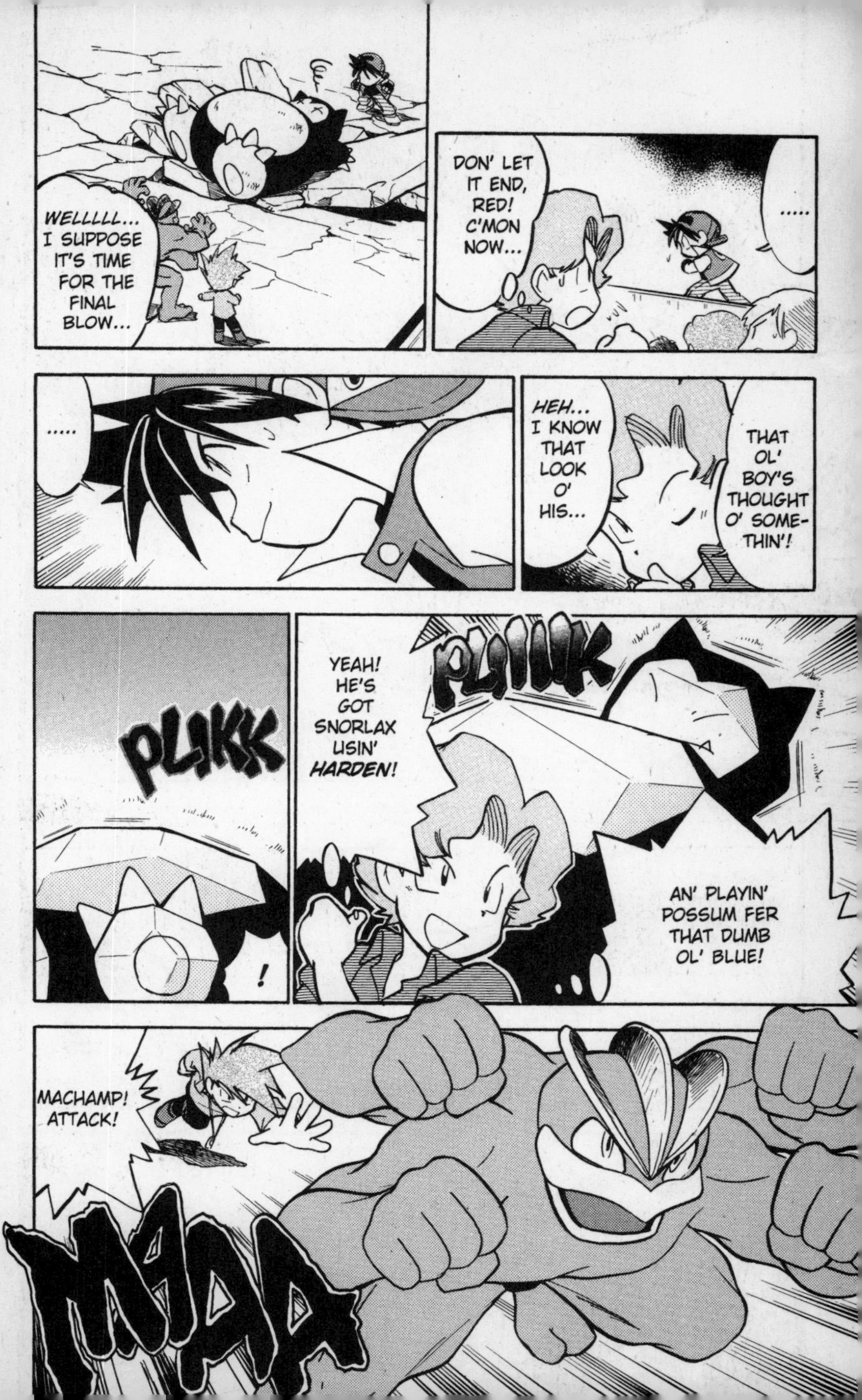
WELLLLL... I SUPPOSE IT'S TIME FOR THE FINAL BLOW...
DON' LET IT END, RED! C'MON NOW...
.....
.....
HEH... I KNOW THAT LOOK O' HIS...
THAT OL' BOY'S THOUGHT O' SOME-THIN'!
PLIKK
!
YEAH! HE'S GOT SNORLAX USIN' HARDEN!
PLIIIK
AN' PLAYIN' POSSUM FER THAT DUMB OL' BLUE!
MACHAMP! ATTACK!
MAAA

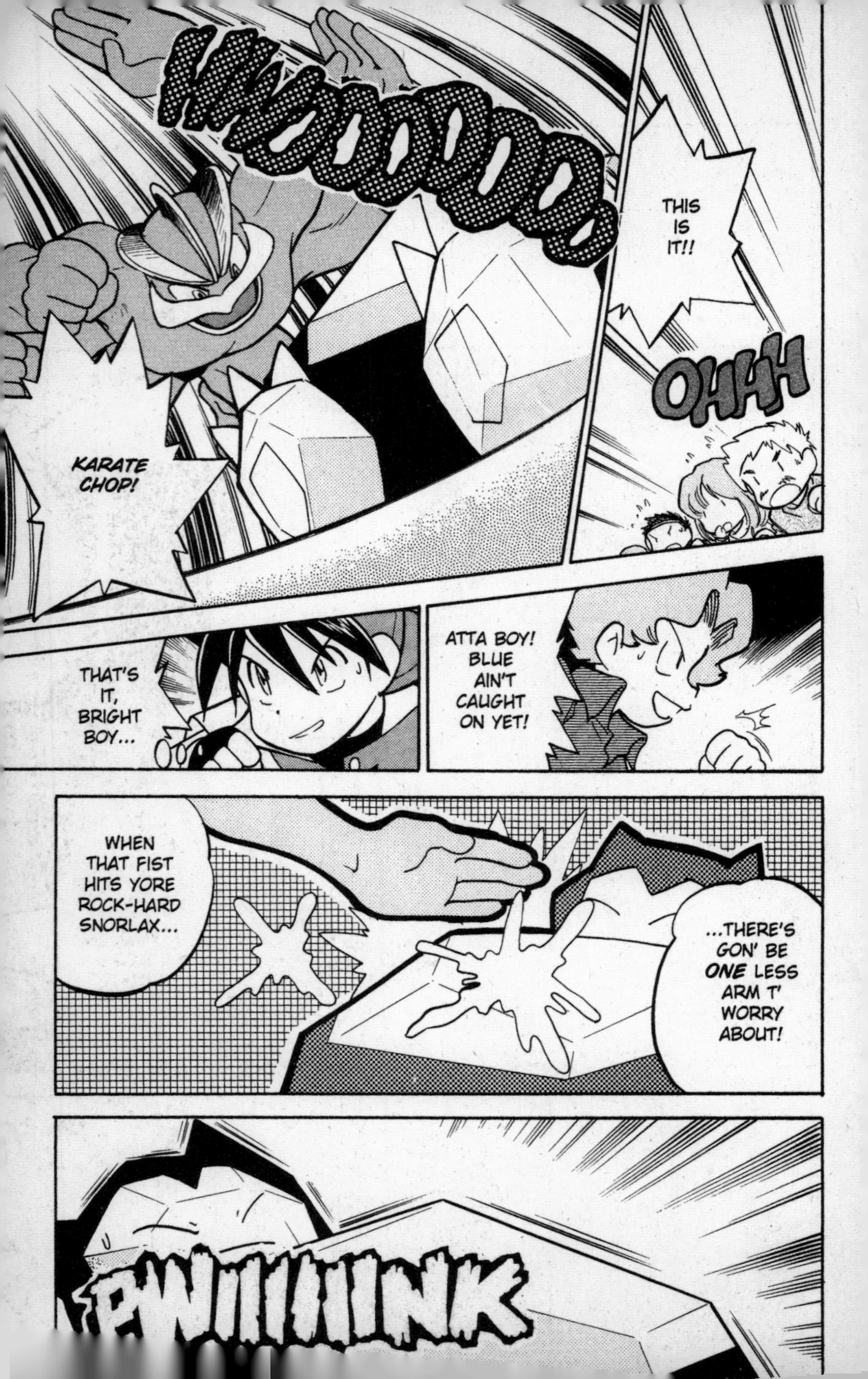
KARATE CHOP!
THIS IS IT!!
OHHH
THAT'S IT, BRIGHT BOY...
ATTA BOY! BLUE AIN'T CAUGHT ON YET!
WHEN THAT FIST HITS YORE ROCK-HARD SNORLAX...
...THERE'S GON' BE ONE LESS ARM T' WORRY ABOUT!

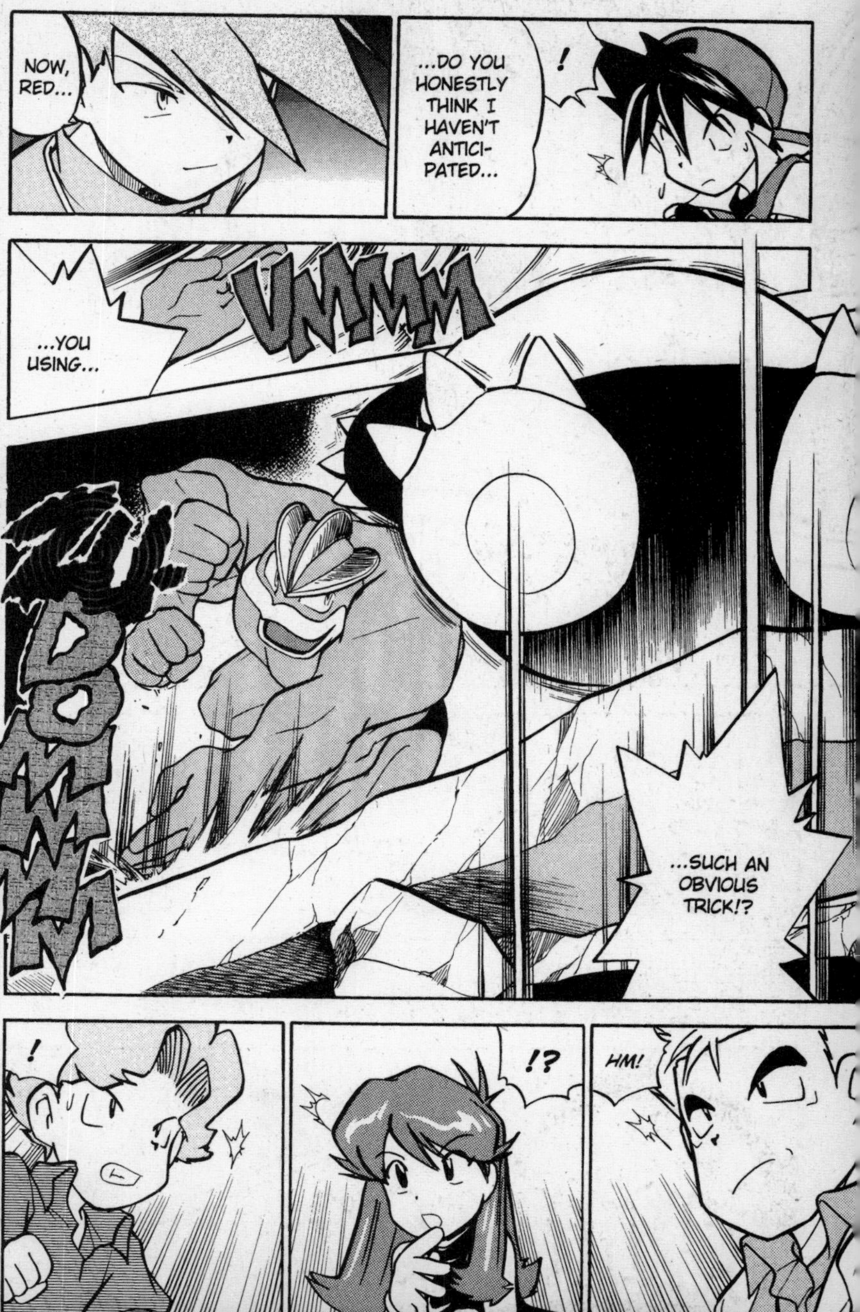
NOW, RED...
...DO YOU HONESTLY THINK I HAVEN'T ANTICI-PATED...
!
VMMM
...YOU USING...
DOMMM
...SUCH AN OBVIOUS TRICK!?
!
!?
HM!

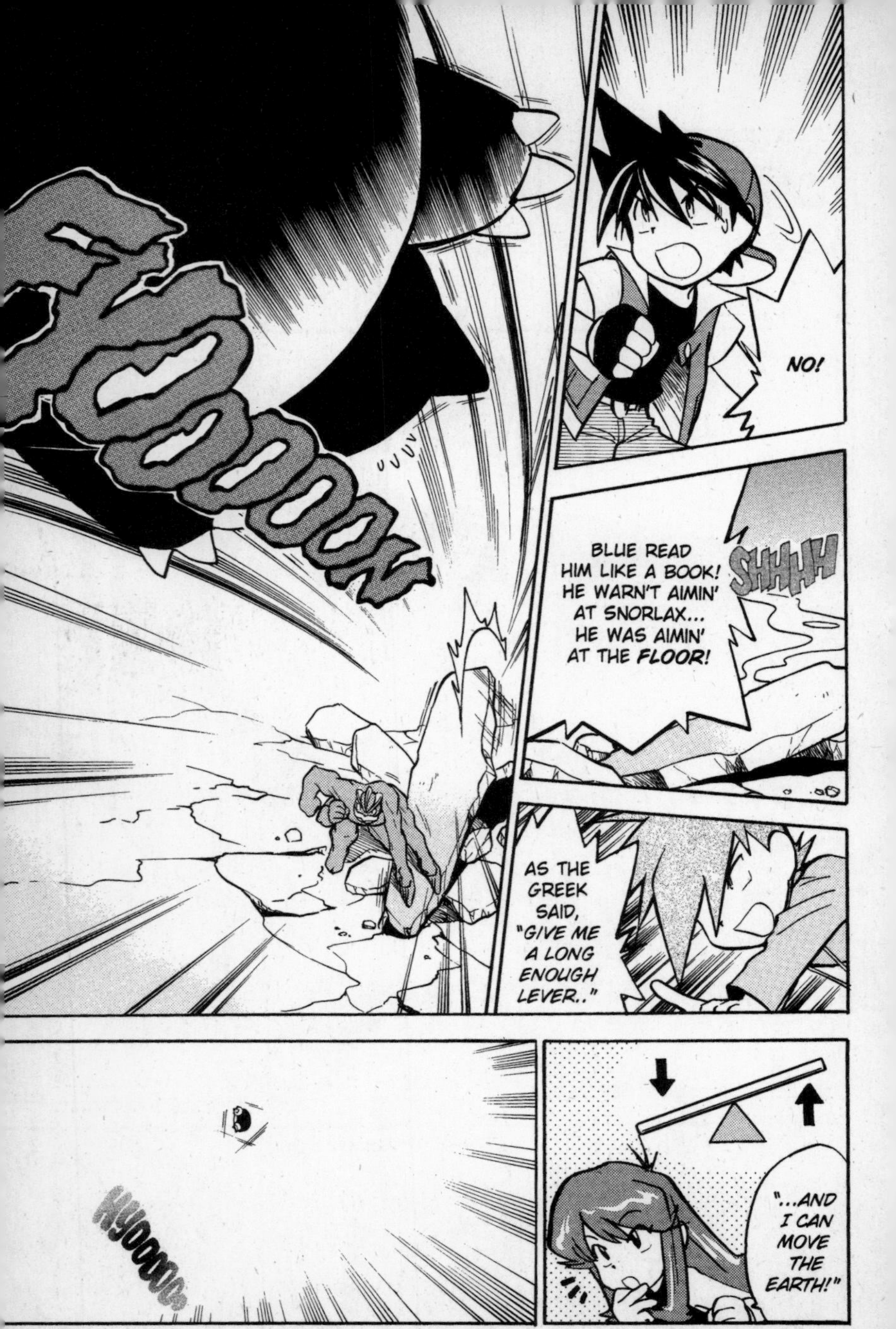
DOOOOON
NO!
SHHHH
BLUE READ HIM LIKE A BOOK! HE WARN'T AIMIN' AT SNORLAX... HE WAS AIMIN' AT THE *FLOOR*!
AS THE GREEK SAID, *"GIVE ME A LONG ENOUGH LEVER.."*
HYOOOO
"...AND I CAN MOVE THE EARTH!"

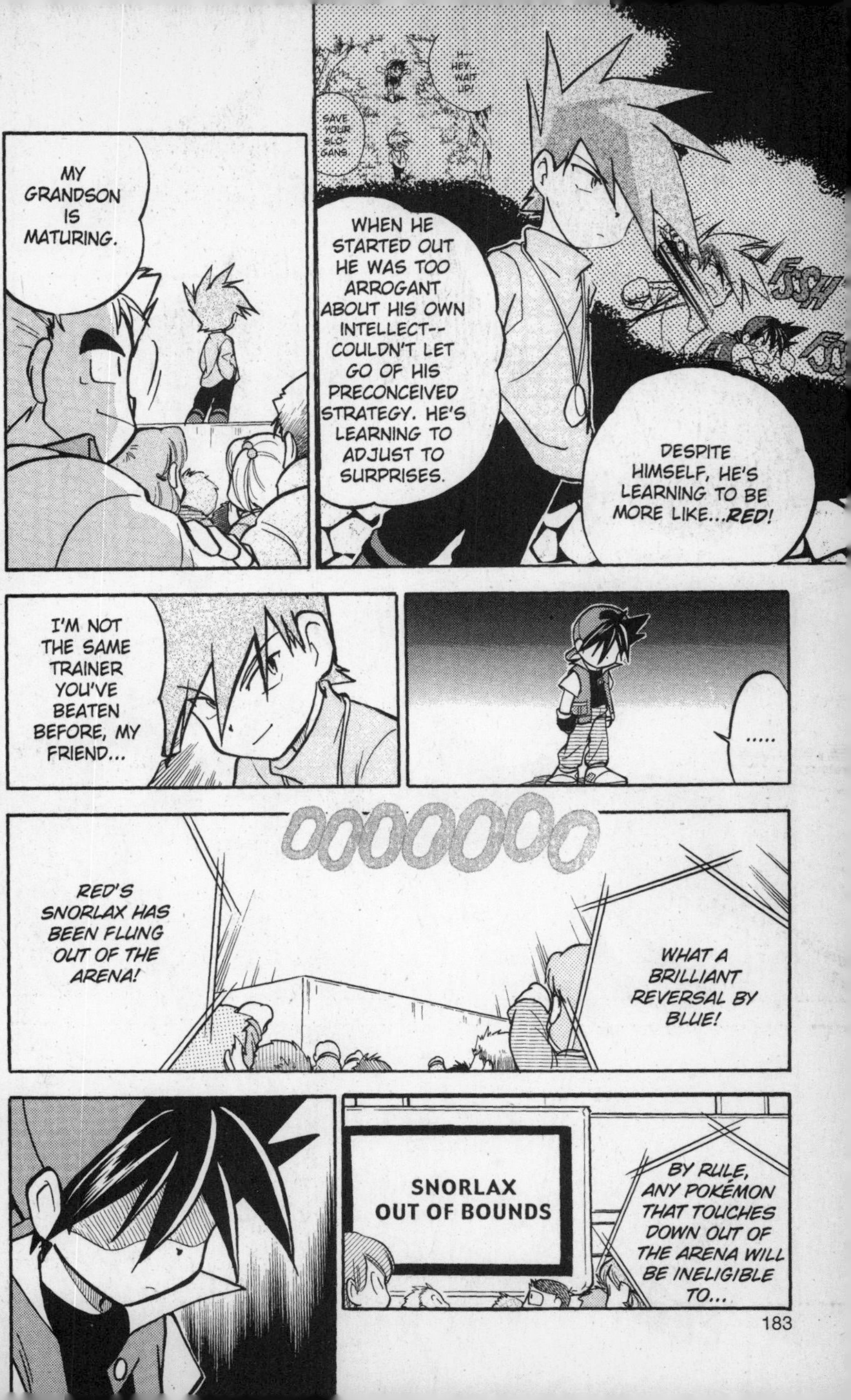
MY GRANDSON IS MATURING.
H-- HEY... WAIT UP!
SAVE YOUR SLO-GANS
WHEN HE STARTED OUT HE WAS TOO ARROGANT ABOUT HIS OWN INTELLECT--COULDN'T LET GO OF HIS PRECONCEIVED STRATEGY. HE'S LEARNING TO ADJUST TO SURPRISES.
FSSH
FSSH
DESPITE HIMSELF, HE'S LEARNING TO BE MORE LIKE...*RED!*
I'M NOT THE SAME TRAINER YOU'VE BEATEN BEFORE, MY FRIEND...
.....
OOOOOOO
RED'S SNORLAX HAS BEEN FLUNG OUT OF THE ARENA!
WHAT A BRILLIANT REVERSAL BY BLUE!
SNORLAX OUT OF BOUNDS
BY RULE, ANY POKÉMON THAT TOUCHES DOWN OUT OF THE ARENA WILL BE INELIGIBLE TO...

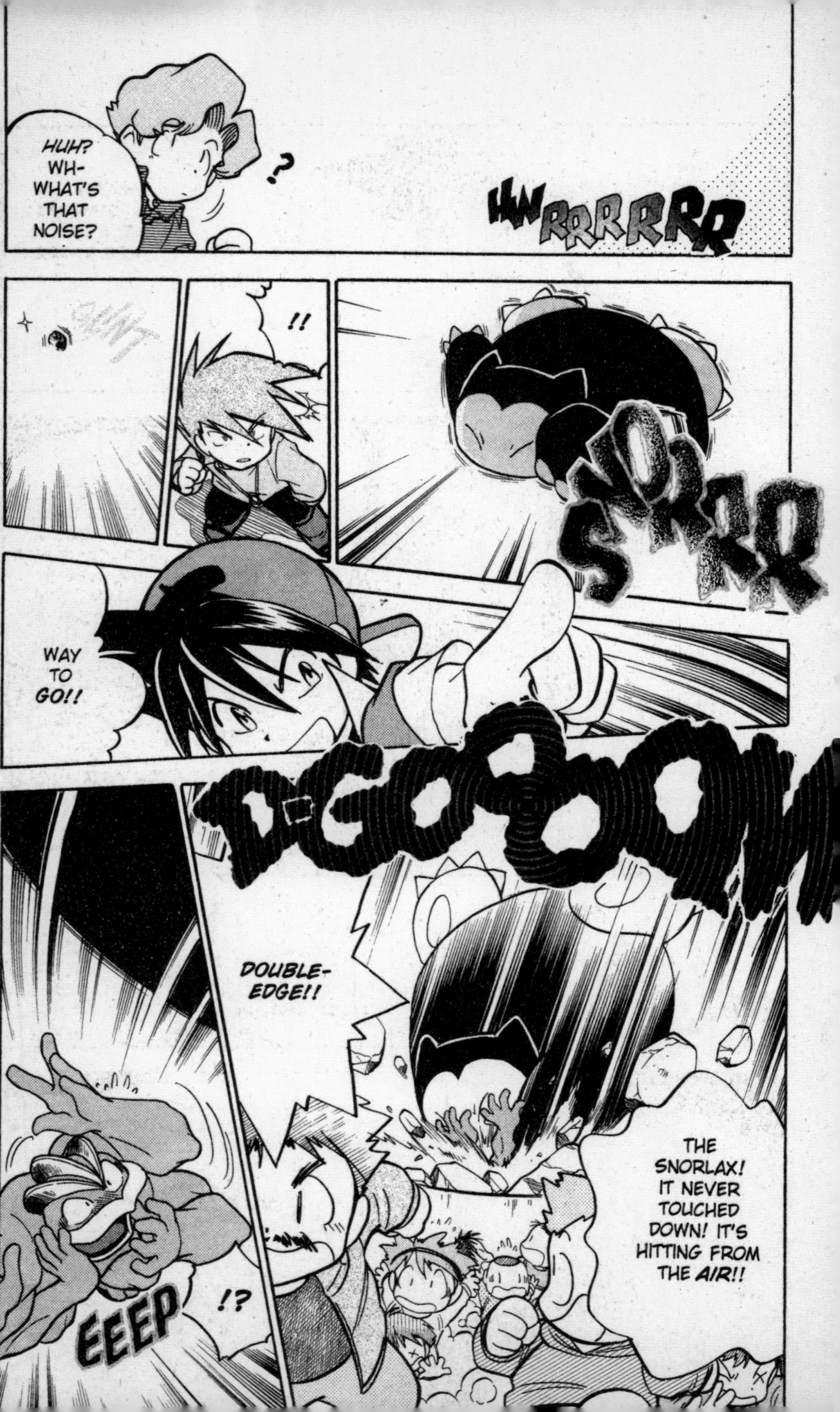
HWRRRRRR
?
HUH? WH-WHAT'S THAT NOISE?
!!
SNORRR
WAY TO GO!!
D-GOOOOM
THE SNORLAX! IT NEVER TOUCHED DOWN! IT'S HITTING FROM THE AIR!!
DOUBLE-EDGE!!
!?
EEEP

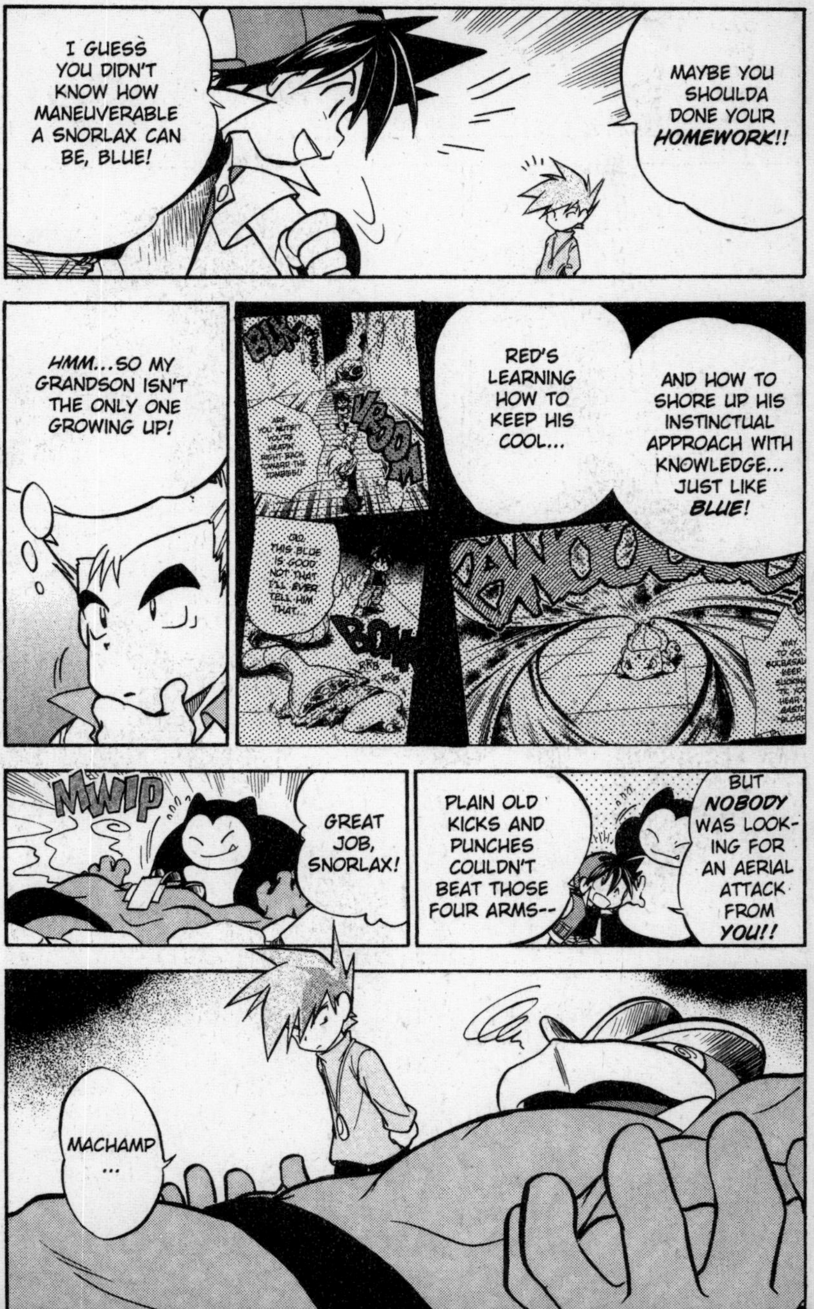
I GUESS YOU DIDN'T KNOW HOW MANEUVERABLE A SNORLAX CAN BE, BLUE!
MAYBE YOU SHOULDA DONE YOUR ***HOMEWORK!!***
HMM...SO MY GRANDSON ISN'T THE ONLY ONE GROWING UP!
RED'S LEARNING HOW TO KEEP HIS COOL...
AND HOW TO SHORE UP HIS INSTINCTUAL APPROACH WITH KNOWLEDGE... JUST LIKE ***BLUE!***
ARE YOU NUTS!? YOU'RE HEADIN' RIGHT BACK TOWARD THE ZOMBIES!!
VROOM
GO. THIS BLUE IS GOOD. NOT THAT I'LL EVER TELL HIM THAT.
BOM
RRB RRB
MWIP
GREAT JOB, SNORLAX!
PLAIN OLD KICKS AND PUNCHES COULDN'T BEAT THOSE FOUR ARMS--
BUT ***NOBODY*** WAS LOOKING FOR AN AERIAL ATTACK FROM ***YOU!!***
MACHAMP ...

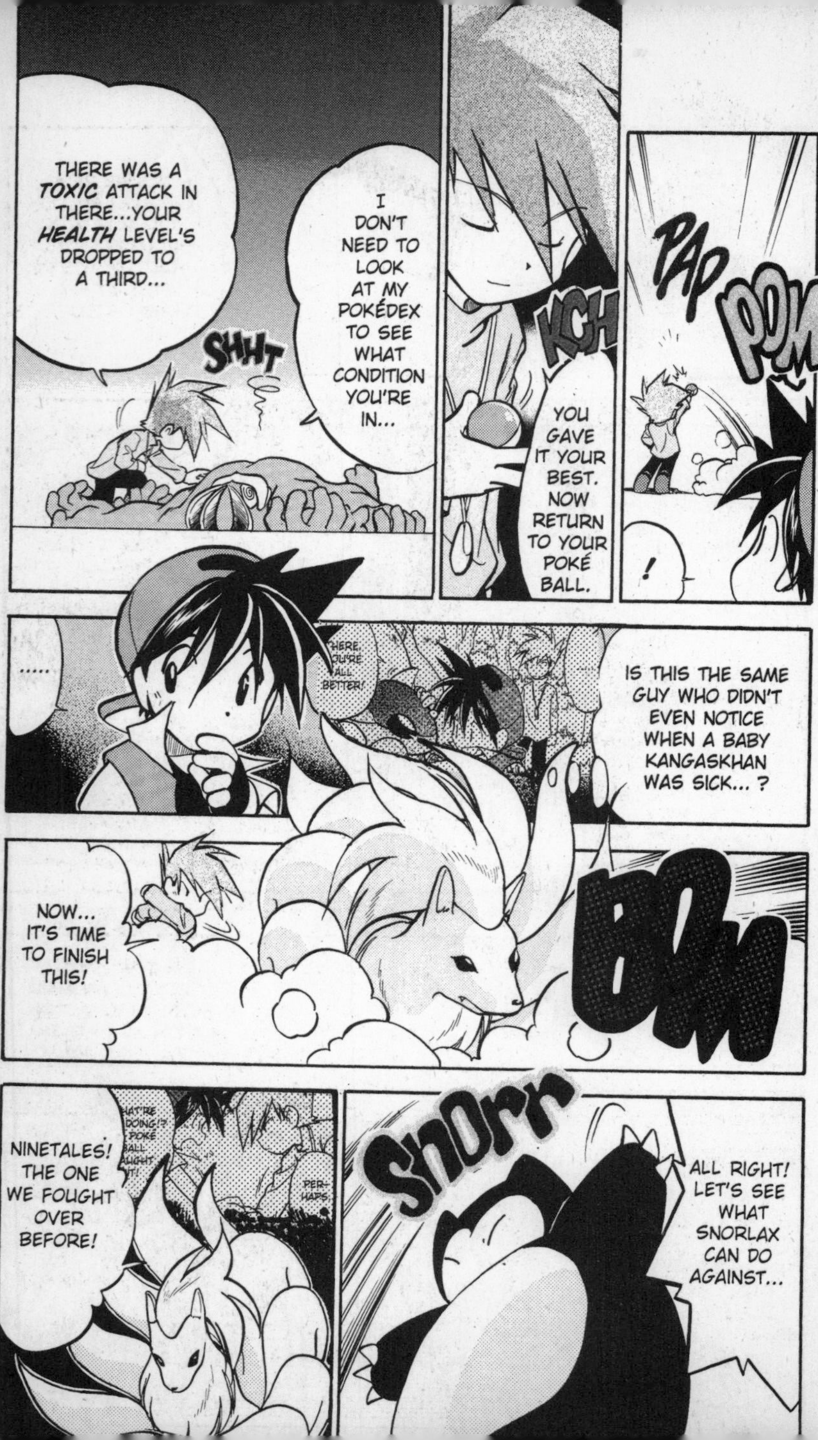
THERE WAS A TOXIC ATTACK IN THERE...YOUR HEALTH LEVEL'S DROPPED TO A THIRD...
SHHT
I DON'T NEED TO LOOK AT MY POKÉDEX TO SEE WHAT CONDITION YOU'RE IN...
KCH
YOU GAVE IT YOUR BEST. NOW RETURN TO YOUR POKÉ BALL.
PAP
POM
!
.....
THERE, YOU'RE ALL BETTER!
IS THIS THE SAME GUY WHO DIDN'T EVEN NOTICE WHEN A BABY KANGASKHAN WAS SICK... ?
NOW... IT'S TIME TO FINISH THIS!
BOM
NINETALES! THE ONE WE FOUGHT OVER BEFORE!
PER-HAPS.
SNORR
ALL RIGHT! LET'S SEE WHAT SNORLAX CAN DO AGAINST...

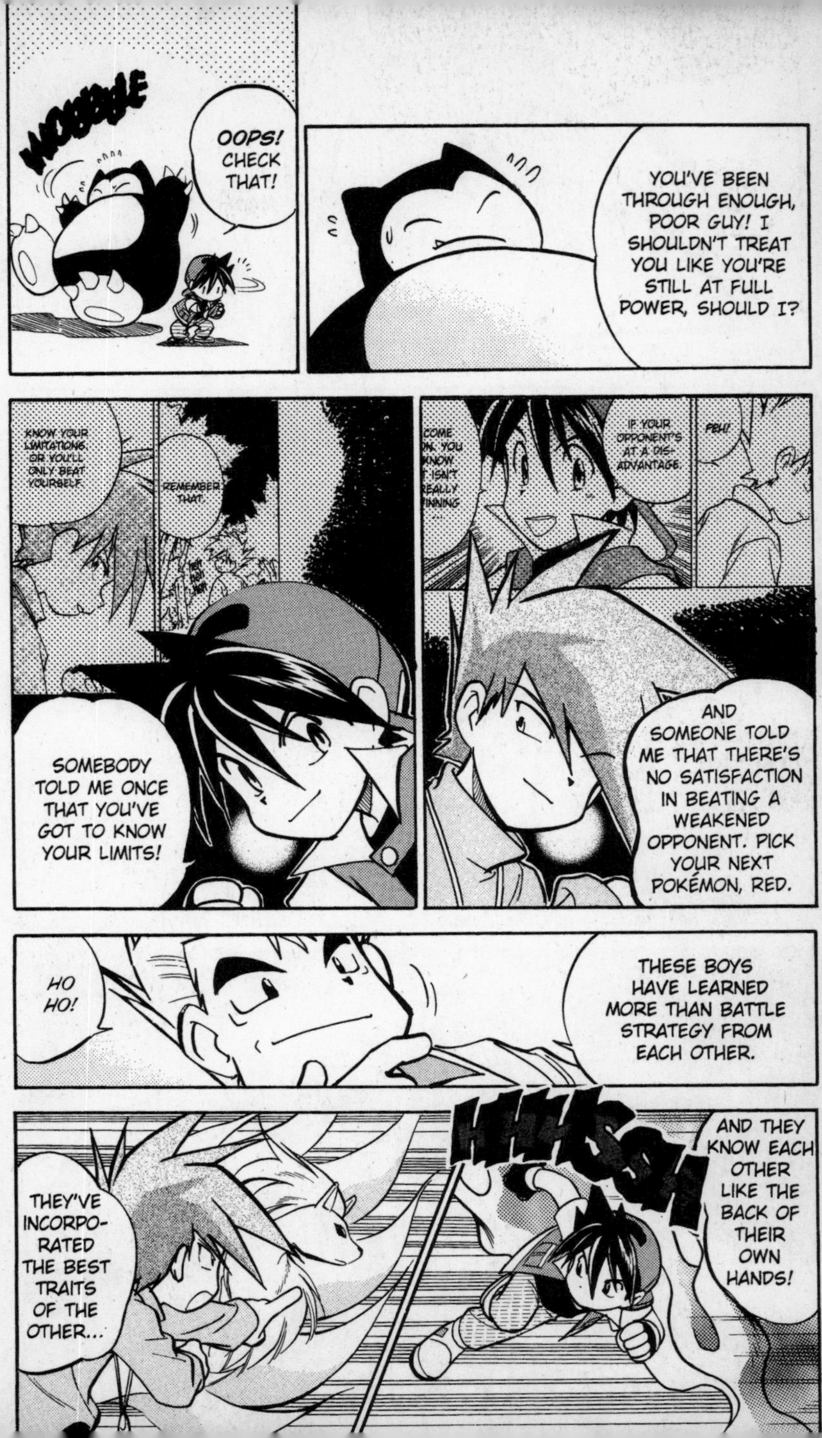
WOBBLE
OOPS! CHECK THAT!
YOU'VE BEEN THROUGH ENOUGH, POOR GUY! I SHOULDN'T TREAT YOU LIKE YOU'RE STILL AT FULL POWER, SHOULD I?
KNOW YOUR LIMITATIONS, OR YOU'LL ONLY BEAT YOURSELF.
REMEMBER THAT.
COME N. YOU KNOW T ISN'T REALLY INNING...
IF YOUR OPPONENT'S AT A DIS-ADVANTAGE.
FEH!
SOMEBODY TOLD ME ONCE THAT YOU'VE GOT TO KNOW YOUR LIMITS!
AND SOMEONE TOLD ME THAT THERE'S NO SATISFACTION IN BEATING A WEAKENED OPPONENT. PICK YOUR NEXT POKÉMON, RED.
HO HO!
THESE BOYS HAVE LEARNED MORE THAN BATTLE STRATEGY FROM EACH OTHER.
THEY'VE INCORPO-RATED THE BEST TRAITS OF THE OTHER...
HHHSSH
AND THEY KNOW EACH OTHER LIKE THE BACK OF THEIR OWN HANDS!

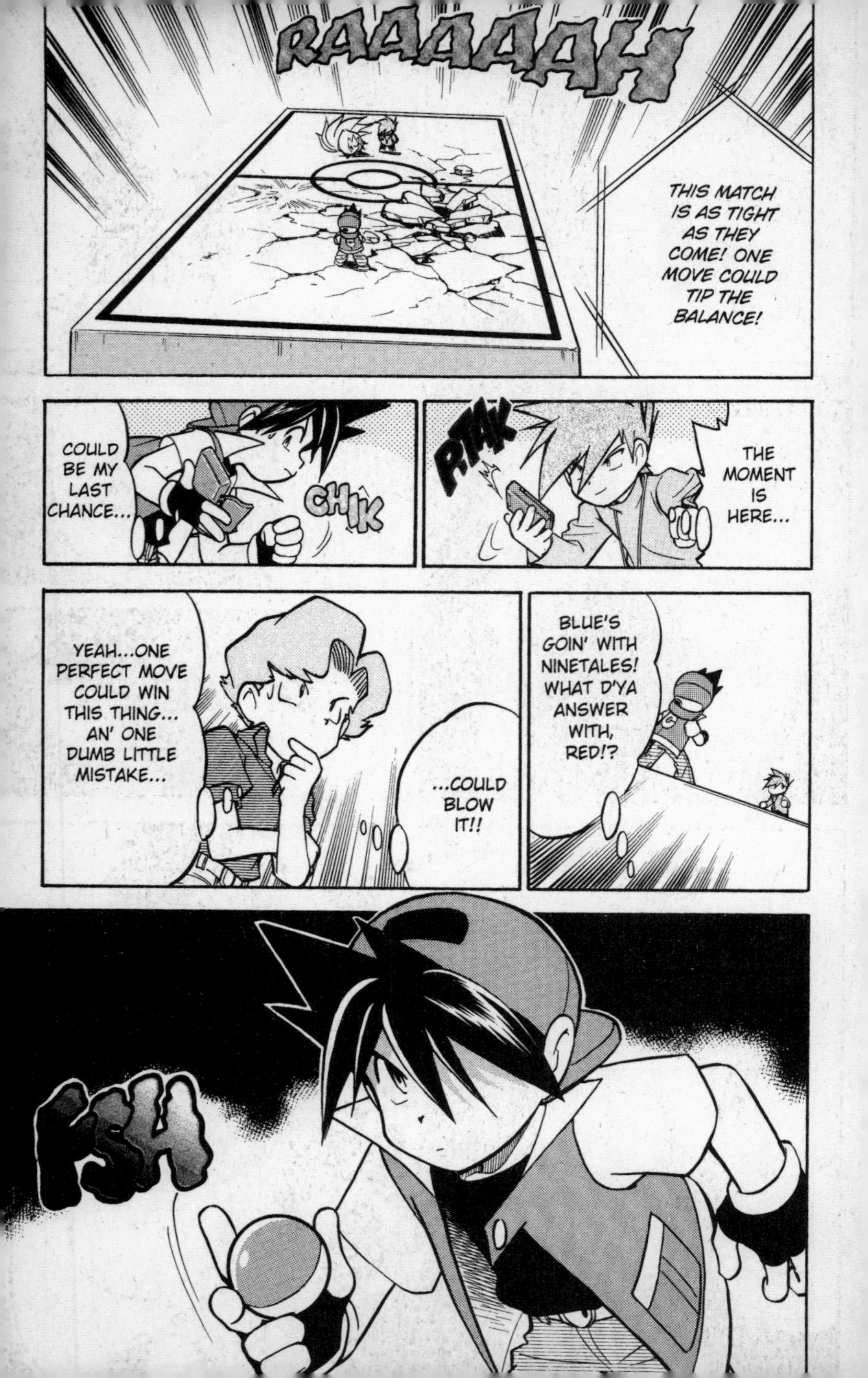
RAAAAAH
THIS MATCH IS AS TIGHT AS THEY COME! ONE MOVE COULD TIP THE BALANCE!
COULD BE MY LAST CHANCE...
CHIK
PTAK
THE MOMENT IS HERE...
YEAH...ONE PERFECT MOVE COULD WIN THIS THING... AN' ONE DUMB LITTLE MISTAKE...
...COULD BLOW IT!!
BLUE'S GOIN' WITH NINETALES! WHAT D'YA ANSWER WITH, RED!?
FSH

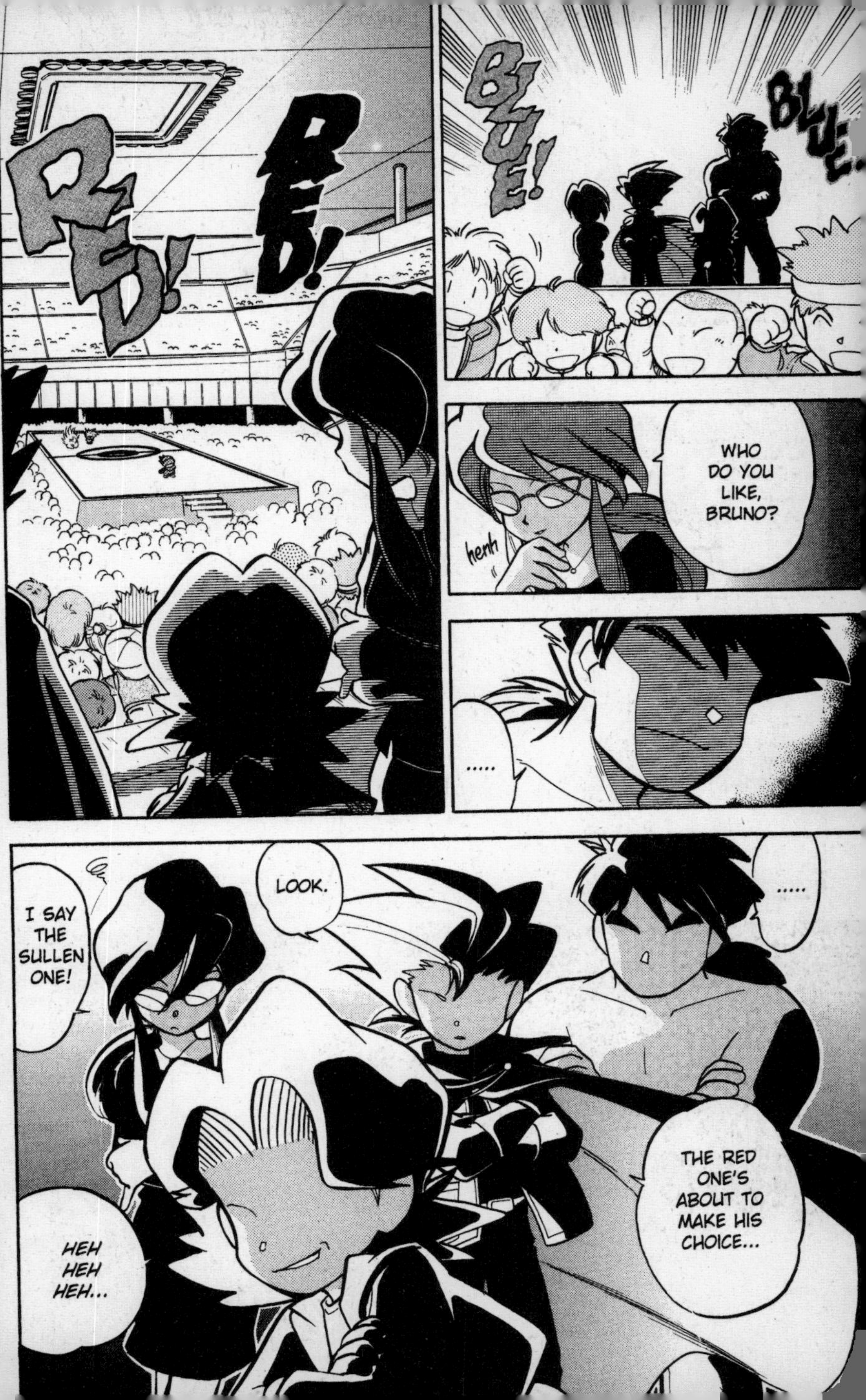

BLUE!
BLUE...
RED!
RED!
WHO DO YOU LIKE, BRUNO?
henh
.....
.....
LOOK.
I SAY THE SULLEN ONE!
THE RED ONE'S ABOUT TO MAKE HIS CHOICE...
HEH HEH HEH...

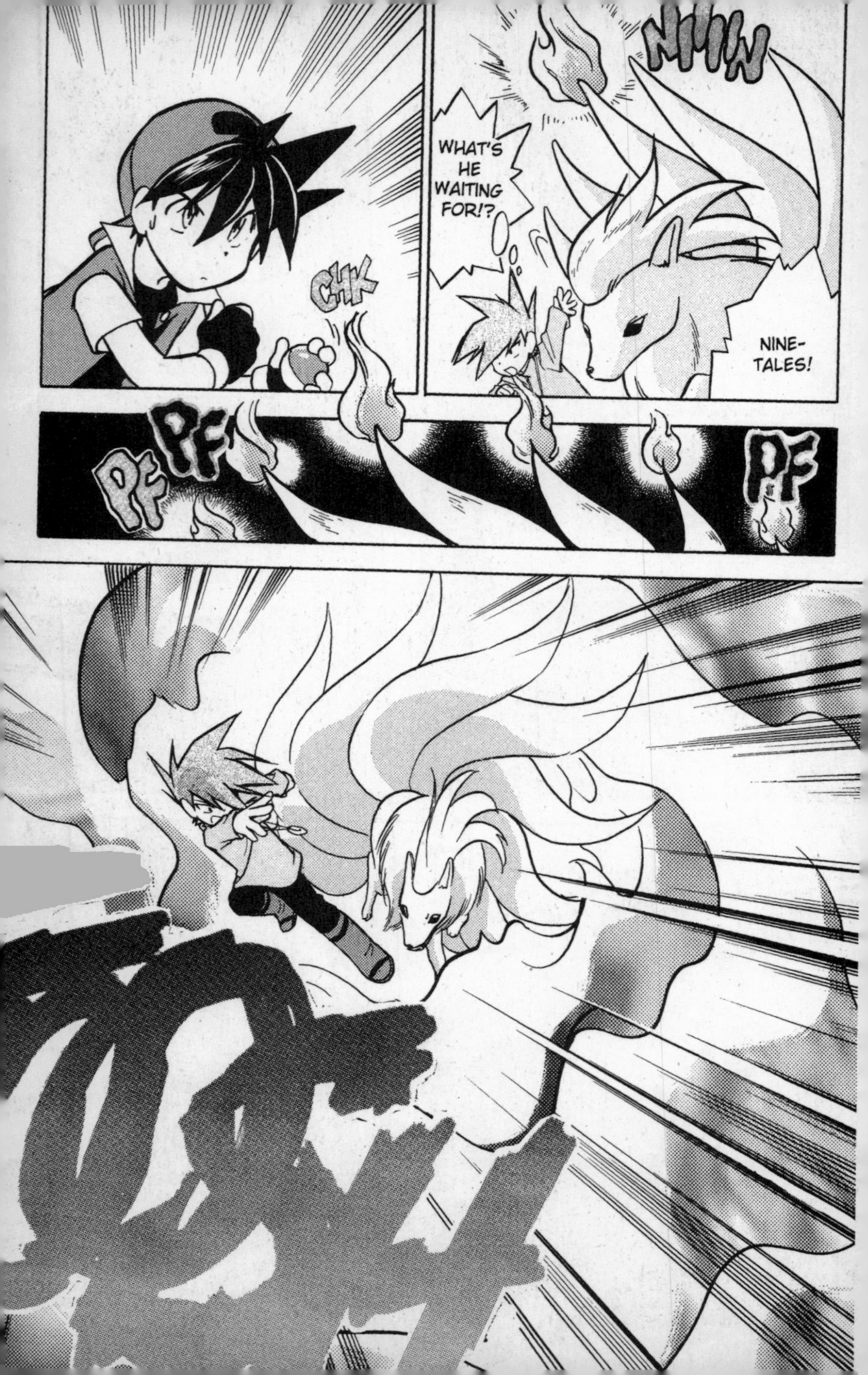
NIIIIN
WHAT'S HE WAITING FOR!?
NINE-TALES!
CHK
PF
PF PF

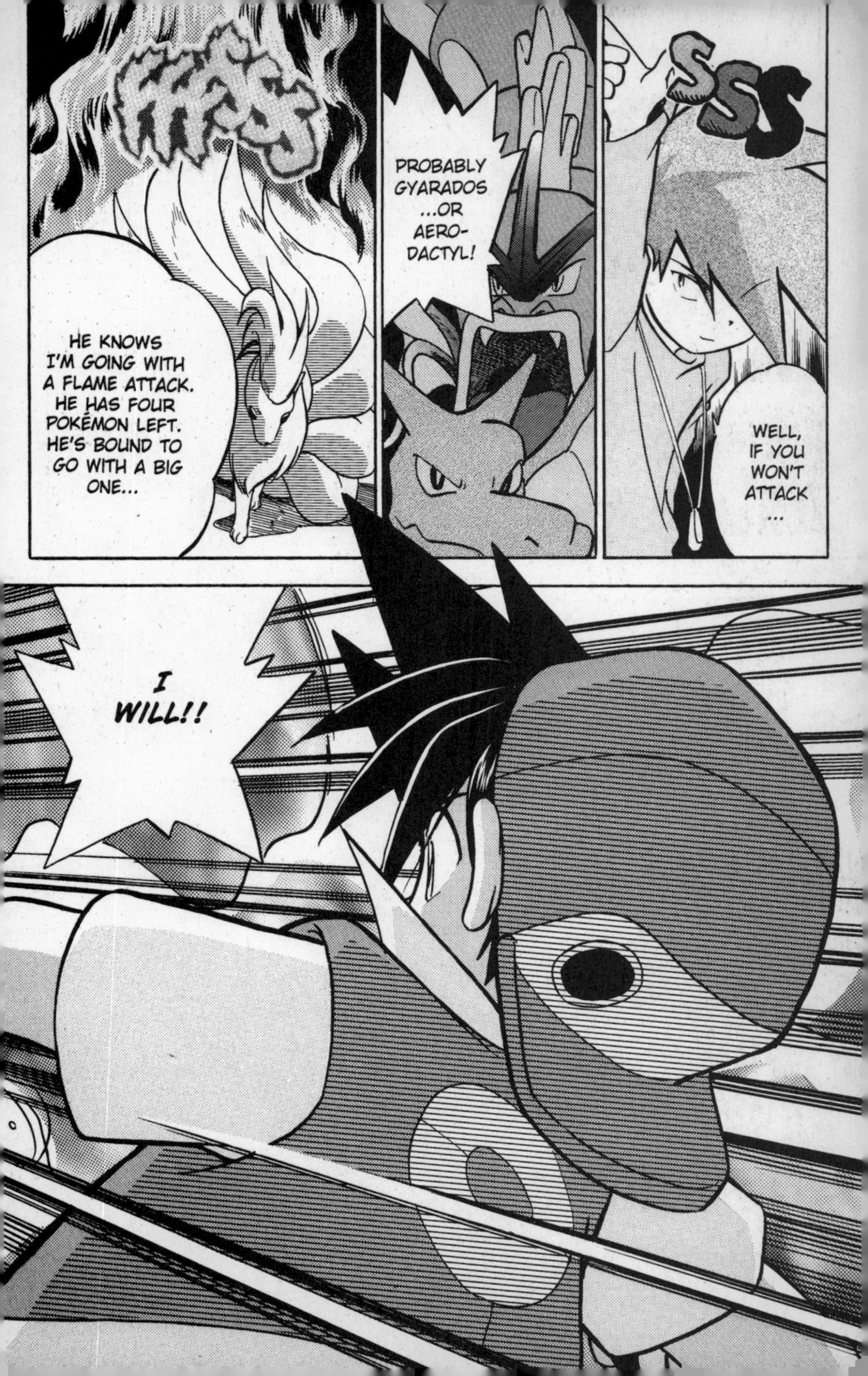
HE KNOWS I'M GOING WITH A FLAME ATTACK. HE HAS FOUR POKÉMON LEFT. HE'S BOUND TO GO WITH A BIG ONE...
PROBABLY GYARADOS ...OR AERO-DACTYL!
SSS
WELL, IF YOU WON'T ATTACK ...
I WILL!!

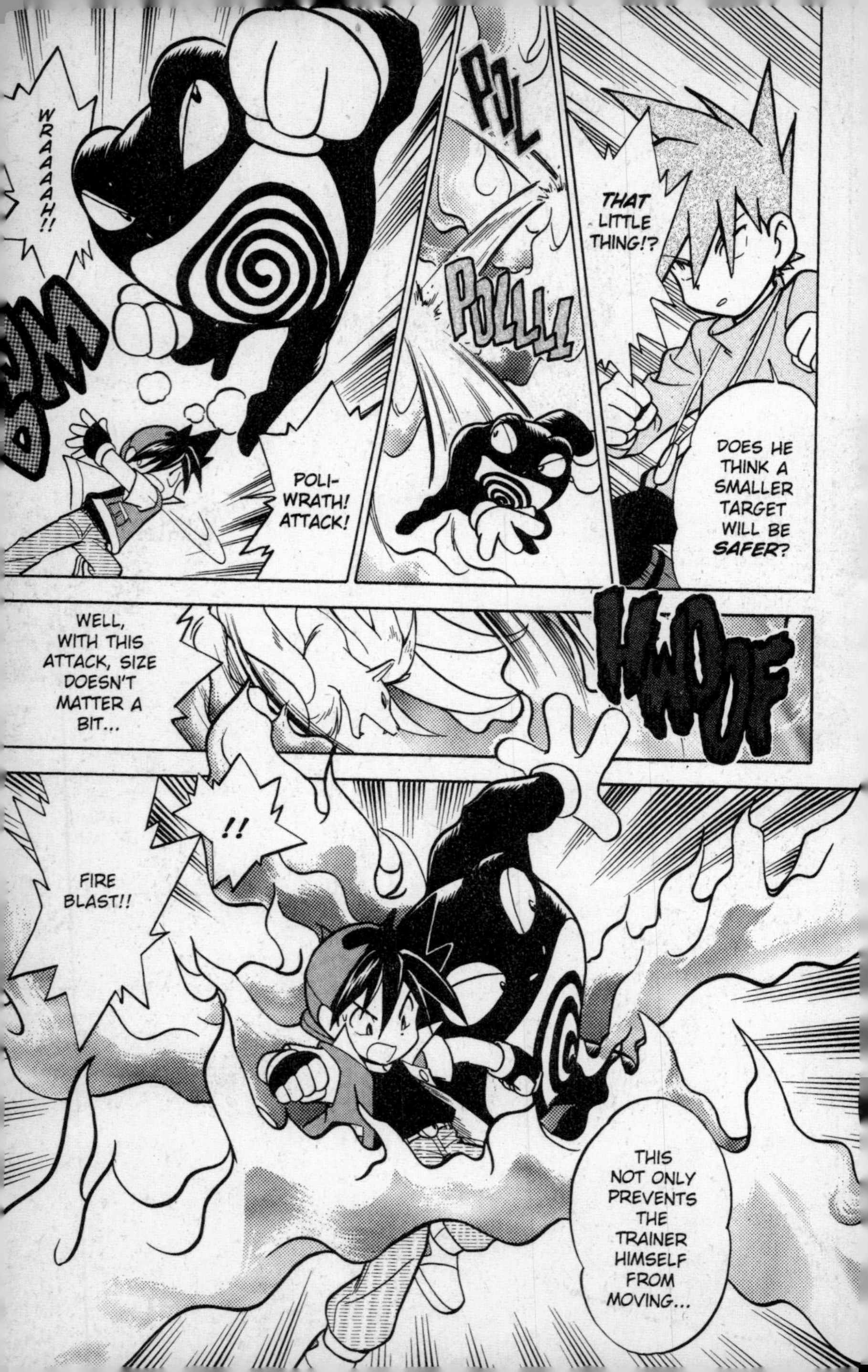
THAT LITTLE THING!?
DOES HE THINK A SMALLER TARGET WILL BE SAFER?
POL—
POLLLL
POLI-WRATH! ATTACK!
WRAAAAAH!!
WELL, WITH THIS ATTACK, SIZE DOESN'T MATTER A BIT...
!!
FIRE BLAST!!
THIS NOT ONLY PREVENTS THE TRAINER HIMSELF FROM MOVING...

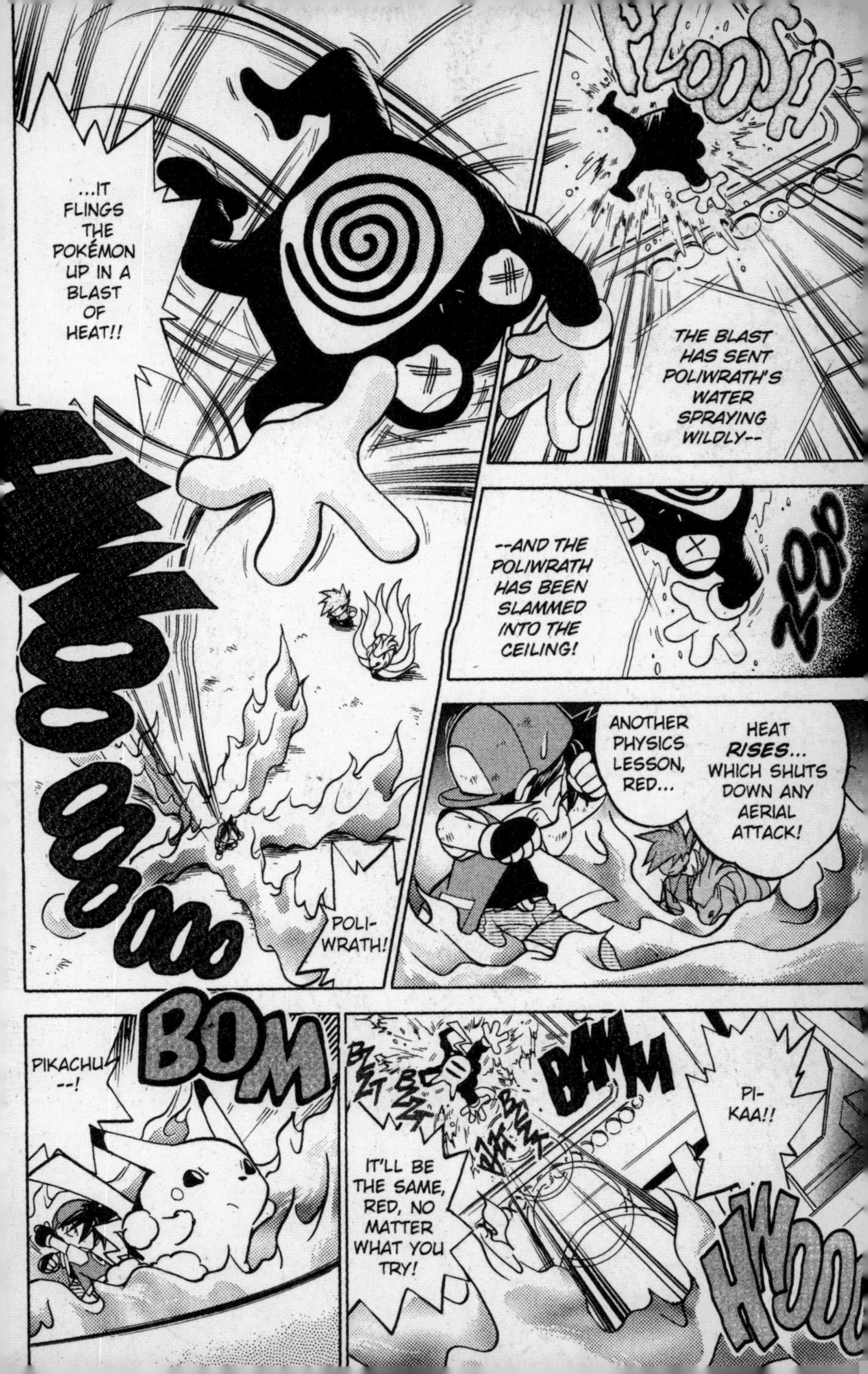

PLOOSH
...IT FLINGS THE POKÉMON UP IN A BLAST OF HEAT!!
THE BLAST HAS SENT POLIWRATH'S WATER SPRAYING WILDLY--
WHOOOOOOOOOO
--AND THE POLIWRATH HAS BEEN SLAMMED INTO THE CEILING!
POLI-WRATH!
HEAT RISES... WHICH SHUTS DOWN ANY AERIAL ATTACK!
ANOTHER PHYSICS LESSON, RED...
PI-KAA!!
BAMM
IT'LL BE THE SAME, RED, NO MATTER WHAT YOU TRY!
BOM
PIKACHU--!

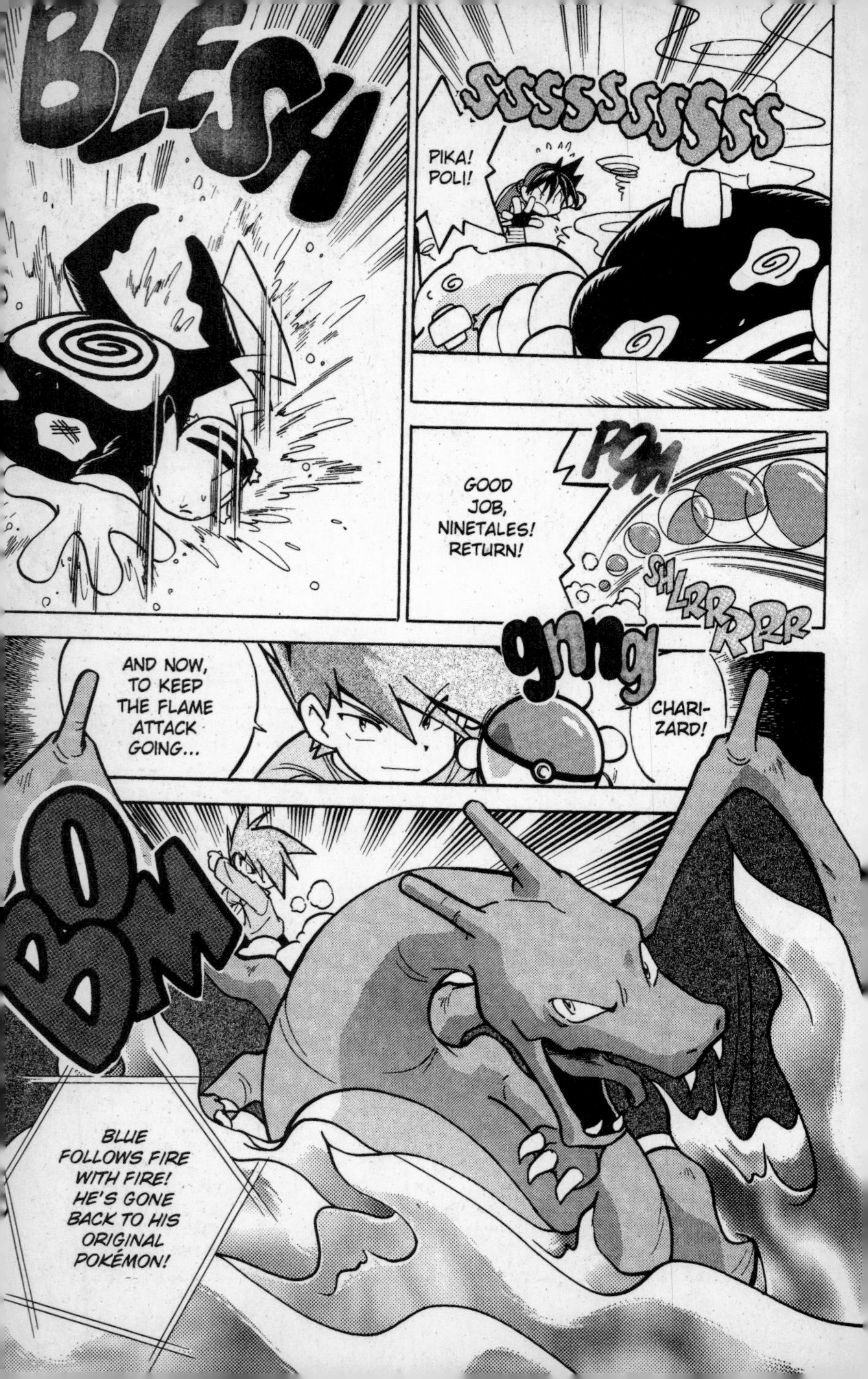
BLESH
SSSSSSSSSSS
PIKA! POLI!
POM
GOOD JOB, NINETALES! RETURN!
SHLRRRRRR
gnng
AND NOW, TO KEEP THE FLAME ATTACK GOING...
CHARI-ZARD!
BOM
BLUE FOLLOWS FIRE WITH FIRE! HE'S GONE BACK TO HIS ORIGINAL POKéMON!

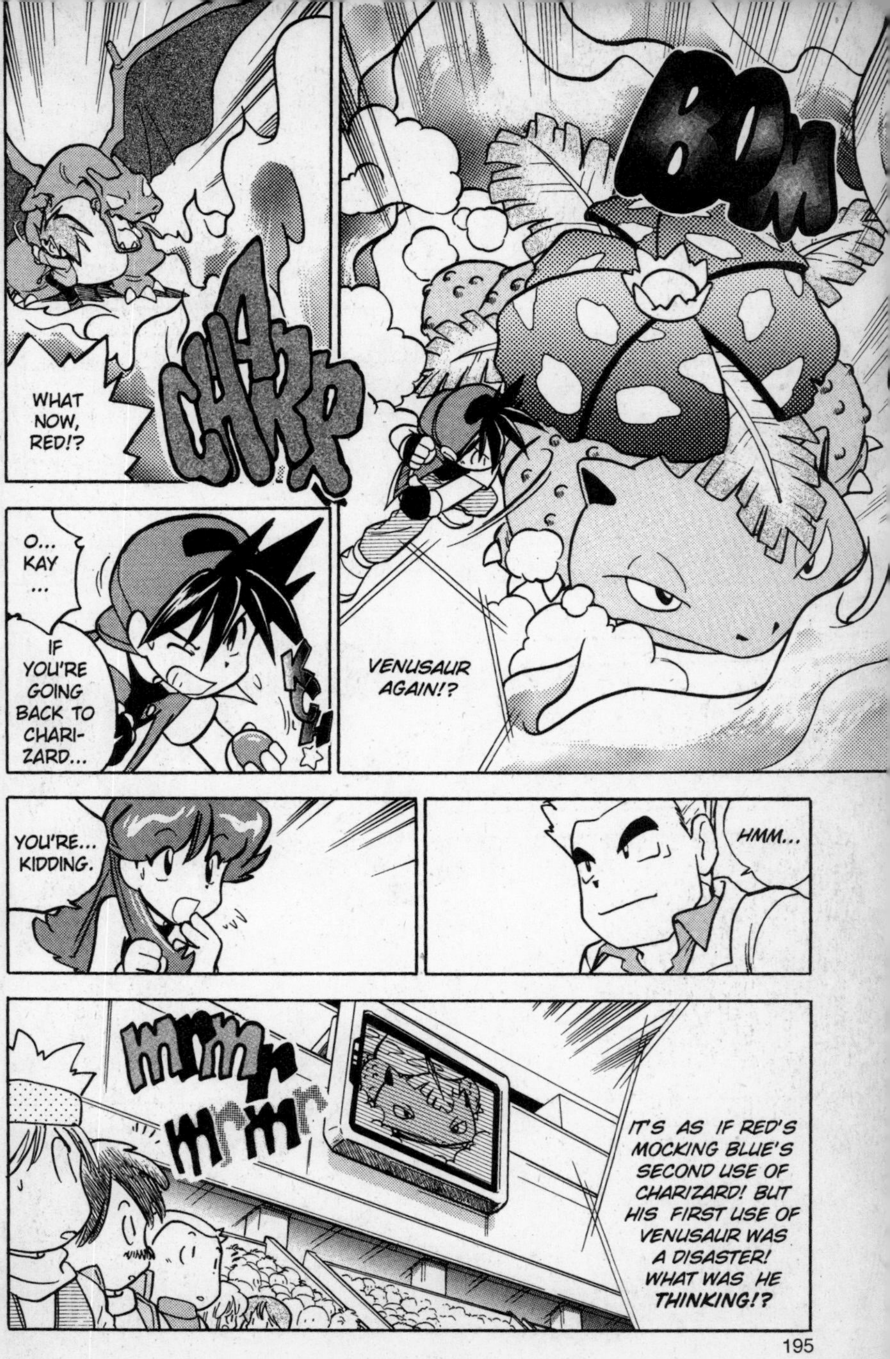

BOOM
WHAT NOW, RED!?
CHOMP
O... KAY ...
IF YOU'RE GOING BACK TO CHARI-ZARD...
VENUSAUR AGAIN!?
YOU'RE... KIDDING.
HMM...
MMMR MMMR
IT'S AS IF RED'S MOCKING BLUE'S SECOND USE OF CHARIZARD! BUT HIS FIRST USE OF VENUSAUR WAS A DISASTER! WHAT WAS HE THINKING!?

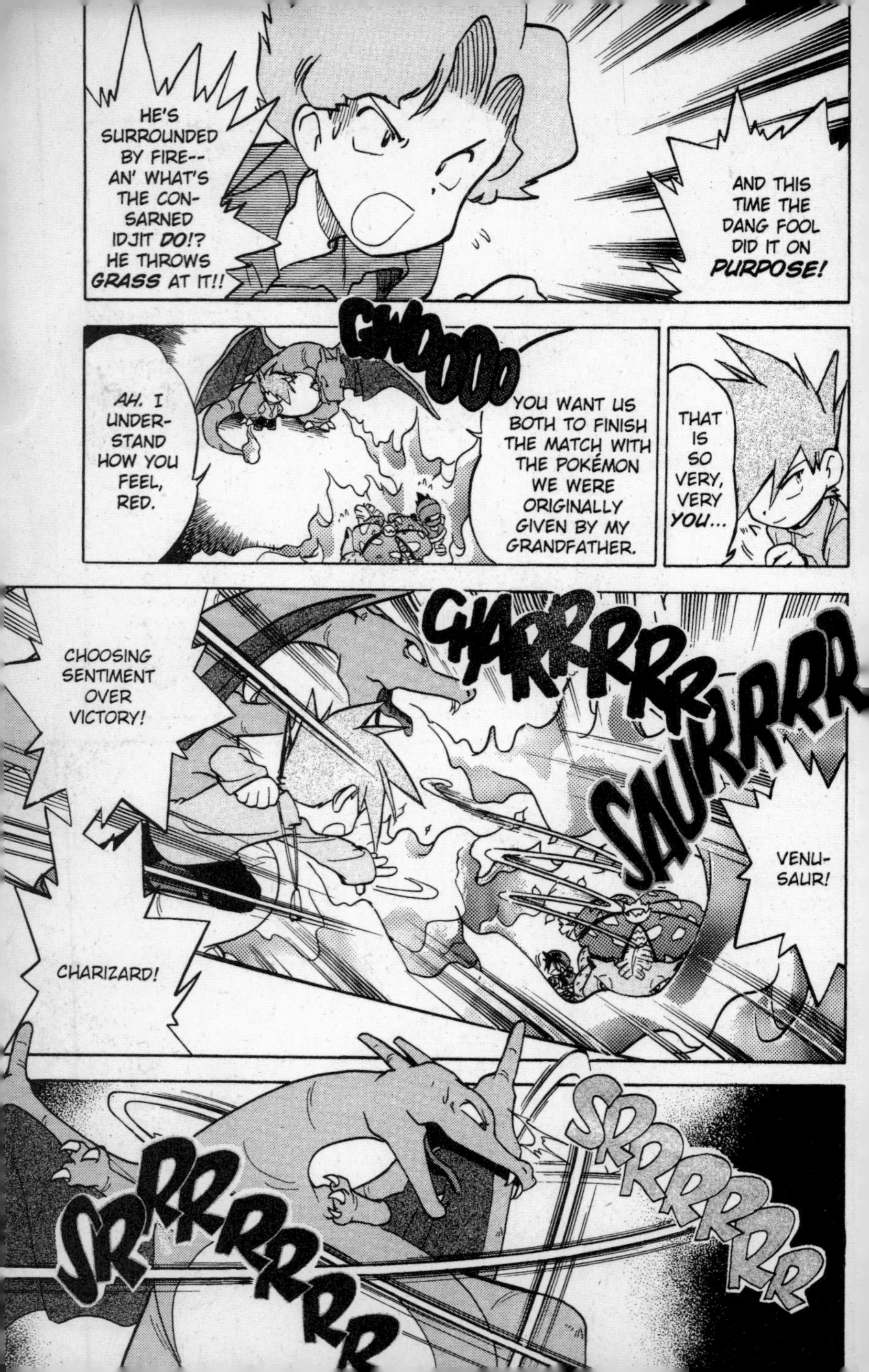
HE'S SURROUNDED BY FIRE-- AN' WHAT'S THE CON-SARNED IDJIT DO!? HE THROWS GRASS AT IT!!
AND THIS TIME THE DANG FOOL DID IT ON PURPOSE!
GWOOOOO
AH. I UNDER-STAND HOW YOU FEEL, RED.
YOU WANT US BOTH TO FINISH THE MATCH WITH THE POKÉMON WE WERE ORIGINALLY GIVEN BY MY GRANDFATHER.
THAT IS SO VERY, VERY YOU...
GHARRRRR
SAURRRRR
CHOOSING SENTIMENT OVER VICTORY!
VENU-SAUR!
CHARIZARD!
SRRRRRRR
SRRRRRRRR

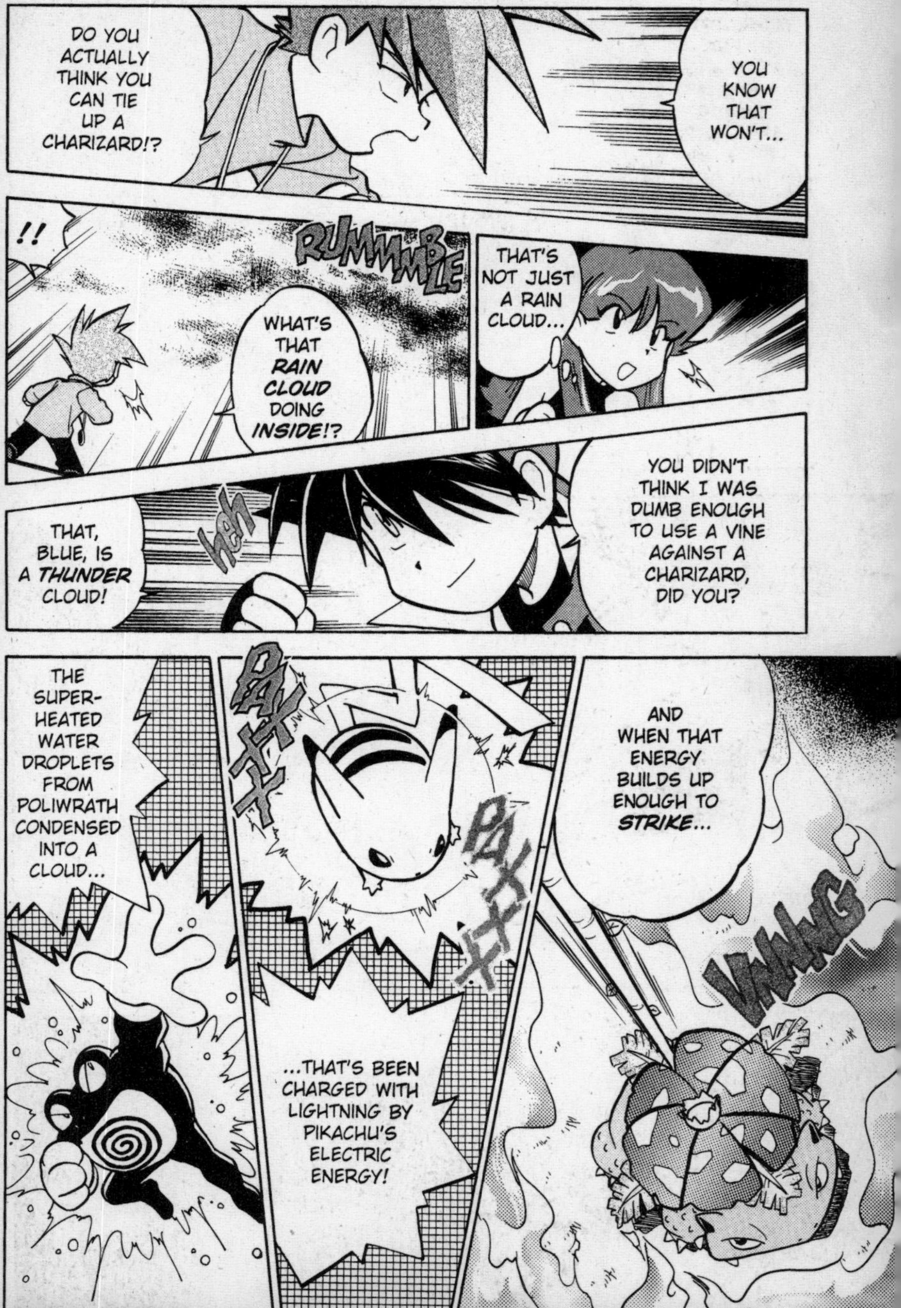

YOU KNOW THAT WON'T...
DO YOU ACTUALLY THINK YOU CAN TIE UP A CHARIZARD!?
THAT'S NOT JUST A RAIN CLOUD...
RUMMMMBLE
WHAT'S THAT RAIN CLOUD DOING INSIDE!?
!!
YOU DIDN'T THINK I WAS DUMB ENOUGH TO USE A VINE AGAINST A CHARIZARD, DID YOU?
heh
THAT, BLUE, IS A THUNDER CLOUD!
AND WHEN THAT ENERGY BUILDS UP ENOUGH TO STRIKE...
VWWNG
PAK
PAK
...THAT'S BEEN CHARGED WITH LIGHTNING BY PIKACHU'S ELECTRIC ENERGY!
THE SUPER-HEATED WATER DROPLETS FROM POLIWRATH CONDENSED INTO A CLOUD...

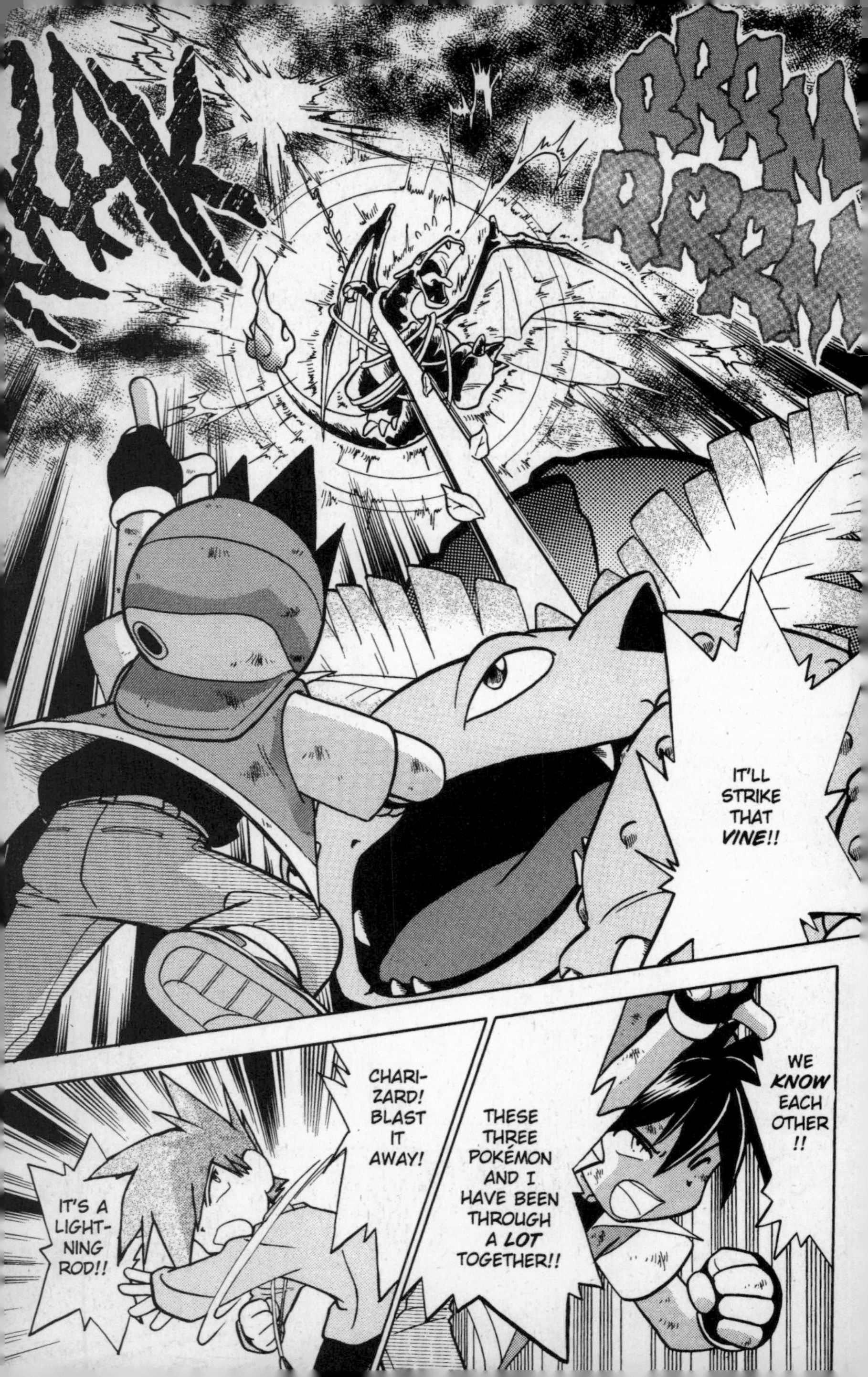
IT'LL STRIKE THAT VINE!!
IT'S A LIGHT-NING ROD!!
CHARI-ZARD! BLAST IT AWAY!
THESE THREE POKÉMON AND I HAVE BEEN THROUGH A LOT TOGETHER!!
WE KNOW EACH OTHER!!

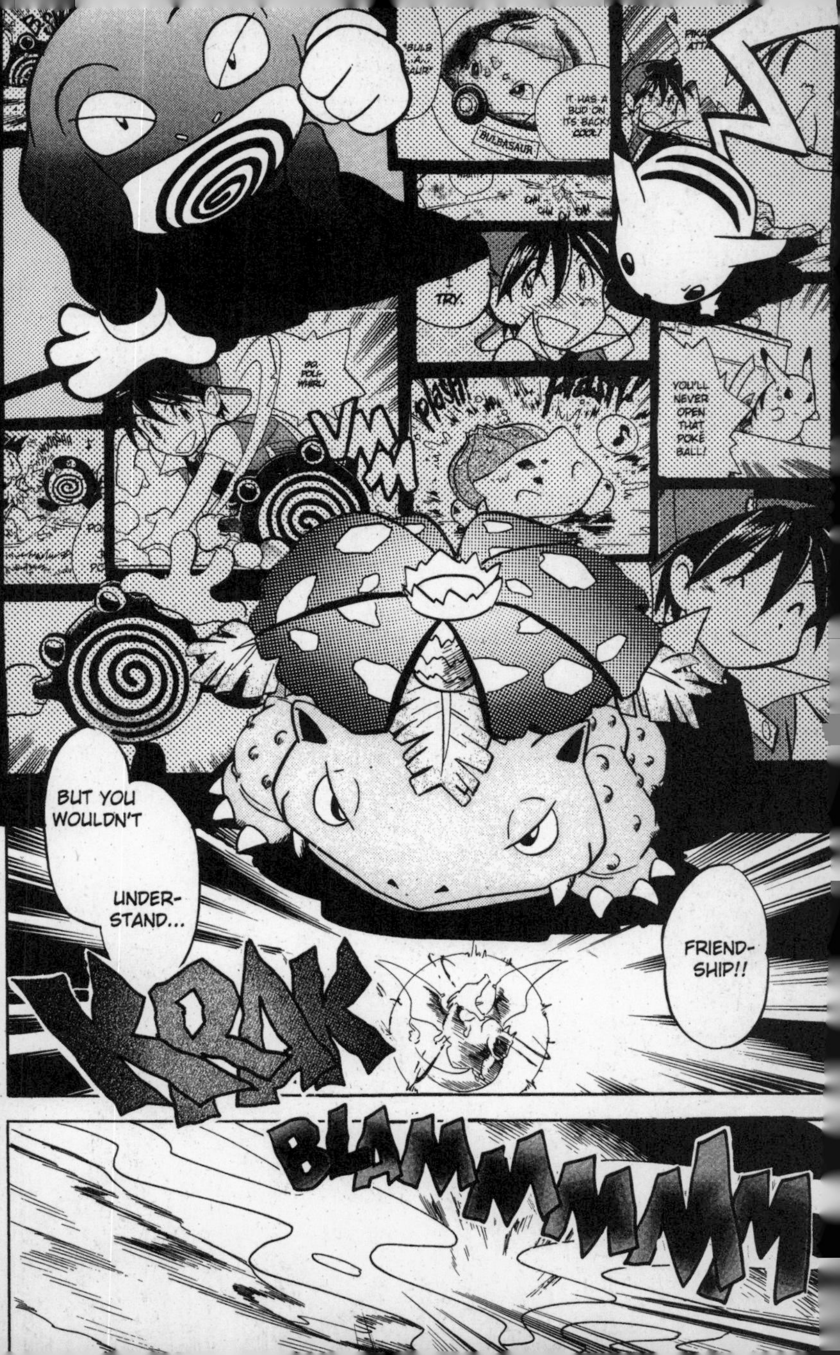
"BULB A SAUR"
BULBASAUR
IT HAS A BUD ON ITS BACK! COOL!
I TRY.
GO, POLI-WHIRL!
VMM
PLASH!
YOU'LL NEVER OPEN THAT POKé BALL!
BUT YOU WOULDN'T UNDER-STAND...
FRIEND-SHIP!!
KRAK
BLAMMMMM

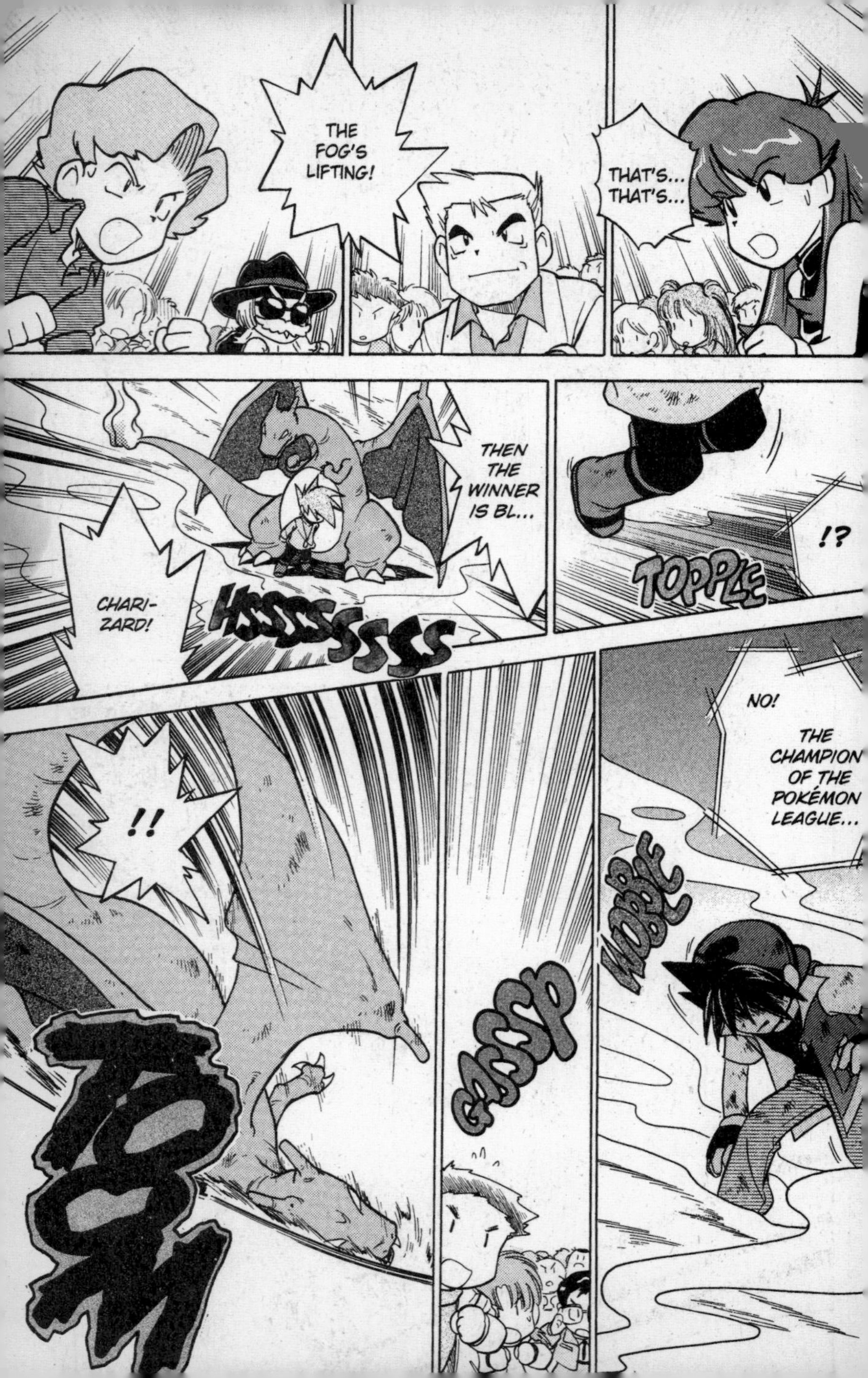
THE FOG'S LIFTING!
THAT'S... THAT'S...
CHARI-ZARD!
HSSSSSSS
THEN THE WINNER IS BL...
TOPPLE
!?
!!
GASP
WOBBLE
NO!
THE CHAMPION OF THE POKÉMON LEAGUE...

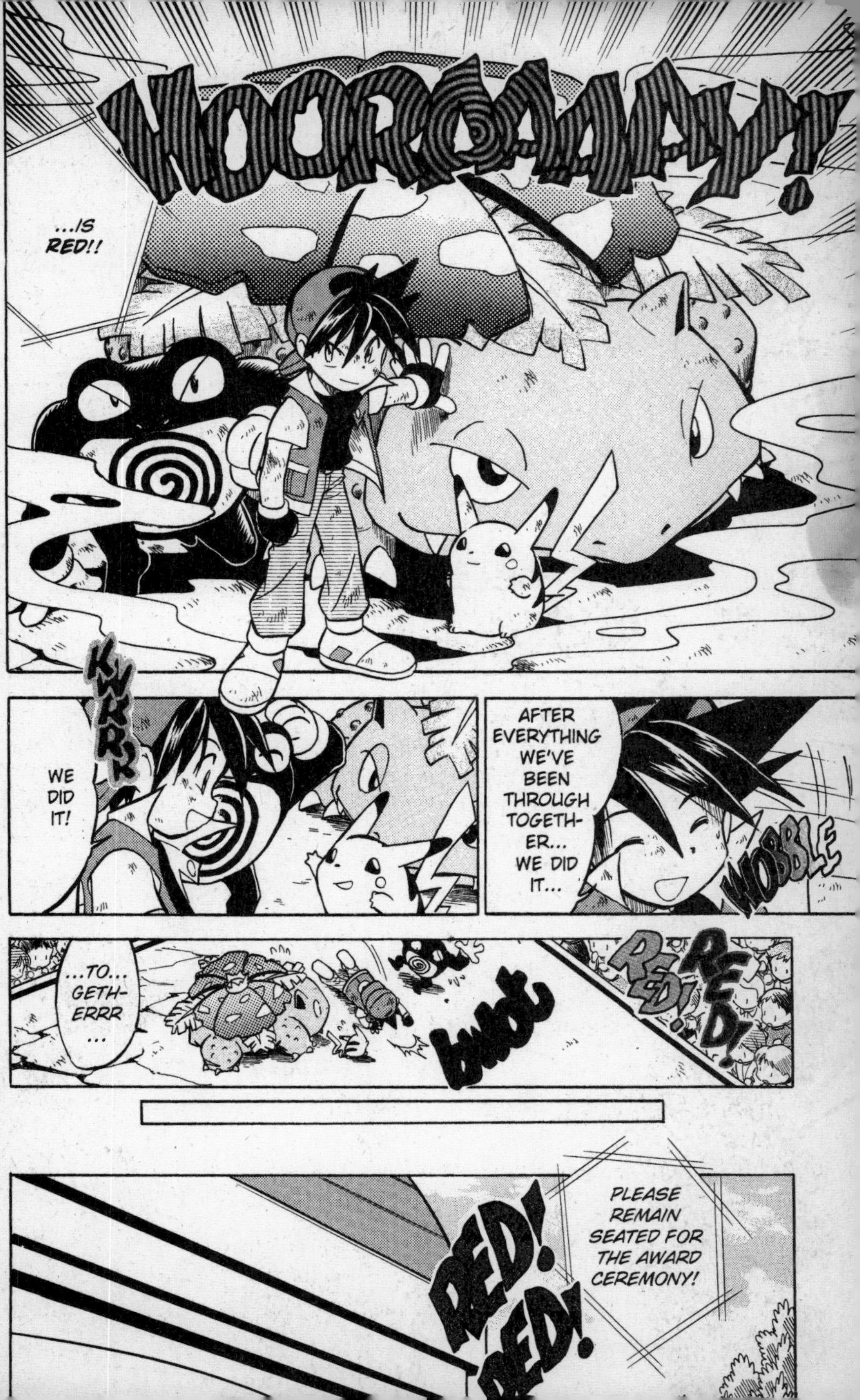
WOOROAAAAY!!
...IS RED!!
KWRRK
WE DID IT!
AFTER EVERYTHING WE'VE BEEN THROUGH TOGETH-ER... WE DID IT...
WOBBLE
...TO... GETH-ERRR ...
bwot
RED! RED!
PLEASE REMAIN SEATED FOR THE AWARD CEREMONY!
RED! RED!

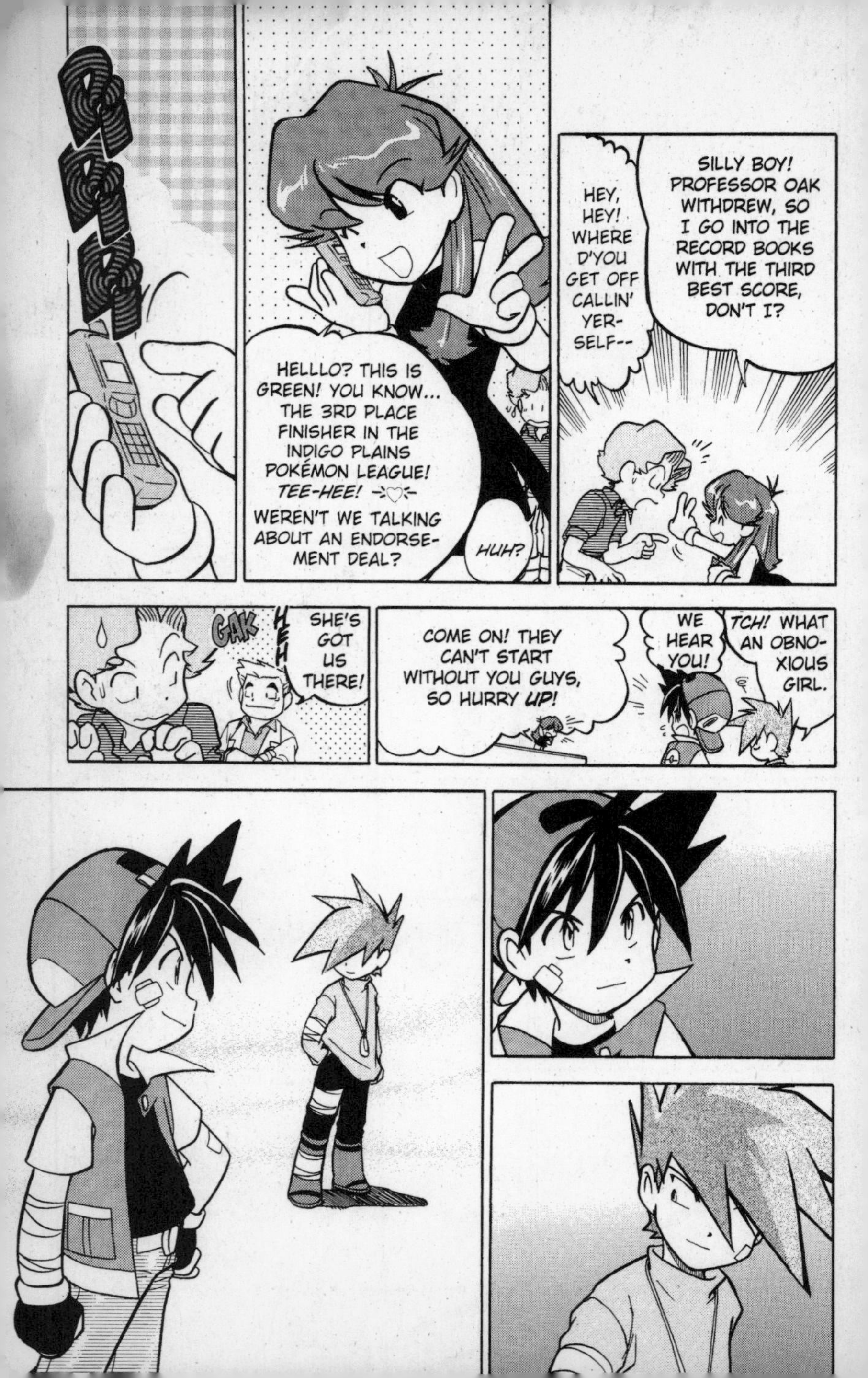
HELLLO? THIS IS GREEN! YOU KNOW... THE 3RD PLACE FINISHER IN THE INDIGO PLAINS POKÉMON LEAGUE! TEE-HEE!
WEREN'T WE TALKING ABOUT AN ENDORSEMENT DEAL?
HUH?
SILLY BOY! PROFESSOR OAK WITHDREW, SO I GO INTO THE RECORD BOOKS WITH THE THIRD BEST SCORE, DON'T I?
HEY, HEY! WHERE D'YOU GET OFF CALLIN' YER-SELF--
SHE'S GOT US THERE!
HEH
GAK
TCH! WHAT AN OBNOXIOUS GIRL.
WE HEAR YOU!
COME ON! THEY CAN'T START WITHOUT YOU GUYS, SO HURRY UP!

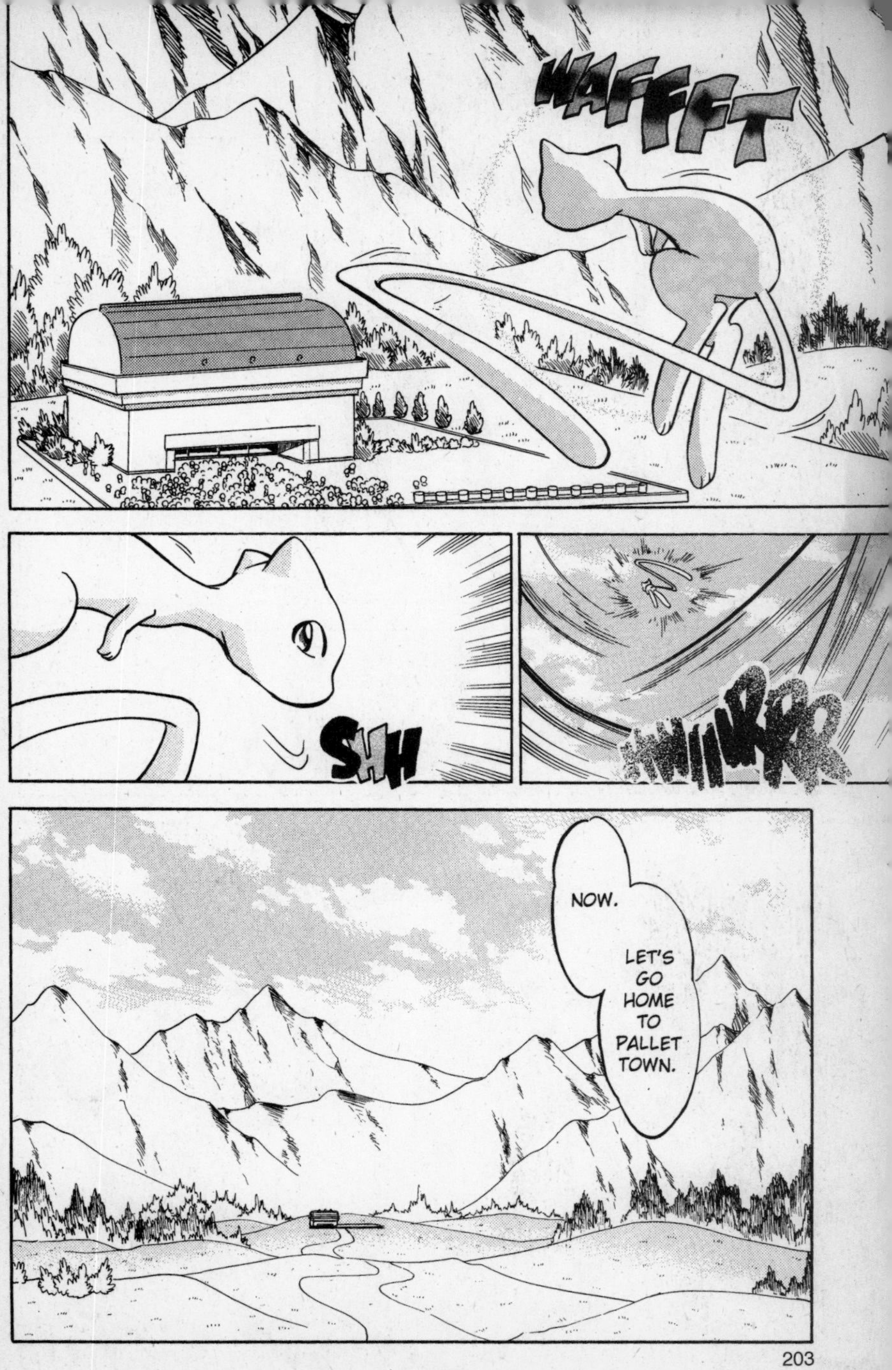
WAFFFT
SHH
WHIIRRR
NOW.
LET'S GO HOME TO PALLET TOWN.

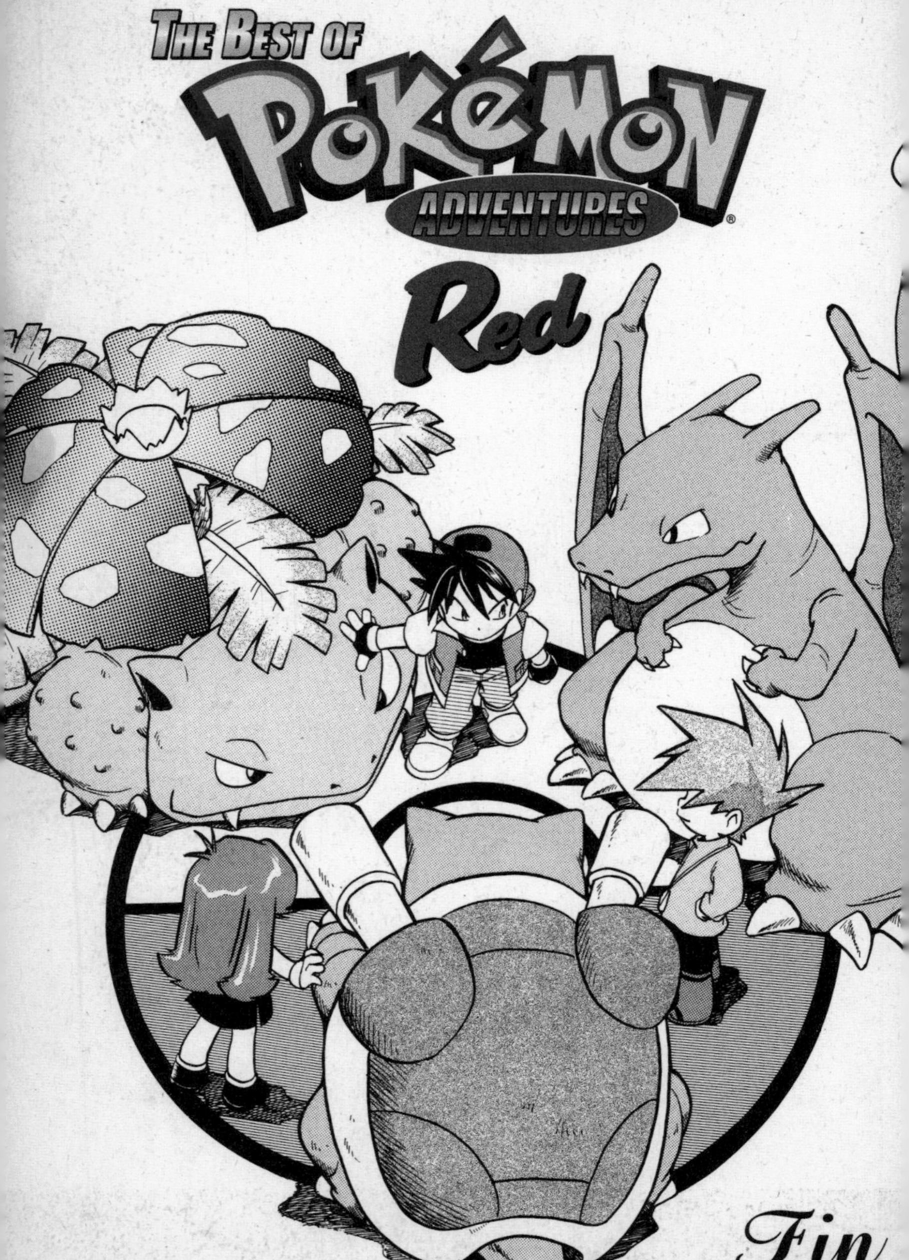
THE BEST OF
POKÉMON
ADVENTURES
Red
Fin

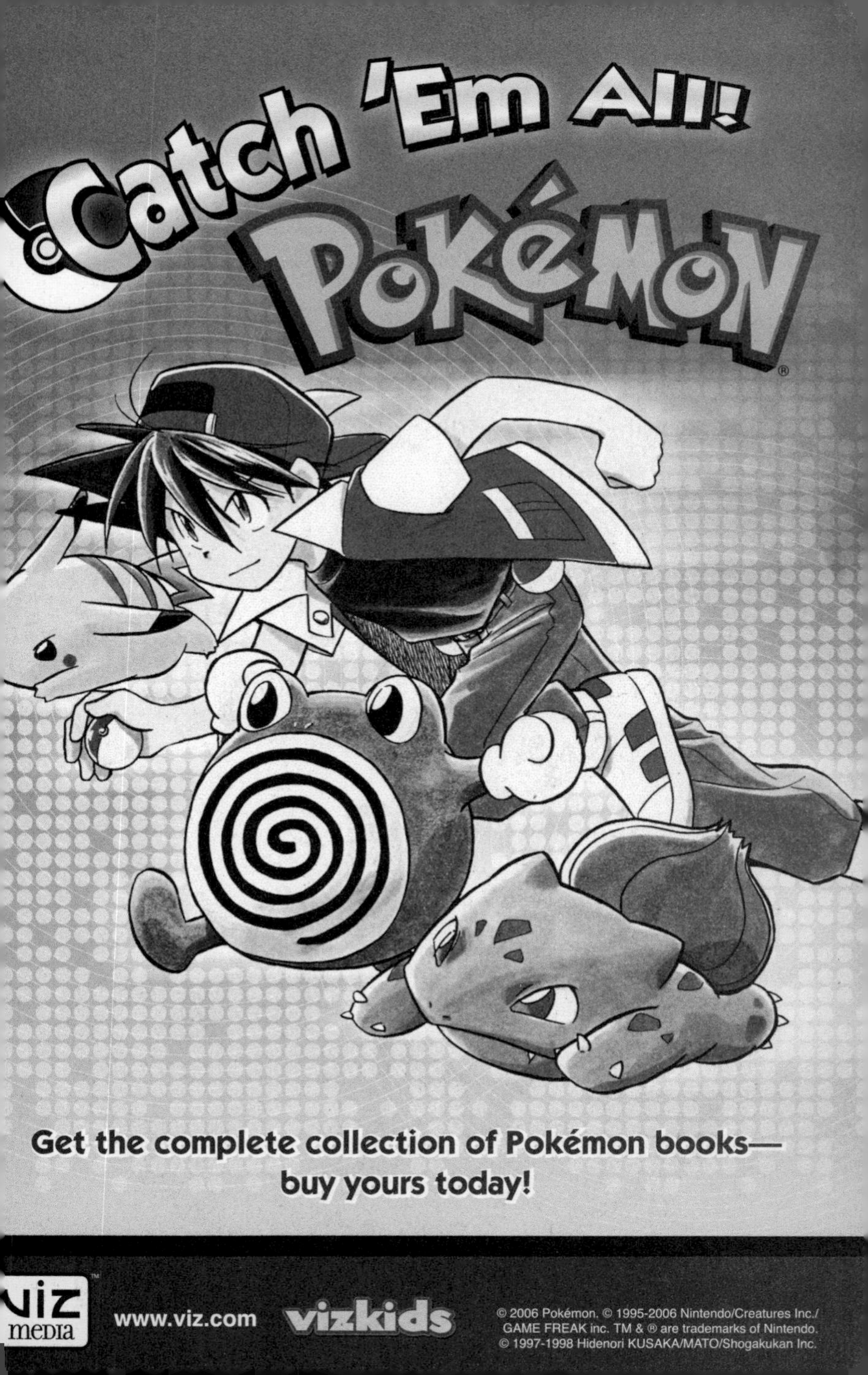
Catch 'Em All!
Pokémon®
Get the complete collection of Pokémon books—
buy yours today!
viz media™
www.viz.com
vizkids
© 2006 Pokémon. © 1995-2006 Nintendo/Creatures Inc./
GAME FREAK inc. TM & ® are trademarks of Nintendo.
© 1997-1998 Hidenori KUSAKA/MATO/Shogakukan Inc.

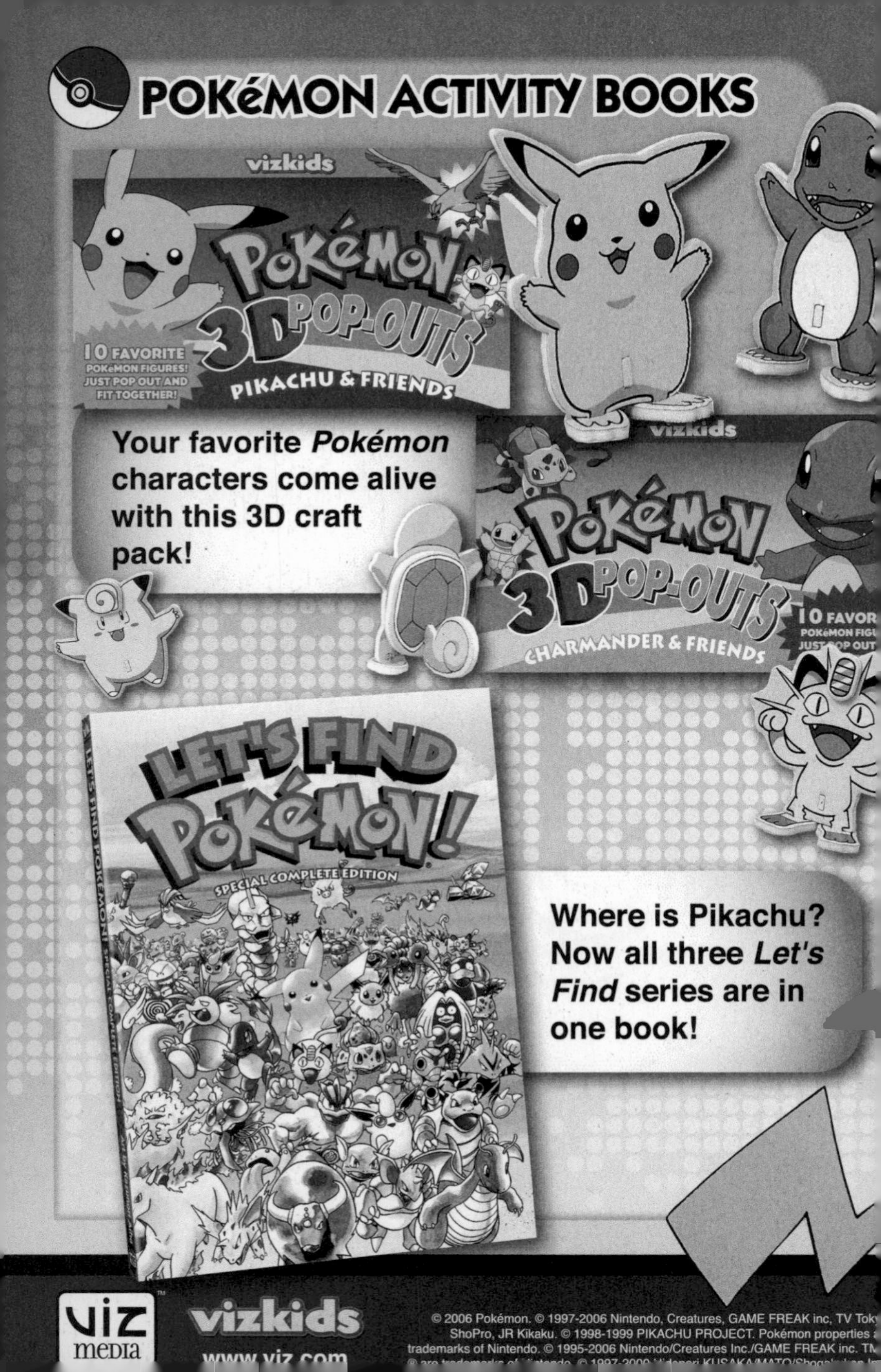
POKéMON ACTIVITY BOOKS
vizkids
POKéMON
3D POP-OUTS
PIKACHU & FRIENDS
10 FAVORITE POKéMON FIGURES! JUST POP OUT AND FIT TOGETHER!
Your favorite *Pokémon* characters come alive with this 3D craft pack!
vizkids
POKéMON
3D POP-OUTS
CHARMANDER & FRIENDS
LET'S FIND POKéMON!
SPECIAL COMPLETE EDITION
Where is Pikachu? Now all three *Let's Find* series are in one book!
VIZ MEDIA
vizkids
www.viz.com
© 2006 Pokémon. © 1997-2006 Nintendo, Creatures, GAME FREAK inc, TV Toky
ShoPro, JR Kikaku. © 1998-1999 PIKACHU PROJECT. Pokémon properties a
trademarks of Nintendo. © 1995-2006 Nintendo/Creatures Inc./GAME FREAK inc. TM

POKéMON STORY BOOKS

Follow the manga adventures of Red and Yellow!

Two complete Pikachu short stories in one full color manga!

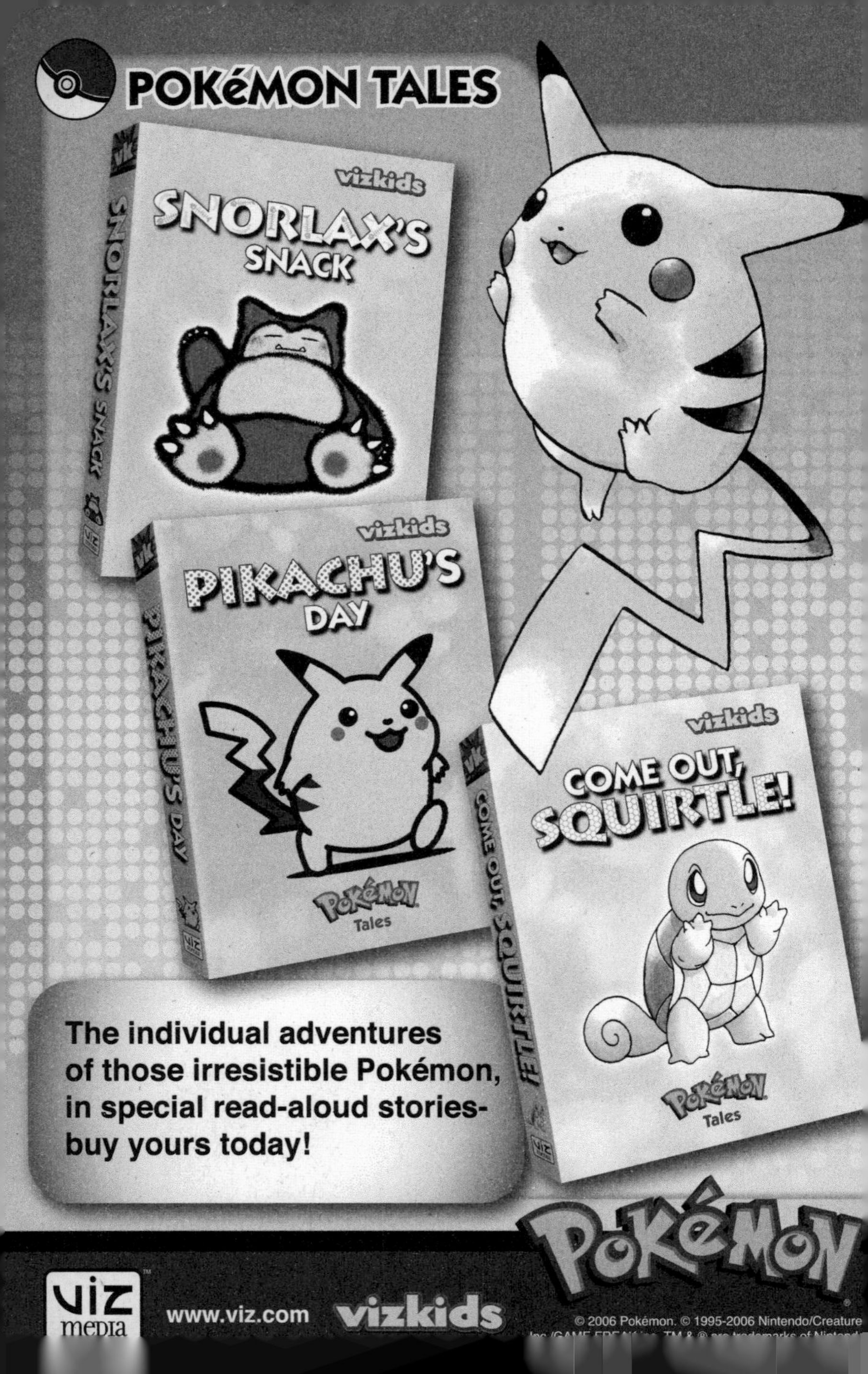
POKéMON TALES
vizkids
SNORLAX'S SNACK
vizkids
PIKACHU'S DAY
Pokémon Tales
vizkids
COME OUT, SQUIRTLE!
Pokémon Tales
The individual adventures of those irresistible Pokémon, in special read-aloud stories- buy yours today!
Pokémon
viz media
www.viz.com
vizkids
© 2006 Pokémon. © 1995-2006 Nintendo/Creature